The
Little Shop
on
Silver Linings
Street

BOOKS BY EMMA DAVIES

The House at Hope Corner
The Beekeeper's Cottage

The Little Cottage on the Hill
Summer at the Little Cottage on the Hill
Return to the Little Cottage on the Hill
Christmas at the Little Cottage on the Hill

Lucy's Little Village Book Club

Letting in Light
Turn Towards the Sun

Merry Mistletoe
Spring Fever
Gooseberry Fool
Blackberry Way

Emma Davies

The
Little Shop
on
Silver Linings
Street

Bookouture

Published by Bookouture in 2019

An imprint of StoryFire Ltd.
Carmelite House
50 Victoria Embankment
London EC4Y 0DZ

www.bookouture.com

ISBN: 978-1-78681-847-8
eBook ISBN: 978-1-78681-846-1

For Dol

Wednesday 4th December

Twenty-one shopping days until Christmas

Daisy checked her watch and rested her spoon back in the bowl. So far, only eleven minutes of the twenty she allotted herself for breakfast had elapsed and, with a happy sigh, she turned the page of the book she was reading. She still had nine more precious minutes to enjoy. The book was one she started on the 1st of December every year and, although its love story was bittersweet, the lingering feeling of hopefulness it left behind was always the perfect start to Daisy's Christmas. She'd been carefully rationing her time with the book, but even so she had almost finished it. A few moments later, however, she acknowledged that she would have to wait until the evening to do so and, reluctantly, she closed the cover, rising to carry her bowl back to the kitchen.

Daisy was a tidy creature, so there wasn't much to clear up, but she dutifully ran a sink full of hot water and suds and carefully washed her bowl, spoon, mug and the measuring jug she had used to add milk to her Weetabix. She had long ago worked out the exact quantity of milk needed to cover her cereal, and not a drop more.

Once washed, Daisy dried and put away her things before returning to the sitting room to check the fire. She had already re-laid it in readiness for that evening, but she checked it again, making sure she had sufficient logs to last her. Another sweep of the room ensured that her book was returned to the small table beside her chair and the cushion on it rearranged to her liking. Finally, once order had been restored, she crossed the room to turn off the twinkling fairy lights on her tree. At seven forty-five precisely, Daisy was ready to leave for work.

It was still dark when she left the cottage, but in a matter of minutes the sun would peep over the horizon to set the day in motion. The night's clear skies meant that the temperatures had plummeted, leaving a sparkling hoar frost covering the world outside her door. Every blade of grass, branch and leaf stood out in glittering relief, and the cobwebs that hung from her gate were beaded with diamonds, glittering in the silvery light. Even the canal just beyond it was transformed with a layer of glacé icing. Her steps crunched as she walked and the icy air seared her chest, but the beauty that surrounded her more than made up for the discomfort. Being outside was when the world made the most sense to Daisy. Time seemed to expand and she had room to breathe, freed from the anxieties that filled her mind; fear had no hold over her out here in the wild open space.

It was just a short walk to the local town where Daisy worked. Apart from her little cottage, Buchanans jewellery shop was the only other place where she felt she belonged. Leaving this early in the morning meant that she would arrive there well before opening time, but the quiet moments before the hubbub of the day were precious to her. It was often hard to feel festive after she'd been on her feet all day dealing with frazzled shoppers, tempers fraying under the pressures of the season, but out in the dark quiet lanes, with just the dawn for company, Daisy could still savour the thrill this time of year always brought. It hung expectantly in the air, the promise of what was to come always more enjoyable than its arrival.

A few more minutes' walking brought her to where the towpath disappeared under a bridge, and she climbed the steps up onto the road above, following the route through the quiet streets. The market square was still deserted but a giant, twinkling Christmas tree at one end lent a jolly air until the stallholders arrived to transform it with their bright wares and seasonal good humour. The shops around the square's edge, however, were already glowing with life, their windows enticing with warm light and splashes of bright colour against the dark buildings and pavements. Some were gaudy and garish, others restrained and elegant, but Daisy loved them all. She had grown up around them and they were like old friends, comforting and familiar.

She turned a corner, seeing the familiar dark shape of the fine red-bricked Georgian building where Buchanans stood. The double-fronted shop had been there for longer than most people in the town could remember, its woodwork still painted a rich cherry colour, the ornate curlicues above the door arches picked out in gold relief. Daisy had always thought that these small details set it apart from its plainer neighbours. The imposing front door was recessed between deep bay windows, displaying a big brass number seven and matching letterbox, which had both been polished until they gleamed. It was a job Daisy undertook every Monday morning, along with cleaning the windows so that the gold and diamonds, emeralds, sapphires and rubies they displayed sparkled even more brightly.

She had worked there for the past eight years, ever since she was seventeen and Beatrice Buchanan had taken her in and given her a reason to get up in the morning. Because Buchanans was a place where magic still happened, where young lovers bought rings to cement their union, or where grey-haired men came in search of something to tell their wives, *I'm still in love with you, even after all these years.* The jewellery that Buchanans sold was too ostentatious for Daisy's tastes, but what she did love were the stories behind each purchase. They made her feel… hopeful… that maybe one day someone might give her a gift of love and she would know how it felt.

By arriving first each morning, Daisy could make sure that items were taken from the safe in the right order so that the display cases were filled from the back to the front. Given half a chance, her co-worker, Kit, would remove jewellery at random so that everything had to be endlessly rearranged at the other end, leaving smudgy fingerprints behind. He never seemed to mind when she pointed this out, simply smiling and polishing away the offending marks, but she was bemused by the fact that he would still do exactly the same the next time around.

Kit was the youngest of Bea's three sons and the only one, thank goodness, who worked on the shop floor. But even though she was grateful for this fact she couldn't really understand why he was there at all. Most of the time he showed a complete lack of interest in the business that his father had set up years before he was even born. Times were tough right now, but Buchanans had once sold jewellery to a very noteworthy client list and, when his father sadly passed away, Kit's inheritance had pretty much set him up for life. How he could be so uninterested in the family firm was hard to fathom.

Unlocking the shop door, Daisy pushed it open and stepped inside, pausing as she always did to breathe in the familiar smell. Warm and old-fashioned, a mixture of wood and glass polish that always reminded her of stately homes she had visited. But today there was a new layer to it; resinous and spicy overlaid with the sweeter scent of cinnamon and orange. She felt her heart lift as she crossed the room to turn on the Christmas-tree lights, running her fingers through the bushy branches and inhaling. A noble fir indeed.

Her gaze swept the room as she stood back to admire her handiwork. Decorated only the day before, the room looked resplendent in all its Christmas glory. In the rear corner of the shop, two five-foot-tall wooden Nutcracker figures stood guard beside a huge Christmas tree covered from head to toe in sumptuous gilded ornaments. Each of the Nutcrackers held a golden tray, on which shallow cut-glass dishes were filled with pearlescent sugared mice and, at the soldiers' feet, a tumble of brightly wrapped presents spilled out into the space in front of them. Huge swags of greenery hung from the picture rail, encircling the room with bright ribbons, candy canes and smaller bright-red Nutcracker figurines.

The theme for the decorations was the same every year, but for Daisy that was part of their charm. Christmas could only begin once Bea, a lifelong devotee of ballet, had concluded her annual visit to see The Royal Ballet perform *The Nutcracker*, her absolute favourite of all their productions and one which she had been to see every Christmas for nearly twenty years.

There was a reverence to the decorating process; when collecting the boxes from the storeroom Daisy would sigh with happiness as her fingers unfurled each beloved ornament from its place of safety. They were things that had come from all over the country, collected by Bea on her travels, and each held a special importance for Daisy. She could remember where each and every one had come from, and which year it had been added to the collection. Seeing them all again was like revisiting old friends and Christmas wouldn't have been the same without them.

Leaving the shop lit by just the twinkling fairy lights, Daisy went through to the back room to take off her outdoor things and collect the safe and cabinet keys. She knew exactly how long it would take her to have everything ready before Kit arrived and, despite the fact that they hopefully had a busy day ahead of them, she doubted that he would arrive any earlier than usual. Checking first that she had relocked the shop door, she opened all the display cases and began to unload the safe, comforted by the familiar routine.

She was just giving the glass one final polish when she heard Kit's quick knock at the door followed by the sound of his key in the lock. He usually knocked first so that she would know it was him arriving; he always said you couldn't be too careful. She looked up as he came in and met his shy smile with one of her own. He walked to work just like she did and the cold air had lent a sparkle to his green eyes, tinging his cheeks pink.

'Hello, Daisy,' he said, standing there for a second before he glanced away and moved past her, his slender form appearing bulky under a thick coat. It was the same every day – the split second when he looked as if he might say something else but then the moment was gone, again. She picked up the bottle of glass cleaner and, giving the nearest cabinet another spray, began to polish the already immaculate surface. Sometimes she wished she had the courage to say something more to Kit, something that wasn't related to their work, but, try as she might, she could never find the words. He was only a sales assistant, like she was, but he was also Bea's son and for some reason that made her incredibly tongue-tied. Or perhaps it was just that he was even quieter than she was, softly spoken and pensive, which made the whole thing excruciatingly awkward. Still, she reminded herself, Kit wasn't the reason she enjoyed coming to work; for her it was all about the customers and the wonderful stories of love they brought with them.

The morning dragged with only a few unremarkable sales and it was nearly lunchtime before a customer appeared who Daisy could tell instinctively was looking for something special. There was something about him, an air of excitement that gave his intentions away. She just knew he would be leaving with one of their signature midnight-blue bags in his hand. Daisy stepped forward.

'Is there anything I can help you with?' she began. 'If not, do feel free to have a look around. We don't bite.'

He smiled, only a trace of nerves showing. 'I think I am going to need some help,' he admitted. 'I know what I want, but not *what* I want, if that makes any sense at all?' He bit his lip, eyes twinkling.

'You'd be surprised, but it makes perfect sense. So, you know you want to buy an engagement ring… just not which one…' She grinned at the stunned expression on his face. 'I saw you looking in the window,' she explained. 'And seeing as you're here by yourself you're obviously going to need a little help in picking what may well turn out to be the most important present you've ever had to buy.'

He rolled his eyes. 'Oh, God, the pressure. But yes, you're absolutely right. Hopefully my girlfriend has no idea I'm here, but I want to make sure what I get is absolutely perfect.'

'Then let's see what we can do,' replied Daisy. 'Why don't you come over to the counter where a further selection of rings is displayed and you can tell me all about her.' She leaned in a little closer as if to whisper. 'I generally find that people do know exactly what they want, they just don't always realise it.'

She gave him a few moments to take in the contents of the case before asking her next question. It gave her an opportunity to see in which direction his eyes strayed, and which rings he peered longest at.

'Now before we start,' she said quietly. 'There's one question I have to ask before we go on. It's awkward, but it's got to be done if I'm to be of any real help to you.'

He looked up to meet her raised eyebrows. 'The budget…? Not as much as I'd like,' he said.

Daisy smiled. He was more perceptive than most.

'And may I ask how much that is?'

'Around three thousand? I don't know… Is that even enough?'

She nodded. 'Well, it does depend somewhat on your expectations… but yes, I can find you the perfect ring for that.' And she smiled reassuringly, just to show she wasn't kidding.

'So, what do you think?' he asked, scanning the display case. 'Because they all look pretty. Where do I start?' He looked up, holding her gaze, his blue eyes intense.

She cleared her throat. 'Well first, I think you're incredibly brave buying a ring in secret. That takes a lot of courage, but it's also incredibly romantic, if you don't mind me saying. Your girlfriend will know how special that makes it.'

He blushed. 'Do you really think so? It seemed like the right thing to do. You see, she's the most thoughtful person I know. She's always doing things for other people, organising surprises, going that extra mile even when she doesn't have to. She makes sure everyone's all right before she even thinks about herself and never asks for reward, or even any thanks. Just once I'd like her to have something that she isn't expecting and that shows her how much I love her.'

Daisy could feel her insides begin to melt and she looked down quickly to hide how she was feeling.

The next few minutes were spent discussing what the man's girlfriend liked, disliked, what shape of stone she might like, the number of stones, indeed which type of stone. And Daisy nodded and smiled, filtering the options in her brain before she began to really fine-tune things.

'And you say she doesn't like fussy things? Then I think a single stone would suit her best. And definitely a diamond you said, so...' She lifted two boxes from the case. 'Brilliant cut diamonds are the most expensive,' she said. 'And possibly the most sought after. They're usually what most people think of when they say a solitaire.' She pushed forward the first of the boxes, pausing while he took in the detail of the ring, a glittering stone in a very traditional platinum setting.

She was about to add something else when the shop door opened, distracting her for a second. It was Bertie, Kit's elder brother and not someone she expected to see today. Her heart leaped into her mouth. Bertie was incredibly good-looking; he had only to look at her to tie her tongue into a series of knots. But he was bad news, a reckless party animal who fascinated her and scared her in equal measure. Though that wasn't the only thing making her anxious; Bertie also looked after administration and accounts at Buchanans, and his arrival usually heralded big discussions about the business. Change was not something Daisy embraced. At all.

Kit jumped off his chair as soon as Bertie entered, but she tried to ignore them both and turned her attention back to her customer.

'And then you have something very different in style such as this emerald cut stone,' she continued, showing the man another ring. 'The stone is larger but they're a little less... well, bling, and often appeal to people who like a more vintage look. I'm showing you two extremes of style deliberately as both rings say something very different. I think that's a really important thing to consider when you're choosing the ring for someone else.'

The man smiled. 'You can say that again, but that's where I'm going to struggle.' He pointed to the larger emerald cut diamond. 'Suzanne has beautiful hands, long graceful fingers that would really suit a larger ring.' He pulled a face. 'And I would love her to have something like this – she's definitely an individual rather than a follow-the-crowd sort of person – but I just don't have the money for it.'

Daisy hoped he would say something like that.

'Then would now be a good time to mention that this ring is actually slightly cheaper than its brilliant cut, but much smaller, neighbour. Only by twenty-five pounds, but well, you could buy a bottle of champagne with the difference.'

The man laughed. 'Not very good champagne,' he said.

'No, well, diamonds I'm good with,' she replied. 'Champagne… not so much.'

'I'm beginning to see that.' He grinned at her, picking up the larger of the two rings. 'Did you honestly just say that I could afford this? I'm not sure I quite believe it.'

'Well, it's true,' she said, very aware that Bertie was watching her. She could see him out of the corner of her eye. 'Brilliant cut diamonds are probably the most popular, which in itself pushes up the price, but they are also the most expensive because of the way they're cut – most of the rough diamond goes to waste during the process and so you get a lot less stone for your money. But with an emerald cut stone that doesn't happen, and this difference allows for a much larger stone for the same price. Plus, as in the case with this ring, that means that extra detailing can often be included in the setting itself.' She took the ring from its box and held it up so that he could see the beautiful shank. 'This one is quite unusual.'

He took the ring from her, his eyes widening. 'Would you have told me any of that if I said I preferred the other one?'

She smiled. 'Perhaps not, but only because I want you to feel good about your choice, and it is *your* choice. There are plenty of others to choose from apart from these two. I only offered them to illustrate the two very different styles.'

He looked down at the display case. 'And yet all the time I was talking to you before you selected those two, I could see you were taking in what I said and weighing up what would, and wouldn't, be suitable. Why do I get the funny feeling you've picked the only two that come close to fulfilling what I'm looking for?'

Daisy blushed. 'Well, that is my job.' Her cheeks began to grow hot, both from the compliment and the weight of Bertie's presence.

There was silence for a moment and Daisy let it continue. They were now into serious thinking time and these things couldn't be rushed.

'Could I ask you a favour?' he said after another few minutes or so had passed by. 'It's probably a bit cheeky, but could I ask you to try this on for me, so that I can see what it looks like?'

He was still holding the ring and she held out her hand so that he could slip it on her finger. Her face felt as if it was on fire and she was glad the man was looking down instead of up.

She could see his eyes soften, his expression turning to one of wonder as he saw the possibilities of his future opening up in front of him.

'I can try the other on as well if you like?'

Her remark drew him back to the present. 'Oh yes… you better had, just to be sure…'

Daisy slipped off the ring and replaced it with the smaller but far more sparkly solitaire. But almost immediately her customer shook his head.

'No, that's not right at all. It would get lost on Suzanne's hands.' He looked up at Daisy then, a full-on gaze, accompanied by a high-wattage smile. 'It's the first one. Definitely. Mind made up.' He blew out his cheeks. 'I can't believe it was that simple. I thought I was going to be in the shop for days...'

Daisy smiled. 'Sometimes things just fall into place, don't they?' She tried to keep the wistful note out of her voice and almost succeeded. She cleared her throat, continuing quickly. 'Now, I don't want to throw a spanner in the works but there is just one more thing I should mention...'

'Oh... yes?' She could almost see Bertie lean closer as if to hear her better.

She reached back down into the cabinet to select another ring. 'So, we looked at this ring in a platinum setting but it's also available in eighteen-carat gold which makes a huge difference to its appearance. Do you know which your girlfriend prefers? Or what metal she generally wears?'

He looked panic-stricken. 'Oh God, I'm not sure.' He scratched his head. 'I got her sister to check her ring size for me, but I didn't really think about that... she has a...' He trailed off, obviously trying to recall what he'd seen her wear before. He looked confused for a second and screwed up his face. 'Gold... I think...'

Daisy smiled. 'Okay, so what colour hair and eyes does she have?'

'Like yours, brunette, and beautiful amber-coloured eyes...'

'And what colour clothes does she generally wear?'

'Erm... sort of reddish... or brown... green sometimes. Earthy kinds of colours, I guess.'

Daisy slipped on the ring with the gold band. 'Then I would say that this would almost certainly suit her better.' She held up her hand beside her face for a moment so he could see how it looked before putting the identical platinum ring on the other hand and then holding it up instead. Then she held up both hands so that he could see the contrast. 'Do you see what I mean?'

'I do!' He looked astonished. 'Oh God, I can't believe I almost fell at the last hurdle. I'm not sure what to say… except thank you. Thank you!' He looked so overjoyed that Daisy thought for a split second that he was going to kiss her in gratitude, but instead he just beamed, his eyes shining.

Daisy took off the ring and handed it to him. 'And the best thing is that because this is set in gold rather than platinum, it's that bit cheaper as well. Now you can buy a really expensive bottle of champagne!' She swallowed a little nervously before leading him over to the sales desk, studiously avoiding Bertie's eye.

Ten minutes later her customer left the shop a very happy man, swinging his little blue bag with a spring in his step. Daisy couldn't help but sigh with happiness at the thought of the young woman who would very soon be receiving the most wonderfully romantic surprise. She returned the sales pad to the desk drawer, passing by Kit as she did so. He was doodling on something and idly eating a sugared mouse, but he looked up as she drew level.

'That was beautifully done,' he said, his voice hardly more than a whisper. 'I don't know how you do it.'

She looked at him in surprise, wondering if she'd even heard right, but Kit's eyes had skittered away from hers and his head was already bent back to his drawing.

'Yes, well done, Daisy, well done! Oh, and hello too, of course.' Bertie was leaning up against the counter on the other side of the room.

She blushed. 'Thank you,' she said, immediately flustered. 'Erm…
I didn't know you were coming in today. Bea didn't say anything.'

'Didn't she? Oh… Well, never mind. She asked me if I could pop
in one day this week to bring the sales figures up to date. Just to see
how the land lies, I guess, before the big push up to Christmas.'

Kit exaggerated a yawn. 'Sales figures time,' he added. 'Whoopy do.'

Daisy ignored him, realising belatedly that, despite the light tone
of Bertie's words, he looked worried.

'Was that okay?' she asked nervously. 'Just now I mean. I know I
probably could have sold that man a more expensive ring, but it didn't
seem right somehow… and he was so nice.'

She flashed Kit a quick glance but he still had his head bent, intent
on his doodling.

Bertie glanced at his watch. 'Isn't it time for your lunch break,
Daisy? Why don't you come through to the back, and we can have a
little chat about the run-up to Christmas.'

He was smiling and didn't look particularly cross, but Daisy's heart
sank as she mutely followed him through. She was in for it now.

'I won't beat around the bush,' he said as soon as he was sitting behind
the small desk which occupied the far corner of the room. 'I'll update
the figures but I don't think it's going to make any real difference to what
I've already told Mother. Which is that we need to have a *really* good
Christmas, Daisy. I probably don't need to tell you, but sales have been
dropping off over the last couple of years, and this year worse than ever.'

She hung her head, feeling her cheeks colour again. 'Is Bea going
to be cross with me?'

His voice was kind. 'No, Daisy, she's not going to be cross with
you. How can she be when you're the only one who seems capable of
selling anything?'

She still couldn't look at him. 'But I let that last man buy a cheaper ring. That's what you mean, isn't it? That I should do better?' She peeked up at him, feeling the intensity of his gaze on the top of her head.

'You have a real talent for dealing with customers, Daisy. And I think you're right in that he went away very happy. Maybe now he'll be a customer for life, who knows? But I guess Bea would be happier if today you'd sold him the emerald cut in the platinum setting, or even the brilliant cut stone.'

She nodded, stroking the back of one hand with the other in comfort. It was kind of him to say that about her even though she wished he wouldn't. She was far happier talking with customers than to people she knew, especially people like Bertie.

'You have the ability, Daisy, I know you do, so all I'm saying is that, while it's really lovely that you take so much care over our customers, the bottom line is that we need more money coming in. And I think you're the person to make sure that happens, but you might need to be a little less...' He searched for the right word.

'Honest?' she blurted out, immediately regretting it. He hadn't been about to say that. It was what he'd meant but he'd been trying to find a word which didn't make it sound so bad. And although he wasn't exactly her boss, he was close enough. How could she possibly say that she disagreed with him?

He smiled. 'I know it isn't always easy with Kit... well, just being Kit... but we can't keep on losing money. There might have to be some changes and Kit is, well he's...' Bertie trailed off, a sheepish expression on his face. He hadn't the heart to say it, but Daisy understood him very well. Kit was family, and if anyone was going to lose their job it wouldn't be him.

'Yes, I understand,' she said. 'And thank you, I'll do my best.' She dipped her head. He was only trying to be kind.

'Sorry, I'm keeping you from your lunch, Daisy,' he added. 'Please go ahead and eat, don't stop on my account.'

She stared at the fridge where she had placed her lunchbox that morning. She ate the same thing every day, but even so she usually looked forward to it. Now, she really didn't think she could stomach anything.

Bertie pulled a face. 'Listen, I might just pop out and get a proper coffee before I make a start. I can't drink the instant rubbish we have here. Can I get you anything? One of those nice hot chocolates with cream and marshmallows?'

Daisy shuddered at the thought. 'No, thank you. Honestly, I'm much happier with just plain tea.'

'Okay, well, I'll leave you to it then. I won't be long.'

And he left her, staring at his back as he returned to the sales floor, feeling like her world had just been cleaved in two. Whatever would she do without Buchanans?

*

Despite the cold, Daisy took her time walking home that evening. She paused as she reached the end of Silver Street and turned to look back at the shop that had been the biggest part of her life for so many years. It seemed like only yesterday that Bea had joked to her that it should be called Silver Linings Street, offering her the job that had been a much-needed lifeline. The thought that it might no longer be there was unbearable.

The busy rush of the market square soon receded, replaced by the stillness that hung over the water particularly in the winter, and by the time she descended onto the canal path, it was almost completely silent, and very dark.

Few people would even contemplate walking the path at night without a torch, but Daisy knew her way as much by instinct as familiarity. Her tiny two-bedroom cottage had originally belonged to her grandparents when they were the lock-keepers, and she had been a regular visitor after school and in the summer holidays when she was younger. Set a little way back from the towpath, it was well hidden, but there wasn't an inch of the canal that Daisy hadn't explored and, even though the job of lock-keeper had long since disappeared, she still helped boats through in the busy height of summer.

By the time she reached her front door, Daisy was already feeling calmer. The walk had been just long enough to restore some of her equilibrium and, once inside, her evening routines would serve to settle her even more. She closed the front door behind her and laid her back against it for a moment, breathing deeply, hearing the soothing tick of the mantel clock from the sitting room. Then she crossed the hallway into the kitchen to set the kettle to boil and took off her outdoor clothes to hang them by the back door. With a satisfied nod she went back to the sitting room and put a match to the fire that she had laid ready that morning. She was home.

Upstairs was one large bedroom, with a tiny one beside it, both nestled under the eaves, so that in summer Daisy could hear the rustle of leaves against her windows and, in winter, the light scurry of the mice with whom she inevitably shared her home. It was altogether the most perfect place in the universe as far as she was concerned and in it she felt safe and sheltered from the storm that was the outside world.

She slid off her work clothes – a white blouse with a Peter Pan collar, which she consigned to the laundry basket, and a long black skirt, which she hung beside two other identical ones in the wardrobe. She touched a hand to the other white shirts also hanging there, mentally counting their number while straightening them and, once satisfied that there were sufficient, she closed the wardrobe door. Her reflection stared back at her and she frowned. Not at her slender figure or pale alabaster skin, or at the soft brown ringlets of her hair which had formed as the day had gone on, but at the intricate sapphire necklace which hung from her neck.

Almost purple, it accentuated the dark violet of her eyes, but even though Daisy could appreciate its beauty, she took it off; it had no place here in her home. And if she was still wearing the necklace then she would also be wearing the matching bracelet which she had removed from Buchanans' safe earlier that morning. She wore them so often that she sometimes did forget to take them off before leaving work, and the fact that she had done so tonight was an indication of how distracted she had been. There was an odd sock which she kept in a drawer for just such an occasion, however, and she slipped the items inside without another thought. Tomorrow she would wear them again, just for the time she was at work. Outside those hours Daisy wore no other jewellery, indeed she hardly owned any.

Dressed in her pyjamas and dressing gown she returned downstairs to feed the fire with logs. Then she made herself a cup of tea and took down a tin of tomato soup from the cupboard. A line of labels faced her; three tomato, and two mushroom soup in case she fancied a change. The shelf below held a packet of rich tea biscuits, a box of Weetabix and a jar of peanut butter, together with three tins of peaches and a pot of custard. All exactly as they should be.

It wasn't until later that evening, once Daisy had eaten, washed up, read for exactly one hour and made a mug of warm milk, that she allowed herself to think about Bertie's words of that afternoon.

Thursday 5th December

Twenty shopping days until Christmas

Daisy tried to concentrate on what Mr Bennett was saying but the young couple with matching jackets were edging ever closer to the shop door and, unless someone said something, they would slip away at any moment. Of course, it didn't help that the 'someone' in question was currently idling behind the counter opposite, lost in thought as he so often was.

'Yes, but the last necklace you looked at was a garnet, Mr Bennett, and this is a ruby, they're really not the same thing at all…' She dragged her attention back to her customer, and fixed a smile on her face. 'Well yes, both are red admittedly, but rubies are special; they're not in the same league at all, and I really don't think your wife would get them confused.'

She shot a glance over the shoulder of her customer. Something had held the couple's attention momentarily – now would be the perfect time to ask them if they needed help. She tried to get Kit to respond by the sheer force of her will, but nothing… *Oh for goodness' sake.* Bertie's message from yesterday couldn't have been any clearer and he must have spoken to Kit about it too. They needed to make every sale they could, not ignore their customers.

'You see, garnets are a much deeper colour, darker and more earthy, sometimes with distinct orange tones, whereas a fine ruby such as this one should be a vivid red…' She held the necklace up to the bright overhead light, watching it sparkle, and angling it so that Mr Bennett could appreciate its vivacity. She turned the word over in her head, one which he had often used to describe his wife. They had recently celebrated thirty years of marriage and were both still so much in love. He was so romantic…

Daisy frowned as the shop doorbell tinkled, admitting another customer; not for the first time that afternoon, she willed Mr Bennett to hurry up and make up his mind. He would buy the necklace, he always bought whatever she recommended, but the process could not be rushed, and there was a certain reverence to his visits which occurred three times a year, and had done for as long as Daisy had worked at Buchanans. Each May, for his wife's birthday, every September for their anniversary and at Christmastime, Mr Bennett would visit the shop and select a gift of jewellery and, while he was a very good customer, Daisy already knew all about him and his wife. The young couple, however, were still a closed book as far as their love story was concerned, its pages to be plundered.

She handed the necklace to Mr Bennett so that he could scrutinise it one more time and smiled at him expectantly. His eye returned to the midnight-blue velvet pillow that lay on the counter in front of him, where several other almost identical necklaces lay. He would pick them all up again, put them down and then repeat the process a couple more times, and all the while she would wait patiently, knowing that the young couple could slip away from her at any minute.

She glanced across at the man who had just entered the shop. He was wandering the counters, peering down at their contents with a bewildered expression on his face. He was not used to being in a jewellery shop at all, that was easy to see. Distinctly uncomfortable… Perhaps she could excuse herself from Mr Bennett for just one moment and offer her help. She took a step to one side and was about to say something in greeting when Kit looked up in surprise as if suddenly realising where he was and beat her to it.

'I'll take this one,' said Mr Bennett.

Daisy nodded, looking back to see that he had indeed chosen the very necklace she had suggested, but she smiled and told him that he had made an excellent choice, just as she always did. She took the pendant from him and withdrew its presentation box from under the counter, carefully nestling the gem inside before holding it up for inspection one last time. Then she closed the lid decisively.

'Do come over to the desk,' she said, trying to listen to what was being said to Kit. She ushered Mr Bennett to a seat and took the one opposite, pulling the sales pad towards her. Buchanans had never operated a till in the shop. Bea said that was far too common, so sales were handwritten and the customer provided with a proper written receipt. Then again, Mr Bennett was just about to hand over one and a half thousand pounds, so perhaps he did deserve a little more than a torn-off slip of paper.

Kit was shaking his head. 'A flower, did you say? Um…' He looked vaguely around the shop. 'I don't think we have anything like that really. What sort of flower?'

Daisy rolled her eyes as she wrote. Kit was lovely, but he had no imagination, that was the problem. The shop was full of precious stones, set into rings, bracelets, necklaces, earrings, any one of them could be described as being flower-like… almost… if you knew how to tailor your description of a piece to match the customer's expectation. She

signed the receipt with a flourish and passed it across the desk, holding
out her hand for Mr Bennett's credit card. Just a couple more minutes
and then she would be free to attend to the gentleman herself – if he
was still around, that was.

The shop door tinkled again as she got to her feet – the couple had
gone – and she glanced at the clock on the wall. It was half past four
and dark outside now; she doubted very much that they would see
many more customers that afternoon. But short of dragging them in
off the street there wasn't much that Daisy could do.

'Oh, I see... No, sorry, nothing like that...'

Daisy looked up as Kit spoke again, smiling at his customer who
was still looking very unsure. He held her look for a moment and
then turned away.

'Well, thanks anyway. It was just a thought.'

The man nodded at Kit and his bright red boots had almost carried
him to the door when he turned back for a moment, his face suddenly
transformed by a brilliant smile as he beamed at Daisy.

'Merry Christmas,' he said. And then he was gone.

Daisy stared down at the credit-card reader in her hand, momentarily
blown off course by the intensity of the stranger's gaze. They hadn't
even spoken and yet Daisy felt as if she knew him, or, rather curiously,
had known him, for a very long time.

She shook her head, concentrating on the task in hand, and seconds
later she was standing by the door, her own face wreathed in smiles.

'And you have a wonderful Christmas too, Mr Bennett, and Mrs
Bennett of course. It's been lovely seeing you as always.' She held the
shop door open for her customer, feeling a blast of frozen air from outside
as she did so. She watched him leave, staring after him lost in thought
as he disappeared almost immediately into the throng of shoppers.

With a shiver she closed the door and returned to where Kit had sat back down again, an open book in his hand. She went and stood in front of him.

'Um…?' she said.

He looked up, a wary expression crossing his face. It often did whenever she spoke to him directly.

'I think we're supposed to be asking everyone who comes in if we can help them,' she said. 'Like that couple… I think they might have been looking for wedding rings.'

'Were they?' he gulped. 'I just thought they wanted to be left alone to browse.'

Daisy sighed. 'Well they spent most of their time by that counter,' she added, pointing. 'The one where the rings are… You could have asked them.'

He regarded her for a moment with his pale green eyes, light-brown hair flopping over his face. 'Well, yes, I suppose I could have done. But I decided that between the two of them, one at least would have asked for help if they needed it.'

'Yes, but sometimes people don't know what they want, and they need a little encouragement.'

He dipped his head slightly, in acknowledgement, but not necessarily in agreement, she noticed.

'And what about the other man – the one you did speak to? What did he want? Only if it's something we don't have I always like to let Bea know.' She fidgeted nervously.

This time it was Kit's turn to sigh. 'He didn't know what he wanted actually… something floral possibly, or botanical, something light…' He paused for a moment, thinking. 'Something *ethereal* was what he actually said.'

'Ethereal?' Daisy frowned. 'In a jeweller's shop?' She looked around her, grudgingly acknowledging Kit's difficulty.

'He wondered whether we might be able to make him something,' added Kit. 'Although he realised that might be difficult seeing as he had no way of describing what he wanted, only that he would know it when he saw it.'

Daisy nodded, but by now was no longer listening. If only she hadn't been busy with Mr Bennett, she might have been able to help the man with the beaming smile. He was after something special, that much was obvious, and she would have loved to find out more. She turned away, a wistful expression on her face. Maybe one day she might be able to help him with a design of her own...

She could feel Kit's eyes on her back as she crossed the room to put away the necklaces she had left out. He probably thought her soppy, and she had a sudden cheeky impulse to turn around and stick her tongue out at him to see if she could make him laugh. But she daren't; he was Bea's son, after all. A glance at the clock confirmed that the afternoon was coming to a close and she automatically collected the glass polish from under the counter so that she could clear away the greasy smudges from the display cabinets in readiness for the following day.

Daisy was just about to start on the second cabinet when the doorbell's jolly tinkle announced another customer. Except it wasn't a customer, it was Bertie. Twice in as many days was unheard of.

'Is Bea here yet?' he asked without even so much as a hello. The slightly forced lightness in his tone made Daisy's ears prick up.

'No, should she be?'

Bertie checked his watch. 'She's popping in apparently.' He shivered. 'God, it's raw out there today. I don't suppose it's anything other than a rallying the troops speech, and her annual inspection of the Christmas decorations, which look superb as usual, Daisy.'

Kit wasn't fooled either. 'And the fact that she chooses to do it the day after you provided her with sales figures is a coincidence, is it?' His eyes narrowed. 'What's going on, Bertie?'

He shrugged. 'Nothing that I'm aware of. Sales are down, but you know that, it's not a secret. I think it's more a case of Mother wanting us all to pull together on this one. Not something we're especially good at, as well you know. She's asked Lawrence to drop in too, lend some weight to the argument and all that.'

Kit's head shot up. 'Lawrence is coming in?' He rolled his eyes. 'Oh, fantastic… Never mind the weight, but we can certainly count on him to lend the argument.'

Daisy ignored him even though he was right. Lawrence was the eldest Buchanan brother, an arrogant bully who treated her with very little respect most of the time. Not like Bertie, who at least acknowledged that she did do some things right.

'Are you really sure that's all it is?' she asked anxiously.

Bertie was about to answer when Lawrence strode in, looking most put out at having to make an appearance. He was much taller than his brothers, his height accentuated by his formal suit and long, imposing overcoat, which flapped about his legs as he walked. He nodded at both Kit and Bertie and then, sweeping the room with a critical gaze, he focused his attention on Daisy. He opened his mouth to say something and then thought better of it, instead carrying on through into the back room.

'I do hope that someone has bought some decent coffee,' came his voice through the door.

'No, I…' Daisy looked anxiously at Bertie. That was normally her job, but she'd had no idea that everyone would be coming in today and wasn't at all prepared. In fact, she wasn't sure there would even be enough milk left.

Bertie raised a placatory hand and disappeared after his brother, leaving Kit staring at her, his expression unreadable. She turned away and continued with her polishing.

Bea arrived moments later, dressed for the Arctic, her habitual tweed trouser suit topped with a plum-coloured cloak, its deep fur ruff matching the mittens she also wore. Despite her diminutive size she cut an imposing figure, jet-black hair piled high on her head, held with any number of diamante clips. They gleamed under the bright lights as her piercing blue eyes swept the room.

'Daisy,' she said, smiling broadly. 'You've done a marvellous job, as always. It all looks quite delightful.'

Daisy smiled, thankful at least for the normality of the greeting from Bea. She was about to add her agreement when the door to the back room opened and Bertie and Lawrence stepped through. She groaned inwardly. Judging by the uneasy atmosphere and the fact that all three brothers were present at once, it could only mean one thing. Bea was about to make an announcement.

Bea's announcements were always highly theatrical and invariably meant more work for Daisy. Work which supposedly would be shared, but which somehow only ever fell to her to put into practice. As the eldest brother, Lawrence was particularly good at bending Bea's ear but, because he rarely stepped foot on the shop floor and his ideas had no grounding in experience, they usually came to naught, despite Daisy's best efforts.

Daisy looked across at Kit who was standing a little awkwardly, a watchful eye on his brothers. She realised why as she took in the expressions on their faces. There was none of the usual arrogance that Lawrence displayed, and Bertie looked most sombre. In fact, they looked bewildered to have found themselves called to a meeting at all, which meant that they also had no idea what Bea was going to say... Daisy's heart began to beat a little faster.

Bea pulled her mittens from her hands and swung her cloak from her shoulders, dumping everything on top of one of the counters. She placed a hand reverently on the glass and then looked about her with an expression of wonder. Her fingers lifted from the counter and, as if she were a small child exploring a magical kingdom for the first time, she glided around the room, touching here, and stroking there. Small gasps and sighs punctuated her movements until she had completed a full circuit of the room and was back where she started, standing in front of the Christmas tree. She raised both arms in the air, looking at her audience expectantly, her bright blue eyes sparkling with excitement.

'Oh, I shall miss all of this!' she announced, her face lit by an enormous smile.

Daisy was so busy watching the theatrics of the show Bea was putting on for them that she almost missed what she had said.

'Why, where are you going?' Daisy couldn't remember when she had last seen Bea so animated.

Bea's eyes twinkled even brighter as she looked from one expectant face to the next. 'I'm going to retire!' she said gleefully. 'After Christmas. Charles and I are going to live in Spain.'

Daisy looked at Kit, who was white as a sheet, and then at Lawrence. As the eldest brother he normally assumed the role of spokesperson for the family, but she could tell that this had come as much of a shock to him as it was to her. Daisy opened her mouth to speak but Lawrence beat her to it.

'Who the bloody hell is Charles?' he said, glaring at his mother and looking at Bertie for clues. But even Bertie, the unacknowledged favourite, looked stricken.

Bea drew herself up. 'Charles is my new beau,' she replied. 'He has asked me to marry him and move to Spain, and I have agreed.'

'Since when?' exploded Lawrence. 'This is utterly ridiculous, Mother. None of us even know who this man is—' He broke off to glare at Daisy. 'Oh, I bet you knew though, didn't you?' he accused her.

Daisy shook her head rapidly, wondering why it felt as if her whole world had suddenly fallen apart.

Lawrence looked across at Bertie and Kit and, receiving confirmation that neither of them knew anything about Bea's new boyfriend either, turned back to his mother. 'Well how long have you known him? You can't just up sticks and disappear like that.'

But Bea had held up her hand for silence, excitement still gleaming in her eyes, but framed with a steely determination Daisy knew of old.

'And this, Lawrence, is precisely why I didn't tell you. Because, I knew you would react in exactly this way and, quite frankly, it's none of your business.' She looked at each of her children in turn. 'As you know I have been on my own for eighteen years since your father died and, in that time, I have had very little in the way of male company. Bringing you up and running the business has taken all of my energy but, as you are also very well aware, I am sixty on New Year's Eve and the time has come to put my own needs first.' She smiled at Daisy. 'Don't look so worried, dear, everything is going to be all right.'

Daisy failed to see how it could be. Buchanans was all she had known since she left school, and Beatrice Buchanan her only boss, and possibly the only real friend she had ever had. What on earth would she do now? And who would run the business? Her head was filling with questions but Lawrence was, as always, one step ahead.

'Mother,' he said firmly. 'I'm sure none of us begrudges you a life outside of this place. Nor do we discount the sacrifices you have made in looking after us all these years, but to say it's none of our business… For goodness' sake, it's *absolutely* our business; we're standing in the middle of it. You can't just give this all up on a whim because of some fly-by-night romance and—'

Bea silenced him with a withering look. 'For your information I have known Charles since before your father and I were married. In fact, had things turned out a little differently…' She paused. 'Well, they didn't, and so I married your father and we were happy right up until the day he died. And I never told any of you about Charles because, if I had, it might have made things somewhat awkward for him. But we kept in touch, and when, two years ago, he found himself in, well let's just say in a different personal situation, we rekindled our friendship.'

'Two years!' Bertie's indignant tone rang out around the shop. 'You've been seeing him for two years and you didn't bother to tell any of us about him.'

'I *chose* not to tell you, Bertie. There's a difference.' She glanced at the clock on the wall and then nodded at Daisy. 'It's five o'clock, dear,' she said. 'Perhaps you could turn the sign to closed now and lock the door. I'd rather we weren't interrupted.'

Daisy did as she was asked, walking back to stand behind the counter on trembling legs.

'So, as I was saying,' continued Bea. 'Charles is not someone I have only just met, about whom I know nothing. Neither is he the scoundrel you all seem to be implying, and I have already made up my mind about our future arrangements so there's really no point in discussing it further.' She smiled directly at Daisy. 'What we do need to discuss, however, are the arrangements for the continuation of the business.' She smoothed down the jacket of her suit and patted the back of her hair to check that all was in place.

'Perhaps we should go through to the back,' she continued. 'So that we might be a little more comfortable. I have one or two things more to say.'

Daisy sneaked a peek at the brothers – at Kit who looked like he was about to be sick, at Bertie who was staring at his mother open-mouthed, and at Lawrence who was bright red and seemingly about to explode. Daisy had no idea how she was feeling. She was used to Bea being rather eccentric, but she had never acted quite so peculiarly before. How had the afternoon changed from being one of fairly mundane routine to one of utter chaos all in the space of half an hour?

Daisy waited until everyone had filed past her and then picked up the bottle of glass polish. She had a feeling that the meeting would go on for quite some time and she might as well get on and clean while she could. She was about to spray the surface of the counter nearest to her when Bea's voice floated back through the doorway.

'Heavens, Daisy, whatever are you doing? You of all people need to come and hear what I have to say.'

Daisy groaned softly. She would really rather not; much better to pretend it wasn't happening at all. But she went through into the other room just the same.

Bea wasted no time in taking centre stage once more.

'Now, as I mentioned, I have some things I would like to say. And I would like to say them without being interrupted – Lawrence, bear that in mind, dear – and I would also like to point out that, despite the fact that you all clearly think I have finally gone and lost my marbles, I have taken a good deal of time to think about all of this and I have considered it very carefully. As such, I would like you to respect my decision. It is final, and I will not be entering into any discussion over it.'

The words *have I made myself clear* hovered in the air between them.

'First of all, I would like to apologise to you, Daisy. And I would also like to thank you. You have been my right-hand woman, my confidante, my friend, and the glue that has held Buchanans together for a very long time. Quite simply, I could not have managed without you these last few years, and indeed neither would my little shop. It would have closed long before now had it not been for your loyalty and hard work. I know that what I have to say will affect you as much as the others, if not more, and for that I am sorry. I would like you three boys to recognise that fact before we proceed.'

Daisy blushed bright red as three pairs of eyes turned to scrutinise her. Bertie, as she knew he would be, was the first to react.

'Hear, hear,' he said, smiling at her, which made her knees feel weird. Lawrence glowered at her, but quickly changed his expression and gave her a tight smile. Kit gave an odd little wave of his hand.

'So then, without further ado: I'm sure you've all worked out that once I retire there will be no one to run Buchanans. You have all had your part to play in the business but clearly someone has to take the helm... and, as the eldest, Lawrence, it would seem that that mantle should fall to you...'

Daisy's heart sank as a supercilious smile crept over Lawrence's face.

'However…' Bea held up her hand. 'However… you all have qualities which make me think you could be up to the task… just as you all have rather less desirable attributes which make me consider that you could not. And yes, Lawrence, that does include you, dear.'

She paused for a moment, frowning. 'And there is also the fact that none of those things really address something which I have been considering for some while now, and that is the indefinable something that Buchanans needs if it's ever going to survive. I don't need to tell you that shops are finding it tough at the moment. Times are changing and we need to change with them, be prepared to take risks, and to think about things a little differently. Whoever takes over the reins will truly need to know what will make Buchanans remain special going into the future, someone who really understands what the business is all about. So, I have come up with a way to help me find that person.'

'Why do I get the feeling we're not going to like it…' muttered Lawrence.

Bea clapped her hands together in delight. 'Oh, Lawrence, don't be such a baby. Of course you're going to like it because it's going to be *such* fun.' She beamed at them all in turn, clearly delighted with herself. 'And it's obvious, really, when you think about it. What better way to decide who should run the business than by having a little competition! I want you all to choose a Christmas gift – and whoever chooses most wisely will be the one to whom I shall pass the reins.'

She took a step towards Daisy. 'And I know that I have a very important birthday coming up, but this gift is not for me… it's for Daisy.'

Daisy looked up in shock.

'A gift? But what kind of gift?' Bertie's voice was tinged with mild panic.

'Well an item of jewellery, obviously,' replied Lawrence, his tone scathing.

Bea smiled. 'Yes, Bertie dear. It should be an item of jewellery… what kind will be up to you. Now, it can be an item from the shop, or it can be something you design yourself. In which case you don't need to have the piece made up, but I will need to see drawings, and to know the materials used, together with costings. Whichever option you choose, you have a budget of five thousand pounds. But the absolute, most important, thing is that I shall want to know *why* you feel it is the perfect gift. In the end that is the only criteria I shall use to make my final judgement.'

There was a stunned silence, during which Daisy had to remind herself to breathe. She could feel all eyes turn on her.

'Does anybody have any questions?' asked Bea. 'Because if you do, ask them now. Other than what I have just told you, there are no further rules and any other considerations will be yours alone. So, to recap – one item of jewellery – five thousand pounds – and the perfect gift. Do all that and the business will be yours. Your gifts should be presented to Daisy at our normal celebrations on Christmas Eve.'

'But *you* get to choose which is the best gift, and not Daisy herself?' asked Kit. 'How is that fair? Shouldn't she choose?'

Daisy looked between the two of them, horrified at the thought, but, to her relief, Bea simply smiled. 'No, because I shall be asking Daisy to help all of you as it is, and to make the poor girl have the final say would just be too much. I don't want anything to be more difficult than it already is.'

'But none of us really know Daisy that well,' said Kit, frowning.

'Then I suggest you get to know her,' replied Bea. 'You have between now and Christmas Eve.'

She looked at her sons in turn. 'Now, does anyone have any questions? Because if not, I really think we ought to let Daisy get home for the evening.'

Daisy daren't even look at anyone. She didn't need to, the air surrounding them was bristling with simmering anger and indignation. An atmosphere that Bea seemed utterly unaware of.

'I have a question,' said Lawrence, his deep voice loud in the hushed room.

'Yes, dear.'

'I'm sure I speak for all of us when I say that this evening's… turn of events has been rather a surprise. I can understand you wanting to retire, Mother. I can accept, just about, your relationship with someone we know nothing of, but what I find utterly bizarre is this rather childish competition. To pass over the running of Buchanans based on something akin to a parlour game seems foolhardy and completely unfair. Surely having us put forward a proper business plan together with financial forecasts would be a far better way of ascertaining who is fit to run the company?'

Bea fixed him with a steely look. 'I can see how that might favour you, Lawrence, but perhaps your brothers, less so… And I have made up my mind about this. You each should have a fair and equal chance of winning and I believe my solution provides this. Assuming of course that each of you wishes to enter the competition; there is no rule to say you have to…'

She held Lawrence's look for a moment and, although he glared at her, it was clear he had nothing more to say. The thoughts in Daisy's head were rushing around at a breathless pace and she was having enormous trouble trying to catch hold of one for long enough to listen to it. But what would happen to her was not her only worry right now.

What did Bea mean when she said the brothers should get to know her? Daisy had no desire to know them any better than she did now. And as for having to ever work with Lawrence… She shook her head. No, she couldn't bear to even think about it. She had a sudden urge to run, to get as far away from the shop as she could. To return to the quiet calm and order of her little cottage.

As if reading her thoughts, Bea moved forward and swept Daisy into a hug.

'Now, you must go home, my dear. It's your day off tomorrow which will give everyone a chance to settle down and then the day after, well, the fun can really begin! Oh, I do so love Christmas.' She looked around her. 'I can't believe that this is going to be my last one here, but I know you'll do everything you can to make it extra special, Daisy. I've always been able to rely on you.'

Daisy looked about her, speechless. Did Bea even know what she'd done? How could she do that to her when Bea had been the one to save her all those years ago? If it hadn't been for her… Daisy shuddered to think what would have happened. She felt utterly disconnected from everything, as if she'd been cast adrift.

Mistaking her silence for indecision, Bea gave her a reassuring smile. 'And you don't need to worry about closing up. We can take care of that tonight. It's the least we can do, isn't it, boys? And have a lovely day tomorrow. I can't wait to hear all about it.'

Moments later, having collected her coat and bag, Daisy found herself standing outside the front door of the shop, feeling rather lost. She took a step forward, looking about her, surprised to find that the world was still turning, that people were still bustling about their business, and that the huge tree in the square opposite was still sparkling with coloured lights.

She pulled her coat more firmly around her, tilting her head and blinking as something cold landed on her eyelash. Looking up into the sky she could see the first soft flakes of snow drifting down, their shapes illuminated under the glow of the street lamp. The windows of the shops around her twinkled with lights and, just across the street, the market was alive with sounds and smells as the traders packed up for the day, their stalls still gathering crowds.

Daisy watched for a few moments, transfixed by such ordinariness; a scene that she had seen hundreds of times over and yet which this evening seemed to hold such poignancy. It was nearly Christmas; a time of goodwill and good cheer and she was usually its biggest fan. Except that this year it seemed as if everyone had started the festivities without her.

Friday 6th December

Nineteen shopping days until Christmas

Daisy already knew where to find Hope Corner Farm. She had seen an advertisement for it a few months ago in the local paper's wedding pages and, since a flower farm sounded like the most beautiful place on earth, she'd driven over to take a look.

Daisy hadn't been disappointed. One of the lovely owners had shown her around, explaining that they hadn't been open for long and not everything they planned was up and running yet, but she'd let Daisy have a look at the field where the flowers were growing in neat rows, bursting with blooms. The owner had also let her take home a huge bouquet for a fraction of the price that it would have cost her elsewhere. 'Hope Blooms', they called themselves, and Daisy had smiled at the pun. If she ever got married, she would like to come back and order her wedding flowers from the owner, who funnily enough was called Flora.

Today she was on her way there to learn how to make seasonal decorations, but it had been all she could do to drag herself out of bed. She hadn't slept at all well and her head was muzzy from lack of sleep and unshed tears. She had seen the course advertised a few weeks ago and had booked it straight away in a surge of Christmassy enthusiasm, but the thought was laughable now.

She had tried to think logically about Bea's decision last night but, try as she might, she still felt incredibly hurt. Bea had given her the job shortly after she'd left school and they'd hit it off immediately, despite Daisy's shyness and Bea's very individual personality. A year turned into two, and then three, and now she had been at Buchanans coming up to eight years.

Daisy had been just as shocked as any of the brothers to learn of Bea's romance and impending retirement, even though she knew that her boss often did things just because she considered them outlandish and wanted to shock people. More than once Bea had hinted that good things were in the pipeline for Daisy's future at the shop, but now the time had come and all Bea wanted was for her to act as referee between her three sons, one of whom Daisy would ultimately end up working for. That's if she even had a job at the end of it all. With Bea leaving and the business failing, it didn't take a genius to work out what would probably happen. It was every man for himself, and that clearly didn't include Daisy.

There were another couple of cars already parked at the farm by the time Daisy pulled up in front of the gates, but there was still fifteen minutes to go until the course started. She clenched her fingers into her palms and, inhaling deeply, reminded herself why she was here. Buchanans could wait until tomorrow, otherwise the day off Daisy had so been looking forward to would be a waste. Pulling herself together, she climbed hesitantly from the warmth of her car and looked out across the yard in front of her.

Almost immediately Daisy spotted a tall woman coming towards her, her face lit by a warm smile of greeting. It wasn't the same person who had shown her round before, but someone at least twenty years older, wearing jeans and a thick red jumper. Hardly the riot of clashing colour and pattern that Flora had worn, but it suited the woman's tumble of long grey hair and brown eyes. The smile grew even wider as she drew near.

'Hello,' she said, extending a hand. 'I'm Grace. Are you here for the course?'

Daisy nodded, shaking hands. 'Yes, I'm Daisy Turner. I hope I'm not too early. It's a bit of a habit of mine, I'm afraid.'

'Is it?' replied Grace. 'Mine too actually. Hence why I'm hovering looking for people. Flora said no one would turn up until the last minute… but…' She tapped the side of her nose. 'I knew there'd be people like me.' She smiled, instantly putting Daisy at ease. 'Why don't you come on down and you can get settled in out of the cold. Have a drink too if you'd like.'

She led the way across the yard, giving Daisy her first opportunity to look around. When she had visited in the summer there had been flowers everywhere she looked but even now, in the middle of winter, the place was still full of colour. A line of half a dozen Christmas trees stood in bright coloured pots along the length of the yard, their twinkling lights cheery against the gloomy grey sky. The doors to various outbuildings that they passed were hung with ribboned wreaths and, towards the far end of the yard, a long low building was covered in more coloured lights. It was towards this that they now walked.

'Have you been here before?' asked Grace. 'The farm hasn't been open all that long.'

Daisy nodded, her head still swivelling at all there was to see. 'I came to have a look around at the end of the summer and Flora explained that this was their first year as commercial growers. I thought it was such a lovely thing to be able to walk among the flowers. When I get married I will definitely be coming back.'

'Well, Flora will be delighted to hear that. When is your wedding?'

Daisy blushed. 'Oh... I don't even have a boyfriend yet. I just meant that when I do get married, if I do, then...'

Grace smiled. 'I might be a little biased, but I couldn't agree more. I'm not about to get married...' She paused, pulling a face. 'I've been there and done that, but I certainly wouldn't dream of going anywhere else. Flora's my friend but she's also an incredible florist. What that woman doesn't know about flowers isn't worth knowing.' She stopped, looking Daisy up and down. 'And can I just say that I absolutely adore your cloak. But make sure you keep an eye on it during the day, otherwise when you come to go home later you'll find that Flora has pinched it. You might have noticed that her sense of style is somewhat unique.'

Daisy returned the smile and nodded at the compliment. 'She's very... colourful, but it suits her. I'm not that adventurous, I'm afraid, but my cloak was...' She faltered at the sudden welling sadness brought on by the realisation of what she was about to say. 'A gift, from my boss.'

'It's tweed, isn't it? Such beautiful colours.'

Daisy looked down at the flecks of blue, green, grey and teal, thinking of the Christmas two years ago when Bea had given it to her. She had been extraordinarily touched by the gesture. She blinked hard. 'Yes, made in Bute. My boss is Scottish and rather eccentric. She has these made specially for her by a woman on the island.'

Grace was still admiring her cloak. 'Well, eccentric or not, she has excellent taste. And what does your boss do... what do you do?'

'I work in the jewellers in town; Buchanans,' she replied.

Grace's eyes widened. 'Wow,' she said. 'A little out of my price range.'

'A little out of most people's,' Daisy replied. 'But I'll have to see what the new year brings,' she added. 'My boss announced her retirement yesterday and so someone new will be running the business.' She let her expression say the rest.

Grace studied her for a moment. 'Well then, hopefully today will help to take your mind off things,' she said warmly. 'Here we are. Come and say hello to Flora.'

Grace opened the door and ushered Daisy inside.

'Oh…' Daisy's hand went straight to her mouth as she gazed around her in wonder, catching Grace's eye who was grinning at her.

'Kind of gets you like that, doesn't it? Amazing to think this place used to be a milking shed.'

It was the smell which hit Daisy first. Rich, intoxicating, verdant… no, more than that… *alive*. It was the only word she could use to describe it. Here, in the middle of winter, was a room positively brimming with life. Every surface held flowers and foliage. It lay on the tables, stood in huge buckets dotted around the floor, even hung from the walls.

The room was long and quite narrow, with whitewashed walls, and open to the rafters which towered above them. It should have been a cold and draughty space but, right at the far end, a large log burner was ablaze, casting a warm glow into the room.

It took Daisy a moment to spot Flora, her forest-green jumper embroidered with big white daisies almost camouflaging her as she arranged more bunches of greenery on a table. But almost at the same instant as Daisy noticed her, Flora looked up and grinned, putting down the foliage and coming forward.

'Hello,' she said, her smile of greeting changing almost immediately to a quizzical look. 'We've met before, haven't we?'

Daisy was impressed. 'You have a good memory,' she said. 'And you're right. I came to have a look around a few months ago. Just being nosey, I'm afraid, but when I saw today's course advertised I knew I had to come back.'

'And in the most gorgeous cloak I've ever seen. Don't leave that lying around, will you, or I'll have to snaffle it.' She laughed as she caught Grace's grin, obviously knowing that her friend was well aware of her penchant for such things. 'I can't remember your name though, I'm sorry.'

Daisy held out her hand and introduced herself, surprised to find she wasn't half as nervous as she thought she would be.

'Come down to the far end,' added Flora. 'It's much warmer down there, and I've put a few chairs around so that we can have a bit of an informal session before we start on our own projects. And besides, very importantly, there's tea and biscuits, cake too. And hot chocolate… coffee… water… fruit juice.' She rolled her eyes. 'I got a bit carried away,' she admitted.

'I might just go and see if anyone else has arrived,' said Grace. 'Save me a biscuit though, Amos has eaten all of mine… again… and I'd kill for a Jammie Dodger.'

Flora stood back to let Daisy go on ahead, leaning in as she passed. 'Grace's partner has a very sweet tooth,' she whispered. 'He's the world's biggest biscuit thief.'

Daisy nodded although she didn't really understand; she and food had rather an odd relationship. As she got closer to the table she could see it was groaning with dishes. How did people *choose* when there was just so much to choose from?

To her immense relief, however, she spied a plain digestive on one of the plates; she could cope with that. And plain tea too, that was okay. She took a seat, basking in the warmth from the fire, and began to think about what the day might bring.

It didn't take long to find out. As soon as everyone had arrived and was clutching a hot drink, Flora sat in front of them all, a basket of materials at her feet, and explained that the day was all about finding their own way of working. There were no right or wrong ways to make a Christmas wreath, or other floral decorations for that matter, and it was all about experimentation; with colour, shape and texture. Everyone had different ideas about what worked for them, be it friendly, fun or flamboyant, and what Flora wanted was to show them some basic skills so that they could go off and apply what they had learned. And that was exactly what Daisy needed.

Daisy had never made a wreath before. She had bought them, at Christmastime, but they were always a little lacking in something. And yet the first one Flora showed them made Daisy's eyes light up. Gone were the traditional colour scheme and ribbons. Instead, it was full of flower heads, silvery foliage and what looked suspiciously like popcorn of all things. Daisy sat entranced while Flora described the process involved to shape the wreath and what elements she was going to add to it, binding the foliage not with wire, but with whips of curly willow which themselves added to the design. The texture it created was so intriguing. Before she had even finished, Daisy was thinking of the silver clay she had brought with her. It wouldn't hurt to ask, surely…

After three quarters of an hour, Flora had shown them how to wire bunches of a huge variety of materials so that they would stay secure, how to make bows and rosettes, and how to start weaving flower heads and foliage together to make a garland. It was enough to get them started and, standing up, she ushered everyone back through to the tables that were heaped with all the things they could choose from to create their own wreath. Daisy felt like a small child in a sweet shop.

Her eye was immediately taken by some huge hydrangea heads, dried to a soft lilac colour, some of the petals slightly more grey, others more pink.

'Beautiful, aren't they?' said Flora. 'They make the most amazing centrepieces.'

'Did you grow these?' asked Daisy, rather in awe.

'Yep, and dried them.' Flora looked up and Daisy could see bunches of flowers hanging from the beams. 'We didn't intend it this way, but the building turned out to be the perfect place to do it.'

'I would never have thought of using anything like this.'

Flora smiled. 'Most people discount them because they're so big, but actually once they're used in a design they look really delicate and, as long as you pick complementary colours, everything blends together beautifully.'

Daisy cast her eye along the table. 'So maybe some of this eucalyptus would work…?'

'That would be perfect. And you can either weave it around the wreath or just take small pieces and bunch them together to use as an accent. Have a play and see what you think.'

Daisy nodded, her fingers lingering over some ivy and small balls of something woven. She turned one over in her hand, thinking, before taking her finds back to the table she was working at. And then she sat for a few minutes letting her mind create the images she would need. The morning passed in a blur.

Daisy was so wrapped up in what she was doing that it took a few moments to realise that the atmosphere in the room had changed. Glancing up, she realised that the hum of industry had stopped and most people were looking around them expectantly. She hadn't noticed, but where the tea and biscuits had been laid out earlier, the table was now groaning with platters of sandwiches and other savoury nibbles. Daisy had almost forgotten that lunch was being provided.

Flora waved a hand from the other end of the room.

'Well, lunch is here folks, if you're ready. There's no set timetable for the day, so we can stop now. Or, if you want to carry on for a bit, that's fine too.'

A woman closest to Flora got to her feet.

'Oh, and feel free to wash your hands, there's a sink in the corner.'

Daisy looked back at her wreath. She would have preferred to carry on, but she would stop if everyone else was. She bent down and took the clay from her bag, placing it on the table. She would ask Flora about it once lunch was out of the way. And if the clay was there, ready, she couldn't pretend to herself that she had forgotten about it. She got to her feet somewhat reluctantly and was about to go and join the others when the door behind her banged.

Grace appeared in the doorway trying to manoeuvre a tray of glasses through the opening while simultaneously holding it open. She caught Daisy's eye and grimaced.

'Sorry, I'm letting all the cold air in.'

Daisy shot to her rescue, grabbing the door and settling a glass which looked about to topple.

'Thanks so much, the door's heavier than it looks. Would you mind holding it for a moment, Amos is just behind me with the drinks.'

The moment she said it, a foot braced itself against the opening and, peering around the door, Daisy came face to face with a broad smile that she had seen only once but would remember anywhere. The man's face lit up with recognition.

'Oh, hello again,' he said, the smile widening even further, then dipping slightly when he realised where he had last seen her. Because this man was Amos, Grace's partner, the man with the bright-red boots she had last seen only the day before enquiring about jewellery. It could have been for his mother, or a sister, a friend even, but Daisy would lay money on it being for Grace. In which case the last thing he would want was for Grace to know that they had already met or, more importantly, *where* they had met. Far too many surprises had been ruined in similar fashion, and Daisy's nose for such things was finely tuned.

Daisy flicked an anxious look towards Grace, but she had already moved down the room, intent on carrying her cargo safely, and if she'd heard Amos's greeting she made no show of it.

Daisy smiled and whispered hello, passing a surreptitious finger across her lips as she nodded towards Grace. There was a flash of understanding in Amos's eyes.

'Thank you,' he replied, and they both knew it was for more than holding open the door.

She closed the door carefully behind them and followed Amos to the far end of the room, where everyone had gathered.

'Right, come and grab something to eat, everyone,' announced Flora. 'Don't stand on ceremony. This is Amos, who lives next door with Grace and, among other things, transformed this lowly cow shed into the fabulous space we have now. But for today, he's just going to give a hand with the drinks.'

Amos gave a courtly bow. Hanging back to let everyone else go first, Daisy was able to watch him for a moment.

There was nothing especially remarkable about him. He was of medium height, with jet-black curly hair, and was wearing jeans and a thick Guernsey sweater plus the red boots of course. But there was something about his face that seemed so familiar to Daisy, as if she had known him all her life. He looked up and caught her watching him, forcing her to look away quickly, but not before she saw a flash of something in his eyes too. Part of her wanted to find out what, but the other part was terrified.

Soon, everyone else had filled their plates and Daisy went forward. Not to have done so would have looked odd, but she was always nervous of any food she hadn't made herself, and if it wasn't plain then she would struggle.

'Everything is vegetarian,' said Flora. 'I hope that's okay. It just seemed easier in the long run…' She smirked. 'Actually, I forgot to put dietary information on the booking forms,' she admitted. 'So it's my fault.' She looked up at Daisy, sensing her hesitation. 'Oh God, you're not a vegan, are you?'

Daisy shook her head, smiling hesitantly. 'No… just a fusspot, I'm afraid. I don't like things that are… complicated.'

Most people usually pulled a face when Daisy said that or, at the very least, told her that she didn't know what she was missing. 'Go on, just try it', was another phrase she cringed at. But Flora just smiled.

'Cheese?' she suggested. 'Or there's egg sandwiches, which make me shudder personally but I'm told everyone likes. Everyone but me, obviously. There's nothing else with it, only a little salad cream. And the quiche is mushroom if you fancy that.'

Daisy stared at her in wonderment. Two of her favourite fillings, and the sandwiches were made from thick doorsteps of granary bread which she would have sworn was homemade. Daisy couldn't abide white bread. It really was the strangest thing. Growing up, she had worried endlessly about all the things that made her different from everyone else, but her brother always told her that one day she would find the others, as he called them – people just like her who had little oddities – and she would instantly forget that she had ever considered herself different. And now here she was, and it was happening just as her brother had said it would. It couldn't have come at a better time. She nodded enthusiastically and began to fill her plate.

Once it was full she really had no other excuse for not saying what was on her mind and, screwing up her courage, she turned to Flora.

'After lunch, would you mind helping me with something?' she asked. 'Or rather, would you give me your opinion on it? I've had an idea and I'm really not sure whether it's good… or bad.'

'Of course,' Flora replied. 'Sounds intriguing… but that's what we're here for, isn't that right, Amos? We like intriguing ideas.'

Daisy started, realising that Amos had come to stand right beside her.

'Oh, we do indeed,' he replied, looking straight at Daisy, his eyes twinkling with amusement. 'And, in fact, I've had an idea of my own and I'm absolutely certain you're the person to help.'

Friday 6th December

Nineteen shopping days until Christmas

It was all Daisy could do to finish her lunch. Although they all sat in front of the log burner chatting excitedly about the morning's progress, she only really had half her brain tuned in; the other half was busy trying to work out what on earth Amos could have meant.

Almost as soon as everyone sat back at their tables following their break, Flora came to join her, pulling out a chair and sitting down. She leaned forward, a conspiratorial look on her face.

'Well, this is all very curious,' she said, her voice low. 'Apparently Amos wants to talk to you about some jewellery, but it's a bit hush-hush, which is code for Grace mustn't know. So he can't come over until the coast is clear. I didn't know you were a jeweller.'

'I'm not,' replied Daisy instantly, immediately pulling a face. 'Well, not in the way Amos means, I don't suppose. I work for Buchanans in town,' she clarified. 'And Amos came into the shop yesterday, obviously needing some help, but I'm afraid I was busy serving another customer and so he got my hapless assistant who is about as much use as a chocolate teapot.'

'Oh, I *see*… well, that explains it.' Flora beamed. 'I don't suppose Grace will mind my telling you, but she and Amos haven't been together that long; only since the summer actually. And you couldn't meet two nicer people, they are absolutely made for one another. It's so romantic.'

Daisy gave a little inward sigh of pleasure. Vicarious pleasure or not, it was still pleasure.

'So, Amos has obviously got a Christmas present for Grace in mind,' added Flora. 'I wonder what he wants to get her?' She grinned. 'Oh, that's got *me* excited now.' She looked down at the table. 'Sorry, that's not helping you at all, is it? What was it you wanted to ask me?'

But before Daisy could even reply, Flora spotted what she'd been working on and picked up one of the clay leaves Daisy had just made.

'What are these...?' Flora asked, looking up. 'How on earth did you make them?'

The leaf that she had picked up was one that Daisy had pressed into clay just a few moments ago – an ivy leaf, its rich veining perfectly transferred onto the surface. She had then cut out the leaf shape from the clay, leaving an almost exact replica of the original.

Daisy cocked her head to the side, looking at it critically. 'I'm not sure whether what I have in mind will work,' she said. 'But I wondered whether it would be possible to make a wreath that would last indefinitely, and to which I could then add these.' She fingered the clay shape.

Flora frowned slightly, but nodded. 'Well you could, but...'

Flora was interested, but Daisy could see that she didn't understand what she was looking at. And then Daisy realised that she hadn't explained herself at all well. She picked up the clay leaf again. 'This is silver,' she explained. 'Or at least, it will be, once it's fired.'

Flora's eyes widened. 'Silver?' She turned the leaf over, seeing only the dull grey surface. 'Do you mean you paint it?'

Daisy shook her head. 'No... hang on a minute.' She fished inside her bag, taking out the little cloth pouch she kept there. She laid its contents on the table: an assortment of shimmering flower heads, leaves and tiny buds. 'These are all made from silver clay,' she explained. 'Just like the ivy leaf I've just started. But they've been fired with a gas torch so that the clay burns off, leaving just silver behind. It's polished and then, well, you can see what it looks like.'

Flora stared, her eyes roaming the table. 'Oh my God…' She peered closer at the leaf in her hand. 'So once this is finished it will look like those do, like silver?' She looked up at Daisy, a hand held over her heart in wonder. 'But these are so incredibly beautiful…'

'Are they?' Daisy blinked at her in surprise.

Flora nodded rapidly. 'I've never seen anything like them before. I thought you said you weren't a jeweller?'

'I'm not, goodness… me?' Her cheeks flushed red. 'No, this is just a hobby and I—'

Flora snorted. 'Well you damn well should be. These are stunning, Daisy, I mean it.' She sat back, still holding the leaf in her hand. 'Tell me what you see,' she urged. 'When you said about making the wreath more permanent and adding the silver. Explain.'

Daisy looked at her, astonished, but Flora wasn't kidding – she actually wanted to know. She took a deep breath. 'I've always loved the idea of jewellery being like a living thing, representing some part of yourself, something you love. And, for me, I'm generally happiest when I'm outside.'

She paused for a moment trying to gather what she needed to say. 'There's so much there that gives me joy – the teeniest detail on a petal, the gossamer threads of a spider's web, or the beads of dew on a summer morning. So what I like to do is merge the two – natural items combined with silver work.' She pulled a face. 'It doesn't always work, but here on this wreath, the colours and textures are just so wonderful I thought that if I could preserve all the materials then I could add small silver details. A bunch of ivy leaves for example, or a cluster of holly berries...'

She lifted up the wreath, peering at it. 'I haven't quite worked it all out yet, but I'd design the silver element so that it could be taken off and worn as a piece of jewellery if you wanted...' She trailed off, not quite sure how to express herself.

'So that the piece exists in more than one place,' said Flora. 'It becomes so much more than just a wreath. Wow... I have never ever thought of doing anything like that, but it's inspired, Daisy. Really, it would look amazing.'

'But is it even possible?'

Flora grinned and nodded. 'Oh yes! The hydrangea heads are already dried, the willow is, well willow... and you could preserve the eucalyptus in glycerine before you used it; that way it would keep its colour and suppleness.' She darted a look further down the room to where Grace was sitting at one of the other tables. 'That's actually a trick that Grace taught me. You can preserve all kinds of leaves that way.'

Daisy's brain was already beginning to conjure numerous different possibilities. She looked down at her work and then back up at Flora whose eyes were shining with excitement, and she felt a tiny shiver run through her.

Flora reached out a hand and touched her arm. 'I have got to get Amos down here to see this. Without Grace,' she added. 'This could be just the kind of thing he's looking for.' She stood up before Daisy could protest. 'Wait here and I'll go and fetch him. Act casual.' She grinned at Daisy and winked before nonchalantly strolling back down the room to where Amos was still sitting, eating a sandwich beside the fire.

Daisy's heart was hammering. This wasn't supposed to happen. It was the first time she had ever shared her thoughts about the things she made, but Flora had liked them. No, Flora had loved them! She sat back and looked around her at the amazing space full of things that Flora had grown. There was a row of gorgeous prints on the wall, too, which added to the overall effect and, with so much else to look at in the room, Daisy realised that she had scarcely noticed them before. Now that she looked, she could see instantly who had created them – a woman with wild dark hair, wearing the brightest jumper that Daisy had ever seen, and who exuded such… joy… about everything she did. Daisy felt quite breathless from the feeling.

She took a deep breath, trying to damp down her feelings. Don't get too carried away, she told herself; this wasn't the kind of thing that happened to her. But further down the room she could see that Flora had sliced a piece of cake and was casually nibbling at it as she chatted to Amos. She was standing side on, so Daisy couldn't see her expression but, as she watched, Amos looked straight down the room at her, a huge smile suddenly breaking out across his face. It was like having a spotlight shone on her.

Amos looked away quickly, placing his hand across his face, and Daisy recognised it as something she did when trying to hide how she felt. He nodded a couple of times and then Daisy saw Flora cross to where Grace was sitting and bend to say something in her ear. Grace got to her feet and with an easy smile made purposefully for the door at the far end. Seconds later, with Grace now gone, Amos came to sit beside her.

He fell on her silver pieces with undisguised glee. 'See, I knew you'd be able to help me,' he said.

'I'm just sorry I couldn't help you the other day, in the shop. Kit isn't always very… helpful.'

Amos regarded her evenly. 'I think he had his mind on other things, that's all. But then he was reading a very good book, so I can see why that would be the case. Actually, you should ask him about it one day, I think you'd like it too.'

Daisy frowned. What a peculiar thing to say. She was about to reply when Amos continued.

'Anyway, it was no matter. I don't have the kind of money that would allow me to buy anything from Buchanans but, in fact, none of the things there were really what I was looking for. That kind of jewellery is—'

'Ostentatious? Showy? For people who have money and would like the world to know it…' She clamped a hand over her mouth. 'Sorry, that was really rude.'

Amos smiled. 'Just not for me,' he finished, dipping his head in acknowledgement of her comment. 'And not for Grace either, which is more important.'

'No, of course,' said Daisy quickly. 'I don't know her, obviously, but anyone can see that she's… well, just lovely.'

Amos sighed. 'Yes, she is. And I'd like you to make me something that tells her story, that tells her why I fell in love with her too.'

'But do you really think I can do that? You haven't even seen any of the things I've made, not really, and I—'

'Daisy, I know that you are the perfect person to make me a gift for Grace. But if I had any doubt at all, that disappeared the moment I saw you here today. A feeling that has now been completely borne out by the fact that you actually make your own jewellery. People cross your path for a reason, I firmly believe that.' He sat back and grinned. 'See, it's fate. You are destined to make something for me.'

She looked up at him. She'd never really thought about it before, but if Amos thought she had crossed his path for good reason, then that would also mean that he had crossed hers for a reason too... But the whole fate shenanigans... She tried to remain focused.

'I think Kit mentioned that you were looking for something... ethereal? That's not a term most people would use to describe jewellery.'

Amos smiled. 'Maybe not, but Grace has this thing about her, a way of being that fills the space a long time after she's left it. I'm not sure how else to describe it.'

Daisy leaned forward. 'Ethereal,' she murmured, thinking how wonderful it must be to have someone describe you in that way. 'What a fabulous word...' She trailed off, thinking. 'So, the jewellery should be a reflection of who Grace is, but more than that it should also reflect something back to her, something that's important to her, that makes her feel whole. Does that make sense?'

Amos just smiled.

'So, what would do that?'

'Oh, heavens, so many things... her bees, her garden, me hopefully...' He grinned. 'You'll have to get to know her a bit better.' He looked down at the wreath she was making. 'And there's just not enough time to do that today.' He beckoned Flora over.

'Are you nearly done?' Flora asked, still grinning with excitement. 'It's just Grace will be back in a moment. I only asked her to fetch some things from the house.'

Amos nodded. 'But I need to concoct a little plan so that Daisy can get to know Grace better. And what simpler way to hide a secret than in plain sight…' He narrowed his eyes at Daisy. 'How about we tell Grace that Flora's husband, Ned, has commissioned you to make something for her? And so you need to speak to Grace in secret to find out what Flora might like. But all the while you're really observing Grace.'

Daisy looked between Amos and Flora, both of them caught up in the illicit thrill of the surprise they were plotting for Grace. Which was all very well except that it relied on her being able to make a piece of jewellery in the first place, and she really wasn't sure that she could. Her face fell as the enormity of what this might involve raced through her mind. It was one thing to tinker with a few bits of clay, and another entirely to design an individual piece of jewellery to which enormous importance was attached. What on earth had she been thinking? She wasn't a jeweller. She worked in a jeweller's shop and that wasn't the same thing at all. Plenty of people had an eye for what looked good and what didn't, there was nothing special about her.

She suddenly realised that Amos was looking at her, a concerned expression on his face. 'Oh God, I've terrified you, haven't I?'

Daisy gave a weak smile, but it was hard to know what to say. Flora and he both seemed so excited and she didn't want to let them down.

Flora touched her arm. 'Is this the first commission you'll have undertaken?'

Daisy managed a nod.

'Then would it help you to know that this time last year, right about where you're sitting, this place was full of cows. I'd only just met my husband and wasn't even living here, and my florist's shop in Birmingham had just had to close. I never dreamed that so much would happen in the space of less than a year, but I had a hope that they might, and that was enough. Sometimes all it takes is one small step.'

'And people who are prepared to take that one small step with you,' added Amos. 'Listen, I have no idea what I want for Grace, not really, but I'll know it when I see it. And I've seen enough today to know that you have it in you to find what I'm looking for. So how about we undertake that journey together? We can both learn as we go along. No pressure, no expectation, but a dollop of hope and a trust in the power of possibility. How about that?'

A slow smile crept over Daisy's face. Put like that it didn't sound scary at all. 'I think I can manage that,' she said.

Amos got to his feet. 'I'm going to make myself scarce, but can you let me have your number so I can get in touch about what we do next?'

Daisy rummaged in her bag, pulling out a card and handing it over somewhat shyly. 'I had these made a while back in a fit of enthusiasm. In fact, I think you might be the first person I've ever given one to. But my number's on there.'

Amos studied the card and then held out his hand. 'I'm very glad to have met you, Daisy Turner.'

She shook his hand, staring at him open-mouthed as he turned and walked back down the length of the room.

Flora laughed. 'I know,' she said. 'He gets you like that, doesn't he? There's something rather magical about Amos that you can never quite put your finger on. He turned up here one day at the start of summer looking for work, and sort of stayed. Of course, it helped that he and Grace fell in love, but I feel like I've known him my whole life too. One thing's for sure though, whenever he's around things start happening, so you better prepare yourself for an adventure, Daisy.'

She paused, checking her watch. 'I can't believe the time has gone by so fast. I'm going to whip around everyone else now and check they're

okay, but will you carry on with what you're doing? I really want to
see how your wreath turns out, so I'm afraid you're going to have to
bring it back to show me once you've fired the clay. I can't wait to see
the finished article.'

Daisy blushed slightly, but nodded, picking up the clay. She could
see just how she needed to continue with the wreath now, and what
it might look like once she had transformed the dull grey clay into
sparkling pieces of silver.

An hour and a half later she walked back to the car, carrying not
only a beautiful natural decoration, but also something inside of her
that simply hadn't been there before.

Saturday 7th December

Eighteen shopping days until Christmas

Daisy took her time walking to work the next morning. Part of her didn't want to be there at all. She'd had such a lovely day yesterday, returning home to sit beside her warm fire and dream about all the lovely things she could make. In the quiet room, with just her little Christmas tree for company, it was easy to imagine that everything was exactly as it should be. But more than that, she had found a little hope and didn't want to let it go. The wonderful thing about hope, however, was that anything seemed possible after it had worked its magic, and this morning she had reminded herself of Flora's story and resolved to have a little more faith in herself.

Daisy always arrived extra early after a day off. The end-of-day routines were never done quite the way she liked them when she wasn't there, so consequently it took a little extra time to get everything ship-shape for the day ahead. She would take her time, in between sipping a cup of tea, and when eight thirty came around and it was time for Bea or Kit to arrive, soothing order would be restored.

Her fingers tightened automatically over the big bunch of keys that she held in her pocket as she readied them for use. Today though, as she neared the front door and was about to pull them from her pocket, she could hear raised voices coming from within, and she stopped dead. It was only just gone half past seven and no one ever got there that early. She stood back, surveying the door and windows, but everything looked as it should. Had they been broken into? She could see no signs that the door had been forced and, leaning closer once more, her ear to the door, she realised with horror that the voice she could hear belonged to Lawrence. What on earth was he doing here?

She tentatively pushed the door open and took a step inside. The main shop floor was still lit only by the small interior lights on the display cases, but standing in the middle of it, their tall figures casting huge shadows against the walls, stood the three brothers, forming an almost impenetrable wall in front of her.

The voices stopped abruptly as the sound of the doorbell jangled loudly in the expectant space.

'Right, well now we might get some answers,' said Lawrence, his face like thunder in the gloom.

'Thank goodness you're here.' Bertie spoke this time, his usual genial manner gone.

'Hello, Daisy,' said Kit simply.

She stared at them in turn, her heart thumping at the harshness of their words, the coldness of their greeting. She had half a mind to turn tail and walk straight back out of the shop again but, instead, she took her bag from her shoulder and, holding it in front of her as if it were a shield, she marched straight through the middle of them and on into the back room. She closed the door behind her and as calmly as she could went to hang up her coat and hat. Then she filled the kettle and set it to boil. She took down her mug from the cupboard and placed her keys beside it, just as she always did, and then she stood, one hand bracing herself against the countertop, eyes closed and breathing deeply. Behind the door the voices started up again and she swallowed, praying that it stayed closed just for a moment. She had expected some degree of reaction following Bea's news of the other day, but obviously her absence yesterday had not allowed heels to cool as Bea might have hoped they would. Instead, it seemed to have inflamed things even more. It really was too much.

When she felt as if she had herself marginally more under control, she quietly opened the door.

'Good morning,' she said, immediately holding up a hand. 'And if any one of you raises your voice at me again, I'm putting my coat back on and going home.' To her surprise she sounded far more fierce than she felt and it had the desired effect. Even Lawrence fell silent. 'Would anybody like a cup of tea?'

The staffroom filled with bodies behind her as one by one the brothers trooped through. Bertie was first to speak.

'I'm sorry, Daisy, we're a bit... preoccupied this morning, as you might have guessed. The fact that our mother seems to have taken complete leave of her senses is rather concerning.'

'Is that what you think she's done?' asked Lawrence archly. 'It's not madness, Bertie, it's malicious and you know it. Mother acts like she's constantly on stage, and you can call it eccentricity if you want to, but I'm calling it what it is, manipulative and divisive.'

Daisy winced. She'd known that Lawrence would be the most upset by Bea's announcement. He had almost certainly assumed that the business would pass to him, but to find that he was now going to have to jump through a considerable number of hoops to secure his future was a hard pill to swallow.

He had a point. Bea did behave as if she was constantly in front of an audience, but Daisy had never known her to be malicious, just incredibly shrewd. And if Daisy knew her at all, there would be a very well-thought-out reason why she was doing this. Yet Daisy herself had been incredibly surprised by Bea's actions on this occasion, so maybe she didn't know Bea as well as she thought she did. Worse, if there was a point to all of this, just how did that involve Daisy?

'Scared you're not going to win?' taunted Bertie.

'Scared I am?' Lawrence fired back.

Daisy rolled her eyes. It was going to be a very long morning. She poured hot water into each of the four mugs and began to prod the teabags, thinking.

'One thing I do know is that it's pointless to try and change Bea's mind,' she said. 'Whatever her reasons are for doing this, I'm as much in the dark as you are, but if you want a chance to run Buchanans in the future, you may as well get used to the idea that it's going to be on her terms. I don't see you have much choice but to do as she's asked.'

'Oh, come on, Daisy, don't act all innocent,' added Lawrence. 'What did she say? You must have known all this was going to happen.'

'I didn't actually. And I can assure you I'm not thrilled about the idea either.' She turned to fish out the teabags, adding milk to the mugs once she had done so.

Lawrence coughed the word 'bullshit' into his hand. 'Sorry, but you must really think I'm stupid if I believe that.'

'You said it.' Kit's voice dropped like a soft sigh.

'Oh, he speaks…' retorted Lawrence. 'I suppose you think you've got it all sewn up too. Mummy's little boy who gets away with everything. I can see why you're happy with the arrangement.'

'Happy?' Kit's voice was scathing. 'Why would I be happy? What could I possibly want with a shop that sells nothing but greed and materialism?'

Daisy stared at him; she had never heard him speak that way before.

'Yes, but holier than thou ideals or not, you still need a job, don't you,' replied Lawrence, sneering.

Kit glared at his brother. That scored home, thought Daisy.

'Leave her alone, Lawrence, that's all I'm saying. Daisy said she didn't know what Mum was planning, and I believe her. Just back off.'

Lawrence looked at Bertie, who just shrugged, casting his eyes downward. Lawrence was on his own. He squared his shoulders. 'Well, I'm sorry, but I don't believe you, Daisy. You've always had Mother's ear, she must have told you something. And why pick you as the person we have to make the gift for, why not choose herself? No, there's something in it for you, there has to be.'

'Shall I tell you what's in it for me?' she said, her anger flaring. 'The only thing that I stand to gain is the joy of working for one of you. Forgive me if I'm not turning cartwheels.' Then she turned on her heel and stalked back out to the sales floor.

There was silence for a few moments and Daisy retrieved the glass polish and cloth from under the counter. As she suspected, no one had bothered to clean the glass yesterday evening. She gave the counter nearest to her a good squirt and began to rub at the greasy marks, continuing long after the glass was clean.

After a few minutes' determined polishing she realised that a figure had come to quietly stand beside her, and she wasn't altogether surprised to find that it was Kit.

'I've brought your tea through for you,' he said, placing it gently down on the desk.

She was aware that he was watching her but she kept her head bent low, avoiding his look.

'Thanks,' she muttered.

He was so quiet that she thought he might have retreated back into the other room, but then she heard a long breath expelled.

'Daisy?' He put a hand out towards her. 'Look, would you stop for a minute?'

She looked up at the exasperation in his voice.

'I'm really sorry, we all are, it's just that… well, we're used to Mum's antics but this, this is something else. It's rather taken us all by surprise, and I don't need to tell you it's causing problems… For you as well.'

Daisy sighed. She was tired and they weren't even open yet. 'Look, I do understand, Kit, but, yes, you're right, it is causing problems for me. I've worked here a long time and, while I don't think that automatically entitles me to anything, I did think that your mum and I had a good working relationship and, as such, she would discuss with me anything which affected the running of the business. I certainly didn't think she was going to retire any time soon, or make me party to some game she wants to play with her sons. I'm not looking forward to it any more than the rest of you.'

Kit nodded. 'No, I can see that and, again, I'm sorry. Tempers got a little frayed this morning. I guess we're still just trying to take it all in.'

Daisy glanced back through the doorway where she could see that Lawrence and Bertie were hovering.

'Oh, for goodness' sake, come in,' she said, picking up her mug of tea and wrapping her hands around it. 'But stop bloody arguing with one another or you can all leave.' She paused, looking at Kit. 'Not you,' she added. 'You can do some work for a change.' To her surprise Kit flushed bright red and she suddenly wished she could take back her words.

She softened her voice. 'I think we're all agreed that none of us are thrilled by the challenge that Bea has set us, but there's no point bickering and backbiting with one another, or me for that matter. It's going to get us nowhere.' She took a sip of her tea, looking at the three of them over the rim of her mug. 'Come Christmas Eve, one of you is going to end up running this place, assuming you all want to enter Bea's little competition, so you had all better have a think about what that means, for you individually, and as brothers. Whether you want to use this opportunity to unite the family or split it apart.'

Her words hung in the air between them but she knew it was what they had all been thinking. None of them worked in the business full time but Bea had promised their father that she would look after them financially and so she had, paying them all handsomely. Bertie looked after the accounts and administration, Lawrence looked after the buying and merchandising, and Kit worked on the sales floor. But, they did all at least have a job and, even before Bertie's pronouncement of a few days ago about their financial situation, they must have known that the present arrangement was simply not sustainable. Something had to give, and Daisy suspected that this was the real reason why Bea had done what she had.

'So, first things first, is anyone going to bow out gracefully now?'

The brothers looked at each other, and one by one they all shook their heads; even Kit, which rather surprised her.

'Then you are going to need to come up with the perfect present for me and it strikes me that we can either do this the hard way, or the not-so-hard way.' She rubbed a hand across her forehead. 'I must be mad but, for what it's worth, I think I need to help you. Whether you like it or not, I'm stuck in the middle of this too.'

Lawrence took a step forward. 'I'm not sure we're even deserving of that, but thank you, Daisy.'

His words sounded a little forced, but it was an apology of sorts, and would have cost him dear.

'I'm not sure you're deserving either,' replied Daisy evenly. 'But it struck me that perhaps this is as much about me as it is you. As you rightly said, Kit, none of you know me that well. You will each need to decide how you're going to run the business, whether you're going to do it alone, or whether there will still be a place for the others, or for me.' She sighed. 'Besides, there's less than a month to go until Christmas and I can't stand the thought of having what might turn out to be my last month here ruined by unpleasantness. There's quite enough of that in the world already.'

'That's really kind of you,' said Bertie. 'And, under the circumstances, very generous. This is going to be difficult enough, without us at each other's throats the whole time. But there's a lot at stake, and I think we need to all agree, here and now, that there's to be no funny business, nothing underhand… We should at least all try and behave like decent human beings.'

Kit narrowed his eyes, but he nodded, holding out his hand. Daisy waited to see who would take it first.

'I agree,' said Lawrence. 'But it's not quite as simple as that, is it?'

'It's as simple as you care to make it, surely?' replied Daisy.

'Except that the playing field isn't what you'd call level.'

Kit's hand dropped slowly to his side. He flicked a glance at Daisy and then looked uneasily at his brother.

'How so?' she asked.

'Well, because clearly Kit already knows you much better than the rest of us,' remarked Lawrence. 'That's obvious.'

Daisy stared at him. 'I doubt that,' she said. 'In fact, I wouldn't say Kit knows me at all.'

'But you work together all day.'

She was beginning to feel increasingly uncomfortable again. She didn't want to say anything to Kit's detriment, that hardly seemed fair, but how did she explain to Lawrence that she and Kit barely spoke when they were at work, and certainly not about anything that mattered?

'Yes, but we only really talk about work-related things, and—'

'Daisy's just being polite,' broke in Kit. 'What she should have said is that I have my head stuck in a book all day and she does all the work, so I rarely give her any opportunity to talk to me, although actually I doubt that she'd want to anyway.'

Daisy stared at him. Now what did she say? She could hardly agree with him.

'Which is a point in itself, isn't it, Kit? Everyone knows you don't want to be here, so why even bother with the competition?' asked Lawrence. 'Or are you just doing it to piss me off?'

'I don't hear you asking Bertie the same question,' Kit replied. 'And yet, forgive me, but I can't see him tied to the shop either, it would put a serious dent in his lifestyle.' Kit held Lawrence's look defiantly. 'But yeah, now that you mention it, maybe that's why I am doing it. It would do you good to lose every once in a while.'

Daisy looked anxiously between the three of them. 'Kit, that's hardly helpful.'

'What? And Lawrence's comment was?'

'And what I do in my own time is no concern of yours,' put in Bertie. 'Not everyone wants to live the way you do.'

Daisy put her hands over her ears. 'Stop it!' she yelled. 'Just stop it, all of you!'

There was a stunned silence for a moment as Daisy stood with her eyes shut, close to tears.

'Jesus, she's right,' said Bertie coming to her rescue. 'We can't keep doing this to one another. There has to be an element of trust and acceptance that we each have as fair a chance as the other. I take your point about Kit, but—'

'I have every right to enter the competition,' growled Kit. 'And whether you like it or not, I'm bloody well going to. I have my reasons, same as you do.'

'Which is exactly what I was going to say,' argued Bertie, his exasperation clear. He held up a placatory hand. 'Look, this is getting us nowhere. Can we all please calm down and think about what Daisy said.' He softened his expression as he turned to her. 'We were talking about the fact that none of us knows you that well and you mentioned that you would help us… Did you have something particular in mind?'

'Not really,' she muttered, opening her eyes now that she was sure the danger of making a fool of herself by crying had passed.

'Then surely the easiest way to accomplish that is if we each get an opportunity to spend some time with Daisy,' suggested Lawrence. 'Or how else can we possibly choose a piece of jewellery for her?'

'Okay…' said Daisy slowly. 'And how are you proposing you do that?'

'I don't know,' replied Lawrence, looking around him. 'Maybe spend a day working here… or…' His eyes suddenly widened and he clicked his fingers. 'I know, why don't we each take Daisy out for the day? Christmas is coming so there are loads of things to do… Where we go could be up to us, wherever we think will reveal the most about Daisy. We could ask her as many questions as we like but we'd all get the same opportunity as each other that way.' He gave her a challenging look, obviously pleased with his idea. 'What do you think?' he prompted.

She was still trying to work out what his idea would mean for her.

'It's not a date,' he added.

She could feel her cheeks growing hot. 'Good. Because I certainly wouldn't be going on a date with you, Lawrence... but yes, I think that might work.' She had meant what she said about getting to know the brothers herself. Her very future depended on it. 'But only on one condition.'

'Go on,' said Bertie.

'That you all promise not to ask me what has been discussed on any of the trips. I don't want to be accused of giving anyone unfair advantage.'

'Fair enough,' said Lawrence. 'Kit? Bertie?'

The other two brothers nodded.

'Then shake on it,' said Daisy. 'And at the same time do as Bertie suggested and swear to behave like decent human beings, for goodness' sake. And you can draw straws to see who gets to go first; that way there can be no argument about that either.'

Bertie smiled and held out his hand. 'You heard the lady,' he said.

'And please hurry up and get on with it,' added Daisy, glancing at the clock. 'I'm way behind with everything and there's a shop to open up in case you'd forgotten.'

Saturday 7th December

Eighteen shopping days until Christmas

They only just got everything done to Daisy's satisfaction before it was time to open and, to her surprise, Kit, having promised to polish everything to within an inch of its life, leaving her to concentrate on the displays, did just that. He was almost as exacting as she was.

It was a Saturday and one of only three left before Christmas, and so the moment the shop opened a customer appeared, and then another and another. Mostly they were just browsers, but it took time to cultivate the natural dialogue that Daisy preferred rather than the forced sales patter that made people sound like they were reading from a script. Obviously she had to judge the length of time she spent with each customer carefully when they were busy, but even so it was nearly an hour later before there was a lull and she could finally speak to Kit.

She placed a sugared mouse on the counter beside him before crossing to fill up the dishes for customers.

'I just wanted to say thank you,' she said. 'For this morning, sticking up for me, I mean. And to apologise as well. I said some things that weren't all that nice, and Lawrence... well, I can only imagine the grief that you've had to put up with from Lawrence.'

Kit looked up in surprise, his fingers sliding over the mouse. 'Lawrence is an arse,' he replied. 'And an entitled arse at that, which is the very worst kind. He's absolutely outraged at Mother for even considering that anyone else should run Buchanans.'

Daisy studied him. 'I should think that rather hurt though,' she said.

'Oh, don't feel sorry for him. He was peculiarly affronted as a child to have been presented with not one, but two brothers, and has behaved that way ever since. Bertie has always tried to be the peacemaker among us, whereas I learned to ignore him at an early age. Which suits me just fine.'

He picked up the little pink mouse and studied it for a moment before biting its head clean off, making a show of chewing slowly, savouring the taste. He gave a sudden smile which lit up his face.

'But you're welcome in any case,' he added. 'Our family is a complicated thing, Daisy. I wouldn't try to get too involved if I were you, and I certainly wouldn't try to make things better. It's unfortunate that Mum thought it was okay to throw you into the middle of all this, but she has, and I'm sorry that's the case. That said, Lawrence still needs to wind his neck in.'

It was probably the longest conversation she had ever shared with Kit about his childhood. 'You're very different from your brothers, aren't you?'

Kit held her look. 'I sincerely hope so, but thank you for noticing,' he replied, a hint of amusement in his eyes.

She dipped her head. 'And maybe I'm speaking a little out of turn, but I'm surprised to hear that you actually want to run this place. I didn't think you'd be interested.'

Not for the first time she wished she could take back her words as the light in his eyes dimmed a little. 'I'm sorry, I… It's none of my business… and rude.'

'No, actually, I don't suppose I've ever given you any cause to think otherwise. I have my reasons though and perhaps one day I'll be able to share them with you.'

She frowned at the strangely wistful tone in his voice. What a curious thing to say. She quickly filled the dishes with the sweet sugary mice to hide her confusion.

'It will be interesting to see what everyone picks for me,' she said, looking down at her wrist where the sapphires she'd been wearing on Wednesday had been replaced by rubies.

'Don't fish, Daisy,' he said, and slid off his stool, nodding towards the window. 'Oh, look, it's ethereal man. Go get him, Daisy, now's your chance.' And he turned away with an odd smile.

'Amos! Hello again,' she said as he came through the door. She really hadn't expected to see him again so soon, or in the shop for that matter. And although she tried to keep the surprise from showing on her face, she didn't quite succeed.

Amos pulled a face. 'Sorry, I feel like I'm ambushing you, but I had to come into town and it seemed too good an opportunity to miss. Much better to come and see you, than ring.' He looked past her into the shop. 'I know you'll be busy today, so I won't be long.'

Daisy recovered herself. 'No, don't worry, it's lovely to see you again. I had such a brilliant time yesterday.' She slid Kit a sideways glance, but he was busy replacing a bauble that had rolled off the Christmas tree. 'I even fired all the clay when I got home, but I haven't had a chance to polish it yet.'

'Well Flora is desperate to see your wreath, as is Grace for that matter. We were talking about it last night. In fact, it gave me the perfect opportunity to explain how you're going to make a piece of jewellery for Flora as a present from Ned, and that it would really help you if you could chat to Grace and pick her brains for a little inspiration.' He laughed. 'Grace thought it was wonderfully romantic of course and just the sort of thing that Flora's husband would do. I can't wait to see her face on Christmas Day when she finds out the gift is really for her.' He leaned towards her. 'I didn't think I'd be any good at this subterfuge lark, but I really rather enjoyed it. I should have been a spy…'

Daisy smiled at his comment but her heart was pounding. Kit still had his back to her but the shop was quiet, there was no way he wouldn't have heard what Amos said. She had to get rid of Amos as quickly as she could.

'Yes, I was thinking about that, actually. Showing Grace the wreath would give me the perfect excuse to see her, and Flora wouldn't see anything odd in that. I should have it finished by early next week, so how about I take it over to show her and then we can have a chat about the other stuff too. Would Tuesday evening be okay?'

Amos smiled. 'Come for dinner,' he said. 'About six thirty? Does that give you enough time after you finish work?'

She hesitated. It was a lovely offer, but even thinking about it was making her anxious. 'Actually, that is a little early for me. And I'd hate to put Grace to all that bother. Why don't I come about half seven instead? Then you can eat first without having to worry about me.'

Amos gave her a very direct look. 'Grace will shoot me if I don't bring you for something to eat, but half seven would still be fine. It can be a moveable feast.' He grinned at her. 'We'll see you then.' He flashed a look at Kit as two customers came into the shop. 'I'd better let you get back to work,' he added.

Daisy watched Amos leave with a sinking heart. She was grateful for the interruption, otherwise who knew where the conversation might have ended up. But it was probably already too late, her secret was surely no longer quite so secret. She gave Kit a nonchalant look as he turned back towards her but he gave her no clue about what he was thinking. He simply stared at her and walked forward to greet one of the customers.

Fortunately the rest of the day was busy and so Daisy had no opportunity to dwell on her conversation with Amos and what Kit might or might not, have overheard. She even cut her lunch hour short so she could help him with the lunchtime rush. If anything, she was far more preoccupied by the fact that Kit was helpful, polite, and showed a knowledge of their stock that she had never seen him demonstrate before. It was all very curious.

Five o'clock arrived before either of them had time to stop and think about anything much and, as she went to lock the door, Kit disappeared through to the back room.

'Sorry, Daisy, but I need a drink before I do anything else. Would you like one?'

She did; she was gasping.

Moments later he returned. 'So then,' he said, handing her a mug. 'Ethereal man is now Secret Agent man. Do tell…' His eyes were watching hers over the rim of his mug as he drank.

Damn, she thought she had got away with it.

'I mean, the day before yesterday you didn't know who he was and yet today, he's inviting you round to dinner. That's fast work, Daisy. I'm impressed.'

'Yes, with his *partner*, Kit. Honestly, Amos is old enough, well not quite old enough, to be my—' She stopped, she didn't want to use the word *dad*… 'Well, he's considerably older than me anyway, and spoken for. I met him yesterday, that's all, on a course. A coincidence admittedly, but nothing more than that.'

'Daisy, I'm just teasing...' He raised his eyebrows. 'Although I would like to know what he meant when he said that you were going to be making a piece of jewellery? Because as far as I'm aware, you just sell the stuff...'

She opened her mouth to protest but nothing came out. What would she say? Kit would see through her in a moment if she attempted to lie. Instead she tried to shrug it off.

'I think calling it jewellery is rather overegging the pudding,' she said. 'I make stuff out of clay, it's little more than a hobby and a bit of fun, that's all. You couldn't even begin to compare it with proper jewellery.'

'I see...' He frowned. 'But then how did Amos get to hear about it?'

She took a swallow of her tea while she thought, fast. 'I was wearing a string of beads on the course yesterday which Amos saw, well, he and Grace both did.' She was thinking on her feet, but it sounded plausible. At least she thought it did. 'Grace complimented me on them and so, later on, when she wasn't around, Amos asked me if I could make her some as a Christmas present.'

'I can't imagine you wearing beads,' he said, his head cocked to one side as he looked her up and down.

Daisy kept the smile glued on her face despite her rising anxiety. 'I do have a life outside of the shop, you know. And I wear all sorts of things, most of them very different from what I wear here. I'm sure you do the same.'

Kit looked down at his jeans and blue linen shirt. 'Nah, this is pretty much it actually. Not always a blue shirt admittedly but, well, you get the idea.' He scrutinised her for a few long seconds. 'Ah well, that explains it then.' He took a sip of his tea. 'Right, so what do you want to do first?' he added, changing the subject.

Daisy heaved a sigh of relief and looked around her. 'Let's get everything in the safe. I polish better when the counters are empty.'

She began to unlock the cabinets, Kit following suit on the other side of the room. It was a laborious process but they had done it so many times that it had a rhythm all of its own and she was grateful that it meant neither of them had to say a word.

'Bit weird though, don't you think?' asked Kit, a minute later.

'What is?' asked Daisy as she stood by the safe waiting for Kit to hand her another selection of jewellery.

'Amos…' Kit paused for a moment, looking up at her, a puzzled expression on his face. 'Or maybe, not weird as such, I dunno, but very indecisive at least.'

'Sorry, Kit, I'm still not following you.'

'Well, Amos comes in here, a day or so ago, has a quick look around and when he can't find what he's looking for, tries to explain what he wants but comes up with the word ethereal to describe it.'

'Yes, but what's odd about that? A lot of people have something in mind but can't quite explain what they're looking for.'

Kit shook his head. 'No, that's not the bit that's odd… It's just that, well, no offence, Daisy, I'm sure your jewellery is lovely, but clay beads aren't exactly ethereal, are they?'

She turned back to place a necklace into the safe, her cheeks burning. She was certain they were bright red.

'No, I guess not…' Aim for casual, she told herself, nonchalant. 'Maybe he changed his mind about that. But then Grace, that's his partner, loves flowers and wears everything in bright clashing colours, so perhaps he thought that my beads were a better fit after all.' Dear God, never let them meet. Or never let him meet Grace and Flora together. 'And, at the end of the day, he's paying me for the present, so what do I care?'

'Ah, materialism at its finest,' replied Kit, and she could hear the grin in his voice.

She gritted her teeth. She wasn't sure what was worse – being caught out in a lie or being thought of as something she abhorred. It was intensely annoying, but she couldn't argue; given what she'd just said, it was a valid response. And if Kit carried on making the kind of observations he seemed to be rather good at, she'd end up telling him everything, and that couldn't happen under any circumstances. She'd never be able to look any of them in the eye again.

'Yes, but you said it, Kit, they're clay beads. It's costing Amos a tenner, that's all. I don't think that's going to put me into the high earners' tax bracket, do you? Blimey, it's probably not even enough to buy your Christmas present with.'

'You've never bought me a Christmas present before…'

It was true, she hadn't. She didn't know what had made her say it.

She snatched the ring box from out of his hand. 'Yes, but this could well be our last Christmas here, Kit, both of us. I thought I might as well push the boat out.'

There was a look on his face that she found hard to fathom.

'Let's get on,' he said quietly. 'I'd like to get home.'

*

It was a relief for Daisy to be back in her little cottage once again, but even the routines which usually soothed and calmed her did little to quell the rushing thoughts in her head. Uppermost of these was the curious way Kit had behaved today. It was partly to be expected of course – Bea's announcement had thrown them all – but there was some change in Kit that she couldn't put her finger on. And then of course he had come so close to finding out her secret, and it didn't matter how many times she tried to replay their conversation in her head, she couldn't be certain that she had got away with it.

She broke off another piece of bread and dipped it in her soup. Before she had left for the evening, Kit had reminded her to expect an email from Bertie advising her of the details of their day out. Earlier that morning Bertie had gleefully pulled out the longest straw from the bunch of three that she held out for them, and wasted no time in fixing up a day to take her out. The forecast was clear and cold for most of the week and, as Monday was scheduled as her next day off, they had settled on that. Friday would be Lawrence's turn, followed by Kit the Monday after.

She would be utterly relieved when the whole thing was over. Apart from the hideous awkwardness of it all, the shop was open seven days a week during the whole of December and it was a busy time of year. She would effectively be losing her days off for nearly two weeks, or at least the opportunity to do what she wished on them.

It was already seven o'clock and Daisy was itching to carry on with the embellishments for her Christmas wreath, but she chased the remnants of her supper around the bowl with a spoon before carrying it back into the kitchen and running water into the sink until it was scalding. She added a generous squirt of washing-up liquid and, pulling on her bright-pink plastic gloves, watched the bubbles rise up until just past the halfway mark. She cut the water off and carefully washed her side plate, mug, spoon and finally the bowl before drying them and returning them to their respective cupboards and drawers. It took ten more minutes to check that the kitchen was as it should be and, after a detour to check again that she did indeed have a clean blouse for the morning, she was finally able to settle herself at the small table to one end of her sitting room.

The pieces of clay she had fired the night before had been polished as soon as she got home, and she picked up a couple of the leaves to inspect them further. They had turned out even better than she hoped. She arranged them on her workspace with a little greenery for contrast and took a couple of photos. Uploading them to her Instagram account only took a moment and, after that, she was free to carry on working on the wreath.

It was half past nine when, with a satisfied nod, she finally stopped and got up to make herself a mug of warm milk. She would check her emails as she drank it, hoping that Bertie had already sent his message and wasn't going to leave it any later. Not only was she intensely curious and more than a little anxious about the kind of day he had planned for them, but her normal routine was to read from ten o'clock and she would rather this were not interrupted.

The day had definitely warranted a rich tea biscuit as well and, as Daisy let the sugary crumbs roll around her mouth, she sighed with pleasure and waited for her emails to load. She leaned forward peering at the screen and then sat up, her eyes widening as she saw a message that could only have come from Bertie... What a stupid email address – BertieBees – but how like him; he never took anything seriously. But then she read the message. It would seem that Bertie was taking things very seriously indeed...

She read the email several more times and was about to close her laptop down when a pinging noise announced the arrival of another email. That was odd... It was a notification from her Instagram account that someone had sent her a message, but it happened so rarely that she was usually a little wary. She'd had one once that was, well... it had made her blush, that was for sure. She clicked on the email to read the message, peering at it through half-closed eyes. But it wasn't what she was expecting at all.

NickCarr1: Hi… I happened across your account today and really love your stuff. Can you tell me where I can buy them from, I'd like to get one as a Christmas present.

She stared at the words, reading them again just in case she got them wrong. But she hadn't. Her heart gave a little leap. Somebody loved her stuff! That's what they had said – not liked, or thought them nice, but actually *loved* them. And wanted to buy something too. She quickly opened her Instagram page to look at it, struggling even to remember what was on there.

There were only about ten finished designs. The rest were just photos like the one she had uploaded earlier; little snapshots of work in progress or, more usually, just images she really liked. It was something she had started up a couple of years ago, thinking that she really ought to try and make a go of things, but she hadn't known how to go about publicising it and so had never bothered with it much after that. Now it was mostly for her own enjoyment. The designs on there weren't even ones that she had been working on recently.

She pulled her phone towards her and opened the Instagram app, tapping to view the message.

Hi, thanks for your message, she typed in reply, her pulse racing. *I make my jewellery to order, but if you tell me which design you'd like I can let you know how much it costs etc.*

She looked at her message. She didn't want to gush, but instead sound like it was the kind of thing that happened all the time. Polite but businesslike… But then again, perhaps she should make it sound more enthusiastic… Pursing her lips, she quickly sent the message knowing that she would dither all night otherwise. Then she placed her phone down again, and turned her attention back to her laptop, feeling a buzz of excitement as she closed it down for the night. She had only just shut the lid when her phone lit up. She had another message.

Thanks for replying so quickly. I'd like something for my girlfriend but although I think she'd love your style, I'm not sure any of these are quite right. I don't suppose you could make me something different could you?

Daisy stared at the message, wondering what to make of it. It was the second time in as many days that someone had shown an interest in her jewellery. She looked up as Amos's words from the other day came back to her. *A dollop of hope and a trust in the power of possibility*, that's what he'd said. Maybe that was all she needed.

Yes, she typed back, a huge grin on her face. *What did you have in mind?*

Monday 9th December

Sixteen shopping days until Christmas

This is not a date. Just remember that, Daisy, *not* a date. She stared at her reflection in the bathroom mirror, her mouth full of foamy toothpaste. She had been telling herself the same thing all yesterday evening and ever since her alarm had gone off an hour ago. But it didn't matter how many times she reminded herself, it still felt like one.

She remembered the day she had first been introduced to Bertie, nearly dying with embarrassment at his classic good looks. Thick dark hair swept back off his forehead, twinkling dark eyes and designer stubble. He dressed to match his image too and, back then, to her, as an even more awkward teenager, he had seemed like an Adonis; self-assured and with a confidence that she didn't think she would ever possess. Of course, over time her opinion had changed slightly when she realised this confidence was a layer he wore like a suit of armour. And, as a string of girlfriends, never-ending parties and hangovers too numerous to mention testified, Bertie was a stereotypical playboy. He was everything she wasn't, and though he fascinated her, she found his wild ways terrifying in equal measure. How she was going to get through a whole day with him she didn't know.

Bertie's email read like an advertisement for a travel company, full of affirmations that she was going to have an amazing time. But throughout the entire message, he never once mentioned where they were going, just that he would pick her up at eight and to wear comfortable shoes and warm clothes as they would be outside all day… and that in itself had caused her inordinate problems.

She had stood in front of her wardrobe last night, staring at the row of blouses and skirts which she wore for work. They were almost identical in design; the blouses white or cream and the skirts black or muted shades of blue and green. Next to them, at the far side of the wardrobe, were a few items of casual clothing: jeans, a woollen skirt, two jumpers, two sweatshirts and a checked shirt which she didn't really like but was brushed cotton and very soft. None of these things struck her as something she should wear on a day out with someone she barely knew. After standing staring at them for quite some time, she realised that something more suitable was not about to materialise and so she pulled out a cream cable-knit jumper and the skirt. She would wear her boots, some tights and her cape. Warm, comfortable and definitely not dressed up like she was going on a date.

Daisy had arranged to meet Bertie in the market square. There was no parking at her cottage, but in any case she had no intention of letting him come to her house, and this seemed the easiest solution. It was quiet at this time of the morning and she had plenty of time to spot him as she made her way through the stalls. He was leaning up against a lamp post at the far side, and she smiled as she watched him trying to look cool when he was obviously freezing. It was a bitter morning, sunny, but with a chill wind, and his navy-blue jacket and beanie hat were doing little to combat the cold. He looked up as he saw her, levering himself away from the lamp post and pulling his hands out of his pockets.

'Morning!' His greeting was accompanied by a bright smile with no trace of the nervousness that she knew would be written across her own face. 'It's a bit nippy.'

She blew a puff of frosted breath into the air. She had walked quickly and knew her cheeks would be rosy but she had not been walking for long enough to get warm and gave an involuntary shiver.

He touched her arm. 'Come on, the car's warm at least.'

She nodded, trying to relax. 'Where are we going?' she asked, but he just smiled.

'You'll see.'

Infuriating.

She followed his quick steps a short distance to where a sleek sports car was parked by the side of the road. She had no idea what model it was, but it seemed barely big enough to contain both of them. Bertie was well over six foot and she had a sudden image of him trying to fold his long legs up sufficiently to enable him to climb inside, rather like a stick insect. It was exactly the sort of car she had imagined he would drive and she quickly saw how at home in it he looked. The dark-blue interior matched his clothes and he sank into the seat just as she had, legs outstretched. By the time she had arranged herself he had slipped on a pair of sunglasses and his hands held the steering wheel lightly. With a grin, he pressed a button and a throaty roar filled the cabin.

'Are you ready?' he asked.

She nodded, even though she wasn't at all sure what for.

He drove quickly, the car hugging the road, and within minutes they were turning onto the main road that led away from the town. She had thought they were going quite fast enough, but Bertie put his foot down and she felt the power surging beneath the car. It was utterly terrifying, but Bertie seemed unconcerned. He was clearly used to driving that way.

They had only gone a short distance, however, before Bertie suddenly eased back on the throttle, glancing at her several times in quick succession.

'Oh God, I'm sorry, Daisy,' he said. 'I forget how fast I drive sometimes. You look terrified.'

'Do I?'

'You're probably nervous as hell too. I know I am.'

She looked at him. 'You don't seem as if you are.'

He grinned. 'Perhaps I hide it better than you. And, right now, I'm in my comfort zone, you're not.'

'No, that's very true. And actually most things are – outside of my comfort zone, that is.'

'In which case you are being extraordinarily generous by coming out with me today.'

She gave him a sideways look. 'Do I have much choice?'

'No... I guess not.'

His voice was laden with apology, which was very sweet of him, but the more she thought about this day and what it meant, it really wasn't about her.

'I'm sorry, Bertie, this must be awful for you. Not this...' She gestured at the interior of the car. 'Although perhaps we shouldn't pass judgement on the day just yet... But I meant the thing with Buchanans. It's awful for all of you. What do you think you'll do, if you don't get the business, I mean? Or even if you do get it...'

'That's rather a lot of questions.' There was a pause as he concentrated on the road ahead of him. 'And the truth is that I'm trying not to think about it. Not a particularly smart move under the circumstances, but there you go, that's me all over. I'm not a businessman, I can only just about manage to do the accounts.'

'But you do want to run Buchanans?'

There was an even longer pause.

'I think that's one of those questions I never thought I'd have to think about. And not something I'm particularly proud of admitting. But when Dad died at such an early age we were all brought up to understand that it was our place to keep the family firm going. We all thought that Lawrence would take the helm when Mum retired of course, but that essentially everything else would pretty much stay the same. Rather naive as it turns out.'

'That might still happen.'

Bertie's head swivelled. 'You really don't know Lawrence, do you? There's no way that he'd keep either me or Kit on the books if he gained control. Not financially viable would be his excuse, but in reality it's because Lawrence likes doing things by himself. I'm under no illusions that I'd be out on my ear.'

Daisy was about to argue but realised there was little point. Bertie's words had an undeniable ring of truth about them. 'But what would you do then?'

Bertie let out a long sigh. 'I have absolutely no idea. I'm not fit for much – bit of a party animal, I'm afraid.'

It wasn't the throwaway comment he meant it to be, and Daisy need only look around her to see that he was being serious about his shortcomings. The car was virtually new, with plush leather seats and a polished wood interior, and an ability to accelerate that came at a price. Bertie himself wore the kind of clothes that only easy money could buy. The designer sunglasses, the boots, a watch that looked like it could launch a rocket – none of it looked like it was trying too hard.

But, despite Daisy's lack of knowledge of such things, she knew enough to understand that beneath the deliberately understated exterior – if you were the right kind of person – these things were shouting at you very loudly indeed. She could see very clearly how Bertie's upbringing had been responsible for the way he lived his life.

'Okay, so what would you *like* to do?'

'Honestly? I don't know that either. You'll think me a poor little rich boy, but I've never even thought about how I would support myself.' He gave a bitter laugh. 'What an admission to have to make.'

'Well, at least you have admitted it,' replied Daisy. 'That's half the battle at least, surely? Plenty of time to get your head out of the sand and contemplate the road ahead.'

'Head out of my arse, more like.'

Daisy smiled. It had been on the tip of her tongue to say that but she had decided on the rather more polite option.

'Well, whichever it is, let's just assume for a minute that you do get to run Buchanans. What would you do then? Would *you* give Lawrence and Kit a job?'

Bertie turned his head briefly to look at her. 'You know, if you could just tell me what would be your ideal piece of jewellery, this would be an awful lot easier. So, come on, what would you like?'

'You didn't answer my question.'

'You didn't answer mine.'

They smiled at one another.

'Come on, I'd like to know. What would you do?' repeated Daisy.

Bertie tapped out a rhythm on the steering wheel with his fingers.

'I'd give Kit a job. Because Kit's as hopeless as I am, just in a different way. Lawrence I'm not sure about. I probably would, just to keep the peace.' He slid a glance at her. 'See, I told you I was a hopeless businessman.'

'Actually, I think you'd be good for Buchanans. You'd bring a little more modernity to the place and because, by your own admission, you don't know what you're doing, you'd come to the business with fresh eyes, rather than being bound by conventional ideas or wisdom about what running the place should entail. I think that might be what it needs.'

'And what else does it need?'

Daisy had often thought about what she would do if she had a business to run, but never about Buchanans; it wasn't hers to consider. She smiled and shrugged.

Bertie gave a frustrated sigh. 'Well, you're no use,' he said. 'But now, as I've answered your question, you can at least give me a clue about the type of jewellery you'd like.'

She grinned. 'I hadn't really thought about it.'

'Favourite colour at least.'

'Blue.'

'Well, that's easy then… sapphires.'

'Ah, but is it? It could be sapphires, but then again it could be lapis lazuli, topaz or aquamarine. Or even tanzanite, a wee bit of chalcedony…'

Bertie groaned.

'I'm sorry. But even if I knew I couldn't tell you, could I? How would that be fair?'

He squinted across at her. 'We could go to a jeweller's or something and you could point out a few things…' He let the sentence dangle between them.

'Bertie, I couldn't. It's not in the spirit of the thing and, besides, Bea's not daft, she'd see through that in a minute. Don't forget, you need to be able to tell her why it's the perfect piece of jewellery for me as well.'

'Well then you could tell me that too...'

'I couldn't, and you know it.' She looked across at him, but he was smiling and she couldn't blame him for trying it on. If she were in his shoes she probably would have done the same.

'I mean it though, I couldn't actually tell you because it's not something *I've* ever really thought about. I don't own things, you see, well not much anyway, and neither do I wish to. I live a very small life, Bertie.'

'So perhaps we're both on a quest then?'

She thought about his words for a moment. 'Yes, perhaps we are.'

It was a curious notion, but maybe he was right. Daisy had thought about Bea's motivation for doing what she had at numerous times over the past few days. Her behaviour was frequently flamboyant, theatrical and seemingly impulsive, but Daisy knew it was often to provoke a particular reaction. So maybe there was more to setting this particular challenge than just finding out who might be best suited to run the company. And, if that were the case, then what were Bea's motives? And, just as importantly, what were her motives for involving Daisy?

She could feel Bertie sneaking looks at her, perhaps mistaking her silence for annoyance.

'You can't blame me for trying though,' he said. 'Quite normal under the circumstances, surely?'

Her smile was warm. 'I don't blame you at all, Bertie. This is incredibly hard on you all, and I wish there was an easier way of doing this. It seems... unkind... is that the right word? Unnecessary? I don't know...'

'But, do you want me to get Buchanans?'

His eyes were fixed firmly on the road and she was grateful that he wasn't looking at her.

'Let's change the subject, Bertie. I think we're on rather dangerous ground. And we are going to be spending the whole day together, after all. Let's not spoil it by talking about the business.' She looked around her, frowning. 'Where are we even going?'

He turned and grinned at her. 'Nottingham,' he said.

Her mouth dropped open. 'Nottingham? Whatever for?'

'Winter Wonderland,' he replied. 'I go every year. It's an absolute necessity at Christmastime. Just the thing to get you in the mood for the festivities.'

She stared at him. 'Is it?' It sounded horrendous: far too busy and full of people.

'Oh yes…' He fiddled with one of the heating controls. 'Are you warm enough? We've still got about an hour and a half to go yet, so make yourself comfortable and just enjoy the ride.'

As soon as he said it, Daisy realised that she was enveloped in a warm fug, and the seat was so comfortable it was like a soft hug. She could even stretch her legs right out. Even if *she* hadn't noticed, her body had; she felt completely relaxed. She turned her head to look out the window at the bright sky outside and smiled. Perhaps the day wasn't going to be quite so awful as she had feared.

*

She came to with a start, looking around her in horror to see that Bertie was grinning at her. She immediately wiped her mouth, terrified that she'd been dribbling in her sleep.

'Don't worry, you were perfectly well behaved,' he said. 'No dribbling, no moaning or making weird noises, snuffling like a pig…'

She wriggled slightly further upright in her seat. 'I'm so sorry, I don't know what came over me. That was incredibly rude.'

'On the contrary, it's quite a compliment. At least I know my driving hasn't scared you witless.'

'Yes, but even so.'

'Don't worry about it, I didn't.'

'Where are we anyway?' They had turned off the motorway and were driving through a built-up area.

'Only about five minutes away. That was perfect timing. And courtesy of a mate's house we can park within a couple of minutes' walking distance from the town.' He smiled. 'I didn't fancy doing battle with all the crowds on the trams.'

He was looking at her and she wondered whether it was him who didn't like the crowds or whether he had realised how uneasy they would make her feel. But that wasn't the only thing that made her anxious. What to eat and drink were two more things and she didn't dare think about everything else the day might involve. She swallowed, the sleepy contentment she had awoken with deserting her in an instant.

She fished around in her handbag, not because she needed anything, but more for the comfort of knowing that everything was where it should be. Her fingers closed around her door keys and she held them in her palm for a moment, reminding herself of her little cottage and what it felt like to be tucked safely inside.

Minutes later they drew up in front of a handsome red-bricked house. A tall tree stood outside covered in red bows, its lights shining even at this time of the morning. A similarly festive wreath graced the front door. It made Daisy smile to herself as she thought of the one at home she had finished last night. It wasn't a patch on hers.

Bertie killed the engine and removed his sunglasses, looking at her for a moment. 'Ready?' he asked.

She nodded, reaching for the door handle, somewhat loath to venture out of the warm space and into the cold. But, before she could open it, Bertie touched her arm.

'No, Madam, let me.' And he jumped out of the car, ran around the bonnet and pulled open her door with a flourish. 'If Madam would care to step this way,' he said with a bow and a broad grin.

'Why, thank you,' she replied. 'Most kind.'

She climbed from the car and they stood looking at one another, silently acknowledging the awkwardness of the day and their mutual desire to make it less so. Their breath was rising in clouds around them.

'Come on,' said Bertie. 'It's too cold to be hanging around.' He indicated the road ahead. 'If we go this way we can cut through the park, and it's only a couple of minutes' walk from there.'

She fell into step beside him. 'So, this Winter Wonderland, it's on every year, is it?'

Bertie nodded. 'I'm not sure how long it's been running, but I've been coming for the last five or six years. My friend who owns the house back there is involved in organising it, so it's a good excuse to meet up. There's a bunch of us here most years.'

She looked at him in horror. 'Are they going to be here today?'

'No, don't worry, it's just us. I'll come back a bit nearer Christmas to meet my mates. But I've managed to pull a few strings and lined up a little VIP treatment. I hope that's okay? I wasn't sure what kind of a day out this should be, and I know my way around this place. It seemed sensible.'

'Bertie, I'm sure it will be great. It's very kind of you to go to so much trouble.'

'Well, I hope so. There has to be some bonus to this game we're all playing, doesn't there?' He paused for a moment indicating that they should cross the road. 'So, if you could choose, what would be your ideal day out?'

'I don't know…' She pulled a face. 'Something else I haven't really thought of. I don't go on many days out.' Make that none, she thought, but didn't say.

'But you must know what you like, or where you like to be?'

She nodded. 'Well, that's easy… somewhere outside, like the canal for example.'

'The canal? What, full of floating beer bottles and old supermarket shopping trolleys?'

She shook her head, laughing. 'No, it's really not like that. I live quite close to the canal and in summer I like to sit and just watch people go by. You can't hurry when you're on a boat and people are more relaxed, they have more time for others. They notice things they wouldn't otherwise do and they seem, I don't know, just happier to be alive than they do elsewhere. I like that. It makes me think that the world is not such a bad place after all.'

She didn't mention that one of the reasons she liked it was because she knew that she could chat to folks quite happily and probably never see them again.

'Put like that, I guess it sounds lovely, in some ways… but not all that much fun?'

'I didn't say it was fun, but then it depends what you mean by fun. I have a feeling that your idea of it and mine would be very different. But the canal is lovely. There's a spot where I can sit and dangle my feet in the water, feeling the eddies lapping against my legs as the boats go by. And there are kingfishers too, if you're lucky. It's very beautiful.'

'Okay… maybe that's fine in summer, but where would you go in wintertime then, at Christmas? Not the canal, surely?'

Daisy's eyes lit up. 'Oh, it's even better in the winter. The water can freeze over, like glass, and the frost lies on its surface, turning it into a glittery mirror. There are rushes and grasses that grow by the water's edge and on a frosty morning like today every single leaf stands out in sharp relief.' She closed her eyes. 'I love all of that, but most of all I love the stillness. The way everything seems frozen in a moment of time. You can breathe it in on a winter's day, until it claims every part of you...' She stopped. 'Sorry. That probably sounds... well, weird.'

Bertie was searching her face. 'It doesn't actually. When you say it... I think it sounds wonderful.' He grimaced. 'I'd never think of going anywhere like that and I've got a horrible feeling you're going to hate today.'

Daisy cocked her head to one side. 'Perhaps,' she said. 'But only because it's very different to what I'm used to. I'm interested to see it through your eyes though.'

They had reached the end of another road and, as Bertie turned left, Daisy could see the gates ahead to a rather elegant-looking park. The trees that hung over its edge were barren of leaf but strung with coloured lanterns instead; red, blue, green and yellow in repeating patterns, right along the edge of the road. The street had been quiet but as soon as they turned onto the path that led into the park, Daisy could see lines of people up ahead, all following the same route, and undoubtedly all heading for the same destination. She felt rather like a sheep.

'Are you hungry?' asked Bertie, suddenly.

She shook her head. 'Not really...' She glanced at her watch; it wasn't quite yet ten o'clock. 'I've not long had breakfast, but if you want something don't let me stop you.'

'A drink then?'

She wasn't really that thirsty either and was about to say so when she realised that the expression on Bertie's face held more than just casual enquiry.

'Possibly,' she replied instead. 'What did you have in mind?'

'It's just that there's this great place I always go to first. It's called the Altitude Bar and is made of glass. Sitting way up above everything else you can look down on all the festivities below. It's a great way of getting your bearings and if you like people-watching… Well, actually, I have a VIP table booked.'

'Then that's where we'll go.'

'Only if you're sure, I don't want to—'

'Bertie, you've gone to all this trouble. Of course we'll go.'

She smiled at him confidently, ignoring the little voice in her head that was screaming *have you gone mad?* A bar at ten o'clock in the morning. What on earth was she letting herself in for?

Monday 9th December

Sixteen shopping days until Christmas

As soon as they emerged from the other end of the park, Daisy could hear the noise swelling around her. The crowds were growing thicker almost with every step they walked and, as they came to the end of a road, Daisy could see why.

'Oh, my word!'

A sudden cacophony of noise and light hit her as she stared out across the market square ahead of her. Everywhere she looked were strings of lights, dancing in the breeze. Ribbons of green and red entwined lamp posts and two golden angels with flutes hung suspended above their heads. Huge neon stars flashed on every corner.

Right in the centre, towering above it all, was the biggest Christmas tree Daisy had ever seen. As a child she had longed to go to Trafalgar Square to see London's famous tree but, despite all her pleading, she had never got to go. And then it wasn't long after that that the thought of going there, to that huge city, with all those millions of people, mingled with Daisy's worst nightmares. Here, though, was a tree that fulfilled all of her childish dreams and more. Even in the daylight it glowed with myriad sparkling lights, so many the tree beneath was scarcely visible, but it seemed to Daisy symbolic of something that she had forgotten long ago.

She could feel her heart begin to beat faster as everything else came rushing in at her; the good-natured shouts from the market traders, the hum of cheerful chatter, piped music and something undefinable that just felt like energy, as if the very place was alive with it. Perhaps it was; Daisy had never seen anywhere so vibrant before. Her eyes darted one way and then the other. She lifted her head, smelling something intensely savoury, smoke, and then... something so very familiar to her, something from her childhood that she could scarcely remember. It tugged at her memories and she had to put out a hand on Bertie's arm to steady the swirl of sensations and emotions. It was sweet, so very sweet...

'Isn't it amazing?' he said, his voice raised against the clamour.

She nodded, feeling the infectious excitement of the crowd around her, almost overwhelming her.

Seemingly without thinking, Bertie grabbed her hand. 'Come on!'

He led her straight through the middle of it all, not stopping until they were standing in front of a building that looked as if it had been transplanted from Switzerland. He pointed up at the huge expanse of wood and glass above them, like a chalet on stilts.

She stood, gazing up, her breath coming in pants; a reaction to the speed with which they had rushed through the market. Bertie was like an overexcited schoolboy, grinning from ear to ear.

'I take it that's the Altitude Bar,' she said, smiling as he nodded enthusiastically.

'And we're just in time for our table. Wait until you see the view from the other side...'

It took a moment to get through the throng of people milling about but they had only just stepped inside when there was a loud shout from in front of them.

'Bertie!'

An enormous man completely blocked Daisy's field of view before lifting Bertie clean off the ground in an enormous bear hug.

'It's so good to see you again, my friend.'

The man settled Bertie back down and she was able to look properly at the giant for the first time. His face was almost hidden by a huge bushy black beard and thick curly hair which, had it been white, would have given Santa Claus a run for his money. Piercing dark eyes twinkled with amusement and the roundness of his apron-clad stomach was matched only by the width of his beaming smile.

'Luka!'

Bertie was equally delighted to see his friend and, still grinning, waved Daisy forward.

'Daisy, this is my good friend, Luka, who has always been this size, even when we were at school together. And now, having been thrown out of countless bars in his youth, has decided to run one... Luka, this is Daisy.'

'Ah, the English rose...' He lifted her hand in his huge paw and kissed it softly. 'I have heard so much about you.'

Daisy faltered, unsure what to say, confused and more than a little embarrassed by Luka's comment. She looked at Bertie, but his expression gave nothing away and then she realised that if Luka was the friend he seemed to be, then he would know everything about the competition.

'Ah yes,' she said, smiling. 'I can only imagine what Bertie's been saying about me; the pain-in-the-bum shop assistant who's making his life a misery...'

It was Luka's turn to look confused. 'I can assure you I've heard only good things about the beautiful young lady who knows so much.' He reached forward to pummel Bertie's arm. 'I love this man, but, sheesh... he has much to learn.' His laughter boomed around the room as Bertie blushed bright red.

'Don't you start, I can get this kind of abuse at home,' he quipped.

Luka bowed. 'Then I will show you to your table, and the drinks are on the house of course...' He held up his hand. 'And I will hear no argument,' he said, firmly.

He led the way up a long flight of wooden steps whose glass sides caused the staircase to seemingly float up the middle of the room. Above them Daisy could see the criss-crossings of wooden rafters that twinkled with tiny white lights, but it wasn't until they neared the top that she got her first inkling of what was ahead. She took in a sharp breath.

'They're trees...'

She turned to look at Bertie in confirmation, who simply nodded. 'Yes they are.'

Arranged around the room were huge trees, bare of leaf, their branches threading upwards to the lofty ceiling, and each of them was wrapped in shimmering lights. It was magical. She stood underneath one of them, looking up through the branches; and had it not been for the noise and the people, she could have been at home. She had done that once, in the stand of silver birch trees that stood behind her house. She had lain on her back, despite the snowy ground, and gazed upwards through the tree's slender limbs. They were pale against the dark of the sky but sparkling with frost and the countless stars that peeped between their branches as she looked up. It had seemed like heaven.

'Are they real?'

Luka laid a hand against one of the trunks. 'I call them my ghost trees,' he said with a smile. 'Sadly the trees are no longer alive, but I brought them here so that their spirit could live on.'

'Oh, that's beautiful, they're beautiful.'

She looked back at Luka to see Bertie watching her. He smiled and rolled his eyes. 'Luka, you're such a romantic.' He took her arm. 'Shall we sit down?'

Luka waved them ahead and slipped back into the crowd as they made their way to a table at the far end of the room, underneath an enormous arch of branches. They couldn't have chosen a finer place to sit and, as soon as Daisy saw the view from the window, her mouth dropped open for the second time in as many minutes. She shuffled along the fur-draped bench so that she was closer to the glass and peered through. Hidden by the building, but standing resplendent in among another square of stalls and other fairground rides, was a brightly painted helter-skelter.

'I don't believe it,' she said. 'That's incredible.'

'I thought you might like it.'

'Oh, just to look at – I don't think I'll be going on it.'

'Why not?'

A sudden memory of a fairground flashed through her mind. One that she hadn't thought about in years. She swallowed. 'I'm just not very good with things like that,' she answered, turning back and looking out across the room. 'This place is beautiful though. Your friend seems like he's a real character.'

'Luka's one of the good guys. Had a terrible upbringing, but still managed to turn out to be a thoroughly decent human being, and his business is doing really well too. Of course at this time of year he makes a fortune, but he's doing well the rest of the year too; even looking to set up a mobile business.' He grimaced. 'Kind of makes me wish I'd got on board with him when he offered, right at the start.'

'Why didn't you?'

There was a sigh. 'Too busy having a good time. And back then, it probably would have been the world's worst idea. I wasn't ready to pull my weight and you can't start off a business without giving it one hundred and ten per cent. I suspect my lack of application would have cost me my friendship with Luka too, so, all things considered, it was probably a smart move.'

Daisy could see the pull within him of what might have been. He still wasn't absolutely convinced he'd made the right decision.

'And what about now? If working with Luka were still an option, might things be different?'

'Possibly. I reckon I could be ready to settle at something, but here?' He looked around him. 'It's nice to come and visit but it feels like a lifetime away somehow. In any case, I have Buchanans to consider, and who knows what's going to happen there.'

'Who indeed…' Daisy fell silent, the weight of what was facing them hanging heavy in the air. She searched for something to say that would change the subject but, just as she was about to speak, a waitress approached them, carrying a tray.

'Hi,' she said brightly. 'Luka has sent these over, and he said to shout if you want any more. On the house, naturally.'

She lowered the tray and placed a tall mug in front of Daisy, before unloading several plates full of food and an identical mug which she placed in front of Bertie.

'Enjoy,' she said. 'And Merry Christmas.' She backed away with a wave, disappearing almost instantly amid the crowds of people moving through the room.

Daisy looked down, biting her lip.

'I wasn't sure what you'd like,' said Bertie. 'But these are Luka's famous hot chocolates and it seemed a bit too early in the morning to start drinking, even for me.'

It was a flippant comment, but Daisy's stomach contracted. 'I don't drink,' she said faintly.

'Don't you... oh.' He looked down at the table and then up again, grinning. 'Just as well then. They normally have rum in them, but I erred on the side of caution.' He pushed a plate towards her. 'I ordered a few of all my favourites nibbles too, some savoury, some sweet, just in case.'

Her eyes roamed the table. 'What are they?'

'Spiced cashews – they have a bit of a kick to them but they're great with hot chocolate. Then there are big old pretzels, which are just, well, you know, pretzels, and these are like mini cheese on toasts, but Luka puts some magic ingredient in them, I think, because they don't taste like that when I make them at home.' Bertie looked up at her and she nodded. 'The stars are gingerbread and these... these are called rugelach. They're little pastries stuffed with cinnamon and raisins, walnuts too.' He picked one up and popped it into his mouth whole, closing his eyes and groaning with pleasure.

'I see, and what's in this?' She looked down at her drink where a mountain of cream was slowly oozing over the side of the mug.

She saw his eyebrows knit together. 'It's just hot chocolate, honestly. None of your rubbish though. It's made with the good stuff; seventy per cent cocoa solids, and then a dash of vanilla syrup for sweetness, all covered in a ton of cream, and more chocolate of course.' He was grinning as he picked up his spoon and plundered the top of his own drink. 'Dig in, you don't have to be polite.'

'I'm not really...' She trailed off.

Oh, this was awful. Bertie had gone to so much trouble so that she could enjoy herself, and if she were anyone else she would have fallen on these things with undisguised glee, just as Bertie had. But she was not anyone else, unfortunately.

'Is everything all right?' He thudded a hand against his forehead. 'Don't tell me, I've managed to pick the one thing you absolutely hate?'

'No,' she replied quickly. 'I like hot chocolate. It's just that I usually have it… well, plain. I've never tried it with all these *things* in it before, I'm not sure…' She gave an involuntary shudder, trying to turn it into a cough.

Bertie gave her an easy smile. 'No worries,' he said. 'Give it a try and if you don't like it I can get you a plain one.'

Just like that. But she couldn't, it would be so wasteful.

She picked up her mug and tried to dislodge some of the cream with her spoon but she couldn't even see the liquid underneath. She looked around her, at all the happy, smiling faces – people drinking from mugs, glasses, huge tankards even, and all without a care in the world, and here she was, couldn't even manage a dollop of cream. She swallowed, took a deep breath and a mouthful of her drink… and almost gagged. It was so, so… She couldn't even put it into words.

A couple of napkins lay next to the plates and she snatched one up, holding it to her lips pretending to be concerned that she had a cream moustache. She dragged a smile onto her face. 'What am I like?' she said.

Bertie popped a nut into his mouth. He was watching her, but made no comment. She picked up a pretzel and waved it nonchalantly.

'So, what are you doing for Christmas?' she asked, trying to deflect attention from herself.

He rolled his eyes. 'What, apart from working out how to run Buchanans, you mean? No, I'll be in Scotland for most of it. A mate of mine has a big house up there; more of castle, actually, so as soon as I'm fit to drive after the big day I'll be heading up there for a week of food, booze and general debauchery. New Year up there is amazing.' He stretched out the last word until it had at least five syllables.

She looked at him, puzzled. 'But it's your mum's birthday on New Year's Eve. Won't you be spending it with your family?'

'God, no!' Bertie laughed. 'I can't think of anything worse. Been there, done that, most definitely bought the tee shirt but I don't think I could stand another family bash – Lawrence being his usual pompous self, muttering about standards and tradition, ordering everyone around, Kit trying to make himself invisible, disappearing for hours on end, while muggins here tries to keep the peace and inject some fun into proceedings, while all the time Mum watches the clock.' He broke off, frowning. 'Of course, I know *why* she was watching the clock now; couldn't wait to get rid of us all so that Charles could come round. Why she didn't say anything I don't know.'

'Maybe she was just trying to protect you. To keep Christmas special for you guys so that it wouldn't feel like Charles was trying to muscle in on the family.'

'Do you really think that?' Bertie sounded incredulous.

'I don't know. It just strikes me that whatever she was like as a mum, with your dad dying so young, Bea has brought you up virtually on her own. Okay, so your dad left a huge pot of money which helped, but most single mums I know are very protective of the family unit, especially when there's a new partner on the scene.'

Bertie popped another nut in his mouth and chewed thoughtfully. 'Do you know, I'm not sure I ever really thought of it like that. Mum just always seemed keen to get rid of us all.'

'Or nervous of someone arriving…' Daisy picked up her drink and took another swallow.

'Yeah… maybe you're right.'

'Of course I'm not sure about Lawrence being pompous or Kit pretending no one can see him, I think those might just be character traits.' She grinned and Bertie laughed, knowing he was being teased.

'So, come on then, Miss Turner. If you have family dynamics sussed, what's your Christmas like?'

She looked up sharply, not having expected the question. 'Oh, quiet,' she replied, heart thudding. 'Very boring, no dramas at all, in fact.' She smiled and took another sip of her chocolate.

'Well then, big family, small?' He glanced up at the tree above their heads. 'Are you a lonesome pine or part of a thicket?'

His description made her smile, and relax somewhat. 'One of a pair,' she replied. 'I have a brother, well, half-brother, but he doesn't live around here, so we have a long phone call on Christmas Day but that's about it. I shall go for a walk along the canal, which will be heavenly, and then go home to sit in front of the fire with my new book. I always treat myself at Christmas,' she explained.

She could see that Bertie wasn't quite sure how to frame his next question. It was the one that always came after, so she thought she would save him the bother, and embarrassment.

'I don't see my parents,' she said. 'My dad left with my brother when I was about five and my mum… It's a long story, but we had a bit of falling-out, so I don't keep in touch.' It wasn't quite the whole truth, but it would do. She pulled a face. 'So you see, I'm not quite the expert on family dynamics that you thought I was.'

'Your mum was a single parent though,' replied Bertie. 'Just like mine.'

'Not like Bea,' said Daisy. 'But, yes, you're right, she was.'

She picked up her drink again so that she wouldn't have to look at Bertie or answer another question just at that minute and, without thinking, took a huge swallow. Her eyes widened and she pulled the mug away from her lips to stare at its contents.

Bertie grinned. 'It's good, isn't it?'

She looked across at him. How on earth had that happened? Was it because she had drunk several mouthfuls already, and got used to the flavour? Or drunk without thinking, bypassing her brain's normal resistance? Whichever it was, the drink was delicious. She took another swallow, letting the velvety smoothness roll around her mouth. It was sweet, but not sickly, creamy and rich all at the same time.

He pushed a plate towards her. 'Try it with a rugelach, it's gorgeous.'

She hesitated. Perhaps she was pushing her luck trying one of the pastries as well, but… She took one before she could think about it any more and bit it clean in half. Her mouth filled with a luscious buttery richness, the cinnamon reminding her of every Christmas she had ever known. She crammed the last of it in before she had even finished the first mouthful. She looked up, grinning.

'Sorry…'

Bertie's eyes twinkled with amusement. 'Don't apologise. It's nice to see you enjoying yourself. I once had a stick insect for a girlfriend and she drove me mad. Do you know how difficult it is to take someone out for a romantic meal when all they'll eat is lettuce leaves, and hold the dressing?'

Daisy nearly choked.

'Not that this is like that at all…' Bertie groaned. 'Oh God, excuse me while I just take my foot out of my mouth.' He peeped up at her through his lashes. 'This is just too weird, isn't it?'

Daisy nodded and chewed, trying to swallow quickly. 'It is rather. But it's so lovely of you to bring me here, to go to all this trouble.'

'Well, where *do* you take someone when you're trying to get to know them better... but not in a romantic way?' he added quickly. 'I had no idea but, seeing as you're giving up your day off to do this, I thought the very least I could do was bring you somewhere fun. And I know this place, I thought it might help.'

'It's lovely, Bertie, really. So, no agenda, let's just try and enjoy it.'

He smiled at her. 'Deal,' he replied. 'Come on then, eat up, there's plenty more we have to see.'

Bertie had almost polished off the pile of nuts, but Daisy did try one, and two more of the delicious pastries disappeared as well. She gave the mini cheese on toasts a miss, leaving them for Bertie who didn't mind in the slightest. He grinned as he gathered up the gingerbread stars into a napkin and slipped them into his pocket. 'We can munch them as we go.'

Moments later they were back outside, shivering in the sudden blast of cold air that hit them after the warm fug of the bar. Daisy pulled her cloak around her.

'Where to?' she asked, but she had a feeling she already knew the answer. Sure enough, Bertie led them around the building and out into the square they had looked down on. An old-fashioned fairground was in full swing, the jangly music loud amid the laughter and flashing lights.

She lifted her head as the familiar sweet smell drifted past her again. What *was* that? She took a couple of steps forward, before stopping dead. As the crowd suddenly parted in front of her, she saw the candyfloss stall straight ahead, gasping as a rush of memories almost overwhelmed her. The smell filled her nostrils, such a wonderful sweet sugary smell, and in a split second she was seven again, tugging on her mother's arm.

Oh, she craved it so much… just a taste, that's all she wanted. Angry voices buzzed in her ears, voices which got louder and louder. She felt a rough yank on her arm and, seconds later, a hand slapped her cheek hard. It took the breath from her body, the sharp sting turning into a hot bloom of pain that overrode all else. Her eyes filled with tears and she began to cry.

Monday 9th December

Sixteen shopping days until Christmas

'Daisy? Are you okay?'

She looked up, stunned to see Bertie's face in front of her, his hand on her arm, eyes full of concern.

'Daisy?' he said again.

She shook her head and looked around her, confused. Her path was criss-crossed with people, the gaudy helter-skelter rose tall into the sky ahead of her, the lines of twinkly lights still blew in the breeze. All was as it had been before, but for a minute she had been... where exactly?

She touched a hand to her cheek, feeling the memory of the pain she had felt there as a child, the shock of the stinging blow from her mother's hand. She inhaled deeply, trying to calm her breathing. The smell of the candyfloss was still strong, but mercifully she could feel the memory begin to loosen its grip.

'I'm fine,' she managed. 'Sorry. I just came over a bit dizzy there for a minute.'

Bertie had caught hold of her other arm now and was holding her firmly in front of him, searching her face anxiously.

She smiled. It was a bit feeble but the best she could come up with. 'I think maybe it was coming back out into the cold after the heat of indoors. I got that sudden whoosh of light-headedness.'

'I used to get sick in department stores all the time as a kid,' said Bertie. 'Don't worry about it. As long as you're okay?'

'I think so.' She nodded. She was beginning to feel better, but she needed some space. 'Could we just walk for a bit?' she asked. 'Sorry, I think I need to clear my head.'

Bertie looked around him. 'Sure… I tell you what, why don't we walk along the canal for a bit? It's not far from here. I can't guarantee it's all that scenic, but it will be quieter.'

She smiled gratefully. 'Thank you. I didn't realise there was a canal here.'

He grinned. 'Neither did I until I nearly fell in it once after a night out. I was a little bit tipsy if truth be told…'

'Ah.' She smiled and took the arm he was offering, grateful for the support as they began to walk.

'I often think I'd like to live on a canal boat,' she mused.

'Then why don't you?'

'Well only because I have my cottage. If I didn't then I think a canal boat would be the next best thing. My house is only tiny, but it's mine and very special to me. My grandma left it to me when she died and it used to be the lock-keeper's cottage when such a thing existed. I played there as a child. In fact, you probably know it…'

'No, I'm ashamed to say that I've never even been to the canal.'

She stared at him, shocked. 'How can you have never been? It's right in the town.'

He pulled a rueful face. 'Too busy doing other things? I dunno really… just never thought about it, I guess…' He cleared his throat.

'I don't really ever walk, or rather I don't ever go for a walk, just for walking's sake.' He paused when he saw the look on her face. 'Has that shocked you?'

She tipped her head on one side. 'I'm a little surprised, yes. I can't really understand how anyone would choose not to do that. I walk every day, even when it's pouring with rain; not always far, but it's a bit like breathing. I'm not sure I could get through the day without it.'

He nodded. 'Perhaps I might have to try it some time.'

'We're walking now,' she replied, raising her eyebrows.

'So we are…'

They fell silent for a few minutes, both lost in thought, until they turned the corner of a road and came to a little footbridge that crossed the canal. Bertie led her up onto it and paused for a moment, his arms resting on the railing.

She followed suit, staring at the dark ribbon of water that threaded its way through the city. She pointed. 'Look…'

Below them, tucked into the side of the canal was a narrowboat. It was painted cherry red and a deep, almost navy blue. A tiny Christmas tree sat on the stern, a wire trailing from the lights that circled it, over the door hatch and back inside the boat. Further loops of lights hung around the windows and from the metal chimney a coil of scented smoke rose into the still air. Daisy breathed it in.

'Don't you love that smell? It's a winter smell, like steam trains too… It makes me feel so nostalgic, what for I don't know, but still…'

Bertie lifted his head to stare down the length of the canal, inhaling deeply. 'I've often wondered how you keep those things warm in cold weather.'

'Squirrel stoves, they're called. Little pot-bellied wood burners, they keep everything toasty and warm. You really can live on the boats all year round, they're very comfortable.'

'But where would you put everything?'

She gave him a long look. 'I think the idea is that you travel light. But they have lots of little cubbyholes, and cupboards tucked away. Seats lift up for storage, that kind of thing.'

'Yes, but I'd never get half of my stuff in there. In fact, probably not even the contents of one room.'

'And all those things are an absolute necessity, are they?'

He frowned at her. 'Well I guess that depends on what you call a necessity, doesn't it? But they're certainly things I wouldn't wish to live without. I mean, I have a fifty-inch TV for starters, where would that go?'

She didn't answer for a moment, her eyebrows raised in amusement.

He rolled his eyes. 'Go on,' he said. 'I can see you're dying to put me straight about my materialistic tendencies.'

'No, I just wondered why you need to have so many things. Is it the need to own things because they make you feel better about yourself – obvious symbols of your wealth and status – or is it just for practical reasons?'

'Blimey, Daisy, don't pull any punches, will you?'

'Sorry, I didn't mean it to sound judgemental, I'm genuinely interested. There's a man that lives on a narrowboat a little further up the canal from me – we say good morning to one another every day. He has a little garden on his roof, and grows vegetables all year round. He has a bike if he needs to go anywhere, a little shelf of books and a well-used library card, and he shops from the local market every day, buying fresh food from local growers. And he can change the view from his windows any time he wants to. It strikes me that he has not only everything he could possibly need, but everything he could possibly want as well.'

Bertie's eyes were twinkling. 'I bet he doesn't have a job though.'

She smiled. 'He's a writer,' she replied. 'So yes, he does. A very successful one actually, but he chooses to live a simple life. I admire that.'

'Yes, but how possible would that be for the majority of people? Folk who have no choice but to work in factories, nine to five, or night shifts? Doctors, nurses, people with mortgages, children… What you're describing isn't realistic.'

'I didn't say it was a perfect argument,' she replied. 'But it comes down to choice, doesn't it; what kind of life you want to lead? The cost of living is so much less on a boat, so you need to earn less. Maybe too many of us are caught like the proverbial hamster on the treadwheel – we want bigger houses, so we need to earn more. We want better jobs, so when we get them and we earn more, we spend more but then somehow we still need more, and so it goes on… it's a vicious cycle. And that's absolutely fine if you're happy with that, all I'm saying is that some people want different.'

'And you're one of those people?'

Daisy nodded. 'I had my house given to me. I know I'm lucky, but yes, I like things… simple.'

She shivered suddenly and Bertie touched her arm. 'Come on, let's keep walking,' he said. They crossed over the bridge and down onto the towpath, heading away from the town.

'It's an interesting subject,' added Bertie when they had taken a few steps. 'And I'll admit not something I've ever really thought about. But then, in my defence, inheriting a fat wodge of money from my father when I turned eighteen meant all I learned was how to spend it. I'm not trying to excuse my way of life, but having that kind of money at so young an age was a big responsibility to place on young shoulders. I'm not sure I dealt with it particularly well. Looking back, I could have done all kinds of things with the money, used it for real good, but I guess I wasn't old enough to even know what that was.'

'You could now though.'

He paused for a moment. 'Yes, I guess I could.' He fell silent, clearly thinking about her words, but then looked back at her with a grin. 'Now might not be a good time to mention this with all the talk of materialism, but may I remind you that you do work in a shop which sells purely decorative items that cost thousands of pounds.'

'Yes, but if I had my way, we wouldn't sell things like that. I can admire certain aspects of them, certainly, but I hate what Buchanans jewellery stands for – that unless you're wearing something hugely expensive, its worth is somehow devalued. And Christmas is the worst possible time of the year where that's concerned. You've seen folks in the shop, buying jewellery that costs a fortune, sometimes even asking for whatever is the most expensive ring or necklace, as if that will somehow bestow more love, or be a better gift. It isn't at all, it's the worst kind of thoughtlessness. And then on the other hand there are people like this man I know who—'

She stopped dead. She had just been about to tell Bertie about Amos, and his quest to find the most perfect present for Grace. 'Oh well, that doesn't matter, it's a long story, but no, most of what we sell is cold and heartless and if I had my way Buchanans would be very different.'

'Then why work there if you hate it so much?'

Daisy looked at Bertie, weighing something up. 'No, I can't tell you, you'll think I'm stupid.'

'No, I won't.' He elbowed her gently. 'Come on, tell me.'

'Well, if you must know it's because nearly everyone who comes in is buying a gift.' She sighed. 'I'm a sucker for a good love story…' She snorted with laughter at his expression. 'No, I really am!'

He stared at her, trying to decide if she was having him on or not. 'There's a lot more to you than meets the eye, Daisy Turner, did you know that?'

She blushed slightly. 'Is there?'

They had reached another bridge and Daisy indicated that they should walk up onto it. 'Let's get back to the fair,' she said. 'I think I could be ready for a spin on a merry-go-round now. After all, you've brought me all this way and we've ended up walking by the canal, something we could do back home.'

'True, but it is lovely here,' replied Bertie. 'Peaceful.' He stared back down the length of water. 'I might even have to take a walk myself sometime. How's that for a change of tune?'

'Excellent,' she replied. 'I heartily approve.'

*

'You hated every minute of that, didn't you?'

'I didn't hate it,' retorted Daisy. 'It's just not what I'm used to.' She took his hand as he helped her up from where she was sprawled on a pile of mats at the base of the helter-skelter. It had taken pretty much all of her courage to get up there in the first place, but she had agreed to it in a mad rush of exhilaration after actually enjoying the carousel.

She had wondered whether her anxiety would get the better of her again as they neared the fairground for the second time that day but, although the clamour of noise and smells was momentarily disconcerting, there were none of the awful flashbacks of before. Instead she was able to enjoy the sights and sounds around her of something she hadn't seen since she was a child.

'But you don't want another go?' asked Bertie mischievously.

'No, I'll pass,' she replied. 'But there is something else I'd quite like to do...' It was another memory from her childhood, but from happier times, after...

'Oh, God, please tell me it's not the waltzers,' moaned Bertie. 'I am definitely too old for those.'

Daisy shuddered, the thought of being whirled around at what felt like one hundred miles an hour not in the least appealing. 'No, something else. I spotted it when I was up there.' She pointed high in the air, smiling at the memory of what she had seen. It had looked like a fairy tale.

'Lead on then.'

She threaded her way through the crowds of people, checking every now and again to make sure that Bertie was still with her. There was something bubbling in her stomach that felt like excitement, but, surely not... Still, what would it be like? she wondered. Would she even remember how? It was such a long time ago.

Almost breathless, she reached the edge of the square, her hands resting on a barrier as she stared across the space. 'Oh, look... isn't it magical?'

In front of her was an expanse of sparkling ice with bodies twirling this way and that under a canopy of stars. The stars weren't real of course but made up from strings of lights that criss-crossed the space and, although it wasn't dark, she could imagine how it would look if it were. Just like it had one magical Christmas the year after she had gone to live with her grandma and grandad.

She turned to look at Bertie. 'Can we have a go?' she asked. 'Please?'

It was the first time she had seen his face fall the entire day. 'Would now be a good time to confess that I have absolutely no sense of balance?' he said. 'It took me twice as long to ride my bike as all the other kids at school, and don't even get me started on roller skates…'

She pulled at his arm. 'I'll help you,' she said. 'You'll be fine.'

He rolled his eyes. 'Do I take it you've done this before?'

'Oh yes,' she breathed. 'A long time ago mind, but I'm hoping it's like riding a bike.' And to her amazement she found herself winking at him.

Bertie groaned. 'A low blow,' he complained.

A few minutes later they were all kitted out and Daisy stepped out onto the ice. All at once she was nine years old again, standing on the frozen surface of the canal as it shimmered under the light of a full moon and hundreds of twinkling stars. She looked up. This was something she could do.

Bertie was still clutching at the barrier, his feet moving even though he had no wish for them to. He waved at her. 'You go off, if you like. I'll just stand here looking pathetic.'

'I haven't done this in years, Bertie. As soon as I try to move, I'll probably be flat on my back.' But she wouldn't be, she could feel the excitement under her feet, that feeling of utter freedom. 'Just give me a minute,' she said. 'Let me get my balance a bit and then I'll come back for you.'

He nodded. 'I'll be right here…'

She gave a tentative push off with one leg, remembering how to hold her weight, not to look at her feet. And then the other. It felt strange, but there was a feeling of weightlessness that felt so wonderfully familiar. It was as if her body, no longer encumbered by her feet gluing her to the ground, had found what it was like to fly; the slightest movement spun her round, or moved her forward and, even if it wasn't where she wanted to go, she went with the flow.

It was tentative at first, a few wobbles as her centre of gravity shifted, but then she was able to lengthen her stride and glide into each movement. She could feel her smile widening as she looked upwards, remembering what it had felt like to skate under the stars. A young boy and his father turned in front of her and she recognised the scared wonder on the boy's face, knowing how it would feel when the fear receded. She grinned at them, almost feeling her grandad's hand in hers as she took her first baby steps.

Still grinning with excitement, she made her way back to Bertie, her fingers outstretched.

'You *have* done this before!' He was laughing. 'Blimey, Daisy, that was amazing. Where did you learn to skate?'

'Would you believe on the canal back home?'

His eyes widened.

'Yes, I know… it would never be allowed now, but my grandparents were great believers in flouting conformity, plus of course my grandad had tried out the ice first; he didn't just let me go regardless. It's funny but the canal rarely freezes over now, but back when I was little it was a regular thing…' She tilted her head to one side. 'Or maybe I just remember it that way. Anyhow, the one stretch of water between the locks made the perfect skating rink, just the right size for a little girl.'

Bertie looked her up and down. 'I can just picture you, twirling round and around.'

'He used to take me out at night, can you imagine? No light, save for that of the moon. It was the most magical thing. So quiet, everything glittering like it was made from stardust. I can't remember when I've seen anything more beautiful.'

'That's a lovely memory.'

'Yes, it is,' she replied. It was one of the ones that had almost made up for what had gone before. She paused for a moment, her head full of them. 'It's funny, but I haven't thought about that in years. Thank you for bringing me here, Bertie.'

'You're welcome,' he replied, his smile warm. 'It was worth it just to see the look on your face.'

She blushed but held out her hand. 'Come on then, your turn now, I can't wait to see the look on *your* face...'

'What, the one when I'm flat on my backside with you standing over me laughing?'

'No, the one when you realise that all your pots of money can't buy a feeling like you're flying. It's the little things, Bertie, always has been, always will be.'

*

It had been dark for some time by the time Daisy finally got home and she walked the path to her cottage more tired than she had been in a long while, but happier too. She couldn't believe how quickly the time had gone, and what she had been dreading had, quite unexpectedly, turned into the most wonderful day out. And she really couldn't work out how it had happened.

Bertie had always been the easiest of the brothers to talk to, but she had thought him brash and showy, lacking in care. In fact, he had turned out to be very considerate of her feelings and she could see very clearly how his upbringing had encouraged his devil-may-care attitude. What she hadn't banked on had been his playful sense of fun and infectious good humour, which had made even the difficult aspects of the day easier to bear, and she had found him to be extraordinarily good company. She couldn't help but wonder if he felt the same.

She came to an abrupt halt. What on earth was she doing? Today hadn't been a date, so why was she even considering what it felt like? No, today was simply Bertie trying to make the best of a bad situation and, whatever else she felt, she would always be very grateful to him for that. More importantly, she reminded herself, it had been about who was going to end up running Buchanans and at least she felt more comfortable about the possibility that this might be Bertie. He might not have the most sensible of business heads, but at least she now knew that she could stand in the same room as him and not want to kill him. She was very worried that the same might not be true for Lawrence...

She stood for a few moments looking at the reflection on the water. The sky was perfectly clear and a glowing crescent of moon sat low above the horizon. It would freeze tonight and she shivered; it was bitterly cold. She turned to go, pausing just for a second as she caught a glimpse in her head of her small self, turning circles on the ice. She smiled, wondering if she would ever see the canal frozen over again, and headed up the path to her cottage.

Even though the day had been so lovely, it was always a relief to be home. The cottage welcomed her in, shut out the world and instantly things seemed simpler and easier to manage. She took off her coat and scarf and hung them on the peg in the hallway before moving through to the kitchen. She wasn't hungry, but a drink would be very welcome. She giggled in the silent space; she might even have a hot chocolate.

Tuesday 10th December

Fifteen shopping days until Christmas

It hadn't been an easy day. She was tired and the shop had been unusually busy for a weekday, with fractious and impatient customers. It didn't help that, despite her best efforts, nobody had bought a thing. She felt pressured and totally unable even to find any Christmas spirit. And then there were her increasing nerves about this evening's meal with Grace and Amos. She wished she hadn't pushed the meal back until later; it just gave her more hours to fret about their meeting.

She sighed and glanced at her watch for about the twentieth time in the last five minutes. There was only an hour to go. Perhaps a cup of tea would help.

'Cuppa?' she asked as she walked past Kit.

'What?' He looked up as if seeing her for the very first time and she was taken aback by the distraught expression on his face.

'I asked if you'd like a cup of tea?'

It seemed to take him an inordinately long time to answer. 'Yes, okay, if you like.'

'Jeez,' she murmured to herself as she walked through to the back. Kit was in a weird mood as well today. He'd spoken even less than usual, if that were possible.

She was just pouring water onto the teabags when she heard the shop bell go. Ordinarily she would have checked whether Kit needed any help, but today she just ignored it. He could manage by himself for once. She took down the biscuit tin and took out a chocolate chip cookie, cramming half of it in her mouth. And she *never* ate biscuits at work. She didn't even *like* cookies.

'Oh dear, is it that bad?'

She whirled around, her hand going straight to her mouth. It was Bertie, a bunch of red roses in his arms. She swallowed, spluttering as she struggled with the half-chewed biscuit. His look quickly changed from one of amusement to alarm when he saw her face. 'Are you okay?'

Daisy nodded rapidly, her cheeks colouring instantly. 'Yes. Sorry… I wasn't expecting… You startled me, that's all.' She swallowed the last of the biscuit. 'See, no harm done. And that was my fault. I don't normally eat biscuits, I think I…' she trailed off, eyeing the blooms '… don't really need to explain, do I?'

Bertie shook his head, laughing. 'No, you don't. But if you have a biscuit habit that no one else is aware of, don't worry, your secret's safe with me.' He watched her for a moment more.

'How have things been today?' he asked. 'Hard going?' Despite his light-hearted comment earlier she realised that he actually was concerned to find her in the kitchen, stuffing her face with a biscuit.

'Just… I'm tired, I think. And it's been a bit of a slow day. Lots of customers, but no one in the mood for buying much.'

The shop bell tinkled and Bertie nodded, waiting a few seconds until he could hear Kit's voice in conversation. 'Well, I'm sure you've done your best. And it's no wonder you're tired. Yesterday was a very long day, which is entirely my fault, but I do want to say thank you.

Our day out could have been a complete disaster, but I really enjoyed it. I hope you did too.'

She blushed and nodded, wondering if she should just take the flowers. Bertie was still clutching them, a wide smile on his face.

'Thank you, it was lovely.' She reached out a hand just as Bertie lowered his arm to his side.

His face was immediately wreathed in apology. 'Oh God, Daisy, I'm so sorry…' He stared down at the roses in his hand. Flowers that were clearly meant for someone else. 'That was… incredibly rude… I really wasn't thinking.'

'No, no, it's all right… honestly. No, don't apologise.' She could barely speak, she'd never felt so embarrassed.

'I've just come from the market and thought I should pop in to say thank you while I was here. I'm just on my way over to see my… well, it doesn't really matter.' He swallowed, lifting the bouquet. 'Actually, you should have these. I can get some more, I—'

'Bertie, honestly… It doesn't matter.'

He opened his mouth to speak, but then closed it again. He was just as red-faced as she was. And it was all her fault. How could she have been so stupid as to think he would be bringing *her* flowers?

'No, it does matter…' He groaned. 'I should go,' he added, 'before I make things any worse, but I did have a great time yesterday, really.'

She nodded, biting her lip. 'So, did I, Bertie. And please, don't worry… I'm not offended.' She plastered a smile on her face. 'And if you think about it, it's really quite funny…'

He held her look for a moment before, to her amazement, coming forward and kissing her cheek. 'Thank you,' he said. 'You're very kind.'

She stared at the empty doorway as he left, her cheeks on fire and her heart thudding in her chest.

'Right,' she said under her breath. 'Well, that was… unexpected…' Her eyes rolled up towards the ceiling. Could this day get any worse?

She stared at the mugs of tea, huffing a little and, for a moment, quite unable to do a thing. Then she cleared her throat, ran a hand through her hair and took a deep breath. Hastily finishing making the drinks, she carried them straight back out onto the shop floor where their customer was just pulling open the door to leave.

'Phew, what a day,' she said to Kit brightly. 'I don't know about you but I'm ready for this.' She handed him a mug and carried hers back to the counter on the other side of the room.

Kit stared at her. 'Not a red roses kind of girl?' he said. His tone was light enough, but there was no mistaking the challenge in his voice.

A sudden heat bloomed within her. 'Bertie just popped in to say thank you for yesterday. And for your information the flowers weren't for me.' Her voice sounded stiff and pompous but she willed it to stay steady.

'Oh, Daisy…' Kit's voice was gentle. 'I'm really sorry. Bertie is, well, he's…'

But the look in Kit's eyes had caught her completely off-guard. 'What for?' she demanded, flustered. 'That the flowers weren't mine? Or insinuating that there was something going on between Bertie and me?'

He bowed his head, his contrition clear. 'For jumping to conclusions when I had no right to.' He held her look for a second before his face crumpled. 'Tell me honestly though,' he blurted out. 'Have you handed it to Bertie on a plate? Because it's driving me mad not knowing. I mean, I'd understand if you have… Bertie is suave, good-looking, and flash with the cash. I think if I were in your position I'd do the same, but…'

He trailed off as she turned and stood in front of him, her hands on her hips. 'Christopher Buchanan, do you know how incredibly insulting that comment is?'

He winced at the use of his full name. 'I'm sorry,' he mumbled, 'I wasn't thinking, I…'

She glared at him, but he looked so sheepish her anger melted away and she softened her expression. 'Fortunately for you, however, I'm not insulted because I know that you don't mean I would ever stoop so low as to hand things to Bertie on a plate, as you put it. Because that would make me dishonest, disloyal and not a nice person at all.'

He closed his eyes and groaned.

'Plus I can see how, knowing him as you do, there's a very real possibility that he might have sought an unfair advantage and that, flattered by his winning smile and wily ways, I acquiesced… But I didn't, nor will I, and don't you ever suggest anything like that again. For goodness' sake you're—'

'Behaving like a child. Yes, I know.' He looked up at her through his lashes. 'Do you know what I hate most about all of this? It's the fact that I've spent most of my life trying to dodge all the bullets that my brothers fired at each other, and me, if I was around, and now I feel as if I'm back in the nursery. I have never wanted to throw my toys out of the pram so much as I do now.'

She was taken aback by the stark honesty of his words and faltered for a moment, unsure what to make of his statement.

'You know, I do understand how you're feeling, Kit, but you have to trust me, otherwise the next few weeks are going to be unbearable. And in the meantime would it help you to know that Bertie still has no more advantage over the rest of you? We had a nice day, we talked about stuff and, if Bertie is shrewd, he may have deduced certain aspects of my character which may help him with his final design…'

She broke off, giving Kit a telling look. 'What we didn't do is directly discuss what my favourite piece of jewellery is now, or, if I had five grand knocking about, what I'd like it to be. And if it helps I'll remind you of that fact the day after I go out with Lawrence,' she said. 'We'll probably be having a similar conversation.'

Kit nodded, thinking about her words. 'Yes,' he replied ruefully, acknowledging his shortcomings. 'We probably will…' He bent his head to take a sip of his tea and then stopped, looking back across at her with a soft smile on his face. 'And for the record, Daisy, I do trust you. And Bertie's an idiot, he should have bought you the flowers.'

*

Now that she was home, Daisy took out the wreath she had made and scrutinised it carefully in an effort to take her mind off things. She had already fired the silver clay leaves and berries and rubbed the residue away, leaving gleaming metal in its place. Polished repeatedly, it now shone as part of the wintry decoration. Set amid the hydrangea heads, eucalyptus and trails of ivy, Daisy thought it was inspired. The colours and textures complimented one another beautifully and, with some clever wiring, she had managed to make two pieces that were removable. One was formed from entwining leaves so that it could be worn as a necklace and the other as a brooch. She only hoped that Grace would like it. How did you even begin to work out what someone would like when jewellery was so personal?

She stopped, staring unseeing at the wall opposite. It had never occurred to her until now how similar her situation was to that of the Buchanan brothers. Each of them needed to design something for someone they barely knew and she was in exactly the same position, except that her future wasn't resting on the outcome of the competition. She looked down at the wreath in her hands – then again, perhaps it was…

She swallowed. Oh God, now she was really nervous. A glance at the clock showed she still had over half an hour before she needed to leave for Grace and Amos's house; what she needed was another distraction. She pulled her laptop towards her.

She had intended to have a little browse of some of her favourite creative sites, either to source materials or look at design inspirations, but, as soon as she logged on, she saw that she had received a message alert from her Instagram account. She had checked last night when she had got home and been a little disappointed to find that there had been no response to her last message, but now here he was, contacting her again.

Underneath where she had typed 'What did you have in mind?' was now a row of dots, followed by his reply:

NickCarr1: That's a tough one, I don't really know. Sorry to be so useless! I guess the trouble is that I want something a bit different, not like anything you can find in the shops, but something that is really individual to her. So now I'm stuck… how do we do this?

God, he really was serious about this. She had thought she would never hear from him again. Daisy thought for a minute and then typed.

Where are you based? Could you come and see me?

She sat back and stared at the screen. That might not have been the wisest thing, but it would make life an awful lot simpler. And in any case they could always meet somewhere public. He'd better get a move on though, Christmas was only just over two weeks away. She was just about to close her laptop again when a reply came pinging back.

Norfolk... You?

She smiled and flexed her fingers.

No good I'm afraid. I'm a very long way from there.

She tapped a finger on the edge of the keyboard while she thought of what else to say.

So then I guess the only way to do this is for you to send me as much information as you can about your girlfriend: what she likes, dislikes, her hobbies, attributes, favourite colours, that kind of thing. Maybe even some pictures of things she already has? I can sketch you some ideas with prices and maybe take it from there? Oh, and I need to know what you're thinking of – a bracelet, earrings, necklace?

She pressed send, and then, as an afterthought:

And you'd best be quick, sorry, but there's not much time left...

Almost immediately a new message appeared.

I know, I'm sorry. I travel a lot on business and am generally hopeless! Definitely a necklace though – I want her to wear it next to her heart

— Aw! The rest of the stuff sounds good… Can you leave it with me? I'll give you as much as I can, as soon as I can, but I'm away again in the morning for a couple of days. Friday at the latest, I promise!

Okay, I look forward to hearing from you. She typed in reply. *Many thanks.*

Daisy closed the lid of her laptop thoughtfully. Oh, it was so romantic. Imagine having a boyfriend who wanted to do that for you. She didn't think he was hopeless at all, in fact, he sounded wonderful. She glanced at her watch and began to collect her things together. It was almost time to go.

*

Her nerves had been steadily building with every mile she drove and as Daisy approached Grace's house, down an enormous long driveway, she almost turned around again and went home. It was the grandest approach she'd ever seen, winding up a hill through an avenue of trees. Even in winter it had a definite air of the majestic about it.

She was relieved, however, that the house at the top of the driveway was not quite as grand as the approach had led her to believe. More of a large cottage, or possibly two cottages joined together; a jumble of roof lines and warm red walls, but a handsome house, nonetheless. It looked very fine indeed with a pair of small Christmas trees flanking the front doorsteps, each topped with a huge red bow. An enormous wreath hung on the front door and Daisy smiled to herself when she saw it. Of course, what else?

An owl hooted somewhere behind her as she climbed from the car and, as she crossed the gravelled forecourt, it was answered by another.

She stopped to listen but after a moment she moved on, feeling the keenness of the wind after the contrasting heat of the car.

It felt like several weeks had passed since she had been on the course, but the barely contained excitement of Grace's greeting instantly brought back the warmth of their first meeting.

'Come in, come in,' said Grace. 'Oh, this is going to be so much fun!' She led the way down the softly lit hallway, halting when she realised that Daisy was lagging behind. She doubled back.

'Do you like it?'

They were standing by a large wall hanging made from some sort of fine gauzy material. Golden in colour, it shimmered in the soft light, but it was what was contained within that caught Daisy's eye. The rectangle of fabric had been divided into square 'pockets', similar to a sheet of ravioli, but inside of each… Daisy peered closer, yes, they really were… real leaves, bright yellows and reds in colour, some large, some small, some pockets containing more than one leaf. It was beautiful. Underneath it, on a polished wooden console table, stood a huge bowl of winter foliage, rich green ivy and holly, dotted with ruby berries, and all intermingled with gilded pine cones.

'Did you make this, Grace?' she asked, her eyes roving over the stunning details in front of her. She didn't really need to wait for the answering nod. 'I think it's amazing.'

Grace touched a hand to the fabric, smiling warmly. 'I'm really pleased you like it. The leaves within are preserved in glycerine, just like Flora was explaining on the course. It means that they stay pliable, but more importantly they keep all their gorgeous colour.'

Daisy nodded, mentally adding what she had seen to her list of facts about Grace, some of which she was sure would be used to provide inspiration for the piece of jewellery that she would be making. There was colour and texture everywhere in this hallway, but the effect was very understated and elegant, much like Grace herself.

'So, are you a florist too?'

'No, just a keen gardener. Whatever the season I try to bring as much of the outside, inside, but I've always loved finding new ways of using plants and flowers as decoration. That's why I'm so intrigued to see your wreath.' She pointed to the bag that Daisy was still holding. 'Is that it?'

Daisy looked up, spotting Amos at the end of the hallway.

'Hello again,' he said, coming forward. 'Come and get warm, Daisy, it's bitter out there tonight.'

'Yes, do,' said Grace. 'The fire's lit and it's about time someone else hogged it other than Amos.' She smiled at him fondly and Daisy caught a flash of something passing between them.

Amos noticed her slight frown. 'It's a long story,' he said, smiling. 'Let's just say that having done without creature comforts for quite some time until fairly recently, I'm somewhat of a convert to the lure of an open fire and a cosy armchair.'

'I don't blame you,' replied Daisy. 'It's the first thing I do when I get home.' She was about to ask Amos if he'd been away, when Grace touched her arm lightly.

'I'll take your coat,' she said. 'Dinner won't be long, but we've time enough for a little chat first. Can I get you something to drink?'

Daisy could feel herself flushing. She had almost forgotten that she would be eating with them. 'A cup of tea would be lovely, thank you. But I hope you haven't gone to too much trouble,' she said, praying that Grace would say no she hadn't, and was cheese on toast all right?

She really hoped it wouldn't be something complicated or swimming in a sauce, she wasn't at all sure she could cope with that.

'I love cooking,' replied Grace. 'So it's not too much trouble at all, but do you know I often think that just simple things are best, provided they're cooked well. So I've gone with soup, plus some wedges of fresh bread. I hope that's okay. I thought it might be just the thing for a cold night.'

Daisy slowly released the breath she was holding. She hardly dare hope...

Grace grinned. 'Please tell me you like tomato soup, otherwise it might well have to be beans on toast.'

Daisy couldn't quite believe her luck. 'My favourite actually,' she replied, finally beginning to relax.

'Perfect,' said Amos. 'Now, come and get settled by the fire.' He waited until Grace had walked away before giving her a surreptitious wink. 'And we can have a covert chat while Grace is in the kitchen,' he whispered.

Amos led the way into another beautifully elegant space, a large and airy room, but warm and cosy too, with rich coloured throws on the chairs and several thick rugs laid over a polished wood floor. One corner of the room was dominated by a Christmas tree which sparkled with silver stars, its only other adornment huge creamy poinsettia heads. Daisy went forward for a closer look. Surely they couldn't be real? She smiled as she touched one. They weren't real – although she wouldn't have put it past Grace to make that magic happen – but, even so, the effect was stunning. She turned back to look at Amos's expectant face.

'So what have you told, Grace?' she asked, keeping her voice low. 'I don't want to put my foot in it.'

Amos kept one eye on the door. 'Very little. Only that Ned had remarked on what you were making on the course when he passed through the shed at some point and mentioned to me afterwards that he was looking for something unique as a Christmas gift for Flora. It was me that suggested you could make something and naturally I offered Grace as the person who could help you to design something that Flora would really love.' He rolled his eyes. 'Given that us men are all hopeless when it comes to choosing presents…'

Daisy smiled. 'You'd be surprised how many are, actually,' she replied. 'They all stagger into the shop on Christmas Eve totally panic-stricken. Not you though, obviously.'

'Although I haven't given you much time, have I? Christmas is only two weeks away.'

Daisy thought of the other commission that she hoped to gain. It wasn't ideal timing at all. 'It will be fine,' she said. 'Don't worry.' The words left her lips before she even thought about them, but it was such an odd thing for her to say. She wasn't used to reassuring anyone; it was usually her in need. 'Hopefully this evening will give me plenty of ideas and I'll be inspired.' She looked around her. 'Even just being here helps actually.'

There was a rattle of crockery from the hallway and she exchanged a look with Amos. He put a finger to his lips, grinning.

Moments later Grace appeared, carrying a tray laden with mugs and a plate of mince pies.

'We'll probably all be heartily sick of these come Christmas, so I won't be offended if you don't take one,' said Grace, putting down the tray onto a coffee table. 'Even though they are homemade and I've been slaving over a hot stove all afternoon.' She broke into a broad smile. 'Just teasing, although if you do want one, be quick or Amos will beat you to it.'

Amos patted his stomach, which was as flat as a pancake. 'I have a dreadfully sweet tooth, I'm afraid. I'll be the size of a house soon.'

Daisy sat down on the nearest chair. She hadn't the heart to tell Grace that she couldn't cope with the gloopy mess of mincemeat inside the pie. The pastry was lovely, but the rest…

'Just the tea will be lovely, thank you. I'm really looking forward to my soup, I don't want to spoil it.'

'Well, I can't wait to see what's in that bag, Daisy,' said Grace, handing her a mug. 'I didn't get much of a chance to look at what you were making the other day but, from what I've heard, it sounds like just the sort of thing that Flora will love. Have you been making jewellery long? I guess working in a place like Buchanans must be heaven for you. Is that where you trained?'

Daisy darted a nervous look at Amos. 'Erm… no, they don't really know about it. In fact, they don't know about it at all. It's a secret…'

Amos shifted in his seat. 'A secret?' His voice was tinged with anxiety.

Daisy was caught. Amos would surely realise that he had let the cat out of the bag the other day in the shop and, although she didn't wish to make him feel bad, she couldn't possibly say anything to reassure him. Grace mustn't even know he had ever been in the shop.

Grace shot Amos a look. 'Why is it a secret?'

'It's a bit awkward really,' Daisy replied. 'Buchanans isn't the kind of shop that would sell the things I'd make. The things they sell are...'

'Well out of my league,' said Grace, picking up her own drink. She smiled. 'And fortunately, not my cup of tea. I hope you don't mind me saying but I find that style of jewellery rather cold and clinical – I don't think I've ever seen anything in their window that could beat the beauty of a flower or the dewdrops on the grass of a morning, and I can get those for free. Sorry,' she added, looking a little sheepish.

'No, don't apologise,' said Daisy. 'They're really not my thing either. I can appreciate the quality of the workmanship, and the stones do have a beauty, in their own way, but... it often seems to me that people buy things simply because of their expense, as if that says almost as much as the piece of jewellery itself, if not more.'

She took a sip of her tea. It was strong, just how she liked it. 'I've worked at Buchanans for eight years and the one thing I do love is hearing people's stories, and there always is a story. People tell me all these very personal things, and yet the jewellery itself seems so impersonal. I've never been able to figure that out about what we sell; surely the very least it should be is personal?'

Amos was studying her, frowning a little. 'So wouldn't what *you* could offer provide their customers with a very real choice? Your boss might be very keen to see what you design.'

Daisy laughed. 'Trust me, she wouldn't. Bea wears diamonds like other people wear a coat if it's cold. And it has to be of the very highest quality, that's always been her watchword as far as Buchanans goes.'

'And quality equals expense, does it?' queried Amos.

'In her world, yes, I'm afraid it does.'

Grace nodded. 'And this is why you've never opened up about your own skills, is that right? Because you think people will laugh at the things you make?'

'I know they would,' said Daisy. She could almost hear Lawrence's sneering voice now. 'They'll think what I do worthless.'

There was silence for a moment and then Grace cleared her throat, exchanging a look with Amos that she couldn't quite fathom. 'When I first met you, Daisy, you mentioned that you'd been to see Hope Blooms not long after it first opened. But I'm not sure if you were aware that just a few short months before that the place was full of cattle.'

Daisy nodded. 'Yes,' she replied. 'Flora mentioned it on Friday.'

'Well then it might also interest you to learn that around the same time I was going through some considerable changes of my own. My marriage had fallen apart and I was facing the very real possibility of losing this place.' She looked around her at the beautiful room. 'And that was a huge problem for me because during the thirty-odd years of my marriage I'd lost so much self-esteem, and thought myself so worthless, that I had become practically a recluse. My house was all I cared about. In fact, I didn't think I could exist outside of it, but, mainly due to this wonderful man here, I found out that what I had thought was my shield and protector was actually my prison cell...'

Daisy swallowed. Grace had just described her almost to the letter.

'... And I'm wondering if perhaps the same is true for you. Buchanans offers you safety, but it might also be holding you back.' She sat back, smiling. 'I think you should show us what you've made now because, if I'm not much mistaken, there is something inside of you that's desperate to make itself known, and talent like that shouldn't ever be hidden away.'

Daisy didn't know what to say. They were such lovely words and she never imagined she would ever hear anyone say those things about her. She dipped her head in acknowledgement and grinned, taking another sip of her tea to fortify herself. Then she bent down to the bag at her feet and lifted her wreath free from its covering. Shyly, she handed it to Grace.

Grace lifted it, holding it a moment at a slight distance before resting it lightly on her lap, her eyes roving over the detail. Her fingertips danced across the foliage, tracing a leaf here and a petal there, and then when she had had her fill, she angled the wreath towards the light, holding it closer so that she could study what lay at its heart.

The seconds ticked by and, as a log shifted on the fire, Daisy realised she was holding her breath. She tried to let it out slowly, remembering to take another as she did so. Eventually, Grace lifted her eyes.

'I don't think I have ever seen anything like this before,' she said, her face lit up with a warm smile. 'The wreath itself is beautiful, stunning actually – the colours you've used, the placement of the pieces and the way you've contrasted everything.' Her fingertip rested lightly on one of the leaves. 'And these are actually silver?'

Daisy nodded, her own eyes tracing the trails of ivy she had made and woven in among the foliage.

'They're wired, so you can take it out and wear it. I've designed it as a circlet – there are clasps on the end which are hidden at the moment. The centrepiece can clip onto it as well, so, if you want, you can wear the whole thing as one piece, or wear one as a necklace and the other as a brooch. In my mind, I pictured it as something a bride might wear, you know, for a winter wedding or something. I don't know though…'

Grace was staring at her. 'That's… incredible… I don't know what to say.' She looked back down and then up again before switching her gaze to Amos. 'Did you know they were like this?' she asked.

He shook his head. 'Described, but…' He held out his hand so that Grace could pass the wreath across to him and Daisy realised that this would be the first time he would see what she was capable of.

'Do you want me to unfasten it, so you can see the whole thing?'

Two heads nodded in unison.

Turning the wreath over, Daisy gently unclipped the centrepiece and handed it to Grace so that she could have a closer look. Made entirely from the silver clay, it had started off life as a silver disc about the size of a fifty-pence piece, but Daisy had added a series of tiny flower heads to it, each made from a number of petals, formed to resemble those of the hydrangea heads. The edges of the disc were softened with leaf shapes, some flat, some with curling edges. It was such a simple design but so exquisitely intricate.

It took only a moment to unwind the ivy trail and Daisy began to gently reshape the central wire so that it formed a circular shape, the leaves turning this way and that along its length. She fastened the clip and held it up for inspection. On Grace's elegant neck it would look beautiful all by itself but, even as she contemplated how it might look, she realised that she had begun to form an idea of what she could make for Grace. Her eyes widened in excitement at the possibilities that filled her head. She would try and put her ideas to Amos if they had a few minutes alone again during the evening, but she was sure he would agree; she'd only had to listen to Grace's words to know that she was on the right track.

'Flora is going to absolutely love this,' said Grace, shaking her head in wonder. 'I know you wanted some more information about her so that you could create something unique, but heavens, Daisy, this is perfect.'

Daisy had almost forgotten that that was supposed to be the reason she was there. 'Do you really think so?' she asked. 'I know she loves flowers obviously, but…'

'No, the ivy is perfect too,' broke in Amos. 'Because it symbolises growth, opportunity and determination. Friendship too, actually, and I never met anyone for whom that was a more perfect description.'

'Oh, yes you're right!' said Grace. 'I'd forgotten that. But Flora will definitely know the associations. I've often heard her referencing things like that when she's chatting to brides about their bouquets.' She grinned. 'It's so romantic, it sways the punters every time.' She rolled her eyes, and Daisy laughed.

'Is it really as easy as all that?' she said. 'I thought I was going to leave today having written pages of notes about Flora and then spend ages trying to come up with something. But from what you're saying you think this might actually be it, I can't quite believe it.'

Amos leaned forward. 'Ah, but you're forgetting that when something is meant to be, it's usually very simple…'

He held her look, his expression easy to read, and she blushed. His faith in her was quite astonishing given the relatively few times they had met, and she had to remind herself that there wasn't actually an intended recipient of the necklace; this was just a trial run, a prototype to see if her idea actually worked, if anyone other than her thought it was beautiful. And her real job was only just beginning. Except that… She looked across at Grace, who was still holding the necklace in wonder, and she realised that actually she didn't need any more insight into Grace's character; if the gift she was going to make were a song, then she already had all the notes.

Grace ran her finger across one of the silver ivy leaves before handing it back to Daisy with a soft sigh. 'I'll just go and check on the soup,' she said. 'But we're also going to have to work out what we're going to say to Flora, because I know she's dying to see how your wreath turned out, Daisy, but there's no way we can let her see this.'

'Oh…' Amos grinned. 'Oops, I hadn't thought about that.' He picked up his mug and took several swallows, waiting until Grace had left the room and was out of earshot.

'Well, that didn't go quite the way I thought it would,' he said, still keeping his voice low. 'I thought it would take ages for you and Grace to work out what would make the perfect gift for Flora, and that by hearing Grace talk about her own likes and dislikes it would help you. Now what do we do?'

His look was full of apology, but Daisy just smiled. 'Don't worry,' she said. 'It's quite the strangest thing, but I already have in my head the image of how I want Grace's necklace to look. Now all I have to do is translate what I can already see into reality.' She pulled a face. 'That's the scary bit.'

'Or the exciting bit…?'

Daisy bit her lip. 'Maybe.'

Amos sat back in his chair, his dark eyes twinkling. 'No, I think you're going to be just fine. Didn't I say that right from the start?'

She gave him a quizzical look and was about to ask him how he could possibly know that, when Grace reappeared.

'Won't be long,' she said. 'Now, tell me why you don't think your jewellery and Buchanans would be a good fit, because honestly I can't see how they could possibly fail to be blown away by the things you make. I understand that it would be radically different from the things they sell, but surely at the very least they would encourage you with it; you're a loyal employee. They could even offer you a small space to sell from – goodness only knows the retail sector is struggling at the moment and maybe a little diversity would be a good thing?'

Amos was nodding in encouragement, but Daisy pulled a face. She had thought endlessly of the possibilities that Buchanans could offer her, if only they had a mind to, but every time she considered it, she still came back to the same point – that she honestly didn't believe they would find any merit in what she did. And she wasn't about to make a laughing stock of herself.

'It isn't that easy,' she replied. 'Especially now.'

'Why, because your boss is retiring?' asked Grace. 'But, if you think about it, the fact that someone new will be taking over Buchanans could also make it the perfect time.' And then she stopped. 'Oh…' Her eyes widened. 'You will still have a job, won't you?'

'Possibly… I'm not even sure about that any more.'

Amos's face was full of sympathy. 'Then it would really help you to get your own business up and running now, wouldn't it? Whether you tell them about it or not. Do you know yet who'll be running the company?'

'Not exactly,' she replied. 'It will be a family member – there are three sons all waiting in the wings, but it's not as straightforward as it sounds. Bea is a little, shall we say, eccentric… She has a love of the theatrical. So, whereas anyone else might make a decision about who is to be their successor based on logic and careful consideration, Bea has decided that the only way to separate the relative merits of each brother is to hold a competition.' She went on to quickly explain the rules of the task that Bea had set.

Amos's eyes widened. 'I can't decide whether that's absolutely monstrous, or the best idea I've ever heard.'

'No, well you should try being in the middle of it all,' muttered Daisy. 'They all squabble like little children and, although I had a lovely day out with Bertie, he's completely clueless when it comes to business, Kit hardly speaks, and I'm dreading my day out with Lawrence. What's worse is that I don't think I'd like to work with any of them.'

'Oh, how come?' asked Grace.

Daisy shot Amos a quick look. He had met Kit but Grace shouldn't know that, and she hoped he wouldn't put his foot in it.

'Well, Lawrence is an arrogant bully, Bertie is a party animal, and Kit… well, he isn't always… how can I put it, full of initiative. The business needs someone with a passion for what they do, and the vision to see an idea through. I just don't think that's Kit.'

Amos smiled. 'Maybe he'll surprise you.'

Daisy gave him a puzzled look but he avoided her eyes, concentrating on his drink.

'Perhaps... I mean he's nice enough...' She trailed off, thinking about Kit's words earlier that day, and the look in his eyes... 'He's just very quiet,' she finished, feeling an unexpected colour in her cheeks.

'Not a nice position for you to be in, though,' added Grace. 'And I can quite see why you're a little reticent about confiding in them. But, perhaps when you've got to know them better, you might think differently. There's still every chance that they'd be open to new ideas.'

'Not mine they won't,' replied Daisy. 'Not when I tell them what I really think.' She glanced across at Amos but he was eating a mince pie. 'You asked me before how I started making my own jewellery, and the simple reason is that I see things differently from Bea. She's been very good to me over the years and gave me a job when I needed it most but I don't want to make the kind of jewellery that Buchanans sells. Whether you have pots of money, or none, people are mostly the same when it comes to matters of the heart. I deal in love, you see, day in, day out, and what matters most when you're giving a gift is not the cost of it, or what it says to anyone else, but that it speaks only words of love.'

She blushed at her words, fearing that she had become carried away by her emotion. 'And that's why I make the things I do, because I don't think Buchanans sells things that speak only of love. Their jewellery speaks only of wealth and possessions and status, and that's not the same at all.'

Amos looked up. 'That jewellery should speak only words of love,' he echoed. 'I think that's the most beautiful sentiment I've ever heard.'

Friday 13th December

Twelve shopping days until Christmas

Friday the 13th December – how could a trip on this day be anything other than a disaster from start to finish? Daisy stared at herself in the mirror, sticking out her tongue and tugging at her skirt. She felt scratchy and uncomfortable but Lawrence's instructions had been very clear. She should be well dressed, smart, no trousers and, if she had them (this was what irritated her the most), good quality or designer clothes. She almost cancelled the trip right there and then. She took in a deep breath. And *relax*, she urged herself. For goodness' sake, Daisy, you will have the most horrendous day if you carry on like this.

They were travelling by train, so Daisy had arranged to meet Lawrence at the nearest station, a half hour's drive away. She drove slowly, glancing anxiously at the sky which was heavy and looked laden with snow. She spotted Lawrence's silver Lexus the moment she pulled into the car park. It was in a reserved space, leaving her to trawl the rows looking for a free slot among the rank and file. Mercifully, she found one, and hurried from the warmth of her car across to where Lawrence was parked. He was reading a newspaper, the broad sheets almost filling the interior of the car. His tan leather driving gloves curled around its edges. How he turned the pages, Daisy had no idea. She stood there for a moment feeling increasingly foolish while she waited for him to notice her but then, deciding that he was either ignoring her, or just incredibly unaware of his surroundings, she rapped sharply on the window.

He turned, frowning at first but then quickly rearranged his face into a smile. She watched as he folded the newspaper meticulously into smaller and smaller sections, revealing – *Oh, dear God* – he was wearing a suit and tie. Where on earth did you go out for the day that necessitated wearing something so formal? If Daisy had been nervous before, now her anxiety levels were going through the roof.

She waited while he organised himself, hopping from one foot to the other to keep warm. The newspaper was tucked away, the driving gloves were removed and swapped for a black pair, a phone was collected, a coat and scarf slid from a hanger above the rear door, until finally Lawrence was suitably dressed and ready to greet her.

'Daisy,' he said briefly, nodding. 'Thanks for coming.' He checked his watch. 'We should go,' he added, 'and I'll brief you on the train.'

She stared at him. 'Hi Lawrence, it's nice to see you too.' She couldn't help herself. Pompous idiot.

He coloured slightly and cleared his throat. 'Yes, of course. My apologies… This is all rather… awkward, isn't it?'

He actually looked so uncomfortable that Daisy suddenly felt rather sorry for him. She smiled. 'It doesn't have to be,' she said. 'I'm nervous too, but we can still have a nice day. I was just as nervous when I went out with Bertie but—'

'Well yes, of course… life and soul of the party, Bertie – what's not to like about a day out with Bertie? I should imagine it's just fun, fun, fun, morning, noon and night.'

Daisy felt herself colouring, but she bit her tongue; arguing with Lawrence would only make it worse.

'I agree, you're very different,' she said cautiously. 'But Bertie is struggling with this competition just as much as you, believe me. Perhaps he just shows it differently, that's all.'

Lawrence raised his eyebrows. 'Yeah, by refusing to take it seriously. That's pretty much his stance on everything.'

He indicated that they should start walking, his mouth set in a straight line. Whatever Daisy might have wanted to say in response would clearly have to wait and she watched his retreating back in dismay. It could well turn out to be one of the longest days of her life.

It wasn't a big station and there were only two platforms, connected by a footbridge, but both were already thronged with people. She glanced up at the departure board as she hurried after Lawrence; she still had no idea where they were going. He was headed towards the far end of the platform and, to her surprise, pushed open a door that she didn't remember ever seeing before. He held it open for her as she passed inside into a smallish room with plush seating and a temperature far exceeding that of outside. It was also empty. She looked back towards the door and the milling people outside on the platform, their faces animated as they chatted, rubbing hands and stamping feet to keep warm. It seemed far preferable to her than the silent space she would have to occupy with Lawrence.

She sat down, pulling her bag around her so that she could cradle it in her lap. Her hands reached automatically for the keys inside, her fingers folding around them, so that they might keep her safe. She swallowed and looked around.

The room was a strange mixture of corporate hospitality on the one hand, with advertisements boasting unrivalled levels of service for the modern business person, and on the other, soft furnishings and watercolours more usually found in hotel foyers. There were also no windows. Daisy looked towards the door a little uneasily.

'I've never been in here before,' she said. 'In fact, I didn't even know it existed. It's a bit of an odd little room though.'

'Is it?' replied Lawrence. 'I've never really thought about it.'

'But how do you know when the train is coming?' she added. 'If you can't see out.'

Lawrence silently indicated a small screen set in the wall next to a painting of some geese. It was so incongruous it made her want to laugh. She didn't though.

'Ah, I see...' She looked about her again. 'No one else seems to know this room is here either. You'd think they'd put a sign on the door or something.'

'It's the first-class lounge,' said Lawrence, inspecting his gloves, his tone just crossing the line into condescension.

Daisy rolled her eyes. 'Oh, silly me,' she muttered. Her fingers gripped her keys even tighter. She chewed at the inside of her cheek. 'So where are we going then?' she asked, grinning. 'To see the Queen?'

She expected a smile, possibly even a chuckle, or at the very least for her comment to be parried with another in similar fashion, but instead Lawrence gave her a look that was not far off a glare.

'We *are* going to London,' he replied, stiffly. 'But not to sightsee. Under the circumstances that would be rather a waste of time. And I would imagine that even were the Queen at home she wouldn't be keen to spend her afternoon discussing the price of fish.'

Daisy could feel her cheeks flushing again, but was saved from having to find a suitable reply by a soft ping from the monitor on the wall.

'That's us,' said Lawrence. 'Come along, and once we're settled I can explain what's going to be happening today.' He got to his feet and crossed to the door.

Daisy stared at his back. Just like that, she thought. No, *Where would you like to go?* or *What would you like to do?* She had imagined that the day would be very different from the one she'd spent with Bertie, but at least he'd tried to consider what she might like. Here she was simply fulfilling a function.

She took her seat on the train, grateful to at least be sitting by the window, and watched as Lawrence settled himself, taking off his gloves and coat and laying them carefully on the rack above his head.

'Right,' he said purposefully the minute he was seated beside her. 'I've made a list of things I shall need to know about you.' He reached for his inside jacket pocket. 'So let's get these ticked off first, it shouldn't take too long. And it would be helpful if you could answer as fully as possible. I shall make notes.'

Daisy pressed her lips together. 'Can I just ask you something?'

Lawrence tilted his head. 'Is it relevant?' he asked.

She stared out of the window as the train began to pull from the station. 'To me it is, yes. You see, you seem to be under the impression that today is just about extracting as much information about me as you can, thinking that this will give you everything you need to create the perfect gift. But today should work both ways, Lawrence; it's also an opportunity for me to get to know you. After all, if you're successful in winning this competition, I might be working for you, and I need to be sure that I'd want to. It's my future at stake here too.'

'Yes, yes, but it's hardly the same thing, is it? Your future, working in the shop, against mine running the company. The stakes are somewhat higher in my case.'

'Are they?' she argued. 'Are you sure about that? Because from where I'm sitting, they're exactly the same. This is important to me too, and it might help you if you stopped to consider why that might be the case instead of just assuming that running a business is more important than working in one. Just in case you don't end up in charge.'

He stared at her. 'But I have to gain control of the business.'

'Why?'

His jaw was working.

'Because it's my birthright, Daisy. I don't expect you to understand about such things, but I'm the head of this family and I was made that way a long time ago when my father died. I've carried that weight, this responsibility, most of my adult life and, as such, it's only right that Buchanans comes to me...' He broke off, pouting slightly. 'I was promised it.' He shook his head. 'Look, that hardly matters now, my father died a long time ago.' He gave her a puzzled look. 'And I don't see what that has to do with anything.'

Daisy held his look for a moment. 'Probably everything.' But she smiled. 'All I'm saying is that I'd be very grateful if you could do me the courtesy of remembering that, while you're interrogating me, underneath is a person who could also stand to lose a great deal when this competition finally comes to an end.'

He gave the slightest of nods, acknowledging her point. 'Although I have to say that's another thing I don't understand...' He broke off as an announcement came over the train's tannoy, before continuing. '... Why you've been involved in all this in the first place. It's not as if you have any final say in the matter...'

His eyes narrowed as he inhaled a sharp breath. 'Oh, I get it...' he said, slowly. 'Of course, this is all a bloody set-up, isn't it? You *are* choosing who wins, that's exactly what this is all about! For God's sake, you and Mother have been as thick as thieves all these years, I knew there must be more to it than she was telling us.'

Lawrence's face had twisted into a sneer while he was talking and Daisy could feel herself growing hotter and hotter. 'It's not like that at all,' she whispered.

'I might as well bloody give up now, because we all know who's going to win, don't we? Bertie-charm-the-birds-out-the-trees-Buchanan – enjoy your day out with him, did you?'

Daisy felt tears sting her eyes. 'At least he was nice to me, and didn't accuse me of cheating. And if you must know, yes, we did have a nice day out, but that in no way means he is any more or less likely to win than either you or Kit. In fact, he even asked me if he could take me to a jeweller's and just point out what I liked, but I told him I couldn't do that. Apart from not being fair, it also wouldn't give him any clue about why a particular piece was the perfect gift for me. And no, I wasn't about to tell him that either.' She fished a tissue out of her bag. 'The difference is that Bertie just accepted what I told him instead of becoming utterly obnoxious. And he's just as scared of losing as you are.'

'Bertie? Scared? What on earth could Bertie possibly have to worry about? He's never had to take responsibility for anything his whole life.'

'Maybe he's never been allowed to, Lawrence, with you ruling the roost. So for your information he's really worried about what he's going to do if you get control of the company because he's under no illusion that you'll give him a job. And in his words, he's fit for nothing. I think that's a pretty big admission to make, so don't you dare laugh at him.'

She was about to say something else when there was a hiss and swish from the end of the carriage and a uniformed steward moved along the aisle towards them.

'Good morning, Sir, Madam, and welcome aboard.' He nodded deferentially. 'Breakfast will be served shortly but, in the meantime, if you'd care for some refreshment, we have a range of beverages on offer.'

The man wore a broad smile, looking backwards and forwards between the two of them, seemingly unaware of the dispute he had just interrupted. His manner was so overtly cheerful that it burst the bubble of Daisy's anger in an instant. She was mortified. She had no right to speak to Lawrence like that and, apart from anything else, he would never give her a job if she kept picking fights with him.

She shot Lawrence a look, expecting to see irritation still written across his face. Instead, like her, it seemed that the arrival of someone else into their space had rather taken the wind out of his sails and he was struggling to rearrange his face into a smile.

'How about you, Madam, what can I get you?'

It was on the tip of Daisy's tongue to answer with an automatic 'Tea please' but then she had a sudden thought. 'Do you have any hot chocolate?' she asked.

'Yes, indeed. Always popular on cold mornings.' The steward smiled again. 'And would you like it with the addition of some cream and marshmallows?'

'Oh, yes please, that would be lovely.' And to her surprise the thought of it *was* quite lovely.

'And for Sir?'

'Just coffee please. Black.'

'Excellent, right away. And if you'd like to take a look at the card on the table, we'll soon be serving from the breakfast menu. If you'd care to make your choices I will be back shortly to take your orders.'

The steward nodded, smiled and slipped away, leaving Daisy looking nervously at Lawrence. 'I'm sorry,' she said. 'I should never—'

Lawrence held up a hand. 'Please… I ought to apologise. Perhaps I've been approaching this in an… inconsiderate manner. I can see how it could have come across as unfeeling and maybe we ought to start again. We could be in for rather a long day otherwise.'

The same thought had been occupying Daisy's head almost constantly. She nodded. 'Should we start with breakfast? I had no idea they did this sort of thing on trains.' She handed Lawrence the card.

'I believe it's just in first class,' he replied, bending his head to see what was on offer. 'Ah, excellent. You wouldn't think so, but the eggs Benedict is surprisingly good.' He tapped the card. 'I can recommend it.' His eyebrows were raised in enquiry.

'I don't even know what that is,' admitted Daisy. There was no point trying to pretend. 'I always have Weetabix.'

Lawrence smiled, a sideways twitch of his lips. 'Eggs Benedict is a breakfast muffin served with a poached egg on top, bacon, and hollandaise sauce.'

Daisy was still none the wiser. 'Um…' She scanned the menu, looking for something that would satisfy her simple palate.

'Why don't you try it?' suggested Lawrence. 'I doubt they do Weetabix.'

She looked up at his comment, but his expression hadn't changed. She thought back to her day out with Bertie. 'Okay,' she said. 'I'll give it a go.' She slid the card back into its holder on the table and looked around her again. 'Is it always this quiet in first class? We're the only ones here.'

'Not usually. I would imagine that other people will get on. It's quite a long journey.' He gave a brief smile. 'We should make London by half eleven though and I've arranged transport at the other end. We'll arrive at our destination soon after.'

'So where *are* we going then?' she asked. 'You still haven't told me.'

Lawrence's face brightened. 'Where every woman wants to go. To Harrods, of course.' He sat back in his seat, a triumphant expression on his face. 'And not only that but we have the services of a personal shopper for the entire day. Monique is wonderful. We wouldn't ordinarily be able to do this of course, but she knows why we'll be there and won't expect us to buy anything. Extraordinarily generous of her, particularly at this time of year.'

Daisy kept the smile plastered on her face, but her heart sank. She couldn't think of anywhere she'd less rather be than a swanky department store, being waited on hand and foot. It was Buchanans multiplied one hundredfold. She swallowed her dismay. 'Oh, I've never been before,' she replied.

'Well I know what you ladies are like,' said Lawrence. 'And I thought that taking you shopping would be the best way to get to know what you do and don't like.'

Daisy wanted to reply that she didn't like shopping, but she kept her thoughts to herself. She was well aware that she wasn't like most women, but Lawrence wouldn't know that.

Moments later the steward arrived with their drinks and she was saved from having to make any further comment.

'Thank you,' said Lawrence. 'And we'll both go for the eggs Benedict, please.'

'Of course, Sir, an excellent choice.'

'May I ask you a question?' said Lawrence, as soon as the steward had retreated.

'As long as it's not one off your list.'

He grimaced. 'It's not. I just was wondering about what you said earlier. And you're right, I didn't consider that come the new year things could be very difficult for you... So, if you're not able to carry on working at Buchanans, what will you do?'

It was a question that was beginning to fill more and more of Daisy's head space as time went on. It would be so wonderful to confide in one of the brothers about her dreams of running a business of her own but, out of them all, Lawrence was probably least likely to understand. Besides, how could she possibly convince him she could make it work when she hadn't yet managed to convince herself?

'I honestly don't know,' she said. 'Rather naive of me, but I didn't think I'd ever need to find another job; there's just always been Buchanans. It feels as if I've been there a lifetime... and I guess, in a good way, it has been.'

He tipped his head to one side and gave her a searching look. 'Which is odd, because I always thought you hated your job.'

'Hated it?' She gave him a puzzled look. 'Why would you think I hated it?'

'I don't know exactly. It can't be much fun working with Kit.'

She frowned. 'But Kit doesn't bother me,' she replied.

'No, Kit doesn't bother anyone.'

'Well, that's hardly surprising, is it? I mean, in between you bossing everyone around and Bertie trying to hold you all together, what space could Kit possibly occupy?'

Her hand flew to her mouth. Where had that come from?

'Oh God, I'm sorry, Lawrence. I didn't mean it the way it sounded... It's just that you're each so very different, but that's a good thing, I guess.' She closed her mouth. There was a whole lot more she could say, but if she carried on she'd only be digging herself a deeper and deeper hole.

To her relief, however, Lawrence smiled too.

'There seems to be something about me that brings out the worst in you,' he said, a slight twinkling of amusement in his eyes. 'Or perhaps it's the best... Are you always this argumentative?'

'No, not usually,' she said with a chastened smile.

Lawrence shrugged. 'Must be me then.' He ran a hand through his hair. 'But I'm curious... When I asked what my dad dying had to do with anything, you replied, "Probably everything." What did you mean?'

Daisy groaned. 'I don't know... Please, just ignore me. My mouth was clearly running away with me.'

But Lawrence's look pinned her to the chair. 'I don't think it was,' he replied. 'Come on, tell me what you meant, I'm actually interested to know.'

She picked up the spoon that was sitting on a saucer beside her drink and buried it in the foamy mountain of cream that was oozing down the glass. 'Let's at least have breakfast first, shall we?'

She put the spoon in her mouth, praying that the steward would appear soon. She didn't think she would ever be more happy to see a plateful of food in her life.

Friday 13th December

Twelve shopping days until Christmas

Daisy's mouth hung open and they hadn't even got inside the shop yet.

She was standing on the pavement, trying to take in the sheer spectacle of the window displays that seemed to run the entire length of the street. The decorations at Buchanans had always been her domain – under Bea's direction of course, with the familiar *Nutcracker* theme – but it was always her responsibility to interpret Bea's ideas and ensure that the displays looked as good as they could be. And up until now she thought she'd always done a good job. But these... these were another kind of display entirely.

'Quite something, aren't they?' said Lawrence, standing by her side, an amused expression on his face. 'I've already seen them of course, I came to the unveiling, but they're quite magical.'

Daisy was utterly dumbstruck.

'Of course, when you have the kind of budget these stores do, pretty much anything goes.'

She swept her eyes along the row of windows, marvelling at the incredible imagination and talent they displayed. Glamorous, intricate and executed like the finest works of art, they were on a level she'd never seen before but she dreaded to think how much they had cost. Despite their jaw-dropping quality, this fact made her feel slightly uneasy. It didn't seem right somehow.

'Shall we go inside?' she said faintly.

Lawrence had obviously been there before, on many occasions. He dipped his head at the doorman and walked through the doors with absolute assurance while Daisy was feeling more and more like a fish out of water with every step, and struggling to keep up with Lawrence's long stride. There was just so much to take in, so many *things*, all leaping out at her, shouting their availability for purchase at the top of their shiny, sparkly lungs. She trailed after him in a daze as he steered them away to the right.

Daisy saw immediately why he had taken her this way first. In front of them lay the entrance to the fine jewellery room; acres and acres of gilt and glass, gleaming gold, marble and finely detailed panelling which surrounded a series of large glass cases. She clamped her lips together, not wanting to be seen with her mouth hanging open.

'You might begin to see some similarities,' said Lawrence as he led them through the hall.

Of course… how had she not seen it straight away? Albeit on a much smaller scale, and worlds apart in terms of grandeur, Buchanans was clearly modelled on this famous store. The deep blue cloth inside the cases was almost identical in colour, the panels beneath each of the glass cabinets was wrought with the same ornate scrollwork that looked like burnished metal, and even the gold banding set around the edge of the room was the same. It was very clever. She glanced across at Lawrence.

'Your idea?' she asked.

'Of course, but with Mother's approval, naturally. It fits with her aspirations and inclination towards the theatrical, and – you have to admit – it's the most wonderful piece of marketing.'

Lawrence was surveying the room with undisguised pride.

'But do you really think that any of our customers will even know that Buchanans is modelled on Harrods? I certainly didn't.'

'That hardly matters,' replied Lawrence. 'Those who do will have an appreciation of the finer things in life, and those who don't will think, as you do presumably, that the decor is elegant and refined. Either way, if Harrods has chosen it to enhance the consumer experience and encourage sales, then it will work equally well for us.'

Daisy could see the logic, partly, but she didn't entirely agree. It was true, she did think that the interior of Buchanans worked in some regards, but she had always assumed that it had been designed to fit the beautiful Georgian building that housed it. Now that she could see it wasn't, she couldn't help wishing that Buchanans had its own style, something that made it special in its own right. It could have so much more going for it – the very traditional jewels they sold were fine, but they only appealed to a particular type of shopper, and not everyone was the same. And of course there would be no room for her own jewellery in a setting like this. She suddenly felt very small; this was clearly not a world in which she belonged.

'Pick something,' said Lawrence, gesturing further into the room, but Daisy was rooted to the spot. She could feel the sales staff closing in.

'No,' said Daisy. 'That's cheating. I told you Bertie asked me the same thing, and I refused. The difference is that he was teasing.'

'And I'm not?'

Daisy shook her head. 'No, I don't believe you are. Besides, there's nothing here I would wear.'

Lawrence stared at her. 'How can you possibly say that when you haven't even looked at anything? Daisy, it may have escaped your notice, but we've come to the finest emporium there is. If you can't find anything here you like, you won't find it anywhere.'

She flushed, hearing Grace's words as loudly as if she were standing right beside her. 'Will anything here match the beauty of dewdrops on a sunlit meadow?' she asked. 'Or the hoar frost that makes every blade of grass look as if it's encrusted with diamonds?' She watched his astonished expression.

Lawrence frowned. 'Well, now you just sound like Kit. For goodness' sake, am I the only one with any business sense around here?'

'Kit? What has he got to do with it?'

He ignored her. 'Which as far as I'm concerned is just another example of why it needs to be me that takes over Buchanans. Anyone else and the business will fail within minutes. All this romanticised tosh about greed and commercialism… It has no place within a modern business. Cold hard cash, that's what makes the world go around. Always has done, always will do. And the only way that Buchanans will survive into the future is to have a sound business plan, some savvy buying and marketing and an eye on the finances. Who else can offer that?'

Daisy looked around her again. Perhaps he was right. It was one thing to tinker with a few bits of clay and turn them into jewellery, another thing entirely to run a business. She wouldn't even know where to start as far as business plans were concerned, or any of the rest of it for that matter.

Lawrence softened his expression. 'Look, I can see that this is all a bit, well, ostentatious. But just as there are people like you who disapprove of it, there are also a good many people who aspire to it. And a piece of jewellery from Buchanans is a pretty good place to start. You're a very good salesperson, Daisy. You have an excellent rapport with customers and I've seen you secure sales where I thought all hope was lost. But if Buchanans goes down, you go down with it.'

He let the sentence dangle in the air for just a minute. 'So… all I'm saying is that you might want to think about what side your bread is buttered on when it comes to this contest. You might find it changes your mind about who you want to help.'

A whoosh of heat shot up her neck, and she would have turned and walked right out of the shop, except… She hung her head. Except that Lawrence was right. There was no point having a job in a failing business, and she did still need a job, that much was certain.

She cleared her throat and looked up at him. 'I appreciate your comments,' she said stiffly. 'But under no circumstances am I going to cheat and pick out a piece of jewellery for you. I may be misguided in your eyes, but I do have some integrity and I'd like to retain it.'

She sighed. 'However, I made a promise to Bea that I would help you all out and so that is what I intend to do. We're here for the day, Lawrence, and I suggest you use it to your best advantage, not by asking me to cheat, but by doing as Bea suggested and getting to know me. Right now, that's where your savvy comes in, Lawrence. Now, where do we find Monique?'

*

Monique was much older than Daisy had imagined, and ferociously chic. Her jet-black hair, cut in a sharp bob, just grazed the bottom of her sleek jawline, and a slash of bright red lipstick accentuated her angular cheekbones and bright blue eyes. It was approaching lunchtime and so presumably she had been working all morning, yet her makeup was immaculate, as were her clothes. Her tiny frame was accentuated by a nipped-in trouser suit that Daisy could tell was expensive, and a pair of eye-wateringly high shoes completed her look.

'Lawrence… It's so good to see you.' Monique's kisses, one to either side, landed several inches from his cheek. 'And tell me, how is the darling Beatrice? I haven't seen her in far too long.' A strong French accent accompanied her words.

Without waiting for a reply, Monique fixed her stare on Daisy and studied her intently for what seemed like several minutes. 'And you are Daisy,' she said. 'Of course, and how delightful you are.'

Daisy's hand strayed to her hair and, spotting it, Monique laughed. 'Beautiful… and we shall make it more so. All of you.' She wafted a hand at Lawrence. 'Now, I do hope you're not going to get in the way,' she said. 'Because Daisy and I are going to be very busy, and we don't need any interference.'

'Yes, but—'

'There are no buts, Lawrence, not with Monique; you should know that by now. Now, go and play somewhere and come back in an hour and a half, not a minute before.'

Monique waited with her hands on her hips until Lawrence had moved away before turning to Daisy. 'Ah, thank goodness. Beatrice I adore, but Lawrence… he is so dull!' She bent her head towards Daisy. 'Do not tell him I said that.' And she winked. 'Besides, he will spoil all our fun, and that is not allowed. Beatrice will not thank me at all.'

Daisy gave her a puzzled look. 'Bea knows I'm here?'

Monique laughed, a loud bark of mirth. 'Of course! And I know all about her wonderful little competition. In fact, I hear it twice – once, the truth from Beatrice and, twice, the not so truthful from Lawrence.' She grinned, pointing at her chest. 'I am the double agent,' she said.

Daisy still didn't grasp what she said. She shook her head. 'Sorry, I'm not completely sure I understand.'

Monique took her arm. 'Come with me,' she said. 'We will have the little tea first, and I will tell you all about it.'

She led Daisy through into a room that would have looked like the lounge area of a swanky hotel had it not been for the mirrored walls to each side. Two big squishy sofas in a beautiful duck-egg blue faced each other over a glass coffee table, and it was to one of these that Monique led her. A silver tray stood in the middle of the table bearing two white cups, a white teapot and white plate, on which stood at least half a dozen pastel-coloured rounds of confectionary. Daisy had no idea what they were.

'Please, sit down,' said Monique. 'You like the tea, yes?'

Daisy nodded, hoping it was just ordinary tea and not some strange herbal mixture. She sank into the sofa and looked around while Monique poured their drinks. Her head was twirling with thoughts.

'And the macarons? Ah… Ladurée…' She slid the plate towards Daisy. 'You must have one. They are the best, naturally, from Paris, of course.'

Daisy selected one, pale green in colour, and turned it around in her hand. It was peculiarly smooth on the surface. 'I've never had one of these before,' she admitted.

'Then you have not lived,' said Monique, smiling. 'Try it, I guarantee you will like it.'

Daisy smiled back. It was hard not to like this charismatic woman. She nibbled the edge of the macaron, the outer shell crisp and crumbly in her mouth. It was nutty and she nibbled some more as the texture changed to one of gooey creaminess. It was not unlike the taste of the hot chocolate she'd had with Bertie and she stuffed the rest of the sweet treat in her mouth impulsively.

'See?' Monique grinned. 'We will make an honorary French woman out of you yet.' She paused. 'Of course Ladurée are perfection, but you should learn to make the macaron at home, then you will always have a little bit of extravagance on hand. One must, every day, have one small extravagant thing and that is enough.'

She clasped her hands together. 'Now then, I am interested to find out about you, Daisy. I have heard so much, from Beatrice and from Lawrence, but Monique always prefers to make up her own mind. That is what I do, why I am here.'

Daisy groaned. 'Oh, I dread to think what Lawrence had to say about me.'

'Nothing bad, I assure you… but very plain; the colour eyes, the colour hair, how tall. Nothing that is you. Nothing to tell Monique what fires your soul, what calms it, nor what type of heart beats within your breast.' She tapped her own chest. 'Is that not the most important thing of all?'

Daisy had never even thought about it before, but there was something very powerful about Monique's words. 'I wouldn't even know how to answer that,' she said. And it was true. What type of heart did she have?

'A good one,' replied Monique. 'Of that I am assured.' She tipped her head to one side. 'But perhaps one that needs a little fun? A little joie de vivre, n'est-ce pas?' She took up her teacup. 'So today we will have the fun, yes?'

Daisy could only nod, although the thought was a little alarming.

'And I shall get to know all the wonderful things that are Daisy beyond the colour of her eyes, and her hair, which looks like the silky fur of the otter. All these things are right in front of me, I do not need to know them.' She tapped the side of her nose. 'And when I have found out all these wonderful things, they will be just for us to know. I shall say nothing of them to the grown-up boy who thinks he can outwit Beatrice. Ha!' Her face broke into a beaming smile.

Daisy smiled. 'Do you mean Lawrence?'

'Of course!' Monique leaned a little closer, although there was no one else in the room to hear them. 'It is what I said before. Beatrice and I, we are the very good friends since many years and she has told me all about her plans to run off with the delectable Charles. Oh, he is so handsome! And so she has the task of who is going to run her wonderful little business. But she is clever, you know that of course, and with the three brothers, it is not easy to choose. So she makes it that they will choose themselves.' Monique sat back with a gleeful look on her face.

'I'm sorry, I don't quite understand.'

'It is the one thing that Beatrice regrets, you see. When they were little it was so hard, to look after them all, and to make the business work, that she didn't think about the money. Because the money has always been there, you know. Her husband was a very wealthy man. But now, she is older and wiser and she sees how it made the boys so they did not have to think, or find out what type of heart beat within their chests.' She smiled. 'And so Beatrice, she has the cunning plan, to help them find this out for themselves. And wonderful Daisy, you are helping, are you not?'

'Am I?'

Monique picked up a macaron and brought it to her lips as if kissing it. 'Oh yes, it is magic…' She popped the fancy in her mouth and sighed. 'Just the little extravagance.'

Daisy swallowed. 'So what do we do now?' she asked.

'Ah, that is simple,' said Monique. 'We shop!'

Ten minutes later Daisy was virtually naked.

'You English women,' announced Monique. 'Always the shy. Hiding themselves away behind the buttons and the collars. Let me get a proper look at you.'

Daisy didn't think she had ever stood in front of anyone with so little clothes on, not even the local doctor.

'And the underwear. *Mon Dieu…*' Monique held her hands up as if weighing two melons and it didn't take a genius to work out what she was referring to. 'You have the pert bosom of the young and yet… ah, so sad, to be hidden behind such drabness, such meanness of fabric. Your clothes should be a part of you, they should speak of the person within, and your underwear, well of course that is for your lover. It should be the last layer of delight before kissing you, the unwrapping of the prize jewel.'

'Heavens, I haven't even got a boyfriend,' Daisy said, blushing.

'*Non?* Well then one day soon, and when the lucky man arrives, Daisy will be ready for him.'

'Monique, you do know I won't be buying anything today, don't you?'

She sighed. 'I know, I know, but I can dream, can't I? And more to the point, so can you. Tell me, do you always wear clothes such as this? What other things do you have?'

Daisy shrugged. 'They're mostly like I'm wearing today.' She didn't want to admit that they were identical. 'I think they suit me.'

'Hmmm, *comme ci, comme ça*… But they could be so much better. The colours for example… the cut… and now that I have had the good look at you, I will decide. Here, slip this on, I will be no more than a few moments. Already I can see it.' She handed Daisy a silk robe and disappeared through a mirrored door at the far end of the room.

Daisy pulled the robe around her and sat down with a bump. She felt rather like she'd been hit by an express train, but it was hard not to get swept along by Monique's enthusiasm. Half an hour ago the thought of shopping had been one she hadn't relished at all, now she was quite intrigued to see what would be chosen for her.

She was just nibbling at another macaron when the door opened again and Monique reappeared, almost hidden behind a pile of fabric. She crossed to the far wall and one by one hung up the selection of dresses she was carrying. Then she turned to Daisy with a beaming smile.

'Now we are ready,' she said. 'For Daisy to reveal herself.'

She took down a floor-length gown, the like of which Daisy had never seen before. It was like something from a fairy tale.

'And we will start with this,' said Monique. 'Because I want to see the light on your face and in your heart when you wear it. For you the perfect colour, I think?' She held the dress closer so that Daisy could see it more clearly.

It was simply styled, sleeveless, with a fitted bodice and full skirt, but its beauty was in its colour – a pale teal-blue silk printed with large flowers. A layer of tulle lay over the silk, the bodice embellished with beautiful embroidery to accent the flowers. It softened the whole look and it was quite the prettiest dress that Daisy had ever seen.

Monique slipped it expertly over her head, nodding with satisfaction at her choice. It fitted like a glove and, as she settled the fabric around her, Daisy raised her head to look at her reflection.

The initial shock at seeing herself in something so different was expected, but as she stared at her reflection an unexpected feeling crept over her. She smiled as the word came to her lips. *Ethereal.* Yes, that was it. She felt as if she were made of gossamer, that only the lightest threads still tethered her to earth and that any moment she could pull free and fly...

She shook her head, smiling. How silly. And yet... As she stood there trying to work out what it was about the gown, apart from its grandeur, that made it so very different from anything she had ever worn before, she suddenly realised that it was because it was patterned. And every single thing she owned at home was plain. How had she never even seen that? The things she adored the most were all patterned – the play of moonlight on water, dancing buttercups in the meadow, even raindrops glittering on the spiders' webs that hung from her gate – and yet she had surrounded herself with none of these things.

Monique was watching her. 'You like this, yes? You feel...' She snapped her fingers. 'Yes, like the million dollars?'

Daisy laughed. 'It probably costs that much too.'

'*Non*, not quite the four thousand pounds. A bargain, don't you think?' She laughed at Daisy's reaction.

'I shouldn't even be wearing this,' she said, horrified. 'What if I damage it?' She lifted her hands clear of the fabric she had just been stroking. 'How can a dress even cost that much?'

Monique shrugged. 'We have many that are even more expensive. But how can you put a cost on how this dress makes you feel? If all your clothes made you feel this way then there would be no need for beauty such as this, no?'

She looked around her, gesturing at a large canvas hanging on the wall beside the sofas. 'A work of art hangs on a wall and it justifies its very existence simply by being looked at. And this is all right because it has a famous painter. The man who made this dress has also painted a work of art and yet he has used fabric to do so. So I ask you, Daisy, what is the difference?'

Daisy stared at herself in the mirror, seeing things she'd never seen before, and a small smile crept up her face. One small extravagance every day…

'Can I ask you something, Monique?' she said after a few moments. 'What are you going to tell Lawrence? About today, I mean.'

Monique thought for a moment, weighing something up in her head before holding up a finger. 'One moment,' she said, and slipped back through the door. She was gone for even less time than before and when she returned she was carrying a square wooden box which she placed down on the table. 'Come,' she said. 'Sit down,' and she beckoned Daisy across.

The lid of the box was hinged either side and split down the middle so that it opened from the centre. Pulling either piece caused the sides to expand outwards rather like a grandiose toolbox, except that when Daisy saw what was nestled inside, she gasped in shock.

'They are replicas only,' said Monique. 'The gowns, they are the one thing, but these… I would live in fear of handling them.'

Monique lifted a 'diamond' choker clear from where it was lying alongside an assortment of other jewels, the sight of which made Daisy feel faint. She was used to handling expensive jewellery, but the things Buchanans sold might as well have been tawdry baubles by comparison. Monique handed her the necklace before opening the other side of the box so that Daisy could see the full array of what was on offer.

For a moment Daisy was so busy trying to take in what was in front of her that she didn't really 'see' what she was meant to. After a few more seconds though, the penny dropped and she looked up at Monique.

'I was supposed to choose one of these?' she asked. She didn't even need to look for Monique's quiet nod to know that she was right.

'As an accompaniment to the clothes,' Monique replied. 'For each outfit a new choice, or perhaps the same choice. They are all items which are available in the store and I was to let Lawrence know which you favoured. It's my job to discern these things even when nothing is said.'

Daisy nodded. 'I see… And he didn't think I would see through that?'

Monique shrugged. 'I think Lawrence is used to taking the quickest route to the things he wants.' She really didn't need to say any more.

Daisy laid the necklace back in the box. 'So what *are* you going to tell him?'

'Well now, let me see if Monique has got it right… ' Her eyes were twinkling. 'So… You are wearing this dress, on the most beautiful night of your life, and you want it to be absolutely perfect. What do you choose?'

'None of them,' replied Daisy immediately.

Monique beamed, clearly delighted with her answer. 'Then I shall tell Lawrence that I'm afraid I cannot help him.'

Friday 13th December

Twelve shopping days until Christmas

Daisy was exhausted. And even though she still wasn't at all comfortable sitting in first class on the train, she sank into the seat with relief. The last couple of hours had been draining.

Up until then she'd actually been enjoying herself. Monique was funny and incredibly astute, but she was also very wise and Daisy found herself admiring the woman who had done her very best to put her at ease. Under her gentle guidance Daisy had learned which colours suited her and how to make the most of her figure without resorting to clothes that felt too tight or too revealing. She had tried on a huge variety of styles that had given her ideas for what to wear together and what mistakes to avoid and, most importantly, where Daisy might purchase similar things from ordinary high-street shops if she wanted to. Daisy had twigged almost straight away what Monique was trying to do of course, but she still felt touched that she was even bothering to try and bolster Daisy's confidence. And whether or not Bea had asked her to do it was immaterial; the request, if there had been one, was not at all evident in the way that Monique treated her, and a huge contrast to the way that Lawrence had behaved.

He had been kept at bay for most of the time she had been with Monique, shooed out of the way in no uncertain terms and, although he left with ill grace each time, Daisy noted that on his return he had managed to amass even more purchases. Eventually though, he made it clear that, as he had brought Daisy to the shop, and paid for their day out, including Monique's services, he felt he should be allowed to stay and see for himself the things Daisy had chosen. Monique had had no choice but to relent. When they left, an hour later, Daisy gave Monique a warm hug, whereas Lawrence simply reminded her to get in touch with him as she had promised. This at least made Daisy smile; if only he knew…

It was now nearly five and thoroughly dark, or as much as it ever got dark in the capital. A mean wind had sprung up, making it bitterly cold. The train was sweltering by contrast and Daisy was beginning to feel claustrophobic, both because of the lack of air and because of the atmosphere which had settled around her the moment Lawrence sat down. She could feel him watching her.

She waited until the train had pulled out of the station before turning to him in exasperation.

'For goodness' sake, if you've got something to say, say it, but stop staring at me.'

He adopted an amused expression. 'I'm just wondering if you enjoyed your afternoon, that's all,' he replied. 'You seem to get on well with Monique.'

'It would be hard not to,' she said. 'She's lovely. And I can see why she's such good friends with Bea.'

Lawrence frowned. 'They're a terrible influence on each other, as you might imagine. Today was a bit of frivolous fun, obviously, but hopefully it has given Monique some valuable information.'

Daisy sighed. 'Yes, let's hope so. I'd hate for it to have been a complete waste of time…' Honestly, did Lawrence have no insight at all?

He gave a satisfied smile. 'Indeed… And I'm very grateful to you, obviously, for coming today and giving up your time. And for being such a good sport about it all. I hope it's been useful for you too?'

Oh it had. It had confirmed to her without a doubt that there was absolutely no way she could ever work with Lawrence. And she really didn't know where that left her.

'It's proved most enlightening actually,' she said. 'Although there is just one other thing you can help me with.'

'Yes?'

'Assuming that you do end up running Buchanans, I just wondered how you saw the future of the business. What changes you might put into place?' She gave him a searching look. 'And don't pretend that you haven't thought about it, Lawrence – I bet you have the whole thing planned down to the last detail.'

He gave her a smug look. 'Of course. Like I said, Daisy, Buchanans is my birthright and I fully intend to make it mine. I've thought long and hard about what I will need to implement once I take control, but—' He broke off to give a condescending laugh. 'Forgive me if I don't share my ideas with you. Not just yet anyway. I'd hate for anyone else to have the benefit of them.'

He was smiling but Daisy was under no illusion that he was joking and she wondered if Lawrence could even hear the final nail he'd just hammered into his own coffin. She stared out of the window wondering how he felt he could insult her like that and yet still retain her loyalty. Well, at least Bea had him sussed and, as the first few flakes of snow began to fall, she thought back to Monique's words about how Daisy herself was helping Bea in her quest. Well maybe she could do a bit more than just that.

'Why do you dislike your brothers so much?' she asked.

Lawrence considered the question for no longer than a second. 'Because they're weak. And if you're asking me if there will be jobs for them at the end of all this, the answer is no. I wouldn't expect them to give me a job either, although I suspect that they both would: Bertie because he's so keen never to upset anyone, and Kit because he doesn't care enough to make a decision. In fact, he probably hasn't even thought about it. Simply put, they don't have it in them to run the business.'

'Because they're not like you, you mean,' said Daisy. 'And a person's strength or weakness is only defined by how they measure up to your standards, is that it?' She paused for a moment, letting her words hang in the air. 'Which is odd because I've always found that real strength comes quietly, often when you least expect it.'

Earlier, on their outward journey, she had evaded Lawrence's question about his father out of a desire to get along and enter into the spirit of the day without taking sides. But now it felt as if she had a duty to stick up for both Kit and Bertie. She turned back from the window.

'You see, I get that when your dad died you felt the responsibility for the family passed to you. As the eldest male I guess that made sense, but that's a pretty powerful place to sit for someone so young. And it made it so much easier for you to get your own way, didn't it? To throw your weight around without considering what anyone else wanted because you could always hide it under the banner of someone needing to take charge. So maybe Bertie is the way he is because being the life and soul of the party allowed him some freedom from being constantly told what he could and couldn't do from an early age. Perhaps he gave up trying to have his say and became the family mediator instead. Is that weakness? I don't know... maybe it's a particular kind of strength… I should imagine it's incredibly wearing trying to keep the peace the whole time.'

Lawrence regarded her evenly. 'Are you done, or are you going to give me your expert opinion on Kit as well?'

Daisy stared back. 'I may as well,' she replied. 'I didn't answer your question earlier because I didn't want to be rude, but maybe I will tell you.' She took a deep breath. 'You said before that Kit doesn't bother anyone, but there's a very big difference between not bothering to speak to people, and choosing not to. I'm only just beginning to understand that and I think Kit chooses very carefully indeed. He's already worked out he has nothing to prove, and it takes someone who is very comfortable in their own skin to do that. So, rather than expend his energy trying to make a point to someone who is never going to listen, he simply withdraws. You think he's weak, but perhaps he's actually the strongest of you three brothers. He chooses his battles instead of trying to fight them all. Interesting then that he still considers himself very much in the running where Buchanans is concerned.'

She dropped her head, momentarily astounded by her own words. She had thought she barely knew the brothers, but perhaps over the years she had picked up more than she had realised. Daisy had never been able to fathom why Bea had made her such a crucial part of the competition, but perhaps she saw something that no one else did – not even Daisy herself.

'I asked for that, didn't I?'

She squinted across at him. 'Well, you did actually… But I'm sorry it came out rather more forcefully than I intended. I'm tired…' She blew out her cheeks. 'And boiling hot, it's so stuffy in here… But I shouldn't have said—'

'Probably not, given that I'm expecting to be your employer soon.' He narrowed his eyes. 'But at least I know you're honest.' His gaze flicked to the menu card on the table. 'They'll be serving dinner shortly, perhaps you might like to make your choice.'

It was pretty much the end of the conversation.

*

Daisy woke with a start some while later, staring around her in panic as she tried to work out where she was. The view beyond the window was obscured by complete darkness.

'We should be home in about five minutes,' came a voice from behind a newspaper and Daisy groaned inwardly as the memory of her conversation with Lawrence came rushing back.

She wiped at her mouth and sat up straighter, peering through the fogged-up window.

'It would appear to have snowed as well,' Lawrence added. 'Although how much it's difficult to say.'

'Oh.' She cleared her throat. 'I don't suppose it's that bad, it never usually is.'

Lawrence lowered the paper and looked at her. 'Are you feeling better?' he asked.

As soon as he said it she realised that the ball of pain that had been sitting over her right eye was still there, in fact, if anything it had intensified. It was tension, and the result of being cooped up in a hot stuffy train for too long. The fact that she had slept was a miracle, but now she had a stiff neck as well. She just wanted to be home.

'Yes, a little bit, thank you. It's just a headache,' she muttered. Which would no doubt turn into a full-blown migraine and she had work in the morning. She bit back her frustration. 'Sorry, I didn't mean to fall asleep,' she said. 'Although maybe that was a good thing; it gave you some time to yourself without having to listen to me argue.'

To her relief, he smiled. 'I've been thinking about what you said, actually. I'm not sure I agree with it but, despite your opinion of me, I do admire people who can say what they feel. That takes a certain amount of courage.' He broke off to fold his newspaper in half. 'And, all in all, it's been an interesting day.'

Well, that much was certainly true. Although Daisy wouldn't call speaking her mind courageous, more like stupidity.

'It has, and I need to thank you, for all of this…' She gestured around the carriage. 'And Harrods, the food. Plus, I really enjoyed myself with Monique. I'm not really comfortable with all that extravagance – I find it all rather overwhelming – but, even so, I'm glad I came today.'

Lawrence glanced out of the window as the first lights of the town came into view and got to his feet, proceeding to collect his multitude of bags from the parcel shelf above their heads. He took down Daisy's coat and handed it to her, straightening to look out the window again. 'Oh…'

She turned at his expression, looking out into the darkness which was just beginning to be punctuated by light as the first houses appeared. Spotlit under the halo cast by the street lights, it was obviously still snowing, and hard at that. She had no way of knowing how long it had been coming down but everything was white. The streets were covered. And whereas Lawrence lived in a big house on the outskirts of the town and could probably walk home if he needed to, she still had a half-hour drive ahead of her.

Lawrence pulled his phone out of his pocket. 'I wasn't aware that snow was forecast,' he said.

'Well, it has certainly arrived,' replied Daisy.

'Yes, quite.' He stared out the window again. 'Will you be all right getting home?'

She began to put her coat on. 'Yes, I'm sure the main roads will be fine, don't worry.' She kept her voice light; she really didn't want to give Lawrence any reason to fuss, it would only make her more anxious.

The train was beginning to slow and she rubbed at her temple, rolling her shoulders to ease out the stiffness in her neck. They passed a house ablaze with Christmas lights of every description, the garden full of lit statues, the windows covered with enormous flashing stars, and soon the lights of the town centre rolled by. But Daisy felt as if she was peculiarly misplaced. She always felt that way whenever she'd been away from home; as if life had passed by without her and she no longer fit into it. She pulled her handbag around her and fished for her keys.

Lawrence's car hadn't fared too badly. In his reserved space it had been sheltered somewhat in the lee of the building, whereas hers, exposed in the middle of the empty car park, was covered by a layer of snow several inches thick.

Beside her, Lawrence swore under his breath. 'I'll give you a hand,' he said, but she could hear the exasperation in his voice. No doubt he would have a roaring fire and tumbler of fine whisky waiting for him when he got home, and she couldn't blame him for wanting to get there quicker.

'It's fine…' She waved an airy hand. 'I have a brush in the boot of the car, and only one of us can use it at a time – there's no point us both standing about. You get on home, it won't take me long to clear it.'

She could see the look of relief on his face, and she was glad she hadn't accepted his offer. It was just one more irritation on a long list that had made up Lawrence's day, most of them caused by her, and he wanted to be free of her just as much as she wanted to be free from him. There was too much crowding her head already and the snow at least was clean and calming.

'Thanks again,' she said, taking several decisive steps forward. 'And drive safely!' She waved a hand in salute and, turning swiftly, hurried across the car park.

Several harsh winters had ensured that Daisy always left appropriate clothing and equipment in her car in case of emergencies and she was incredibly glad of that now. The snow had slowed a little, the flakes smaller, but a keen wind still blew and the covering on her car was like icing sugar; light and powdery. It was, however, growing colder by the minute and soon the harsh grip of frost would set in, gluing the snow hard to her windscreen.

She climbed into the car and started up the engine, leaving it running to warm things up and chase the final bits of ice from the screen while she cleared the rest of the car. It took ten minutes, and her fingers were frozen inside her gloves by the time she finished, but, finally, she was ready to go.

She hadn't even noticed Lawrence pull out, but he had already disappeared as she began to manoeuvre out of the car park and towards the bright lights of the town. The streets were deserted, the shoppers all gone, but the festive lights still danced and sparkled above the shops, strings from one side of the street to the other blowing in the wind. It was extraordinarily pretty, the black-and-white timbered frames of the shops rendering the scene like something from a Dickens novel. She drew in several deep breaths, forcing down her shoulders and reminding herself to relax. The day with Lawrence was over, she had the rest of it to herself and her little cottage would be warm and toasty in no time. She might even treat herself to another hot chocolate.

The snow had stopped now but, as she turned off the main road towards her house, the layer of white became more and more dense the further she drove. The earlier winds had whipped along the road, blowing the snow into huge drifts that spilled out from the hedgerows across the narrow lanes. She slowed to a crawl, navigating with difficulty, until she stopped, recognising that if she went any further she was likely to get stuck. Her only option was to turn around and drive back out to the main road again, follow it a little further along and take another route into the town. She sighed with frustration; she was only a couple of miles from home.

She edged forward, turning the wheel so that the car headed towards the hedge. The road was narrow but with a bit of toing and froing she should be able to turn around. When she had gone as far as she dared she put the car into reverse, easing backwards this time, inch by inch, but it was tricky; the lights from the rear of the car weren't strong enough to illuminate anything against the thick bank of snow and it was much harder to see where she was in relation to anything else.

She realised her mistake the minute she tried to move forward again. The snow was powdery and she had gone too far back. The tyres had nothing to grip on and they spun without traction. Daisy backed off the accelerator and very gently applied it again. Nothing. Just the frustrated whine of her going nowhere.

Okay. Think. She had a shovel in the back of the car, she would be fine. All she needed to do was scrape away some of the snow from under her tyres and she would be on her way again. She grabbed her phone and put on the light, opening the car door and preparing herself for the blast of cold air.

And that's when she realised her second mistake. She had reversed too far back and the boot of the car was now firmly pressed up against the hedge – there was no way she could even get it open. Damn. She swore under her breath, kicking at the snow in frustration. She looked down at her boots and groaned. The leather was already sopping and soon her feet would be very wet indeed. Wet and very cold. She wrenched open the rear door and climbed inside, furious with herself.

She bent down in the confined space and began to unlace her boots, her cold fingers struggling with laces that she couldn't see in the dark. She kicked the door open so that the interior lights came on again and thumped the back of the seat in anger. Eventually, after a few minutes more tussling, she managed to get her boots off and pull on her wellies, relieved that these had been on the back seat, along with an old oilskin coat and blanket.

Right, try again. She looked around for something else she could use to scoop away the snow from under her tyres, but there was nothing apart from the scraper she used to clear the windscreen with. It would have to do, and she pulled her gloves on again. The pain above her eye pounded as she climbed from the car and she wriggled her shoulders again, trying to ease them. She was so nearly home.

'Daisy…?'

She whirled around at the sound of her name, her feet nearly slipping out from under her with the force of her movement.

'Kit, you scared the life out of me! What on earth are you doing here?'

Friday 13th December

Twelve shopping days until Christmas

Kit was standing in the lane holding a torch, keeping the beam played at the ground.

'Walking,' he replied. 'I saw the car headlights and thought I had better come and investigate. Isn't the snow amazing?'

Daisy stared at him. Not only had she not heard him coming but what a ridiculous thing to say under the circumstances.

'Not when you're stuck in it, it's not,' she replied. 'Which is all I need after the day I've had.' She aimed a vicious kick at the car's tyre. 'And I'm only a couple of miles away from home.'

Kit looked away to his right across the fields. 'Less, as the crow flies.'

She followed his line of sight. For goodness' sake, what did that have to do with anything?

'I'm going to have to clear the snow away from the tyres so I can get out… but I can't open the boot to get the shovel.' She held up her hand. 'And don't say anything. I know it was stupid to reverse so far back, but I couldn't see where I was going.'

Kit didn't say a word. Instead he flicked the torch off.

The darkness settled around them, instantly soothing. Daisy sighed, feeling the tight ball of tension within her.

'You know that saying, "When life gives you lemons, make lemonade"?' said Kit.

'Yes – usually said by people who could never make lemonade if they tried and just use it as a means of pretending to be something they're not and—' She ground to a halt as she realised that Kit was looking at her, eyebrows raised, an amused expression on his face.

'Oh…' she said. And then despite herself she burst out laughing. 'Which is what you were just going to say if I'd let you get a word in edgeways.'

He grinned. 'Exactly! But the general invitation towards optimism is hard to ignore. It struck me that there are two things we can do in this situation… Actually, there are three, but the third option is for me to just go on my way and leave you here, so I'm not going to mention that one.'

She met his look. 'So, go on then, what are the two options?'

'Well, we could either struggle for half an hour to free your car so that you can drive off and try the other road into town only to find that it's also impassable, or I could walk you home. It's the most beautiful evening.'

Daisy looked around her. 'Is it?'

'Yes,' said Kit more forcefully. 'It is.' And he looked up.

It seemed in that moment as if everything stood still. The darkness swirled around Daisy and lifted as the moon came out from behind a cloud. A bright shining disc of light that transformed everything around her into a silvery shimmering landscape. Sounds rushed in and for a moment she swore she could hear the world breathing.

She looked back at Kit, dumbstruck. Suddenly she wanted very badly to be out in the fields, to leave the tensions and stress of the day behind her and breathe in the calming air.

'But what do we do about the car?'

Kit shrugged. 'Leave it here,' he said. 'The frost is going to set hard tonight and this snow will be going nowhere. It's my day off tomorrow, don't forget. If you leave me your keys, I'll come back early in the morning and free it for you. Provided I can get through, I'll drive it home. How's that?'

It all sounded utterly and beautifully simple.

'Thank you,' she said, before looking down at her clothes. Her wellies would be fine, and the hem of her skirt was already wet so there was nothing she could do about that.

'Are you warm enough?' asked Kit. 'I have spare gloves and another fleece if you want to put that on under your coat.'

She nodded gratefully and five minutes later they were set to go. The fleece was huge on her, but warm and, as Kit hitched his pack onto his back, he smiled. 'My emergency rescuing-a-damsel-in-distress gear,' he said.

Daisy arched her eyebrows. 'Really?' she said. 'Pick up many women out in the wilds, do you?'

'Ah, you'd be surprised… Although actually it's more like a change of clothes in case I fall on my arse and get soaked.'

She laughed. Collecting her handbag and checking she had her keys, she made sure the car was locked and then gestured at the moonlit road. 'And you're sure you know the way?' she asked. 'I don't really ever come out this way when I walk.'

'You'll see,' said Kit, mysteriously. 'Come on.'

They walked back along the lane for a hundred metres or so before Kit led them through a gap in the hedge, helping her pick her way over the drifts that had blown there.

'It's not so deep out in the field,' he said. 'There's no barriers for the snow to collect against, you see, it simply spreads itself out.'

Daisy nodded. 'And did you really just come out for a walk?'

Kit stopped suddenly, looking around him and then finally up at the sky. 'Of course… what could be more perfect?' He touched her arm lightly. 'Listen,' he said.

So Daisy did, allowing the sounds of the world around them to reach her. She could hear the snow being blown across the field and a pair of foxes barking in the distance and, closer to home, something rustled under cover of the hedgerow. But surrounding it all was a deep stillness, not a sound in itself, more a sense that permeated every part of her, so resonant she could almost hear it. And it was so familiar to her. She welcomed it in like an old friend, drawing it deep inside of her with each breath, calming and peaceful. London suddenly seemed a million miles away.

'Better?' asked Kit gently.

'Yes… yes, I am.' She looked at him incredulously, realising that her headache had gone. How did he know? And, as she stood, head angled to the sky, she realised that Kit was very much at home out here in the field, with just the moon as his guide. How had she never seen that before? Today wasn't a one-off, he was a part of the landscape out here, just as she was at home by the canal. It shocked her that she had never even noticed, or perhaps never taken the time to. And yet he had obviously recognised something in her.

'I don't think I realised how tense I was,' she said. 'I was longing to be home, but this is…' She broke off and inhaled a deep cleansing breath. 'Perfect,' she finished.

Kit smiled. 'I find it helps,' he said. 'Being somewhere where everyone else isn't – where there is room for me, and I can be as big as I want instead of feeling incredibly small.'

She stared at him. 'Yes,' she breathed. 'That's exactly it! That's how I feel most of the time. Some people, they just delight in making you feel small.'

Kit slid her a sideways glance. 'Are we talking about my brother here by any chance?'

'Yes,' whispered Daisy. 'But don't say his name, not out here.'

'Where did he take you?'

Daisy pulled a face. 'Harrods…'

Kit burst out laughing. 'Oh, dear God, that's priceless.'

'Yes, most of it was actually, although that didn't seem to stop him from buying half the shop.' She paused to reflect on the day which already seemed to be receding further and further into her memory. 'It wasn't all bad. I met Monique, who I think you probably know. And that was fun at least. Plus, she has Lawrence well and truly sussed. I don't think he's going to find his quest to rule Buchanans quite as easy as he thought he would.' She broke off then, realising that if she were not careful she could reveal what she had learned about the competition. And that wasn't her information to share.

'He'll get by, he always does,' replied Kit, studying her face. 'Do you know the fact that he always got what he wanted used to drive me mad when I was younger. It seemed so unfair and I strove to get the better of him, to have whatever he wanted just so that he didn't win. But then, I realised that all I was doing was hurting myself because I didn't actually want any of the things he did. As soon as I worked that out it freed me from the stupid pattern of behaviour that I'd got myself locked into. Now I don't care what he does. It has no bearing on the way I live my life.'

'But what about the shop then?' asked Daisy. 'I didn't think you cared about it but yet you entered the competition.'

He gave her another searching look. 'I can see how you'd think that. And on the outside I think perhaps that's the message I've been giving.' He gave a rueful smile. 'But actually I care about it a great deal, just not in the way Lawrence does.'

He acknowledged her smile, knowing that he was right. 'Buchanans doesn't interest me the way it is now but, if Lawrence wins, what I think will be immaterial as far as the shop goes. I need to put my energy into making sure he doesn't gain control, but I learned a long time ago that becoming fixated with what my brother does is a sure-fire way to lose out yourself. It's too distracting, and nothing saps your focus quicker.'

Daisy nodded. It was true. She had spent most of the day fighting against Lawrence's points of view, almost out of necessity in case she became tainted by his opinions and the sheer dominance of his personality. There was no room for it in the way she lived her life, and nor, by the sounds of it, in Kit's.

'But you do know Lawrence isn't going to give you a job,' she said, looking across at Kit, whose face was turned to the sky.

'No, I know…' He stopped and smiled at her. 'I wouldn't want him to.'

'But there's only two weeks to go before it's all decided, Kit. What will you do?'

His face fell. 'More time would be useful certainly, but… I'll get by. I have… other options.' He smiled again. 'But more to the point, Daisy, what about you?' He paused for a moment. 'I'm not going to be so insensitive as to ask you who you would like to see run Buchanans, but I'm guessing things could become quite difficult for you if it's Lawrence.'

Daisy sighed. 'After today, it most definitely would. I seemed to spend most of the day arguing with him, and he didn't like that one little bit. I didn't think I wanted to work with Lawrence before, but now I'm certain of it. I guess that just leaves me with two weeks as well. But I'm hopeful I may have other options.'

He held her look. 'Good,' he said simply.

'It's not that I don't want to tell you.' She ground to a halt. 'It's just that I can't say what they are right now, not until I know what's happening with Buchanans. It will make a difference, you see…'

They had been walking across a field, making for a stand of trees at the other side, and now, as they followed their dark line, Daisy was intrigued to see glimpses of light shining between the shadowy trunks. She stopped to peer a little closer.

'Is that a house?' she asked, looking around her as she tried to orientate herself. 'It's in the middle of nowhere.'

Kit nodded. 'Mmm, you can see it better from the other side. Looks lovely, doesn't it, all lit up against the snowy night?'

It looked beautiful. The moon cast a silvery glow over everything in the field but the trees were flecked by patches of golden light which grew brighter towards the centre of the woods. She followed Kit as he began to walk along the line of trees.

'I probably shouldn't say it,' Daisy added, picking up her previous train of thought. 'But I'll be glad when all this is over, even if it does mean I'm out of a job. I feel like I'm keeping far too many secrets at the moment. I know I can't tell any of you about the days out I've had with the others, but it's almost impossible to be impartial. In fact, how can I be when this affects me too? And you haven't even had your day out with me yet. Neither have you mentioned it, Kit. You probably ought to get a move on.'

'I'm getting to know you now, aren't I?'

'I suppose, but it's hardly the same, and certainly not the same opportunity that Bertie and Lawrence have had. That hardly seems fair, given what you've just said.'

'I know…' Kit broke off, squinting at her. 'I just haven't been sure where to take you, but I guess we are running out of time. We decided originally that I should take you out on Monday, so how about we just go for a meal somewhere, in the evening? It doesn't have to be anywhere fancy.'

Daisy could feel her heart sinking. 'I'm not really a big eater,' she said.

'Then eat small,' said Kit, smiling.

She hesitated. It was hardly fair to refuse when she was the one who had prompted his suggestion.

'A drink then?' said Kit, looking at her, an amused expression on her face. 'Cup of tea? Glass of water?'

She laughed. 'Okay, okay, I'll come out for dinner.'

He grinned. 'Great, I'll pick you up at seven.'

'I could meet you in town if you like, save you the bother?'

After a couple more steps, Daisy realised she was walking by herself. She turned to see Kit, feet planted in the snow, his hands on his hips. 'Daisy, I'm walking you home, do you not think I already know where you live?'

'Oh…' She swallowed. 'Do you?'

A smile grew on Kit's face, a smile which widened with a warmth that was plain to see even by moonlight. 'Of course I do. Daisy who lives among the trees, hidden away in her tiny cottage, with only the rustle of grass, the gleam of a blackbird's wing, and the silver on the water for company. I often walk past and see your lights glowing from the windows, with you tucked up warm and safe inside.'

Daisy could feel herself blushing. It seemed such an intimate thing to say and yet strangely it didn't make her feel anxious at all.

'I didn't know that,' she said. 'You've never mentioned it.'

'No,' he said. 'I've often wondered why I haven't. Weird really, when you think about it. We work together most days and yet we never really talk, do we?'

Daisy knew why that was. It was her fault. Because she had never even bothered to get to know Kit, thinking him lazy and uncaring, when in reality that was far from the truth. He was simply misplaced at Buchanans, that was all. Out of his natural habitat, she could see that now. And she of all people should know how that felt. She was just about to say so when, turning to look at him, her eyes were drawn to the scene beyond. Her hand went to her mouth.

'Oh, look at that!' she exclaimed. 'How beautiful.' A break in the line of trees allowed Daisy to see through to a small clearing where a log cabin sat huddled in the snow. 'It's like a gingerbread house,' she added, and she wouldn't have been at all surprised to see Hansel and Gretel come walking towards them.

The cabin windows glowed with light, casting a golden halo that glimmered across the drifts of snow banked against the side of the cottage. She was too far away to see inside clearly, but there was the impression of warm cosiness and, through one of the windows, the outline of a Christmas tree could be seen, its lights twinkling into the night.

She turned to Kit. 'Isn't that the most perfect thing you've ever seen? There's even smoke coming from the chimney, look!'

'And perfect if you don't want any neighbours,' said Kit.

Daisy walked a few steps to the side. 'I'm just trying to work out where we are,' she added. 'But if I'm right, there are no roads across here. How do you get to the place?'

Kit shrugged. 'On foot?' he suggested. 'I should imagine that's part of its charm, the fact that it's hidden away among the trees and the only way to get to it is by walking.' He smiled. 'But then I guess you know all about that.'

'I do… but my cottage is slightly closer to civilisation than this place. Oh, but still, isn't it gorgeous?' She was still staring at the cabin, trying to imagine what it must look like inside. 'You said you come out walking this way quite a bit, didn't you? What does it look like in the daytime?'

'Erm… a log cabin…?' He was teasing her, she could tell. 'But you're right, it's quite something and without the benefit of lights to show its presence during the day, you could easily walk right by and miss it entirely; it blends in almost perfectly among the trees.'

Daisy gave a sigh and turned away. 'Probably owned by a huge bear-like woodcutter, who wears checked shirts and spends his evening polishing his axe collection…'

Kit laughed. 'Let's hope not!'

They carried on walking, striking out straight through the middle of the field, heading for its opposite corner.

'Are you warm enough?' asked Kit as they turned into the wind.

Daisy nodded. 'I am actually, this walk is blowing the cobwebs away too, which was just what I needed. There is something so utterly peaceful about walking in the moonlight.'

Kit pointed at a line of animal tracks in the snow that stretched away in a curve in front of them. They looked fresh. 'Monsieur Reynard is out on his nightly rounds, I see.'

She scanned the countryside ahead of them, but the fox was nowhere to be seen. 'I have one too. She crosses the bottom of my garden most nights. And the year before last, she raised cubs. I used to see them playing on the lawn.'

'So sad that most folks never get to see a sight like that,' added Kit.

'Or don't want to… The most amazing set of tracks I ever saw came from the outline of an owl in the snow. It had come in to land to take some prey, a rabbit I think from the prints. You could almost see every feather on the massive arc of its wings imprinted into the snow as it took off in flight. It was the most breathtaking and heartbreaking thing I've ever seen.'

Kit's face was lit up in wonder. 'I would have felt blessed to have seen something like that. Maybe one day I will.'

Daisy turned to look at him, meeting the wistful expression in his eyes. 'I hope so,' she said.

They fell silent for a while after that, reaching the end of the field a few minutes later. Kit led them through a small thicket of trees and across a lane that looked like a farm track before cutting sharply away to his left through another dense stand of trees.

'Watch your footing here,' he said. 'It's pretty dark in the middle.' He held out his hand as she scrambled over a large log and she instantly felt the reassurance of his grip as she stepped back onto flatter ground. She looked around her but she still had no real idea where she was.

Within another couple of minutes, however, she could see a line of lights through the trees, getting brighter and brighter with every step. Soon it would be time to leave the silvery twilight world behind and she felt strangely disappointed.

'You'll see where we are in a minute,' said Kit, as they emerged back into open space, but Daisy had already spotted the face of the clock-tower at the far end of the market square, which towered above all else.

'We're at the back of the park!' she exclaimed, looking around her to see the trajectory of their walk. They had travelled in the opposite direction to the road that Daisy had been following and yet she'd been amazed how quickly they had reached the town.

'You would have found your way,' said Kit, as if reading her thoughts. 'But it's much easier when everything is not covered in snow, the landmarks are so much harder to read.'

'Even so, it was very kind of you, Kit. I've hijacked your walk.'

He stopped to look at her. 'And yet we've still been walking?' His lips curved upward into a grin. 'So maybe you haven't… maybe, I've just had the pleasure of your company *on* my walk.'

His eyebrows were raised in amusement, but there was something more than just merriment in his eyes, something she couldn't quite fathom.

'Well… thank you, anyway…' She trailed off, a little embarrassed. 'And enjoy your day off,' she added as an afterthought. She took two steps forward. 'Bye then…'

Kit laughed. 'I said I'd walk you home, and walk you home I shall.' He waggled a finger at her. 'And don't argue. I'm not great at a lot of things but rescuing damsels in distress is a particular forte of mine. My success rate is currently one hundred per cent and I should hate to ruin my score by abandoning you here.'

'So how many damsels have you rescued then?'

She grinned as Kit made a show of scratching at his head, thinking hard as he counted on his fingers. He beamed at her. 'One!' he announced.

'Then how could I possibly let you down. Lead on, Sir.'

He bowed and, laughing, caught hold of her arm. 'I'll race you to the swings,' he said, taking off and running across the field.

'You swine!' Daisy raced after him but her wellies were not really made for running in the thick snow and he beat her easily.

'Oh, my gosh,' she panted. 'I can't breathe!' She swept a pile of snow off the top of the swing seat next to Kit and collapsed onto it, grinning. 'I used to come here all the time as a child. My dad used to—' She stopped suddenly. 'It was a long time ago, it doesn't really matter now.' She stood back up, annoyed with herself for breaking the mood, but no longer wanting to swing. 'Shall I push you?' she asked Kit, anxious not to make him feel awkward.

'Go on then,' he replied. 'I think my masculinity can take it.'

And just like that the mood changed again, and Daisy found herself grinning at the ridiculous notion of two adults playing on the swings in the snow.

'Higher, higher,' yelled Kit as she shoved him as hard as she could. He was heavier than he looked, but soon he was soaring into the air and Daisy stood back watching him. His grin was infectious and before she knew what she was doing she had climbed back on her own swing, working her legs furiously to get herself to move.

It had been years since she'd been on a swing and the edges of the seat rubbed painfully at the sides of her thighs, but the sensation was one she remembered keenly. And she was almost there...

And then, without even thinking about it, her swing dropped in line with Kit's and for several seconds they swung together. It seemed for a moment as if time everywhere else stood still and there was just the two of them, their swings carving an arc through the cold still air in perfect harmony. It didn't last of course, Kit had a distinct weight advantage and they pulled apart, but something else had aligned in those few moments and Daisy would have sworn from the expression on Kit's face that he had felt it too.

Daisy automatically allowed her swing to slow, knowing that Kit would do the same. It was getting late and they should probably get moving again. She risked a glance at him, feeling a little awkward, and was relieved to see that he didn't look uncomfortable at all, he looked just the same. He smiled at her.

'Childish,' he said, 'but incredibly good fun.'

She nodded and returned his smile. How had she never noticed before how easy Kit made everything feel? They fell into step once more as they carried on walking across the park and within minutes were passing through the market square.

Daisy turned her head automatically to look at Buchanans. Like all the other shops, it was still twinkling with festive lights, but she didn't want to think about it any more today. Tomorrow would be soon enough.

The town was quiet for a Friday night, apart from a large bunch of people obviously headed for a night out. An office party perhaps, but they seemed to belong to a different world from the one that Daisy was in and she exchanged a look with Kit. It wasn't his cup of tea either by the look of things. They walked the rest of the way in near silence and, almost immediately it seemed, they had left the lights of the town behind them again and the quiet stillness of the canal beckoned.

The moon was still full, but there were more trees here and it was darker than out in the open expanse of the fields. However, Kit walked confidently beside her, navigating the towpath by night just as well as she did.

She breathed in deeply as her hand unhitched the gate into her garden. The cottage was in darkness but it still looked inviting, and she was glad to be home, albeit sad that their walk was coming to an end. She laughed as Kit followed her up the path.

'You really did mean to the door, didn't you?'

He bowed slightly. 'I hope you consider yourself rescued, my lady,' he said.

And the strangest thing was that Daisy did.

Saturday 14th December

Eleven shopping days until Christmas

'Good morning!'

Bea's greeting was as cheerful as ever as Daisy pushed open the door to Buchanans the next morning. She was even earlier than usual, knowing that the day was going to be incredibly busy, but pleased to see that Bea had also made sure she arrived in good time. Bea usually covered for either her or Kit when it was their Saturdays off and Daisy always looked forward to their chats before the shop opened.

'I've made your tea,' said Bea, popping a sugared mouse into her mouth. 'And eaten far too many of these so, before we get down to anything else, can I suggest that you remove this from me and hide it for the remainder of the day.' She handed Daisy the box of festive treats.

Daisy grinned. There was nothing to Bea, and she would eat sweets all day if anyone let her. She went through to the back to deposit her bag and coat and change out of her boots. The streets in the town had been cleared of snow, but it was still thick down by the canal. Ready for work, she returned to claim her cuppa gratefully. She had got up in good time, but somehow she had dithered and fussed about and, before she knew it, it had been time to leave and she'd barely managed her breakfast, let alone a drink. She knew why of course – it had been the same reason she'd been unable to sleep. But with any luck they would be rushed off their feet today and Daisy would have no time at all to think about Kit.

'Right, I'll make a start on the cases, shall I?' she asked Bea. 'I think we should put the platinum diamond collection in the centre for today, don't you? I mean, if we can't sell it at this time of year, when can we? And I'm going to change the cushions if that's okay, the purple I thought, and—' She broke off, aware that Bea was staring at her. 'But we don't have to, of course, I…'

Bea was grinning. 'First things first, young lady,' she said. 'As always, your judgement as far as the business goes is impeccable and yes, we should absolutely do as you suggest. However, do you really think you can come in here this morning and not tell me a single thing about your days out? Heavens, I've hardly seen you all week. Come on, I want *details…*'

Daisy groaned. 'Do I have to?' she replied, sighing. But then she frowned. 'Anyway, isn't that breaking the rules a bit? I mean, if I tell you what's been going on won't that influence your decision about the competition?'

But Bea just laughed. 'Don't be silly. I won't know what piece of jewellery any of the boys is going to choose for you, will I? No, I just want to know how things have gone. You know, how well they got to know you, if you got on… that kind of thing.'

There was a definite twinkle in Bea's eye that Daisy didn't like one little bit.

'But I haven't had all my days out yet,' protested Daisy. 'So I can't really tell you how everything went.'

'Bertie and Lawrence then,' said Bea, pouting. 'You can tell me about them. Start with Bertie.'

Daisy wasn't going to be let off, that much was clear, and past experience had told her that there was no point in arguing with Bea when she was in this mood.

'So Bertie took me to the Winter Wonderland in Nottingham,' she began. 'Which was lovely. Very festive and, I thought, a pretty good place to go for a day out. It was fun, and he was a very considerate companion. I enjoyed it,' she added as an afterthought.

'Yes, yes, but what did you think about Bertie?'

'Bea, I can't tell you that! How is that possibly fair?' Even though it was nearly a week ago, the images from her day out with Bertie were still very clear in her head. As were their conversations. Perhaps most important had been the realisation that she would be very happy to have Bertie run the shop, or at least she had been up until last night… But she couldn't give Bea any indication of who she thought should run the business, that wouldn't be fair to any of them. She felt the weight of responsibility that Bea had placed on her lying heavy on her shoulders.

'All I can say, is that we had some conversations which I think Bertie might find quite useful going forward. It was an opportunity for him to take stock and so I'm sure that Bertie has been thinking very carefully about what he wants to do. In any case he has a friend who runs his own business, doesn't he? I met Luka and he seemed the sort who would be only too happy to help. I'm sure Bertie could go to him for advice if he's successful.'

Daisy took another mouthful of tea, signalling the conversation was at an end.

Bea rolled her eyes dramatically. 'I hardly consider that a full answer,' she said. 'But I suppose you're right in that it wouldn't be fair for you to tell me what you think about Bertie's suitability as far as Buchanans is concerned. Though I am glad to hear that he is taking the competition seriously.' She touched a hand to her hair, her rings sparkling in the bright lights. 'So now, how about Lawrence?'

'Well you already know where he took me,' challenged Daisy.

'Of course I do. Lawrence has very little imagination where certain things are concerned, but I hope that the day was a success nonetheless?'

Daisy was tempted to ask her which part of the day she meant; some parts had been rather more successful than others.

'I've never been to Harrods,' she said. 'So that in itself was a change for me. London at Christmastime too... goodness, the windows were...' She trailed off, wondering how to phrase her feelings; she didn't want to lie. 'Well, they were quite extraordinary. And of course Lawrence showed me the fine jewellery room. I had no idea that Buchanans was modelled on it.'

'A fact that is completely lost on the inhabitants of our little town. Lawrence's idea, naturally.'

Daisy frowned. 'But he made it sound as if you were really keen on the idea.'

'It appeals to my sense of irony,' replied Bea. 'And I find it quite amusing, but I never thought it was going to make us the sure-fire success that Lawrence seemed to think it would.'

'Oh...' Daisy was rather taken aback by her words. She had always thought that Bea had the last word on everything, and yet, from the way she described it, she had simply indulged Lawrence. It was something that seemed to happen far too often in Daisy's opinion.

'Shall I let you into a little secret, Daisy dear?' When she nodded, Bea continued. 'It's no secret that I love London and all that it has to offer. But have you ever wondered why I choose to make my home here?'

Daisy was tempted to say because it was cheaper, but she knew that probably wasn't of concern to Bea.

'You see, I was only young when I met the boys' father and for a young girl like me who had hopes of going on the stage it was a dream come true. William was terribly well connected and we got invited to all the best parties, the shows, the opera. It was like dressing-up and playing pretend all the time, and I loved it.'

Bea paused to give Daisy a twinkling smile. 'I still do, as you are probably well aware. But... it is also incredibly wearing to do it *all* the time. Don't get me wrong, I don't regret any of it for a minute but, particularly as I've got older, I've realised that it's only a part of me and the other part needs feeding too, on trees and fresh air and going the whole day without doing your makeup, making fried-egg sandwiches and sitting in your pyjamas until noon. So that's why I have never lived in London.'

'But Charles? I thought he was—'

'Something big in the city?' interrupted Bea. 'Or a playboy perhaps? No, he doesn't even live in London. Charles is a farmer, actually.'

'Never!'

Bea grinned at Daisy's astonished face. 'It's easy to make assumptions, isn't it? But in fact, not everyone is as you might first imagine.'

No, Daisy was beginning to realise that.

'And so when Charles and I move out to Spain, we're going to live on an olive farm and spend our days walking and watching sunsets, and becoming incredibly tanned and wrinkly no doubt.'

Happiness was oozing out of Bea's every pore. Daisy couldn't quite believe it, but she could see how utterly in love with the idea she was.

'Do the boys know about all this?'

'No.' Bea laughed. 'I should imagine it's going to come as something of a shock... perhaps not so much to Kit, but...'

There was something about the way that Bea said his name that caught Daisy's attention. She had always wondered why Kit was so quiet in comparison to the rest of the family, and why he was so unlike them. Daisy had assumed that he had inherited his traits from his father but now, hearing Bea, perhaps he was a chip off his mother's block after all. And then something else occurred to her. Something that made her smile a little wickedly.

'Lawrence is going to be astounded by your news,' she said.

'Yes, isn't he?' Bea's eyes shone with amusement. 'I probably shouldn't say this, but I'm rather looking forward to seeing the expression on his face when he finds out. Lawrence has some very endearing qualities, but he's such a snob. Sometimes I think I'd like to tell him about Monique too. Just for the fun of it. Oh, I'm so naughty.'

Daisy gave her a puzzled look. 'Monique?'

'Yes, although that's not her real name of course.'

A little thrill of illicit pleasure ran through Daisy. 'Then what is it?'

'Sarah…'

'No!' Daisy burst out laughing.

'She's not from Paris either.'

Daisy groaned. 'Go on…'

'Sussex, a little village just outside of Kent.'

'But that's, that's… Oh, God, that's brilliant!'

'It's also incredibly astute. Personal shoppers can earn a considerable amount of money, particularly at somewhere like Harrods, so, as you might imagine, competition to become one is fierce. Most of them are self-employed and work to contract, so Sarah had to come up with a clever marketing trick that made her stand out from everyone else. And her trick was to become Monique, the oh so chic Parisienne.'

'So really she's no different from a shop window, or any other type of merchandising. It's all about selling the aspiration.'

'Exactly. But she's also very, very good at what she does. And she never makes fun of people. She takes her role very seriously indeed.'

'No wonder I liked her. But she's still playing them at their own game.'

'Of course, but the very best players know how to play so that everyone wins…' Bea put her finger to her lips. 'You mustn't let on though. No one must ever find out. Which is why I won't tell Lawrence – he'd probably think it an outrageous deceit and get her the sack.'

Daisy shook her head. 'I wouldn't dream of saying a word.'

'No, I knew I could rely on you.' She gave Daisy a searching look. 'Oh, this competition is going to be such fun. Now when are you meeting Kit?'

Daisy's head was spinning with all these new revelations. She had almost forgotten she was meeting Kit, and why…

'On Monday night. We're just having dinner. I did ask him if he wanted to go somewhere for the whole day, but he didn't seem to want to.' She would hate for her boss to think she wasn't offering the same opportunity to each of the brothers. But Bea smiled.

'No, I'm sure in Kit's case dinner will be just fine.' She glanced at her watch. 'Heavens, is that the time, we must get on, man the defences and all that.' She held out her hand for Daisy's mug. 'And I don't know about you, but I need another of these before we open and then I'll be ready for anything.'

She crossed the room and had just got to the door when she stopped and turned. 'I'd also just like to say how grateful I am to you, Daisy, for everything. I know how much of a trial this has been for you but, I hope, at the end, you will see it's been worthwhile.'

And with that Bea disappeared through to the kitchen, leaving Daisy staring at her back in wonderment. Any thoughts she had of asking her just what she meant soon disappeared, however, when she realised that unless she got a move on they wouldn't get everything done in time before they opened. She hurried to the safe and began to get the day underway.

*

The morning passed in a blur, and it wasn't until Bertie appeared to help out at lunchtime that she realised how quickly the time had gone, or indeed how ready she was for a break. Bea looked equally pleased to see him, but she wouldn't hear of taking her break first and waved Daisy's suggestion of it away. Daisy did wonder whether Bea might have wanted a little time to talk to Bertie on his own, but the shop was so busy with customers as she went through to the back room that she quickly dismissed the idea.

She opened up her lunchbox and pondered its contents. She was hungry but she really wasn't sure she could eat. The world seemed to be spinning around her so fast that she couldn't settle to anything. Christmas in the shop often did that to her, it was the adrenaline rush from being so busy. But this year was different. There were so many things to think about and this morning had only added to the list. She had anticipated spending her lunch break sketching out her ideas for Grace's present, but now she wasn't sure she would be able to do them justice.

She was about to get her sketchbook out anyway when she suddenly remembered that Grace's was not the only necklace she had to make. She should have heard back from her other customer by now. She fished in her handbag for her phone so that she could check for a message, acknowledging that in all likelihood there would be nothing. His delay was probably just an excuse and she would never hear from him again.

Except that when she looked at her phone there was not one but two messages there. The first was from Kit.

Hi Daisy. Hope you've thawed out after last night. Just wanted to let you know that your car is fine. It was still somewhat wedged this morning, but I went early enough so there was no one else about and was able to retrieve it no problem. Now parked in its usual spot, and have posted the keys through your letter box. Hope that's okay, Kit xx

She couldn't believe she had actually forgotten all about her car this morning. Bless you, Kit. She read the message again, smiling. Two kisses.

Clearing her throat she looked at the second message – a notification from her Instagram account.

NickCarr1: I'm so sorry I didn't get back to you yesterday, my business overran and I missed my flight. I've been wracking my brains all week to think of things to tell you about my girlfriend, but it's even more difficult than I thought! I could tell you that she makes me feel more alive than anyone I've ever known, but how do you make that into a necklace? Or that in certain lights her skin looks like alabaster, so pale that when she arches her neck it makes me want to lay my fingers against her skin to feel her heart beating? That she's the first thing I think of every morning when I wake up, and the last thing at night, and when she smiles at me it's like there's no one else in the room. Sorry, I'm not being any help at all... but she reads a lot, does that help? Also, she doesn't like frilly stuff, except on flowers (which she loves), no lace, plain colours, that kind of thing, and she's very tidy… Please ask me anything you think you need to know, maybe I'll be better at that? Hopelessly, Nick.

Daisy sat back, staring at her phone. And then she reread the message, her heart lifting at the words. Maybe his message didn't help her at all, but how could anything be wrong in the world when you had someone who loved you the way Nick did? She thought for a minute, trying to compose a reply, but realised that she couldn't. She needed a little time to think about things, to let her brain sift through all the information she had and see if it couldn't come up with an idea. After all, that's what had happened with Grace's necklace; she had come up with the design almost without trying. She picked her bag up again and this time she did take out her sketchbook, turning to a fresh page, before rummaging for a pencil.

With Grace firmly in her mind, she started to sketch, committing her ideas to paper with a few light strokes. She was sure what she had in mind would work, it was just a question of getting the design elements balanced so that the piece sat properly. She added another detail and then paused, tapping the end of her pencil against her teeth. She wasn't thinking about Grace now at all, but of her wreath, and how the jewellery she had made to sit at its centre allowed it to be a part of something else. Because something else had been brewing in the back of her mind since the day she had gone on the course at Hope Corner Farm. Framed on the wall of the old cow shed had been a series of Flora's prints; bold botanical designs and, because they were linocuts, very simple in their execution. It had struck her at the time how easily they could be embellished.

She turned a new page and sketched a quick image of a daisy that she remembered from one of the prints. Might she be able to make a simple pendant, for example? Replicating an element of the design and then adding it to the print so that it could be removed if necessary; much as she had designed the brooch at the centre of her wreath. That way the jewellery became so much more than just a pendant and the picture became so much more than just a print.

The excitement was bubbling inside of her. She was on to something, she knew she was. She thought back to the words from Nick's message, and the perfect idea came to her. She sketched it quickly in case it evaporated during the course of the busy afternoon ahead, and then she stared at the sketches she had made. Oh my God, they could be gorgeous! She shot a glance at the clock and picked up her phone.

Hi Nick, thanks for your message. Actually you've been more help than I think you could possibly have realised. I'm at work just now so can't give you all the details yet, but I actually do have some ideas! Can you leave it with me until later tonight and I hope to be able to send you some sketches then. Hopefully, Daisy.

She pressed send before she could change her mind and grabbed her sandwich, praying that the afternoon would go just as quickly as the morning. She was itching to get home and make a start.

Sunday 15th December

Ten shopping days until Christmas

Daisy rolled over and opened an eye to squint at the clock. She hadn't gone to bed until past midnight but, instead of falling into a deep sleep, she had still been so excited that she'd woken nearly every hour, itching to get back up again. She almost did at five o'clock but then willed herself to sleep again until a more sensible hour. The clock now showed six forty-five and she flung back the covers with relief.

It was cold in the bedroom and she thrust her feet into her fluffy slippers, pulling her dressing gown from the end of the bed as she did so. There'd been another light fall of snow in the night and the view from her window was breathtaking. But first things first.

She relit the fire in the sitting room before setting the kettle to boil and contemplated the day ahead. She was meeting Amos at eleven and he was the first visitor she'd had to her little cottage in what felt like years. She looked around it with a critical eye as she sipped the first cup of tea of the day. It was clean and tidy and, beyond that, simple and homely. Besides, there was nothing she could do about it now, and today wasn't about winning awards for her interior design. The thought made her stomach leap in nervous excitement.

She had rushed home from work the night before, eaten several quick slices of toast and got straight to work on Grace's present. By eight o'clock she had done enough to know that she could go no further without Amos's approval. So, with an apology for the lateness of the hour, she had sent a text asking if she could see him. His reply had arrived within five minutes and he declared it to be perfect timing: he would be running some errands for the farm the next morning and so would call in on her if she could provide directions to where she lived. Daisy hadn't given it another thought but sent them straight back. It was only afterwards that she had realised what a first this was for her.

After finishing her design for Amos last night, she had turned her attention to everything else that was humming through her brain, shocked to discover as she had laid her pencil down quite how late it was. But she had covered the pages in her sketchbook with ideas that flowed out of her as if she'd opened a tap. And they were good, she could see that. It was as if something had shifted inside of her but, whatever it was, the results were plain to see. The very last thing she had done before she went to bed was annotate some of her designs and photograph them so that it was clear just what she was trying to achieve. Then she attached them to a message which she sent to *NickCarr1* with a simple query:

On the right track?

She hadn't received a reply yet, but that was hardly surprising given the hour.

Rinsing out her mug, she set it ready for her second cup of tea which she would have with her breakfast and then went to get dressed. She needed some stillness back inside of her and there was only one place she could get that.

The canal path was deserted. Even the regular dog walkers weren't up and about yet, but Daisy was glad of it. Her feet were the first to lay a trail through the soft snow, or at least the first human feet. The blackbirds had been out dancing and, by the look of it, something small and furry had scurried past on more than one occasion. Other than that, however, the landscape was a clean white sheet and Daisy breathed in deeply as she made her way through the wintry world.

It wasn't just the rising tide of excitement about her jewellery that was occupying Daisy's head, there were a whole cast of characters clamouring to be heard, not least of all Kit. The transformation of the day she had shared with Lawrence couldn't have been more pronounced and, ever since, she had found herself thinking about Kit more than she cared to admit. And he hadn't just posted her car keys through the door as he'd described. He'd slipped them inside an envelope with part of a poem by Walt Whitman. How did he even know that she loved his work? It was such a lovely gesture, it made her feel, well, a little bit gooey inside, if truth were told, and that was usually only something that happened to the heroines in the books she read.

And thinking about Kit inevitably led her to thinking about Bertie, and Lawrence too to some degree. Bertie had ended up staying at the shop the whole of the afternoon yesterday and it had been fun – busy, but he was such a natural with the customers that the banter had kept them all going. It made her think what it could be like to have Bertie there the whole time… and what Bea had made of it all.

Daisy had caught Bea watching her and Bertie on a couple of occasions and, given their conversation in the morning, she was dying to know what her boss had been thinking. In fact, it had crossed her mind on more than one occasion to come clean to Bea about her jewellery-making, but she knew she mustn't, it would make a mockery of the whole competition.

Her breath hung in the air as she walked and she lifted her head to scent the smoke which was drifting along from the narrowboat moored further up the canal. A thin coil of it rose straight into the air from the chimney and she'd always loved the smell. As she drew closer she could see that a little Christmas tree had been put up on the stern at some point over the weekend, just like the one she'd seen in Nottingham, and that Robin was already up and about enjoying his first cigarette of the day.

He raised his hand in greeting.

'Land ahoy!'

She smiled. It was his regular greeting.

'Beautiful morning,' she said.

Robin just grinned. 'Still night, I haven't been to bed yet…'

'Oh…'

'The elusive plot twist, which has been missing for days, showed up about nine o'clock last night, leading to the inevitable all-nighter in case the damn thing eluded me again.'

'And did it?'

'No, I nailed the little bugger.'

Daisy smiled. Robin peppered his speech with swear words, but his books were elegant in their use of language. It made her like him even more. She had never been on board his boat and she probably never would. Their brief conversations were all they had, but he was as much a part of her landscape as the trees and water. She waved a hand and walked on.

'Enjoy your sleep,' she called as she passed.

Half an hour later she was home again, refreshed and buzzing with energy. No nearer to resolving the complex thoughts in her head but at least they weren't shouting at her quite so loudly now. Her phone pinged as she opened the front door and a brief message flashed up on the screen.

NickCarr1: Nail hit squarely on the head. You are a genius! Please proceed with the second design and as long as it doesn't cost more than one arm and a leg, I'm good. In awe, Nick.

It looked as if she was going to be rather busy…

*

Amos arrived on the dot of eleven grinning from ear to ear. 'I like your wreath,' he said, pointing to the front door.

'Yes, it's been somewhat inspirational,' she replied, greeting him warmly as she ushered him inside.

'And what an amazing place to live. If it hadn't been for your brilliant directions, I would never have known this place was here.'

Daisy smiled. 'No, it's not every day that directions to your house include the phrase, "Turn left at the lock gate and then follow the hedge."' She took his coat and then invited him straight into the sitting room where not only was there a roaring fire, but her work table, spread with everything she had been working on.

Amos looked around him. 'This is just how I imagined it to be,' he said. 'You suit one another… the house and you,' he added, in response to her curious expression. 'You'd be surprised, but some people don't ever get along with their houses.'

'Yes,' she said. 'I've always thought we make a good pair.' It was something she had always believed, but had never spoken about to anyone else. Somehow when Amos said it though, it didn't seem odd at all.

He headed for the table almost immediately, his eyes lighting up as he approached. His hand reached out instinctively before taking it back at the last moment. 'Sorry, may I?' he asked.

She nodded, pleased. He'd been reaching for the tiny bee she had made yesterday evening and she'd only just finished polishing it. She watched as he held it closer, turning it this way and that to see the detail. He paused in his observation, his eyes sweeping the page of her sketchbook, and she could see him make the mental connection between what he held in his hand and what she had drawn. He looked up, eyes wide.

'Daisy, this is incredible. These things... they're perfect. All of them. And apart from the bee, I don't remember even talking about them and yet, they *are* Grace... you have captured the essence of her beautifully. I really don't know what to say.'

Daisy could see that he was struggling, his emotions very close to the surface but he made no move to hide them. She felt a moment's discomfort that she had caused such a reaction, but then it hit her – *she* had made him feel that way, her jewellery had moved him almost to tears, and a sudden elation rose in her.

She traced a finger across the sketched design on the page. 'This is silver wire,' she said. 'It's very delicate, but stronger than you'd think. I'm hoping it will connect everything in a way that will make it seem as if all the elements are floating. Ethereal, I think you said.'

'I did... but I never thought for one minute...' His gaze was still fixed on the table, but then he looked up at her. 'I can't thank you enough, Daisy. Grace will absolutely love this, and it's everything I could possibly have wished for.'

Daisy smiled. 'Well I haven't made it yet, so hold that thought until I have. It may all go horribly wrong.'

But Amos was shaking his head. 'No, it won't. This has been right from the very start. I knew it the first minute I met you.'

'Yes, you did, didn't you? I wonder why that was?'

'Perhaps I saw a little spark of something.' He was grinning at her. 'And all it needed was feeding, just like your beautiful fire.' He looked back down at the table and then she saw his gaze shifting to another set of drawings. He pulled one closer.

'These look a little like the prints that Flora makes,' he said. 'I didn't know you were a painter too?'

'No, I'm not. I was just messing with an idea I'd had.' She tipped her head to one side, studying her sketch. 'I couldn't remember the detail, but it was more the composition I was after.' She picked up a small daisy head she had been working on, still in its rough clay form. 'You see, I rather thought that if the prints were big enough I might be able to add something... or perhaps if just a part of the design were made bigger, maybe on a card instead of a print. I'm not really sure...' She was still turning the daisy over in her hand when Amos took it from her.

'So where does this go?' he asked.

Daisy pointed to the flower head on the page. Her little clay model was an almost exact replica. 'I think it's going to be a pendant,' she said. 'I just need to work out a way to fix it so that once it's removed it doesn't damage the original artwork, that's if it works at all...'

Amos gently placed the clay against the flower head. 'Like this?' he asked, looking at her to check he'd got it right.

'Yes, you see, I could—'

'No, I get it,' interrupted Amos. 'I'm just not sure why you're being hesitant.'

'Because Flora's prints are so lovely all by themselves and—' She broke off, aware that Amos was no longer looking at the page but at her, searching her face. 'Just that I don't want to ruin them. I wondered if it wasn't a bit arrogant, seeking to add something to her prints when they're already beautiful and don't need any embellishment.'

'But your jewellery stands on its own two feet just as well as her prints, and what you're thinking about here is joining two works of art to make a third and that's something completely different. I don't think it's arrogant at all and, for what it's worth, I don't believe Flora will either. Inspired collaboration is what it is.'

Daisy smiled. 'Well, not yet it isn't but, maybe one day…'

Amos looked at his watch. 'Well, we could always go and find out.'

'Sorry…?'

'I was running errands for the farm this morning,' he replied. 'So I'm going back there soon. If you're not doing anything else, come with me. We can go and ask Flora just what she thinks.'

Daisy's hand fluttered to her cheek. 'I couldn't possibly do that! Not without asking. I mean, it's Sunday and—'

'And Flora will be busy selling Christmas floral decorations, and very much working. So, no, you won't be interrupting her if that's what you're worried about.'

'No, but she still won't be expecting me.'

Amos grinned. 'Daisy, the farm is open to the public…' He raised his eyebrows in amusement. 'Come on, grab your coat.'

Daisy stood her ground. 'Erm, we were supposed to be discussing Grace's present. And I can't get on and make it unless we do.'

But Amos was just as adamant. 'What's to discuss? I think it's perfect and I would like you to make it exactly as you have described.' He gave her a warm smile. 'And I'm not just saying that to get you out of the house. I can't think of a single thing I would change. I'm not sure how you've done it, but it looks to me like a little bit of magic.'

His dark eyes twinkled at her and Daisy knew when she was beaten. She picked up her pieces of clay and closed the sketchbook. 'Give me ten minutes,' she said.

*

She was ready in half that time, snatching the wreath from the front door on their way out as she remembered that Flora hadn't seen it yet. Amos insisted that she bring everything, including the design for Grace's necklace, and minutes later they were on their way back to Hope Corner Farm.

Daisy scarcely had time to think about what was happening to her, something which seemed to be occurring with increasing frequency these days, but with Amos chattering away she didn't have time to be nervous either. By the time they arrived she was more excited than anything. And it was lovely to be back.

They met Flora's husband, Ned, on their way in. He was just coming through the gate, almost hidden under a pile of greenery that he was carrying out to a customer's car.

'Ho, ho, ho!' he called out as he passed.

Amos held back to wait for Ned to finish his task. He would need his help to unload his van, currently stacked with the logs that were the result of his earlier errand. But he waved Daisy on with an encouraging smile, suggesting that she should go and find Flora who would be in the old milking shed. Daisy took a deep breath and walked purposefully across the yard.

There could be no doubt what Flora was selling as Daisy approached the shed. Beautiful wreaths and festive garlands lined the route and there were also small trees and a barrowload of mistletoe tied into sprigs with red bows.

Another two people passed Daisy on her way out but, when she pushed open the shed door, she was pleased to find Flora alone, downing a cup of tea by the looks of things. Flora waved when she saw Daisy, flapping her hand as she finished drinking.

'Sorry,' she said. 'Long overdue and nearly cold, but very welcome.' She puffed out her cheeks which were bright pink and, despite the fact that they clashed rather with her bright red jumper covered in snowy white pom-poms, Daisy thought she looked wonderful. Her eyes were shining with happiness.

'Have you brought your wreath to show me?' she asked. 'I do hope so, I was only saying to Grace the other day that I wondered if you'd finished it, but she thought you'd probably been too busy.'

Daisy smiled. 'I think she was being tactful,' she replied. 'She still thinks I'm making you a Christmas present from Ned, don't forget.'

Flora tapped her head. 'Oh, of course… How's that going anyway?' And then her eyes lit up. 'Have you brought that as well? Can I see it?'

'Well, not exactly. The wreath yes, Grace's present is still just sketches and a few samples at the moment, but that's kind of why I'm here. Amos came to see me this morning to see how far I'd got and, well, he suggested I came…'

Flora nodded, her curls bouncing with excitement, and indicated a table at the far end of the room. 'Come and sit down and you can show me.'

Daisy followed her down the room. 'He seemed to really like what I have in mind for Grace, but there's… something else as well.' She broke off, unsure quite how to continue, or even whether she should, despite what Amos had said.

But Flora wasn't quite so reticent. 'Well, that sounds intriguing. I'm dying to see what you've been up to.' She sat down at the table. 'I want to see it all, so first things first, let's have a look at the wreath.'

Daisy dutifully removed the decoration from her bag and placed it on the table. 'So this is just the floral part…' she began, as Flora immediately picked it up and held it in the air for a better look.

'Look at those colours!' she exclaimed. 'Daisy, you've done so well with this. It absolutely works, all of it. Are you pleased?'

Daisy nodded. 'I've had it hanging on my front door.'

'So I should hope. And the silver…?' She leaned forward eagerly, replacing the wreath on the table, waiting as Daisy fished back in her bag, bringing forth the small pouch that held them.

'It was this that got me thinking really…' Daisy held up the circlet of ivy leaves that she had shown to Grace and, undoing the clasp, began to entwine it with the wreath. 'So there's this, which you can wear as a necklace by itself, or, if you want, I made a centrepiece for it as well, so you can wear them together or this second piece just as a brooch. They attach together, see? Or of course you can leave them both on the wreath. I probably haven't placed it quite right, but you get the idea.'

She handed it back so that Flora could take a closer look, noticing as she did so that her prints were still hanging on the wall. Daisy had misremembered a few of the details from the one she'd tried to copy, but it was pretty close, and would certainly serve to illustrate her design. She was so busy studying the print that it was a few seconds before she realised Flora had fallen silent and was staring at her. She smiled nervously.

'I had no idea that it would ever look anything like this,' said Flora. 'I'm not sure I can take it all in actually. It's incredible…' She broke off, eyeing the bag that was at Daisy's feet. 'And I absolutely have to see what you've made for Grace…'

'It's not finished, but…' Daisy laid her sketchbook on the table and turned the pages until she found the design she wanted. Then she took the little bee from the pouch and placed it down on the edge of the paper. 'It's probably self-explanatory,' she said.

For the second time that day, her work was subject to scrutiny and Daisy sat waiting anxiously for Flora's verdict. Amos's words had been lovely, but Flora was a proper artist and she might view things differently, with a more critical eye perhaps. Daisy could see that Flora was weighing up what to say when the door at the far end of the room burst open and Amos appeared with Ned in tow. He had obviously been telling Ned about Grace's present because the two of them strode down the length of the room and, before she knew it, Daisy had three people crowding around her, all staring at her designs ready to pass judgement. She didn't think she'd ever been more nervous in her life.

Flora's finger was tracing the outline sketch of another element that Daisy had drawn. 'Dewdrops on the grass…' she said softly, almost reverentially. 'And the moon…' She looked up at Ned and Amos and then slowly back to Daisy. 'I honestly don't know what to say.'

Ned grinned. 'Blimey, that's a first!'

Flora poked his arm.

'And she hasn't even shown you the print thing yet,' said Amos. And before Daisy could stop him he crossed to the far wall and took down one of Flora's pictures, bringing it back to the table. Then he sat down and looked pointedly at Daisy, a wide grin on his face.

'I know you feel awkward about this,' he said. 'But you have no reason to. Talent like yours deserves to be shouted from the rooftops and if you won't do it, then I'm afraid I'm just going to have to.' He gave her an encouraging smile. 'Take a deep breath, Daisy, and tell Flora all about it.'

And so she did.

Monday 16th December

Nine shopping days until Christmas

Daisy had scarcely been able to think straight since she had got home. Everything seemed to have become so complicated, and she could feel the pressure around her building. Like a storm that needed to burst, leaving everything clean and fresh in its wake.

She stared at her reflection in the mirror. Wear something warm, Kit had said, but preferably several thinner layers rather than one big one. But how did you do that when you wanted to look nice? It was something that had been troubling her since Friday night. Her wardrobe was just not cut out for choice and, besides, she was keen to try out some of the ideas that Monique had given her. So, armed with these thoughts, Daisy had toured the charity shops and the vintage market stalls and was now trying to choose between a cherry-red cashmere jumper, which she had almost fainted over finding, and a draped cream-coloured top, which was very romantic but probably not that practical.

The jumper won and, with freshly curled hair, clean jeans and boots, Daisy thought she looked okay. At the last minute she slipped a white tee shirt under the jumper, remembering Kit's advice about layers, and went downstairs to wait for him to arrive. She stood in front of her work table, tracing a light finger around the circlet of ivy leaves that lay there. And then on an impulse she picked it up and fastened it around her neck. The metal was cool against her skin, its weight unfamiliar, but it nestled there, following the dips and rises of her collarbone. When she moved, it moved and, fascinated by the way it felt, she crossed to the mirror in the hallway.

She could remember the last time she wore a necklace of her own all too vividly, and since then she had never worn one, the shock of the memories it brought too overwhelming, but perhaps today… The subtle light in the hallway brought a gentle gleam to the metal, dancing as she moved. It was so beautiful, perhaps if she just… but the voice in her head was getting louder and louder, the words bringing a sudden rush of tears to her eyes. Her fingers fumbled with the clasp as a sudden knock at the door made her jump and, flustered, she pulled at it. Kit mustn't see this; if he did she would have to explain and how could she possibly tell him now? It was wrong, she should never have put the necklace on. Rushing back into the other room, she fiddled with the clasp again, anxiety making her rough, and to her horror it came away in her hands. She had broken it.

Another knock sounded and she dropped the necklace on the table with a sob, dashing at her eyes and the tears that filled them. Kit was waiting, but how could she go anywhere now? Daisy took a deep breath and willed herself calm, just like she had so many other times in the past. She was good at putting on a brave face. She sniffed, swallowed and pulled her jumper straight.

'Come in!' she said, opening the door wider and beckoning Kit into the hallway.

He smiled at her in greeting but then a momentary flash of concern crossed his face. 'Is everything all right?'

'Yes, yes, I'm fine.' She sniffed again. 'Sorry, I was just putting some mascara on and I stuck it in my eye. I'm hopeless sometimes.' She dropped her head slightly so that Kit wouldn't be able to see that she wasn't wearing any.

'Right, I'll get my coat, shall I?' she said. He was now looking past her and eyeing up the door to her sitting room, but there was no way she was letting him in there. She smiled and stood her ground, forcing him to stand back slightly so she could reach the row of hooks.

'You might want your wellies,' he said.

She looked down at her boots. 'Oh. I rather thought… Why, are we walking?'

'Only a tiny bit, but there's still a little snow around. I'd hate for those to get ruined.'

The snow had all but melted out by the canal but, she sighed, wellies it was.

Five minutes later they were walking down her garden path and, as Kit went on ahead to open the gate, she realised she was studying him quite intently. For some reason it made her blush. The small hallway had been far too intimate a space to look at one another without embarrassment but she'd never realised before quite how long Kit's legs were. Perhaps it was seeing him silhouetted in front of her, dark against the deepening blue of the night, that made him seem taller than usual. She cleared her throat and looked away.

His car was parked next to hers, in the spot she used just where the road to town rose over the canal bridge. He opened the door for her, apologising as he did so.

'It's very old, and what you might call functional, but I don't use it much, so…' He trailed off, leaving the sentence unfinished. She climbed in, smiling at the contrast between Kit's choice of transport and that of his brothers. Expensive, plush or sporty this was not. And it was freezing.

'I think the heater might have packed up, too,' added Kit, climbing in beside her. 'Sorry, but we won't be in it for long and when we get where we're going, I promise it's warm.'

'So, where are we going? Somewhere in town?'

'Not quite, but close. A little place I know.' He grinned at her, but it was obvious he wasn't going to tell her any more.

She did up her seat belt and smiled back. 'Okay then, let's go.'

Kit wasn't kidding when he said it wasn't far. He took a road away from the town, but they had only been driving a couple of minutes when he turned off the road onto a tiny track that Daisy didn't remember seeing before. Even with his headlights on full beam, there wasn't much to see; tall hedges rose on either side, blocking the view. After another minute, Kit pulled up in front of a small gate and killed the engine. It was suddenly very dark.

She could hear the exhalation of breath as Kit grinned and the creak of his seat as he moved. 'Can I just say that, whatever this looks like, I'm not an axe murderer.'

'Ah, but you would say that, even if you were…'

'Possibly true.' He opened his door, flooding the interior of the car with light. 'Want to risk it?'

She laughed. 'Things can't get much stranger than they've been the last few weeks,' she replied. 'I'll risk it, if only because I have no idea where we are and I'm quite intrigued to find out.'

Daisy climbed from the car and followed Kit to where he came to rest by the gate. The night was like an impenetrable blanket, the moon completely hidden behind the clouds, but she could feel the stillness spreading out around her.

'Would you like the torch? Or my arm?' asked Kit. 'It's almost too dark tonight, even for me.' He switched on a torch he was holding so that its light cast an eerie glow up over his face. 'Although it's not far, you'll see the lights pretty soon.'

She took the torch, but switched it off again, linking her arm through his. 'I like the dark,' she said. 'Just don't lead me into a ditch.'

'Fair enough.'

He opened the gate and she stepped through, sensing wide open space in front of her. There was something darker even than the sky massed some way ahead of her and, as her eyes gradually adjusted to the gloom, she began to make out the shape of a field, hedgerows leading away from her on both sides.

She squinted as they walked, striding out right into the centre of the field. There was something she couldn't quite see yet, but there was a sense of purpose in the way Kit was moving so she knew they must be close.

It all unravelled in her head at the exact same moment she saw the first flash of light. As if her internal compass had suddenly tuned in to where they were. She realised that the road where she had got stuck in the snow must lie on the opposite side to the field, which would mean... And then there was another flash of light, and another, and she understood exactly where they were and where they were going.

She must have quickened her pace or tightened her grip on Kit's arm because she heard him chuckle. 'Worked it out, have you?'

She nodded. 'But I still don't...' And then she stopped. 'Oh, my God, Kit, you *live* there? That cabin in among the trees is yours?' She slapped at his arm. 'You sod, you could have said!'

'And where would have been the fun in that?' Kit replied.

'I don't believe it.' And now that she could see the gap in the trees and the warm glow of the house beyond it, she dropped his arm and began to run, stumbling a little on the uneven surface, but not caring.

She skidded to a halt just at the perimeter of trees and sucked in a breath. Close up it was even more breathtaking. It was a traditional log cabin — a long low roofline behind, with an adjoining apex at the front providing a deep overhang around a porch area surrounded by railings. Twinkling lights were wrapped around the wooden uprights and along the top rail and slightly larger lights hung from the pitch of the roof. At the corners of the building the enormous logs which formed the cabin walls were laced together like clasped fingers, and on the left-hand side a huge tree was covered in coloured lanterns. The recessed windows glowed with warmth and she could smell the smoke from the chimney.

'I don't believe it,' she said again as Kit came to stand by her side. 'I think this has to be the most magical building I've ever seen.' She could hardly believe she was actually going to go inside. 'How on earth did you get lucky enough to find this place?' she asked.

'I had it built,' Kit replied, grinning. 'Or rather, I built it…'

She stared at him. 'But that must have taken… how do you even…?' She stopped. 'And this is going to sound incredibly stupid but, *why* would you even? I don't mean why have a house like this, that's blindingly obvious, but to build it yourself. There can't be many people who would do that.'

Kit smiled. 'I hope the answer to that question will become apparent when we go inside.' He ushered her forward with his hand. 'Shall we?'

The front door opened into a space the full height of the building, rising majestically above them and, as Daisy looked around her, she realised that the whole of the house was open to the roof; there were no ceilings to any of the rooms. Instead, intersecting the space, were walls, made from the same huge logs that formed the outside but these only rose to half height, creating rooms that had an incredibly cosy and intimate feel, while at the same time being light and airy. She moved through the space with her head craned upward to look at the intricacy of the wooden beams above and a growing sense of wonder deep inside her.

She followed Kit under an archway in the wall ahead of her, carved out of the solid logs so that as she passed through she could see the whole ends of the tree trunks that had made it. Her mouth dropped open as she looked around her in a daze. In front of her an enormous log burner was ablaze with dancing flames, and in one corner stood another Christmas tree, at least fifteen foot tall. She scarcely knew what to look at first.

The polished wood floor was partially covered with a huge creamy tufted rug and there were plants everywhere; on surfaces, lining shelves, and even overflowing from a series of pots sunk into a beam that was suspended from the ceiling. Everything was plain and simple in design, rustic some might call it, but the effect was stunning. And as she gazed in wonder at everything around her, Daisy realised with a sudden sharp insight that what she was looking at was Kit himself, his very essence shining through every single item in the room. She was beginning to understand.

She inspected the rug, then looked at a shelf and the objects upon it, the coffee table and the selection of books it held, until, finally, she turned back to Kit who had not said a word since they entered his house.

'You made all this,' she said. A statement not a question. 'Everything here.'

A slow smile transformed Kit's face. 'I did,' he replied. 'Everything you see is either built from reclaimed materials, or recycled, repaired and given a new lease of life. The windows, floors, doors, everything, all the soft furnishings too. You can't see it tonight, but I have a garden where I grow all my own vegetables, and slightly further afield is a borehole which supplies all my water, and a wind turbine which provides most of my electricity. I tread as lightly as I can.'

'How long has it taken you?'

Kit grinned. 'A long time. About seven years all told. I decided on my twenty-first birthday that I needed to do something with my life that I could be proud of.'

'And this is it.'

'Yes, this is it. Most of it anyway. I have a few other... things I support.'

Daisy searched his face, wondering not for the first time how she never knew these things about Kit. She looked at him, at his open expression, and realised that he wasn't showing off, or being boastful of his achievements, he was simply happy to be living the kind of life that held meaning for him. And suddenly she understood perfectly where Kit's quiet strength came from. He had no need to prove himself to anyone, everything he needed was right here.

'How can you possibly bear to be at Buchanans?' she asked.

'Ah...' He gave her a sheepish grin.

'Do you know I used to think you were lazy, or that you just didn't care, about anything much...' She bit her lip. 'I feel awful now, for even thinking those things.'

'No, don't feel awful. That was entirely my fault. I spent so long when I was younger feeling I had to justify my actions with everyone, particularly my family, that in the end I think I gave up bothering to explain. Of course what I should have been doing was looking for the right kind of people to explain it to, people who would understand because of who *they* are. Which is really why you're here...'

Daisy could feel a warmth rising up inside of her. 'Oh, I see...'

Kit smiled. 'I rather hoped you would. And in answer to your previous question, yes, my way of life is at complete odds with everything that Buchanans stands for and yet it would be hugely hypocritical for me to turn my back on it. My father started the business and the money I inherited when he died has allowed me to support certain things that would otherwise be beyond me. So, I have no wish to see the family business die out, but it's a rather curious position to be in nonetheless.'

'Then why go through with the whole competition?'

He was quiet for a few seconds, weighing up his response. 'Because Buchanans doesn't have to be the way it is now,' he replied. 'And I believe there's a better way, but unless the business passes to me there will be nothing I can do about it. It's an opportunity I don't want to let slip by.' He pursed his lips. 'But I don't really want to spend the evening talking about Buchanans, that's not why I invited you here... And I believe I promised you dinner...' He held out his hand. 'Let me take your coat before you start to roast and you can explore while I get some drinks and dinner on the go.'

Monday 16th December

Nine shopping days until Christmas

Daisy was beginning to feel rather warm, whether from the heat of the delicious fire or Kit himself, she wasn't sure. She shrugged off her outdoor things and handed them over, watching as he removed his coat. He was wearing a thick cable-knit jumper and it suited his slim frame. She realised suddenly that Kit was so much a part of this house that it was no wonder he looked slightly awkward outside of it.

He looked down at her feet, an amused expression on his face. 'Feel free to keep the wellies on if you want, but if not, just sling them by the front door.' There were archways on either side of the room and Kit pointed to his right. 'The kitchen is that way, but feel free to have a wander, or just sit by the fire, whatever you prefer. Can I get you a glass of something? I've got some homemade mulled wine on the go, or something lighter maybe?'

A sudden flush rose up Daisy's cheeks. 'I don't drink,' she said. 'Ever.' She paused and swallowed. 'Sorry, what I meant to say was, that sounds lovely, but I'd rather have a soft drink if you don't mind. Actually, just tea would be lovely.'

Kit's smile was warm. 'Just tea it is.' He held her look for a moment before slipping from the room, leaving Daisy rolling her eyes. For goodness's sake, she scolded herself, just relax, Kit's a friend. She bent down to pull off her wellies and, after depositing them by the door as instructed, wandered back into the main room and then through the archway to her left. Something had caught her eye earlier and she was intrigued.

Her face lit up as she entered a room lined with bookshelves. The orange flash of colour she had seen was exactly what she had thought it was; row upon row of old Penguin books. They were all here: Emily Brontë, George Orwell, F. Scott Fitzgerald, John Steinbeck... She ran a finger lightly along the spines, saying hello to old friends, and then she stood back to look around the rest of the room. There was a whole section devoted to books about sustainable building, technical manuals, and books on subjects Daisy knew nothing about. Many of these were new, but only she suspected because they weren't available second hand. Apart from these, pretty much every book in the room had already been loved, and clearly a great many by Kit himself. Two squishy armchairs covered in a rich tweed-like cloth were positioned either side of a tall window. A woollen throw was placed over the arm of each, and Daisy could imagine that, winter or summer, it would be the perfect place to read. She pulled one of her favourites from a shelf and sat down, turning to the last page. Her lips turned upward as she read the final lines – a message to the reader that it was futile to try and move forward when everything was connected to the past. If only she could recapture hers. Done things another way. How different her life might have been.

*

Daisy was still lost in thought when Kit found her with a cup of tea.

'I wondered if I might find you in here,' he said.

She looked up, a query on her face.

'I thought you must be a big reader,' he explained.

'Well, yes I am… How did you know?'

He smiled. 'Call it an educated guess.'

Her brows drew together but Kit shook his head and would say no more.

She cleared her throat. 'I've seen you so many times with a book in your hand at Buchanans but…' She broke off, pulling a face. 'But I always thought they looked incredibly boring, sorry. I never imagined all this…'

Now it was Kit's turn to take a book from a shelf. 'I probably had my head stuck in the mysteries of… *Wind-Powered Water Pumps*… a playful little number if I remember rightly.' He slid the book back where it belonged. 'But it's amazing how if you pick the right book, no one will talk to you.' He grinned at her, a knowing smile that saw right to the heart of Daisy's own subterfuge on occasion. She blushed, but there was something rather lovely about their shared similarities.

She replaced the book she had been looking at and held out her hand for the mug. 'I'll come through, shall I?'

He nodded and she followed him through to the kitchen, her jaw dropping not only at the size of it but the skill with which Kit had put it together. Fitted kitchen it was not, but all the better for it in her opinion. Beautiful old tables and cupboards ranged around the room together with a painted dresser which held crockery of all shapes and sizes. A multitude of pots and utensils hung from a length of chain above an enormous range.

One thing was very clear upon looking around the room.

'You obviously like cooking?'

Kit followed her gaze. 'I like growing, I like cooking, and I like eating,' he replied. 'The three seem to follow a natural progression.'

Daisy narrowed her eyes. 'Growing, I'm okay with...'

He looked back at her. 'You know, if you and food don't exactly get on, the best way around that is to learn to cook. That way you get to eat things you like, cooked just the way you like them. And you can be adventurous in your own home too – try things you never normally would, because who's to know if you spit something halfway across the room because it's disgusting. I started growing my own vegetables for all sorts of reasons, but mostly because I didn't want to keep eating processed foods. I didn't plan it that way but the more I cooked, the more I realised I loved food.'

The way Kit described it made it sound the simplest thing in the world, and Daisy wanted to believe him but... She looked around his kitchen. Maybe it *was* that simple. Daisy had a big garden, and she liked to grow flowers and shrubs, why not vegetables? She had thought that her biggest barrier to eating was that she didn't like many of the things you could buy, but perhaps that was just it; perhaps she just hadn't found the things she liked yet, because they weren't things that could be bought.

'I can teach you, if you'd like?' offered Kit. 'Sometimes it's more fun that way. Or I can just be on hand to ask me anything you want to know.'

She thought for a moment. 'Actually, there is one thing I'd like to know,' she replied. 'And that's quite how you've managed to get inside my head. There seems to be an awful lot about me that you know, and yet I don't remember telling you.'

He shrugged. 'I'm observant, that's all.' And when she pulled a face, he continued. 'Daisy, you bring your own lunch to work every day, and every day you eat the same things. Cheese sandwich, carrot sticks and a yoghurt. It's not that hard to work out.'

She gave a sheepish smile. 'Maybe I'm just not used to people being observant,' she said.

'Of course, it also helps that I'm interested,' added Kit.

She looked up, catching Kit's eye as her heart added in an extra beat somewhere. She hadn't a clue what to say.

'So I thought, today, that I'd start you off gently with something I know you like. Well it has cheese in it, and carrots, so I'm hoping it's a goer, otherwise it may well be a sandwich after all.'

His smile was so warm, Daisy wondered if she might actually melt, but she was incredibly touched that he had put so much thought into what to cook for her.

Daisy took her tea across to the table and sat down. She couldn't trust herself to say anything, but instead busied herself watching Kit's back as he prepared their food. He was still turned away from her when he spoke again.

'Actually, I also wanted to apologise for something, or rather explain about it. When we were out the other day, I mentioned that I'd walked past your house before but never said anything about it to you. I know you weren't aware I even knew where you lived and I wondered if I had made you feel uneasy. It came across as if I was stalking you or something.'

Daisy smiled. 'You're not really the stalkerish type, are you?'

Kit turned quickly and flashed her a cheeky smile. 'I might be,' he said, and then his face grew serious again. 'No, not really... The thing is, though, when I mentioned it I also said how odd it was that we never really spoke, but we didn't finish the conversation. It wasn't until I'd been home a little while that I realised why that was.'

'What, that we didn't finish the conversation? Or why it's odd that we never really spoke much before?'

'Stop avoiding the subject,' said Kit. 'Why we never spoke.'

'Because I'm antisocial?'

Kit smiled. 'No… I asked you once about your family, when you first came to Buchanans, do you remember?'

Daisy shook her head, feeling a little flicker of anxiety. She had no memory of it at all.

'I don't remember exactly what you said, but it was basically "none of your business and don't you dare ask me about them ever again…"'

'I was seventeen,' replied Daisy. 'And obviously going through my final years of being an obnoxious teenager.'

Kit was watching her, a soft look in his eyes. That, more than anything, was making her feel nervous. It was an inviting look, full of empathy.

'Perhaps,' he said. 'But sadly I think I took you at your word and didn't really speak to you much at all after that.'

Daisy dropped her head. 'Yes, I know it was my fault.'

'Hey…' he said gently. 'I wasn't being critical, Daisy, quite the reverse in fact. I've been just as guilty of dodging conversation. You've had a bellyful of my family over the last couple of weeks, and because I've spent a huge amount of time in my past trying to work out how I fitted in between them all, my head has been stuck in the sand so long sometimes I forget it's there at all. Of course being tongue-tied, flustered and painfully self-conscious around you hasn't helped in the slightest. But, no excuses, I should have been a better friend.'

He'd been flustered and self-conscious around *her*? She thought back to all the times she had thought him rude or uncommunicative… and suddenly it all began to make sense. He was just the same as she was and the more time she spent in his company the more she realised what kindred spirits they were. The thought that she might at last be able to share certain things about her past with another person was almost overwhelming, but that didn't mean that Kit was necessarily ready to hear them. Or that she was quite ready to share them.

'Me too,' she admitted. 'But I'm not sure I know how. I don't really have any friends, so…' She wasn't sure how to continue.

'Neither do I…' He grinned at her. 'We make a right pair, don't we?' He turned back to the counter and, after a few seconds, turned back around holding a ceramic dish. 'Twenty minutes in the oven to finish off and it will be ready. Do you want to slice some bread for me while I just wash up a few bits?'

She sidled from the table. 'Okay, but let me wash up, I don't mind.'

Kit waved a bread knife at her. 'Nope. You can wash up after dinner if you like, but not before!'

He collected various pots and pans from where he'd been standing and carried them to the sink, leaving the counter empty apart from a chopping board and the knife. 'The loaf is in the bread bin on your left,' he added. 'And when I said slice, I meant great thick chunks, so we can have it with our food.'

She nodded, pulling out a round loaf that smelled heavenly. It was a far cry from the sliced loaves she ate at home.

'Did you make this?' she asked.

'Yep, when I got home from work. It's soda bread, so no faffing about with yeast and proving and all that. Try a bit.'

She cut a small slice off the end that was virtually all crust and was just about to nibble a bit when Kit strode across to her, a butter knife in his hand. He pulled a dish towards him.

'You're really not good at this eating lark, are you?' he said, swiping the crust from her hand, stuffing it in his own mouth and then nudging her out of the way with his hip. He cut a huge chunk from the end of the loaf and slathered it in butter before taking a bite. 'Oh, that's heaven,' he mumbled through a mouthful of bread. 'Here...' And before Daisy could object he thrust the same chunk of bread at her, so close to her lips that she had no choice but to take a bite.

Her eyes widened in surprise.

'Ha! I told you it was good,' he said, taking another bite himself before offering it back again.

Daisy swallowed, reeling. The bread was good. It was soft and salty, rich in flavour, but she had also eaten something that had just been in Kit's mouth too and that just wasn't something she would normally do. She looked up at his face, split by a grin as he enjoyed his food and she laughed. What did it matter anyway? She opened her mouth to accept the last piece of bread, rolling her eyes.

'That is gorgeous!' she managed after a moment.

'Told you. I can teach you how to make it if you like, it's dead easy.'

She nodded. 'Okay.' And for some reason Monique's words echoed through her head. *One small extravagance every day...* 'Do you know how to make macarons?' she asked. 'Only I had them recently and I thought I should try and have a go myself.'

'No, I've never made them but I'll certainly have a recipe in one of my books. We can have a look after tea if you like.'

Daisy nodded firmly, and turned back to slice the bread, in thick chunks this time.

'So what are you going to be doing for Christmas?' asked Kit after a few minutes. 'I'm guessing something fairly quiet, or will it just be recovering from all the shenanigans at the shop?'

'Hmm, something like that.' She thought of the pieces of jewellery she had yet to finish, the success of which might well help her to decide what she was going to do in the future. And of course all that also depended on who would end up running Buchanans too. 'I have a few decisions to make,' she said lightly. 'But yes, it will be quiet, they always are. How about you?'

There was silence for a moment and Daisy wasn't sure that Kit had heard her question, but then he suddenly turned around.

'Would you like to spend Christmas Day with me?' he asked. 'Here I mean…?' He broke off, looking embarrassed. 'Sorry, that just sort of came out. I had a bit of a speech all rehearsed, but…'

'I'd love to.' The words shot out of Daisy's mouth before she even realised it was open. She stared at Kit, both of them looking rather surprised, until the corners of Kit's eyes began to crinkle and a smile spread over his face. 'Good,' he said. 'I'm glad.'

'I should imagine that Christmas might be a bit different for you this year?' she said.

Kit grimaced in reply. 'We normally all go to Mum's on Christmas Day but I really don't think I could bear it this year. I can't imagine it's going to be the jolliest of occasions and it struck me that I could either do what I normally do and try to keep a low profile, or actually do something I might stand a chance of enjoying.'

Daisy blushed slightly. 'If Lawrence wins he'll be absolutely insufferable…'

'And if I win, I'll end up with a knife in my back,' finished Kit. 'If it's Bertie he'll just do what he normally does anyway which is to get sloshed and pretend we're just one big happy family. Weird things, families…'

Aren't they just, thought Daisy.

'And yours won't mind if you don't spend the day with them? Sorry, I don't even know where they live? Are they local?'

Daisy swallowed and looked at the bread she had just eaten, at the man who wanted to teach her how to cook, who had just offered to share his Christmas with her, and who wanted to be her friend – no, *was* her friend.

'I don't see my family...' she began, her throat closing as if to keep the words from being said. 'I have a brother, actually he's my half-brother, but he doesn't live near me and so I speak to him, but I haven't seen him for years. It's complicated...' Her voice was barely above a whisper.

Kit had stopped what he was doing, and turned back towards her, his hands dripping water onto the floor. 'Daisy, the other night when I walked you home, you mentioned your dad playing with you on the swings, but then you stopped as if you didn't want to remember it. Did something happen? I don't want to pry but...'

'I was five when my dad left, and I haven't seen him since. It wasn't his fault, not really, he just couldn't take the fighting any more.'

Daisy was trembling, but she clenched her nails into her palms and forced herself to speak. If she didn't say these things now, she feared she would never say them.

'Shortly after that my brother got taken into care, and I was left... with my mum.' She sucked in a breath. 'Until I was nine when I went to live with my grandparents at the lock-keeper's cottage.'

Kit had taken two steps towards her. 'What happened?' he asked gently.

'I had no one to look after me.' She could feel the familiar wave of pain beginning to build within her, because the reality was that she'd had no one to look after her for years before that. She thought of the endless days when she had come home from school to an empty house, and an empty fridge. Or worse, her mother passed out on the settee. Because at least if her mother wasn't there, there would be no angry shouts, no beatings as she came around, crazy for more booze or another hit. Even being cold and starving hungry was better than that.

'I had no one to look after me,' she repeated, 'because my mother died from a drug overdose and so my grandparents took me in and they saved my life.' A slow tear began to roll down her cheek. 'Until I was seventeen, when they died, and I was alone again.'

Monday 16th December

Nine shopping days until Christmas

There was a moment when everything seemed to stand still, when Daisy held Kit's look as if she couldn't tear her gaze away. And then the next second she was in his arms, her head cradled against his chest as she gulped for air.

He didn't say a word, but held her, rocking her gently, and it had been so long since anybody hugged her that she hugged him right back, letting the feeling of warmth fill her up. She didn't think about what it might mean, only how it felt. Her tears flowed freely but she let them fall. She was safe here.

'Daisy, I'm so sorry,' he murmured, his lips against her hair. 'I never knew…'

He didn't say anything else, but his arms held her close until her past receded and her tears simply melted away. There was no need for them in the present. Not when she could finally begin to look towards the future.

Eventually she pulled away, amazed that there was a smile on her face. 'I was going to apologise,' she said. 'But instead I think I should thank you. I've never told anyone about my family before.'

He smiled a little sadly. 'Perhaps it's just that I know what it feels like to stand in a room full of people and feel so utterly lonely. I don't think I've ever fitted in, and I realised pretty early on that the things I wanted from my life were different from what other people did. But I always hoped that one day I would meet, not just someone who understood, but someone who was like me, who wanted the same things I did.'

'Oh…' Her hand hovered somewhere around her mouth.

'And some while ago I asked Mum about you, about your family, and she gave me one of *those* looks, you know the ones I mean… She said, quite rightly of course, that if I wanted to know more about you that I should actually ask *you*, not her. I've kind of been trying to pluck up the courage ever since, and when you mentioned your dad the other day, well, I think I just decided that perhaps now was the right time. Because I do want to find out more about you, Daisy. I want that very much indeed.'

Daisy had almost given up hope of ever finding anyone like that, resigning herself to reading about them instead between the pages of romance novels.

'I'm not very good with stuff like this, Kit…'

'Then let's just take it one day at a time.' He turned around to glance at the oven. 'And for now we can simply eat and chat. If nothing else I can amaze you with my culinary expertise.' His eyes twinkled and Daisy realised it was as simple as that.

'Tell me again what's in this?' she asked, as she forked in another mouthful of food ten minutes later. 'Because I can't believe it's as easy as you say it is.' She looked down at her plate of rapidly disappearing food, a little pool of sauce oozing out from under a golden crust. A few weeks ago it would have been her worst nightmare.

Kit paused, just about to take another bite himself. 'It really is. Just some root vegetables; carrots and parsnips, together with some baby onions and mushrooms, cooked in a white sauce and then topped with a cheesy breadcrumb crust.'

'But it doesn't taste like any of those things,' said Daisy. 'There must be something else in it.'

'A little mustard and tarragon to flavour the sauce, but that's all, I promise you.'

'And it all came out of your garden?'

Kit nodded. 'Apart from the mushrooms, yes.'

Daisy shook her head. 'And I go home most nights and heat up a tin of either mushroom or tomato soup. I'm ashamed of myself.'

'There's nothing wrong with that, it's honest enough food, just not as tasty. In my opinion anyway.'

'I guess it's something else that just came about because of how things were… before. There wasn't always a lot of food and I ate what was cheap, or what I could get hold of. And somewhere along the line it became part of the way I am, part of who I am. And I've never had cause to question it before now.'

An agitated expression crossed Kit's face. 'But you shouldn't give yourself a hard time, Daisy. Everything you are is testament to how strong a person you've had to be. Change if you want to, but not because you feel you should. I'm sorry if you feel pressured.'

She was quick to smile. 'No, that's just it. I do want things to change, and suddenly I can begin to see a way through, perhaps to the future that I've always wanted. The last couple of weeks have been… unusual to say the least, but they have helped me to see that I can be different. Maybe it's not quite as hard as I thought it was going to be.' She pressed her lips together, her fork idling on her plate as she contemplated just how much she should tell Kit. But then he knew about pretty much everything else...

'You see, I've been making things,' she continued. 'Jewellery actually, and I don't know, but I'm wondering whether it might be something I could be good at.'

Kit had just been about to take another bite of food and his fork stopped halfway to his mouth. He slowly lowered it again. 'What kind of jewellery?' he said slowly. 'Somehow I get the feeling it's not just clay beads.'

'Not quite,' replied Daisy. 'Made from clay, but silver clay actually. Flowers and leaves and everything I see in the world around me. But they're not proper jewellery, not like Buchanans sells, and I don't even know if they're any good.'

Kit had a puzzled expression on his face. 'But why didn't you tell anyone? We could have helped you, or... something, I don't know.'

'But how could I tell you, Kit? Think about it. If I told anyone now it would ruin the competition, and be tantamount to cheating. I've probably already told you too much. When I first started making things, I didn't tell anyone because I thought you'd all laugh at me. I mean, Buchanans sells gems which cost thousands of pounds, and which are... not my cup of tea admittedly, but still very fine jewellery. By comparison my designs are, well, there is no comparison. It would be like trying to compare a symphony with a child blowing a recorder out of tune. I would have felt so stupid showing them to Bea... Except that in any case, now it's all different, because if I showed any one of you my designs, you would instantly know how to win the competition and that would be the worst kind of betrayal.'

She swallowed, clearing her throat a little. 'None of you know this, but Bea knew my grandmother, and she took me in when I was seventeen, and gave me a job knowing I had nothing. It's what has kept me going all these years. How can I betray her loyalty? I won't do it, Kit.'

Kit nodded as he took in what she was saying, but he still looked confused. 'I can understand that, but this is your future, Daisy.' He thought for a second. 'One thing I am curious about though.'

She raised her eyebrows.

'At work, you wear jewellery from the shop, and I know that you do it just to advertise what we sell. It's not the real you and I can tell you don't like it.' He grimaced. 'And for very obvious reasons I've been paying attention to what you do wear just recently, but you don't, do you? Even tonight when you are definitely off duty, you're not wearing any jewellery, and I wondered why that was…'

Daisy couldn't help but give a wry smile. It was the one thing throughout this whole situation that she had found incredibly ironic. In fact, part of her wondered if it was why Bea had chosen to do what she had – simply because Daisy herself wouldn't be giving any clues. She chewed another mouthful of food thoughtfully, savouring the taste.

'I don't wear any jewellery because I don't own any,' she replied. 'So it's really pretty simple.' She dropped her head.

'Although that's not the whole story of course…' said Kit.

She looked back up, surprised at his intuition. She sighed. 'No… I don't own any jewellery because I learned not to own things from a very early age. Everything I ever had was taken away from me, to sell usually, or as punishment. Birthday presents from relatives, Christmas too, and I never knew where the things went. But there was one thing I'd kept hidden, a tiny silver locket that my grandmother had given to me. I used to wear it sometimes when I knew I was alone in the house but, one day, I must have got distracted and forgotten to take it off, until it too was ripped from my throat. It was the last piece of jewellery I ever owned.'

Kit swallowed. 'Oh, Daisy...'

She lifted her chin a little. 'As I got older I vowed never to own anything just for the sake of it, but only if it really meant something to me. Now I don't own many things because it's not possible for everything to be special. The more you have, the more the sheer weight of possessions dilutes the importance of those you already have.' She frowned. 'I don't know if that makes any sense at all.'

Kit was thinking. 'Although if you lived in a house that had taken you years to build, that indeed you had built yourself, and if you had made everything that went in that house, and what you couldn't make you chose carefully, only on the basis that it either fulfilled a function or brought you joy, then I think you *would* understand.' He reached out his hand across the table. 'I think you would understand very well indeed.'

His eyes were tender as he slid his hand into hers.

'Just as I think that now is the right time for you to finally let go of some of the things from your past and work towards the kind of future that you want. Make your jewellery, Daisy, no one is going to laugh at you. In fact, far from it, how could they when it's so beautiful? Who knows what's going to happen at Buchanans, but things are changing, and maybe now's the time for them to change for you too.'

She smiled and was just about to answer when her breath caught in her throat. She stared at him.

'What did you say?'

'That maybe it's time for things to change for you too...'

'No, before that... You said that no one would laugh at my jewellery designs because they were beautiful... How could you possibly know that?'

She shot up from the table and marched out of the kitchen, the sound of Kit's chair scraping hideously across the floor following her.

'Daisy, wait! Daisy! Look, let me explain. It's not what it sounds like…'

She whirled around.

'No? You've let me just pour my heart out to you. I've told you things I've never told anyone else, because you made me feel—' She threw her hands up in disgust. 'It doesn't matter how you made me feel… and, Christ, you even had your own sob story to share with me. But that's not what this is all about, is it? You knew I was making jewellery all along and you never said anything. This whole… charade… it's been about Buchanans the whole time—'

'No, Daisy please, I would never—'

'And I can't believe I fell for it. How stupid am I?'

She could feel tears beginning to well up and she was damned if she would let Kit see how upset she was. She had to get out, back to her own house and her place of safety.

'No wonder Bea had to come up with a stupid competition to help her decide who should run the business. She wouldn't want to choose between any of you, and neither would I…' She trailed off. 'Actually, I'd give it to Bertie, because he's the only one who's had any shred of decency throughout this whole thing. Lawrence thought he could just outright cheat by using Monique to find out what sort of jewellery I would wear, and you, you thought you could wheedle your way into my affections and, what? Did you think I'd just roll over and tell you everything you wanted to know!'

She was furious with herself. 'I've probably told you far more than I should have anyway.'

Kit was standing six foot away from her in the hallway and, even as she glared at him, she was still aware of how impressive a building it was. He looked utterly dejected, his hands hanging limply by his sides.

'Daisy, why would I even do that?' He sighed. 'I should have told you I knew about your jewellery-making but, just as you had reasons for keeping it quiet, I have reasons for not telling you I knew. And I'm still not going to tell you what they are, but you have to trust me.'

She smiled bitterly. 'Forgive me, Kit, but I'm not big on trusting people for the sake of it – it doesn't take a genius to work out why. People have to earn my trust, and lying to me is not the right way to go about it.'

'I didn't lie, Daisy. I withheld information, exactly as you have done. You had your reasons, just as I have mine. But I promise you it has nothing to do with trying to trick you into giving me the information I need to win the competition. In fact, I'm just as keen as you are that you *don't* tell me…'

She stared at him, trying to process what he'd just said. It all sounded perfectly plausible, but then it would, wouldn't it?

'Then tell me. If it has nothing to do with the competition, tell me why.'

Kit looked as if he was trying to swallow a length of barbed wire. 'I can't,' he said eventually.

'Can't, or won't?'

'Oh, for goodness' sake, what difference does that make? Can't or won't – it's both, because one follows the other. If I can't tell you but then choose to anyway, what kind of person does that make me? Surely not someone you could ever trust and yet it seems as if that's exactly what you want me to do – break *my* trust.'

She frowned. There was something in what he said, but... 'So then it does have something to do with the competition...'

There was silence.

'Thank you,' said Daisy, bitterly. 'Now I have my answer.'

Kit glared at her. He was getting angry now. 'What do you want me to say? Okay, it has to do with the competition... happy now? Except it's not in the way you think and seeing as I don't recall ever giving you a reason to doubt me, it's rather hurtful that you so obviously do.'

He looked up to the rafters. 'Daisy, we're standing in a building that has taken me a quarter of my life to build. Everything in it was either made by me, or I had a hand in making it where I lacked the skill. There is nothing fake or pretend about it. It is everything I believe in and everything I have dreamed of during all that time. You couldn't find anything that's a truer validation of who I am, so why do you find it so hard to believe me?'

She looked around her, at the very visible of proof of what Kit had just said, but trust went a whole lot deeper than just a few words. For all Daisy knew, that was exactly why Kit had chosen his home as the place where he could get to know her better.

'Because I wanted to believe you, Kit. I wanted you to be different. But you're not. You're just the same as everyone else who manipulates the truth to get what they want. You can dress it up any way you want.' She went to put her wellies back on. 'And I'd like my coat, please, I'm going home.'

'Daisy, please. This is silly... It's a misunderstanding, that's all. Can't we just—'

'I said I'd like my coat, please.'

'What? And you're just going to walk out, are you? With no torch, and no moon to light your way.'

'Yes, well, as you so thoughtfully showed me the way the other night, I'm sure I'll manage.'

His eyes narrowed as he searched her face and, just at the moment when she could bear it no longer, he turned on his heels. She stood by the front door, her cheeks burning, not even knowing if he would return. But he did, less than a minute later, holding her coat. He was wearing his own and in his other hand he held his car keys.

'I'm taking you home,' he said. 'If you won't listen to reason, then I'm not being held responsible for you falling in a ditch and breaking your neck.'

'I don't need your help, I said I'd be fine.'

'Tough.'

Walking across the field was bad enough, but the car ride home was one of the most excruciating Daisy had ever experienced. Neither of them said a word the whole way, and yet Kit was unfailingly polite, checking to see she hadn't stumbled, holding open the car door for her. But if anything it made her even more infuriated. She wanted him to scream and shout at her, so that she could feel justified in her anger at him. But he clearly wasn't going to and so, instead, she endured a suffocating silence.

Minutes later he pulled into the space beside her car and turned off the engine. She didn't know what to do. Her anger had cooled on the way and Kit's lack of retaliation had allowed doubt to creep into her mind; with it had come guilt. She risked a tiny peep at him out of the corner of her eye, but he was looking straight ahead, hands resting lightly on the steering wheel. She should say something…

'I think your house is the most amazing thing I've ever seen, Kit, and I want to thank you for showing it to me.' She hated the way her voice sounded, false and somehow insincere. 'And for dinner too, it was lovely.'

'You didn't finish it,' said Kit quietly.

'No... I'm sorry.'

The silence stretched out.

'And for bringing me home too...'

'That's okay. I think you know the way from here.'

She swallowed.

Her hand was resting on the door handle.

'So, I'll see you tomorrow,' said Kit.

She turned then, hoping to see a glimpse of a smile, but instead Kit just looked immeasurably sad, one side of his face ghostly pale in the scant light, the other in darkness. She nodded, choking back her tears, and stumbled from the car.

It was all a far cry from the last time Kit had brought her home. Then she had felt rescued. Tonight she felt as if she was floundering on the rocks, shipwrecked.

She only just made it inside before the dam that was holding back her emotions broke apart. And there, in the quiet dark of her hallway, she cried for all the times she had ever felt alone. For all the times she had tried to love and care for her mother but been pushed away. For all the times the children at school laughed at her because her school uniform was dirty and stained. For all the times she had cried herself to sleep wondering what she had done wrong. And then she cried some more, because since her grandparents had died there was only one person who had made her feel like she wasn't alone, and now she had pushed him away.

The darkness was all encompassing when Daisy eventually stirred, rousing herself from the floor of the hallway. She was thirsty and her head ached. Her limbs were stiff from sitting on the cold tiles and her eyeballs felt rough and gritty. She licked her lips and swallowed, trying to find some moisture as she fumbled for the light switch, flinching when the dark was suddenly banished from the small space.

She poured herself a glass of water from the tap in the kitchen and held it up to her cheek, relishing its coolness before drinking it down in one go. It was late, nearly ten o'clock, but she felt restless now, strangely empty, and there was no way she could go to bed, she would never sleep. She looked around for something to comfort her and impulsively took down the box of macarons she had bought from the delicatessen the other day. The first disappeared in a moment as she stuffed it into her mouth virtually whole. She waited until she had made herself a hot chocolate before eating the second, and the third she ate while sitting at her work table.

As she drank, she looked again at the sketches she had made for Nick's girlfriend and then she took out a fresh piece of silver clay from its packet and pulled her tools towards her. There was only one thing she could do in the circumstances, and so as the hands of the clock crept on towards midnight, Daisy began to make a heart.

Tuesday 17th December

Eight shopping days until Christmas

Daisy felt the colour drain from her face, but for Bertie's sake she plastered on a smile. Kit, on the other hand, had a face like thunder.

'Run that by me again,' he said bluntly.

'I'm pulling out of the competition,' Bertie said, screwing up his face in sheepish apology.

'Yeah, that's what I thought you said.'

Bertie's face fell. He'd looked so happy when he came through the door that Daisy couldn't help but feel a little sorry for him. Now, his excitement was seeping out of him like a punctured tyre.

'I know it's not great timing, but then actually, maybe it is. And it wouldn't be right for me to go along with this thing, not when I've realised that running this place isn't what I want to do. At all.' He took a step forward. 'You made me realise what my life should be about, Daisy, and I'm sorry, it isn't about running the family business.'

Daisy looked up in anguish. 'Don't make this my fault,' she said.

'It's not anyone's fault,' countered Bertie. 'I'm immensely grateful to you. If it hadn't been for you, I would never have realised what I wanted. Or had the courage to go for it.' He smiled at her. 'I'd kiss you if I didn't think you'd hit me for it.'

She sighed, not daring to look at Kit. 'I'll go and put the kettle on,' she said. 'And then I think you'd better start at the beginning.'

Daisy didn't want a drink at all. What she wanted was a private opportunity to take in what Bertie had just said away from Kit's furious stare. How had it all gone so horribly wrong? Only a day ago she had come home from seeing Flora and Amos, fired with inspiration and determined to follow her dreams, and then yesterday, it had all been so lovely to start with until Kit had ruined it all. And now this.

She couldn't blame Bertie for wanting to follow his dreams but, out of all of the brothers, she'd always had the feeling that he was the most likely to win the competition. And she already knew that she could work with him. His news couldn't have come at a worse time.

She added water and teabags to three mugs and held her hands to both cheeks, feeling how flushed they were. Kit was clearly stunned by Bertie's news and she wondered how that was making him feel – more confident about his chances of running Buchanans, or less so? There had just been the two of them in the shop today, and it had been busy, but the atmosphere had been awful, a strained politeness that set her teeth on edge and made her head ache. And Bertie's news would only make it worse. But, whatever happened, she still didn't want there to be any unpleasantness with Bertie. He'd obviously made up his mind up about his future, and that had to be good thing.

Kit was with a customer when Daisy returned to the shop floor and so she and Bertie stood, rather awkwardly, while they waited for Kit to finish. Her tea was far too hot to drink but she tried to sip it anyway, feeling a little self-conscious. She hadn't seen Bertie since their rather embarrassing encounter when he had brought the flowers that weren't for her – only a week ago and yet so much seemed to have happened.

'So how did your day out with Lawrence go?' asked Bertie, blowing across the top of his mug. 'I hear he took you to Harrods.'

Daisy nodded. 'As you might imagine, not my favourite place,' she replied. 'But it was okay. I met your mother's friend, Monique, which was… enlightening.' She smiled. 'Actually, it was good fun. If you ignored the price tags on the clothes, it was just like the dressing-up games I used to play when I was a child.'

Bertie grinned. 'I didn't ever really play at dressing-up…'

'No, I don't suppose you did. What did you boys do then?'

'Ran around shooting at stuff mostly, from what I can remember. That and try to kill one another. Nothing much has changed.' He winked at her. 'And how was Lawrence?'

She tutted. 'He was fine.'

'Just fine? Really?'

Daisy rolled her eyes. 'Okay, he lectured me on his birthright and exactly why he's the one who is going to gain control of Buchanans. Then he told me what he wants to do when he does. Oh, and of course he didn't think I would see through his thinly veiled plot to use Monique as a spy, feeding him with all the information about me that he could possibly wish to know. I think I annoyed him by arguing with nearly everything he said, and then he pretty much threatened me for doing so, implying it wasn't the kind of behaviour he would expect from an employee. Apart from that, we had a lovely day…'

Bertie groaned.

'Well, you did ask.'

'And I've just made everything a million times worse, haven't I?'

Daisy held up her hand to prevent him from saying anything else and was about to change the subject when Kit's voice sounded from across the room.

'That's pretty much the size of it, yes.'

His customer was just walking towards the door and Kit came across to join them, claiming his cup of tea. 'This had better be good,' he said. 'And I don't mean the tea.'

Bertie took a deep breath. 'In a nutshell, what's happened is that Luka has asked me again to go into business with him, only this time, I've said yes.'

'So you'd rather do that than keep the family firm going, thanks Bertie.'

Daisy winced. 'Hang on a minute, Kit. At least let Bertie explain.'

Kit glared at her, wanting to say something else, but then his shoulders dropped and he held his tongue. He nodded slightly in Bertie's direction.

'I've been doing a lot of thinking ever since our day out,' said Bertie. 'I rang Luka the day after to thank him for his hospitality and he mentioned then that I should come on board with him. To be fair, he says that nearly every time I talk to him, and I've kind of got used to just glibly batting his remarks aside. This time, I told him I couldn't because of what was going on here, and he laughed, saying it was about time I grew up and thought seriously about what I wanted to do with my life.'

'Ouch.' Daisy tried to look sympathetic.

Bertie shrugged. 'Luka wasn't being critical, it's a bit of a running gag between us. But given that you and I had been discussing that very thing only the day before, well, this time it rather hit home.' He stroked the stubble on the end of his chin. 'I think I said to you that I wasn't really fit for anything, and in a way that's true, but I think what I am good at is being with people—'

'Party animal…' muttered Kit.

Daisy threw him a sour look, but Bertie held up his hands. 'Yes, in a way, but I hope in a good way too, rather than the derogatory way you mean, Kit.'

'Actually, I would agree with that,' said Daisy, lifting her head a little. 'You do have a natural way with people, Bertie, and you're a born mediator. For heaven's sake it's the role you've played in your own family for years and, I would imagine, a skill that would come in very handy in Luka's line of work. I'd hardly said ten words to you before our day out, but you were the perfect host as it happens. We were both nervous, and you really put me at ease and helped me to enjoy a day I didn't think I would.'

Out of the corner of her eye she could see that Kit was looking at her, probably wondering if she was trying to score points, but she wasn't. This was important to Bertie, and he deserved his chance at happiness, just the same as anyone else.

Bertie smiled and she could see him finally relax a little, his natural excitement growing once more.

'That's a really kind thing to say, Daisy, thank you. And I know that I could use those skills here, but there are two reasons why I've decided I don't want to. The first is purely practical in that I'm not a businessman, not yet anyway. But Luka is, and I need someone like him to show me the ropes. Otherwise I think all I'd be doing here is sinking the ship and that doesn't help anyone.

'And the second reason, as you so eloquently put it, Kit, is that I'm a party animal and this is not, and never will be, my natural environment. I don't want to sell people trinkets and baubles, I want to sell them memories, and friendship, time spent with family, and I think I'd be good at that. You might think that's trivial or worthless, but I don't. I think people need good times in their lives, maybe now more than ever.'

Bertie's words struck a chord with Daisy and she suddenly felt rather sorry for him. All his life he had been portrayed as a rather careless individual, never taking responsibility for anything, his talents belittled because they weren't 'serious' or possibly, more to the point, a match for Lawrence's business acumen. Yet what Bertie had said made absolute sense and she could see that he could be very successful, particularly sheltering under Luka's wing for a while. She was just about to say so when Kit cleared his throat.

'I think that's the most sensible thing I've ever heard you say,' he said. 'I'm sorry, Bertie, I owe you a huge apology.' He held out his hand.

Bertie regarded him a little warily at first, but then took it and broke into a grin. 'I think perhaps I am finally growing up too. It's taken a while, but this feels right. Luka is doing well but he needs help to expand, and I can't think of a better way to invest in my future.'

He broke off, pulling a face. 'But I am sorry, Daisy, I realise what this means for you.' He smiled at his brother. 'No offence, Kit.'

'None taken. We all know that with you out of the competition it's a virtual certainty that Lawrence will get this place.'

Daisy couldn't bear it. Kit sounded so despondent and, despite their argument, she now knew just how much he cared about Buchanans, and why. This was an awful blow for him.

'Listen, just because Lawrence likes to think he has this place in the bag, doesn't mean it's so. Don't put yourself down like that, Kit, you have just as much chance as he does.' She broke off to include

Bertie in her next words. 'And besides, you mustn't worry about me; whatever happens, I'll be fine.'

'But I do worry about you,' replied Kit, his eyes on hers.

'Do you?' Daisy could feel herself blushing. 'Oh.'

Time seemed to stand still for several seconds as Kit's words swelled to fill the space between them.

'But you shouldn't… either of you,' said Daisy. 'Maybe it's just time for things to change. And you mustn't feel bad either, Bertie. You're only doing what I know is right for you.'

'So, what *did* Lawrence say then?' he asked. 'You mentioned earlier that he told you exactly what he would do here.'

There didn't seem to be any point now in not telling them. 'Well, he's going to get rid of you two for starters. Sorry, but that's what he said. Although I don't suppose that comes as much of a surprise. Lawrence definitely sees this place as his and his alone. As to what he intends to do with the business, I'm not so clear about that. But he has it all planned out. And I would imagine, given his taste in retailers, that he intends to take this place up a notch.'

'Which will kill it off completely,' said Kit. 'It's his fault things are the way they are now.'

Daisy nodded. 'I agree with you. But I don't think Lawrence will listen to what anyone else has to say, least of all me.'

'But you're probably the expert among us,' said Bertie. 'That's a rather short-sighted attitude to take.'

'I don't think there's any doubt that you're the expert among us,' countered Kit. 'So what are we going to do?'

Bertie smiled. 'Well I should have thought that was obvious… There's only one thing you can do and that's win the competition.'

'Easier said than done,' replied Kit. 'Lawrence will be pulling out all the stops.'

'Yes, but how is that going to help him when he doesn't know a thing about me, or what jewellery I would like? Despite his conviction that Monique was going to spy for him and divulge all, he'll probably have found out by now that her lips are very firmly sealed.'

'He'll find a way,' said Kit darkly. 'I don't know how, but he will. That's just what Lawrence is like. No point trying to outwit him.'

Bertie swallowed a mouthful of his tea and then put the mug down very carefully, clearing his throat as he did so. 'There is one way to swing the outcome of the competition in your favour…'

Daisy looked at him bemused. 'Well, I don't see how when…' She broke off as she suddenly realised what Bertie meant. She flashed a look at Kit, but he was studying the floor, avoiding her gaze. 'No,' she said firmly. 'Absolutely not, that's cheating.'

Bertie opened his mouth to speak but she held up her hand. 'Don't even think about it,' she warned. 'I could have given the game away at any point over the last couple of weeks, to any of you, but I haven't, nor will I. My feelings about who gets to run Buchanans are immaterial. If they weren't then Bea would have given me a say in who wins, but she didn't. So it's her decision and hers alone, and whatever that is I will just have to accept it.' Kit's gaze was still resolutely on the floor and she kicked his foot to make her point. 'I thought I'd made that perfectly clear.'

He looked up, startled, and threw Bertie a warning look but it was too late.

'Daisy… your loyalty does you enormous credit, and when I was in the running for this place I was incredibly grateful for it, but come on, the whole situation is different now, surely you can see that? Besides, if Lawrence wins then I dread to think what will happen to this place. Despite ducking out of the competition, I still care enormously what becomes of Buchanans; it's been in the family for years for goodness' sake. We owe it everything and I can't stand by and let all that fall by the wayside because Lawrence has ideas above his station.'

He gave Kit a pointed look. 'Sorry, Kit, I don't mean that you're not in with a chance, of course you are, but look, it's the just the two of us here – who's going to know if we stack the odds slightly in your favour?'

Kit groaned. 'Bertie, that's really not—'

'For goodness' sake, what is the matter with you two?' exclaimed Daisy. 'Am I really the only one here with any morals? And I thought better of you, Bertie. I really thought you were prepared to play by the rules, but first Kit and now you!' She banged down her mug and glared at them both.

Bertie was looking confused. 'Have I missed something here?' he said, looking at his brother, and then he gave a wry chuckle. 'Well, Christopher Buchanan… seems like you can't help yourself after all. Pretending to be all holier than thou when really you're no better than the rest of us!'

Kit looked like he was about to explode and Daisy winced. Bertie was only teasing, but whereas Kit would probably have shrugged it off before, now it was all getting a little too personal. And that was probably her fault.

She raised her hands. 'Listen… this isn't helping anybody—'

But Kit wasn't about to heed her words.

'For your information, Bertie, I have never considered myself above anyone in this family. I simply live a different life from the rest of you, but I've never interfered in your choices, I just accept them. And I have certainly not cheated, despite what Daisy seems to think – last night was just a misunderstanding, that's all.'

Bertie slapped a hand against his head. 'Of course, your meal! How did it go?'

'Fine…' Kit's voice echoed just a split second behind her own, but his voice was flat. She looked imploringly at Bertie to drop the subject and was relieved when he winked at her.

'Oh I see, bit of a touchy subject. I'll keep quiet then.'

Daisy rolled her eyes. That was almost as bad, but at least she didn't have to say any more. She fixed both brothers with a steely gaze.

'Right. I'll just make this clear again, shall I? I will not be entering into a discussion with any of you about the competition, on any level, so I suggest you refrain from bringing up the subject again. Kit and Lawrence can both do what has been asked of them and, on Christmas Eve, Bea will decide who is running Buchanans. Following that, I will decide what *I* want to do. And that's it. End of story. And now, if I'm not very much mistaken, Bertie came in to tell us his good news and as such we should be congratulating him, not bickering like small children.'

Kit had the grace to look sheepish.

'She's right, Bertie. Fighting among ourselves isn't going to help, and I am really pleased for you. So if this competition has helped you to work out what you want then it's had its uses after all. I suppose that's something to be thankful for at least.'

Bertie nodded. 'Although I think it was mostly down to Daisy.'

'But I really didn't do anything,' she protested. 'Perhaps it's just that the time is right.'

'Maybe…' He thought for a moment. 'No, it isn't that. I know exactly what made me change my mind – it was seeing you, whirling on the ice, the look of absolute joy on your face as you were reminded what that felt like. It's the little things, you said, and it really is. We were in the middle of a busy town, crowded with people, and the thing that made you happy wasn't the shops, or the food, or the spectacle of the whole thing, but a simple memory of something that meant a lot to you. And I did that, by taking you there, I brought that back to you, and it made me realise that if I could do it for you, I could do it for other people too. Or at least give them the chance to make those happy memories.'

She leaned forward and impulsively kissed his cheek. 'I think that's perfect,' she said.

'But what about you two?' asked Bertie. 'What do you want to do? If you could do the one thing that truly made you happy, what would it be?'

Daisy smiled. 'I'm working on it,' she said lightly.

Kit looked straight at Daisy. 'I already know what I need to be happy,' he said. 'And maybe one day I'll get my wish. I hope so.'

Bertie smiled. 'I hope so too.'

Wednesday 18th December

Seven shopping days until Christmas

The ground was hard underfoot, sparkling like diamonds as Daisy walked, laying a trail through the frosty grass. It was early, only just gone seven o'clock, and the canal path was deserted. Even Robin was still tucked up inside, his narrowboat closed up against the cold and dark.

She stopped for a moment and looked up at the sky still shining with stars. This time next week would be Christmas Day and Daisy would know her fate. Maybe then her life could go back to being how it was before. But then she stopped herself. Did she really want it to?

She thought back to her conversation with Bertie yesterday. He and Kit had parted on good terms and, just before he left, Bertie had told her how excited he was at the thought of his new life. In fact, he wished it was something he had done years ago. On the face of it his news was a disaster for Daisy, and her future at Buchanans hung in the balance more than ever before. There was now only a fifty-fifty chance that Lawrence would lose and those were not odds she was happy about at all. But more than that was the thought that she was just as guilty as Bertie of not doing anything with her life. What had she been *doing* all these years?

And so, tempting as it was to stay in bed an extra hour or two on her last day off before Christmas, she had got up at the usual time and, after a quick cup of tea, headed outside to clear her thoughts. She must finish the piece she had been working on for Nick's girlfriend – if she didn't get it in the post today then he would never stand a chance of receiving it in time. She must not think about Buchanans and, more importantly, she must not think about Kit. If she did then the day would escape her and she couldn't let that happen.

Fortified by the still morning air and the bracing cold, she went back inside to have some breakfast and another cup of tea. Then, and only then, would she start work. She had stayed up the night before last to make the heart, but she had not fired it yet and a fresh look might reveal it to be hopeless. The rest of the design was relatively straightforward, but she didn't want to skimp on its finish either, and so the quicker she got to work the better.

She fed the fire before sitting down at her work table and then she opened up the small pouch where she had stored the clay heart. Her own heart was pounding as she laid it in front of her. It wasn't finished, she could see that straight away, but it was good. Her whole being lifted; it was everything she had hoped for and, as she surveyed it critically, she could see exactly what else was needed to make it perfect. She thrust aside the other thoughts in her head and, with a single-minded focus, picked up a small metal tool and set to work.

Two hours went by before she even moved but, at the end of that time, she straightened, lifting her hands clear of the clay and took a deep breath. The heart was intricate, and it had taken several painstaking attempts to get everything fixed in such a way that firing the clay would strengthen the design and not weaken it. She would obviously have to check everything over again very carefully once it was fired, but for now at least she had something she could work with.

She looked again at the messages Nick had sent, and the sketches she had made when the idea had first come to her. She really had no idea whether it would be a suitable gift or not, only Nick's say-so that he liked it. But somehow, it felt right. She knew nothing about his girlfriend, not even her name, but she had a vision in her head of a petite redhead, with alabaster skin just like Nick had described, and a delicately formed face, just like the flowers she so loved. If any of that were true, then Daisy's design would look beautiful. If not, then at least Nick had cared enough to try to make her gift something special, and maybe that was all it took to make it the perfect present. Daisy certainly thought so.

It was as she was rolling out the clay for the second part of the design that her mobile rang. Not a number she recognised, she was on the verge of ignoring it when curiosity got the better of her. Her mobile never rang. Why would it, when there was no one to call her?

Fumbling the buttons with mucky fingers she managed to connect the call, fully expecting to hear the rehearsed lines of a cold caller. Instead, she recognised the voice straight away.

'Flora!' she exclaimed. 'How are you?'

'Busy, but good busy. In fact, very good,' came the reply. 'Are you at work?'

'No, a day off. Why? Is everything all right?'

'Yes... I was just wondering if you were okay to talk for a minute? And if you were sitting down?' Daisy could hear the smile in her voice.

'Go on…' she replied, wondering what on earth was coming next.

'Good, because I don't suppose you know of a place called The Castle, do you? It's real name is Ravenswick Hall but—'

'What, the swanky wedding place? What self-respecting romantic hasn't heard of it?' She broke off, not wanting to think of anything to do with weddings or romance or relationships or anything that might lead her back to Kit. 'Anyway, go on, sorry, I interrupted you.'

'Well, there's no reason why you would know this, but Hope Blooms supply the hotel with flowers, particularly for weddings. Their events manager and I have become quite good friends over the last six months and she popped in yesterday for a cup of tea on her way home. She wanted to talk about their plans for the new year.'

'Okay…' Daisy still had no idea where this was leading.

'And so, while we were chatting and dunking custard creams, she caught sight of the sketches you had left with me and asked me what they were. I showed her the couple of pieces of jewellery you left and explained who you were, and what you did – she'd heard of Buchanans of course – and well, the upshot is that their plans for the new year include a new bridal room in which they will showcase items from local businesses. She'd like to offer you a space for jewellery.'

Daisy's heart nearly leaped clean out of her chest, but then almost immediately it sank again. 'Oh, but I don't know if that's even going to be possible,' she said. 'It's lovely of her of course, but not really my decision and I have no idea who's going to be running Buchanans yet, or what plans they have, so I—'

'Daisy,' said Flora patiently. 'I don't mean Buchanans, I mean you. Kate would like to feature *your* designs.'

'Wha… what?'

'She absolutely loved them. In fact, she thought they were the nicest thing she had seen in a long time and she also thinks her brides would go for them, big time. Daisy… Are you still there?'

'Yes, I'm here,' she replied faintly. 'Sorry, I just can't quite believe it. She'd rather have my designs over Buchanans, at The Castle?'

'That's what she said. And Kate is pretty decisive, I don't think there's any doubt in her mind.'

Maybe so, but there was plenty in Daisy's. There was a rising sense of excitement deep within her that she would have loved to give free rein to, but this was serious stuff. This wasn't just making the odd piece of jewellery, this was supplying the county's most popular wedding venue, something her competitors would give their eye teeth for. If Daisy couldn't come up with the goods then there would be a whole queue of people waiting to step into her shoes.

She realised she'd been quiet for a little too long. 'Sorry, Flora… I'm just, speechless, actually. It's the most amazing news I think I've ever had, but I'm not sure it's something I can do. I have no stock, nothing I can offer for sale and, apart from the couple of designs I've shown you, nothing to show The Castle either.' She bit her lip. 'I really don't think I can do this…'

'Daisy, a very wise man who lives not a million miles from here once said that there's nothing wrong with fear, it's the place where courage is born, and I think he's right, don't you?'

Daisy smiled. 'Amos,' she murmured. It was just the kind of thing he would say.

'Yes,' said Flora. 'And would it also help you to know that when I first went to see Kate about going into partnership with them, I hadn't even grown any flowers, not a single one? I had a pad of paper, a head full of ideas and the rest I rather rashly made up on the spot. But the wonderful thing about Kate is that she can spot potential. She isn't necessarily looking for the finished article, just the possibility... So, I know this is terrifying and right now you can't think straight, but don't discount it. Have a chat with Kate and let *her* convince you that you can do this.'

Daisy nodded. It made sense, but it was still... 'How do we do this? Do I get in touch with her, or the other way around?'

'She asked if you could contact her, but not to worry until the new year, she's flat out busy as you can imagine – it's wall-to-wall parties at The Castle and they won't be looking to open up this new venture until early spring. That should give you plenty of time to have a think and make a few plans.' Flora paused for a moment. 'And while you're at it, have a think about designing some more jewellery to go with my prints, because that is definitely something we should do. I can't decide whether we should have them as prints, or greetings cards, both probably.'

There was a sudden intake of breath. 'Listen, Daisy, I'm sorry, I've got to run, I have a bride coming to see me in ten minutes, but make sure you let me know when Grace's present is finished, I can't wait to see it!'

Daisy was still holding the phone in her hand several minutes later, staring into the fire in a daze. She slowly replaced it on the table. This was madness. Stuff like this didn't happen to her.

She was getting carried away by the dream of it all, that's all this was – the lure of Christmas magic, the trips out, the experiencing of new things, more than she had ever done over the last few years. Even the possibility of a relationship with Kit that went somewhere beyond friendship. All these things had made her think she was something she was not. For goodness' sake, she had never had one single commission, let alone two. The chances were that once Christmas was over, several years would go by again before anything similar happened. It was time to get real. She had bills to pay, food to buy and none of that would happen by selling the odd bit of jewellery every now and again. Whichever way she looked at it she needed her income from Buchanans to survive, just as she had for the last eight years, and if that meant she would have to work with Lawrence, at least in the interim until she could find another job, then so be it.

The clay was still in its wrapper, but she needed to get a move on and she pulled it towards her, unfurling it from its protective cover. She had lost her focus now but, taking a deep breath, she pushed everything else from her mind save what she needed to achieve. There would be plenty of time to ruminate later, once she had finished. She had a feeling she would be pounding the towpath quite a bit over the next few days.

She took a break for lunch and another quick one around five when she went for a walk to clear her head but, other than that, she worked solidly through the day. At just gone eleven at night, she rose from the table, cold and stiff. The fire had long since died and she had been so intent on her work that she hadn't even moved to collect a cardigan to keep herself warm. But she didn't care, she was finished.

Stretching out her arms and legs, she did a quick tour of the room to get her circulation going again and then she approached her work table, slowly and with a critical eye. The piece had surpassed all her expectations. There had been a moment after firing the heart when she'd thought she'd got it all wrong. It was too fussy, too intricate in parts and looked dull and lifeless. But she'd persevered, she'd had no choice, and, slowly, as she'd polished, its beauty had been revealed. She held her breath and picked up the heart, taking care not to taint its gleam with her fingers, and it nestled in the palm of her hand. It spoke of love, and that was all Daisy wanted.

Laying it down carefully on a soft cloth, she pulled her laptop towards her and began to type a quick message.

To NickCarr1:

Hi Nick,

Sorry it's so late but I have just finished! I'll post it tomorrow and keep everything crossed it gets to you in time... Polishing took a lot longer than I thought, and well, you'll see why. I hope I have given you everything you wished for.

Yours, Daisy.

Sunday 22nd December

Three shopping days until Christmas

'Is everything okay?' Amos's face was full of concern.

Daisy opened the door wider and stood back to let him in, trying to rearrange her face into a bright smile as she did so.

'Yes, I'm fine,' she replied. 'I'm just a little tired, that's all. Come on in.' She held out her arms for his coat.

'Flora won't be long,' he said. 'But for obvious reasons we arranged to come separately. I'm supposedly on an errand for Ned because Flora has had to pop out to one of her brides for some last-minute emergency.' He gave Daisy a long look as soon as he'd removed his jacket. 'You do look tired though. I hope all this extra work hasn't been too much?'

But it wasn't that which had caused Daisy's tiredness, or it wasn't the sole cause of it anyway.

'No, no, it's been fine. Actually, it's given me something to occupy my evenings, so I've been very grateful,' she replied. 'It's been a bit of a tough week for various reasons.' She turned to hang up his coat. 'However, it's nearly Christmas so enough about that.' She smiled. 'I can't wait to show you Grace's present.'

And at that a welling excitement began to grow. It had taken her until about eight o'clock last night to finish it, threading all the separate elements together and finally seeing if her design on paper would look the way she wanted it to. She had cried when she saw it.

Amos smiled but he was still looking at her intently. 'Is it the competition?' he asked. 'It must be getting quite intense now we're so close to Christmas.'

She pulled a face. 'Pretty much... I've had a bit of a falling-out with Kit because of it, but it's a long story.' She really didn't want to talk about it.

'Then why don't you tell me while we wait for Flora?' said Amos, his expression suggesting that he wouldn't take no for an answer. 'Because I've a horrible feeling I might be to blame.'

'You do? Well, I don't see how...' She led him through into the sitting room where she had already laid out a tray ready for tea. 'Have a seat, Amos.'

She added hot water to the teapot and gave its contents a stir, but when she turned back to ask Amos if he would like a cup, she was surprised to find him still standing, an anguished look on his face.

'May I ask what you and Kit have fallen out over?' he began.

Daisy faltered. She had thought endlessly about whether she had simply got on her high horse about the whole issue and overreacted, but she hadn't, it was the principle of the thing at stake. If none of them could be honest, then what was the point of the whole competition? Bea trusted her – that more than anything was what was important – and on it hung everything else. She'd had no choice but to take Kit to task. But, aside from that, what really hurt was the thought that he had used her.

'I told you when I first came to your house why Buchanans were not to know about my jewellery-making, and the competition only complicated that further. But Kit and I got talking over dinner the other night and I stupidly confided a few things in him, one of which was what I've been doing in my spare time. I probably shouldn't have mentioned anything at all but, oh Amos, it was such a relief to talk about it. And Kit was really encouraging too… I know why now, of course, seeing as he let slip that he knew about my jewellery-making the whole time.' She dropped her head a little. 'He was cheating all along, trying to get close to me so he could wheedle out of me what I'd been working on. It all went a bit pear-shaped after that.'

'Yes, I see,' said Amos quietly. 'And it's as I thought.' He drew in breath. 'I rather think I owe you an apology, Daisy, because it was me who told Kit about your jewellery in the first place.'

'Yes, I know, in the shop, the day after I'd been on the wreath-making course. But you weren't to know, Amos, and besides, it wasn't that. Kit asked me about it then and I just made light of it, saying I made clay-bead necklaces. He seemed to accept what I said and we didn't speak any more about it, but this time it was different. He seemed to know *exactly* what I'd been doing.'

Amos looked stricken. 'And you and Kit…?' He left the sentence dangling.

'Yes, me and Kit,' echoed Daisy. 'Well, not any more. I thought there might have been but…'

'And this dinner you shared with Kit, where was this? At a restaurant? Or at his wondrous wooden house in the woods?'

Daisy's eyes widened in shock. 'You know where he lives?'

Amos nodded sadly. 'I do. Which is why I hoped that you and he might find a little spark of romance. You're so alike, it's a wonder you've never seen it before. I met him one day while I was out walking, and listening to him was like hearing him finish your sentences. I'd only met him briefly before then but...' He trailed off, indicating the sofa. 'I think I might sit down after all. Maybe you should join me.'

He rubbed a hand over his face. 'Do you remember when I first met you that day in the shop?'

How could Daisy have forgotten? It was the day when her whole world had seemed to change. She nodded.

'And then the day after, on the course, you mentioned Kit, not in the most flattering terms as I recall.' He smiled. 'But I'd spotted something that first day, not only the title of the book he'd been reading, as I think I remarked to you, but also the way he looked at you. It reminded me of the way I look at Grace.'

He held her look for a moment. 'But it was the book which interested me really, a rather unusual title for a sales assistant to be reading, I thought. Something on the design and installation of wind turbines and water pumps. It caught my attention because I used to be a builder, Daisy – had my own company building houses – and so it seemed only natural when I bumped into him a second time, while out walking one day, to ask him about it. The result was a visit to his house and a quite lengthy conversation, which started off about the marvel of the setting I found myself in, and then, as these things do, traversed a multitude of subjects. One of which was the Christmas present that you were making for Grace. I'm so sorry, Daisy. I had no idea at the time that the fact you made jewellery was a secret.'

Her mouth dropped open in shock. It really was that simple.

She looked up at Amos's apologetic face, thinking about his words. There was a train of thought she was trying to catch, because if it really was that simple then why— A knock at the door interrupted her musings and her thoughts scattered. Flora was here. She shot a look at Amos as a sudden wave of nervous excitement gripped her.

Flora's cheeks were flushed as Daisy ushered her in. 'I'm so sorry I'm late. You wouldn't believe it – I actually did get a call from a panicked bride.' She stopped and looked around her. 'Blimey, Daisy, this place is gorgeous. And how perfect, given what you do.' She smiled at Amos. 'So?' Her eyebrows were raised.

He grinned at her. 'I haven't seen it yet,' he replied. 'We were waiting for you.'

There was a weight of expectation in the room as looks were exchanged and Daisy didn't know what to say. Should she try and explain her thinking behind the piece before she showed it to them? Or suggest that all was not lost and she still had time to make alterations in case they didn't like it? In the end she did none of those things, but beckoned them over to her work table, which had been cleared of clutter. A rectangular space had been left in the centre which she had covered with a cloth and, underneath it, Grace's necklace waited to be revealed. She suddenly felt very hot.

Gently, Daisy lifted the covering, holding her breath, avoiding Amos's eyes as she waited for a reaction. The seconds ticked by, the silence in the room growing incrementally, but still Amos had not said a word. Nor had he moved. A few more moments passed and, unable to stand it any longer, Daisy finally looked at him. His eyes were glued to the necklace and it was only the movement of his eyelids that revealed him to be drinking in the detail. A slow smile spread upwards and, at the point when she didn't think it could grow any bigger, he turned to her, his eyes shining with emotion.

'Daisy…' He bit his lip, and then held a hand to his mouth, laughing at his lack of self-control as a tear rolled down his cheek. 'I don't think

I've ever told you how much I love Grace,' he said. 'But that... that tells me you knew all along.'

He held out his arms and as Daisy moved towards him he pulled her into a huge bear-like hug which enveloped her. 'Thank you,' he said simply. With a final squeeze he released her, holding out a trembling hand. 'May I hold it?' he asked.

Daisy sniffed. Her own cheeks were wet, and she dashed her palm against them. How ridiculous. But yet it wasn't, standing here with these wonderful people, it wasn't ridiculous at all. She nodded and, reaching out, placed the necklace gently in Amos's outstretched hand.

A series of three fine silver wires, each hung successively lower than the last, were joined at uneven intervals by tiny silver beads that themselves glistened like dewdrops on a spider's web. But in the spaces between the beads Daisy had wired all the things which made Grace who she was: a tiny silver bee for her industry and wisdom, a rosebud for her beauty and the love she shared with Amos, an ivy leaf for friendship, a dove for the peace she brought to everyone around her and, finally, a shining crescent moon, not only the symbol for the silver from which the necklace was wrought, but for Grace herself. Each of the items was delicate, neither overpowering its neighbour. Strung from the finest silver wire, they seemed to float in the space that surrounded them.

'Oh, Amos...' It was the first time Flora had spoken and she laid a hand over his as he gazed at the necklace it still held. 'It's perfect. Just perfect. I don't know how you did it, Daisy, but Grace is going to absolutely adore this.' She looked up at Amos and grinned. 'Good job Ned's already given me the best present I could ever wish for, or he could be in a lot of trouble right now.'

Daisy looked at the expression on her face, shining with happiness for Amos. 'Why, what did Ned get you?' she asked, wondering why Daisy had received her gift early.

'Well, admittedly it was a fair few months ago now, but Ned gave me my life back. And then he gave me my flowers. I'd say he's got the whole present thing covered for a few more years yet.'

Daisy nodded and smiled at her new friend. Because that was just the kind of thing Flora would say. And that was perfect too.

'Would you like to see it on?' Daisy asked Amos. 'Flora can be our model, can't you?' Daisy had wondered what it would feel like nestled against her own skin. And she had almost tried it on in the moments after it was finished, but then she'd stopped herself. It wasn't hers and it wouldn't have been right to wear it.

Amos nodded enthusiastically but he didn't need to, Flora was already pulling her jumper off over her head. Underneath she wore a plain scooped-neck tee shirt; it would show off the necklace beautifully. She gathered her thick hair into a bunch and held it away from her neck, so that Amos could fasten the necklace, albeit with shaking hands.

Flora stood back and lowered her hair, pushing it back over her shoulders. She stood up tall, stretching her neck. 'It feels wonderful,' she said. 'Like someone is just lightly touching my skin with their fingertips.' Daisy could see she was itching to explore it with her own fingers, but she held back, not wanting to spoil the effect for Amos.

'Jewellery should speak only words of love… That's what you said, Daisy, wasn't it? But this, this is even better, because these words aren't spoken, they are whispered gently like a lover's sigh…'

Flora snorted. 'Oh, for goodness' sake, Amos, will you stop?' She dabbed at her eyes. 'Or my mascara will be halfway down my face.'

But she grinned at him, and then at Daisy and, in the look that passed between them, was the acknowledgement that he was right.

*

It was the anticlimax, Daisy knew that, but by three o'clock she was pounding the towpath again, trying to rid herself of the restless feeling that had plagued her ever since Flora and Amos had left. Their reaction had been everything she could have wished for but now that the elation had died down, together with the sheer relief that it was all okay, her thoughts turned increasingly to the coming days.

She hadn't heard from Nick yet, nor had she expected to. Her parcel had only been sent on Thursday, and not to his home address, but to the house of his girlfriend's parents near Chester where he would be staying once he was back from his last trip before Christmas. She didn't suppose he would even see it until Christmas Eve. So now she was reduced to playing a waiting game. Not only for his response, but also for the day after tomorrow when Buchanan's fate was decided, and hers along with it. It induced a horrible feeling of helplessness.

The canal was quiet, but the light was already beginning to go and Daisy wasn't surprised. This close to Christmas people were either busy or enjoying a quiet afternoon by the fire in readiness for the mad rush to come. There was now so little time left in which to say something to Kit. But it was unlikely she would get the chance even if she could find the words.

She was on her way back home when she saw Robin clambering from his boat. He was muffled against the cold just as she was, clutching a brightly wrapped package to his chest.

'Land ahoy,' he called. 'I was just coming to see you.'

She grinned. 'Were you? Although I'm not sure you can say "Land ahoy" when you're on solid ground too.'

'Good point. In that case, Happy Christmas, Daisy.' He thrust out the present towards her. 'I know it's earlier than we usually exchange gifts, but I sent my manuscript off to my editor this morning, so I'm a free man and heading to my parents first thing in the morning instead of Christmas Eve.'

'Ah… well then you'd better come back to the cottage with me a minute so I can get your present. I'd hate you to miss out.'

He grinned and fell into step beside her. 'I'll confess I hadn't a clue what to get you this year, but I have it on good authority that you'll like those.'

'Oh?'

'Yes, I bumped into your friend – boyfriend? – the other evening when I was out. Taking the air, as I like to call it, but what is actually one last cigarette before bed, and we got talking. Fascinating chap, I approve.'

Daisy stared at him. There were several things wrong with that statement. 'Hang on a minute… When was this, Robin? And I don't have a boyfriend. What did he look like?'

Robin scratched the end of his nose. 'Erm, tall, dark and handsome? No, let me think… Tall, yes, dark… hard to see at night, but dark-ish… and handsome? Not my cup of tea, obviously, but maybe… friendly looking anyway, with a very open face… and kind of…' He motioned to his forehead. 'A floppy hair thing going on.'

It can only have been Kit. 'When was this?' she asked again.

'Wednesday, I think… yes, definitely Wednesday, but it was late. Your light was still on though.' He paused for a moment. 'I did do the concerned citizen thing because he was stopped by your path, but he seemed to know where he was going. And once I got talking to him it was obvious that he knew you, so I thought it must be okay.'

Daisy gave him a reassuring smile. 'Yes, it's fine. I know who it was. Sorry, I forgot he'd been round for a minute. He comes out walking this way quite a bit and he popped in when he saw my light was on. Bit embarrassing actually, he was busting for a wee.' The lie came easily; she had no wish to make Robin anxious.

Robin laughed. 'God, and I kept him talking for ages. Like I said though, interesting chap. He didn't have a torch with him and, when I commented on it, he said he always walked by moonlight. We got talking about the stars.'

It was definitely Kit.

They had reached her cottage and Daisy pushed open the door. 'Hang on and I'll go and get your pressie,' she said.

She returned moments later and held out the package. 'They're, well, I bet you can guess.'

'Aye, notebooks,' Robin said, a broad smile on his face. 'Same as always, but what would I do without you, Daisy?' It had become a bit of a standing joke between them as Daisy had bought him notebooks ever since she found out he was a writer.

He leaned forward to give her cheek a kiss. 'Well, Happy Christmas. I hope you have a good one.'

'You too, Robin.' She was still clutching her gift from him and she gave it a gentle shake. 'Intriguing...' she said. 'Thank you.'

She watched as he made his way back down the path, giving a farewell wave before shutting the door. She stared at the present, the present that clearly Kit had offered advice over. She couldn't... could she? No, she shook her head. It wasn't Christmas yet and she never opened presents early. She took it through into the sitting room and placed it under the tree.

The walk hadn't exactly chased Kit from her mind but the urgency to think about him at least had lessened as other thoughts crept in too. Now though, he was right back, centre stage. There was something… Ever since Amos had revealed that it was he who had inadvertently told Kit about her jewellery, something had been gnawing at her. That should have made everything simple, but somehow it hadn't and she couldn't work out why. But as she straightened, it came to her.

She had accepted what Amos had said to her, why wouldn't she? He had no reason to lie. It was a simple mistake; unfortunate, but not the end of the world. It explained perfectly how Kit had found out about her jewellery, and yet Kit had chosen not to tell her how it had come about. It was the one thing that she could have understood, the one thing that could have made things right between them. But instead he had refused to tell her how he knew. And that she just couldn't understand.

But that wasn't the only thing, because now she knew that on the night she had finished making the first of her Christmas gifts, Kit had been walking the towpath outside her cottage. He had been standing on her path talking to Robin, and yet she had never known he was there. So why was he? But she already knew the answer. Kit had been there because he had been checking on her, making sure she was safe. She stared at Robin's present for a moment before ripping off the bright wrapping. The sob burst from her lips even before she glimpsed the pastel colours inside, before she even smelled the distinctive aroma. She knew exactly what it was. A box of macarons. How could she ever have thought Kit had cheated?

Tuesday 24th December

One shopping day until Christmas

The man beamed at Daisy. 'I can't thank you enough. You've been an absolute lifesaver.'

She smiled back. 'You're very welcome,' she replied. 'And I'm sure your wife will love her present. Happy Christmas.' She held the shop door open, giving a little wave as the man disappeared from sight.

'Now that *was* cutting it fine,' said Bertie. 'And skilfully done, Daisy,' he added.

'Although to be fair, given the lateness of the hour, he probably would have bought anything.' Lawrence's smile was tight.

She frowned. 'Which was exactly why I didn't just sell him anything,' she replied. 'Because he would have left the shop with a nasty taste in his mouth, knowing he'd just been fleeced and would never come back.'

Kit moved to stand beside her and turned the sign on the door to closed. 'She has a point, Lawrence,' he said breezily.

Lawrence scowled.

'Children, children…' said Bea, tutting in mock consternation. 'Today of all days, let's find a little Christmas spirit.'

The atmosphere in the shop suddenly became serious. It was two o'clock and all morning they had been busy, although mostly with folks popping in to wish them the compliments of the season rather than last-minute customers. It was tradition at Buchanans to serve mulled wine and refreshments during the morning until the shop closed early afternoon. Afterwards Bea would say a few words, thank everyone for another, hopefully, successful year, and present her Christmas gift to Daisy. There would be more wine, which Daisy never drank, and party food, which Daisy rarely ate, but it never mattered. Unlike the majority of shops, Buchanans didn't open on Boxing Day, or the two days following that, so there were always four days off to be savoured and to Daisy it had always felt like the end of term before the long summer holidays, full of delicious anticipation for the days ahead.

Today, however, was obviously rather different from the norm and that in itself made Daisy feel edgy and out of sorts. Christmas Eve at Buchanans had been part of her festive-season traditions for a very long time and she hated having this taken away from her. It was as if someone had died. Kit and Bertie had done their best to keep things light-hearted, even though Kit must have been feeling dreadful too, but Lawrence had spent most of the morning seemingly inspecting things. Whether he found them to be lacking in something, Daisy didn't care. She just wished he wasn't there. She hadn't heard from Nick either, and that only made things worse. Lost in thought, it took a moment for her to realise that Bea was speaking again.

'Goodness,' she said. 'You all look like you're waiting to hear if the patient is dead or alive.'

'Look, can we just get this over with,' replied Lawrence. 'It's pointless trying to pretend that there's anything nice about all this. So why don't we all cut the fake bonhomie and seasonal good cheer and get down to business. We all know it's the end of an era, Mother, so let's find out who lives or dies.'

Daisy swallowed. There was an element of truth in what Lawrence had said, but why did he always have to be so confrontational? She had expected Bea to become somewhat flustered by his remark, but she was surprised at the force with which Bea's reply came out.

'You really haven't learned a thing, have you?' she said, pinning him with a ferocious stare. 'This is not about endings at all, Lawrence, but about beginnings.' She narrowed her eyes. 'And I am disappointed, but sadly not surprised, that you haven't figured that out yet.'

What on earth did Bea mean? Daisy shot a look at Lawrence, who looked like he was chewing a live wire, and then glanced at Kit, who was actually smiling and, worse, staring straight at her. She looked away, dropping her eyes to the floor, her cheeks aflame. Oh, this was horrible.

'Perhaps we had better, erm, make a start,' suggested Bertie. 'It is a little nerve-wracking, and poor Daisy looks like she might pass out.'

'I agree,' replied Bea, smiling at Daisy with twinkling eyes. 'But we will do this with dignity and grace, or not at all. So, let's do as we always have and drink a toast to the year and have a little celebration of our efforts and achievements.'

She led the way through into the back room, where she had been disappearing all morning to lay out plates of food. Daisy didn't think she could eat a thing.

'Daisy,' said Kit quietly. 'Can I get you something? There's some non-alcoholic mulled wine.'

She cleared her throat, her mouth suddenly dry. 'I might just have some water, if that's okay.' But she was touched that he had acknowledged she didn't drink alcohol.

'And something to eat?' Bertie was hovering with a plate. 'I know you like these.'

She glanced at his offering, eyes widening when she saw what he had put together for her. The plate was filled with the tiny pastries she had eaten at the Altitude Bar, some of the pretzels, and spiced cashews too. Someone, and she suspected she knew who, had also added some macarons to the plate. She gave a weak smile and took it, trying to remind herself that she liked these things.

A few minutes later, glasses were charged and an expectant hush descended once more.

'Well, another year is almost over,' said Bea. 'And another Christmas at Buchanans has also come to an end. I know you have all the figures, Bertie, and it's not been as bad a year as I feared, despite certain challenges faced by the retail industry in general. However, I don't think I'd be telling you anything you didn't already know if I said that things will need to change at Buchanans if it is to survive. And now the time has come to find out how. Before we start with the judging of the competition though, I would just like to say my own thank you to Daisy, for everything you have done to put Buchanans first. Your loyalty and devotion to me and Buchanans has never been in question and without that and your unstinting hard work, I truly don't believe we would be in the position we are in now.' She raised her glass. 'To Daisy, may you have the happiest of Christmases...'

She blushed, just as she always did. Bea's speech hardly ever varied, the odd word here or there, but essentially it was the same every Christmas Eve. But she meant it and Daisy was always incredibly grateful. She received Bea's warm hug gladly, knowing that it was likely to be one of the last she received from her. She was just about to pull away, when Bea gripped both her arms and gave her another squeeze. Her eyes were shining as she laid a hand against Daisy's cheek.

'Darling girl,' she said, and it was so quick, Daisy almost missed it, but there was no mistaking the fondness of the look in Bea's eye. It made her feel quite emotional.

Releasing her, Bea returned to the table where the food had been laid out, beside which stood a much smaller table covered with the traditional Buchanans' blue velvet cloth.

'Now, when it is your turn, would you three boys like to place the gifts you have chosen for Daisy on here and I shall open them. As eldest, Lawrence, perhaps you would like to go first. Oh, I can't wait to see them!' She beamed at them all and, despite herself, Daisy felt a frisson of excitement. Bea's mood was infectious.

Lawrence stepped forward, flashing Daisy a look that was a mixture of many things – triumph mostly, but also a warning. He was expecting to be her boss soon and it was a reminder that he would always have the last word. A pulse began to beat in her neck.

His gift was wrapped in a flat square box which she recognised as the same shape as one of their own. Did that mean it was an item from the shop? It couldn't be though, surely she would have known if something was missing? It seemed to take Bea an inordinate amount of time to undo the tape holding the paper closed, but eventually she pulled out the box, dropping the paper onto the floor in her haste. Bea hugged it to her for a moment and then, holding it inches from her face, she lifted the lid and peered inside. Her sharp intake of breath was distinctly audible in the silent room. Eyes wide, she lowered the box.

'Lawrence,' she said. 'I don't know what to say. This is beautiful, truly stunning.'

Daisy wanted to wrench the box from Bea's hands to have a look and she was acutely aware of Kit's eyes on her.

With trembling hands, Bea took what appeared to be a photograph from the box and held it up. 'Lawrence, tell me why you chose this. What's it all about?'

He strode forward and, taking the picture from his mother, turned it around so that they could all see it. Bea was right, it was incredible.

'This is obviously an artist's impression. Although actually it's rather more than that, as I had my design digitally rendered in 3D so you could appreciate it better. There would have been no time to make an object as delicate or intricate as this given the time frame, but you'll find my costings in the box underneath the satin. It comes in at exactly five thousand pounds, although to really create it the way I imagined it, the cost would be somewhere closer to fifteen thousand. I think that you can see how that would be worth it.'

The image showed a series of interlocking flower heads, each with six petals. The centre to each flower was formed from a gemstone, as were the individual petals, using two different gems in alternating colours. Each flower was also different from the other. The flower heads themselves were fused together so that they only just touched and the whole lot was suspended from a gold chain attached to the two outermost flowers. The settings alone would have been incredibly difficult to fix and the sheer variety of colours and stones was astonishing. It was, however, probably the least likely piece of jewellery Daisy would ever choose to wear. It was too colourful, far too brash and it drew attention to itself like a Belisha beacon.

'Good God!' It was Bertie speaking. 'Are you sure you mean fifteen thousand? More like thirty.'

'It's whatever your budget will allow for,' replied Lawrence. 'In my example I've used various types of pretty, but fairly ordinary quartz, to keep the cost down a little, not precious stones at all. But I think you'll agree, it's the effect that is mesmerising. The design is what's important, and what makes it so utterly perfect for Daisy.'

Bea was nodding. She looked ecstatic. 'But what makes it so perfect, Lawrence? Why is Daisy going to love this?'

He looked momentarily taken aback. 'Well, the flowers are like daisies, aren't they? And that's her name… She likes flowers, and all the colours too, bright ones, and I know she likes big bold statement pieces.'

'I rather thought Daisy preferred more muted colours,' said Bea, slowly, as if thinking. Daisy looked down at her navy skirt and tried to hide her smirk. Monique had done her job well.

'No, definitely bright colours. I know that for a fact.' He lifted his head a little, defying anyone to argue with him.

Bea grinned at Daisy. 'Exceptional,' she said. 'Well done, Lawrence.'

Daisy's heart plummeted. How could Bea just accept what he said? She knew Daisy better than that, surely? But then she looked at Lawrence's design again. It was an exquisite piece of work. Not for her, for a million and one reasons, but she had to acknowledge the skill in the design, however misplaced. She didn't dare even look at Kit.

Bea clasped her hands together in delight. 'Now then, Bertie. Let's see what you've come up with.'

It was all a pretence. Following Bertie's shock announcement that he was pulling out of the competition, they had debated long and hard whether or not to tell Lawrence. Bea knew of course, she had to. Not least of all because Bertie didn't want it to come as a surprise to her on the final day, but also, Daisy suspected, because he wanted his mother's blessing.

Bertie put one hand into the inner pocket of his jacket and pulled out a long box which gave an audible rattle as he passed it to his mother.

'Careful,' he warned. 'It's very delicate.'

Bea took the box and eased off the bow. She was grinning broadly. Whether she knew what was in the box or not Daisy didn't know, but she was doing a good job of keeping the suspense going. The paper came next, inch by inch, until, when she was almost there, she gave a little excited whoop and tore the remaining wrapping away. She held the box to her so that no one else could see and peeped inside.

'Oh, Bertie!' She burst out laughing. 'I love it!'

And then she held up Bertie's gift; a string of brightly painted pasta tubes strung together. The sort of necklace that every child learned to make at playschool.

Bertie turned to Kit, who gave him a high five.

Lawrence's face was a mixture of so many things, Daisy almost laughed out loud herself. He looked shocked, hugely relieved, triumphant, but also incredibly irritated.

'Would someone like to explain to me what's going on, as you all seem to be in on Bertie's little charade.'

Bertie put his hand over his heart. 'Whatever do you mean, Lawrence? Is this not the most perfect gift for Daisy?'

Bea tutted. 'Bertie, stop being so naughty. Explain to Lawrence what it is you've decided to do.'

He grinned. 'Well, in a nutshell I've quit the competition.' He rolled his eyes. 'And yes, Lawrence, that does now mean you have a fifty-fifty shot… The longer version of events is that I've done what I suspect Mum wanted all along, which is to work out what I wanted from my life and then go and do something about it. So, I'm going into business with Luka.'

Lawrence's head was swivelling from Bertie to his mum, to Kit and back again. 'You're doing what?'

'Going into business with Luka.'

'Yes, I heard what you said, Bertie, I'm not deaf. But I thought you wanted to run Buchanans. If only to see me ousted from the top spot. Well, that is a turn-up for the books.'

'Not everything is about you, Lawrence,' retorted Bertie. 'I've done what's right for me.'

'And you're going to run a what? A bar…?'

'If that's what you want to call it, yes. I won't even bother to explain. But I think we both know that Luka does rather more than run a bar.'

Lawrence made a dismissive noise. 'Call it what you like. It still sounds like you're going to be serving people all your life.'

Daisy couldn't hold her tongue any longer. 'No, Lawrence. Bertie is going to do what he excels at, which is making people feel special. I can't think of anything more worthwhile.'

He glared at her, but she no longer cared.

'So you all knew…?' said Lawrence. 'Yes, of course you did. Well, you're out of the competition, Bertie, and that's all that matters to me.'

'Yes, you've made that quite clear,' Bertie replied, giving Daisy a warm smile. 'But although you may have heard what I said, Lawrence, you didn't listen. Such a shame you haven't worked out yet what this has all been about.'

Daisy saw the flicker of confusion cross Lawrence's face, but she knew he would never admit to curiosity.

'Shall I tell you? You see, when I said that I thought it's what Mum wanted me to do all along, what I meant was more that this competition was never just about who gets to run Buchanans, but rather who had it within themselves to face up to who they really are.

And stand up for what they believe in. In fact, very cunning, Mum, very cunning indeed. And getting Daisy to help… stroke of pure genius.' He grinned. 'I probably shouldn't say any more, but I just wanted to add my own very personal thank you to Daisy. If it hadn't been for you, I never would have figured out my own part to play. I just hope I'm right about everything else.'

This time it was Daisy's turn to look confused. She knew that Bea had been smart where Lawrence was concerned, guessing quite rightly that he would try and get Monique to help him, but was what Monique had said also true: that the competition had been designed so that the brothers themselves chose the winner, and not Bea? But how could that be so?

Lawrence sighed. 'Can we please get on? I'm happy for you, Bertie. If that's what you want to do with your life, then that's great. But you are now out of the competition and there are still two people here for whom the outcome matters a great deal.'

'Three,' said Kit.

'I'm sorry?'

'You said two, but there are three people here for whom the outcome matters a great deal.'

Lawrence flashed Daisy a tight smile. 'Yes, quite.'

Bea cleared her throat. 'I'd just like to add that I am extraordinarily pleased with your decision, Bertie. This isn't the environment for you, and so I'm very happy that you've come to that conclusion. However, we do need to establish a winner, and thus far Kit has been incredibly patient. I think it's time he had his turn now.'

Kit went to retrieve his present from his coat pocket and Daisy smiled when she saw the long slender box wrapped in silver paper covered with ivy leaves. Despite their argument, she desperately wanted

Kit to win and for his sake there must be no trace of doubt on her face as he walked forward.

She couldn't begin to imagine the thoughts inside Kit's head. She knew he didn't want Lawrence to win but, taking into account everything Daisy knew about him, why on earth did he want to run Buchanans? She was sure now that Bertie was right – that the competition was as much about facing up to who you were, and what you really wanted from life, as it was about taking over the running of the family firm. And, out of all three of the brothers, Kit seemed to have worked this out years ago. So, whichever way she looked at it, she couldn't understand why he was even taking part.

And then a sudden thought came to her. Kit had built his own house for goodness' sake. He had designed and built every element of it. He was an expert at crafting things. God, why had she never realised that before? His design would be nothing less than outstanding, it had to be. Her heart was in her mouth as Bea began to open the box. Oh, please dear God, let him have chosen something amazing.

Underneath the wrapping, the box was made from cardboard, with a simple flap for a lid. It was tied with a piece of raffia to keep it closed until Bea was ready and, as she pulled the bow undone, Daisy craned her head to get a better look. Eventually it was free and Bea pulled back the lid to look inside.

The box was empty.

Tuesday 24th December

One shopping day until Christmas

Bertie groaned. Lawrence laughed. And Daisy nearly fainted.

Kit, on the other hand, stood with an expectant look on his face as he waited for Bea to comment. She looked just as shocked as Daisy was.

'I know you can be absent-minded, dear, but you appear to have wrapped an empty box.'

Kit smiled. 'Yes, I know it might seem that way, but it does, in fact, contain the perfect present that you asked for.'

Lawrence let out a frustrated sigh. 'Oh, spare us the half-baked philosophy, please.'

Kit ignored him, looking at Bea instead. She was still staring into the box as if she imagined something would suddenly appear. 'Perhaps you'd better explain,' she said.

'Three weeks ago, you challenged us to choose the perfect piece of jewellery for Daisy. And to also explain why our choice was the right one. You said that in the end that was the only criteria you would use to determine who wins.' He broke off to look enquiringly at Bea, who nodded. 'And so we all got into a fine old panic because none of us really knew Daisy all that well, myself included. But that was simple too, you said, we should just get to know her. I think we all know what came next.'

'Get on with it,' muttered Lawrence. 'For goodness' sake…'

Bea gave him a withering glare. 'Do go on, Kit.'

'And so, like Lawrence, and for a little while Bertie too, I wracked my brains trying to come up with something that Daisy would like. And I learned a lot about her. I learned that she likes to walk in the moonlight. And that she takes nothing from the world that she doesn't give back in some other form. I learned that she can tell which creatures have crossed a snowy field, and that if she stands in still places she can feel a world most people can't even conceive of. I learned that she is loyal with an integrity I thought was lost in the world, and I learned that even though she has few things, she still has everything she wants, and this makes her happy…' He trailed off, lifting his eyes to Daisy's. 'But I also learned that although she has an incredible ability to choose jewellery for other people, it's almost impossible to choose something for her because Daisy doesn't really like jewellery. She doesn't ever wear any, and so the perfect present is… none at all.'

There was stunned silence for several seconds as Daisy stood, her cheeks burning, conscious that every eye was on her.

Lawrence began a slow handclap. 'Oh, bravo, Kit. I have to hand it to you, you could follow Mother onto the stage. You could at least have had the guts to say you couldn't come up with anything. I've never heard such—'

'Shut up, Lawrence.' Bertie had taken a step towards him. 'For once in your life, just shut up!'

But Daisy scarcely heard him. All she could hear were Kit's words reverberating around her head. The warmth in his voice, the look in his eyes as he spoke them. And the way he described her, it sounded familiar somehow…

'That took an incredible amount of courage, Kit,' said Bea. 'Especially when there is so much at stake.'

And Kit smiled again. 'It's not courageous when there is nothing at stake for me. I don't want Buchanans, I never have. And I'm not the right person to run it. But I know someone who is.'

Lawrence looked like he was about to explode. 'But she's not even family!'

Daisy stared at him, trying to fathom his words. And then it hit her, just what Kit meant. Her eyes stretched wider. Had he just given up the business for *her*?

'What was the point of the competition, if not to find the person most suited to run Buchanans?' added Kit. 'But not as it is now. Instead, how it needs to be if it's ever going to survive. You know that, Mother, I know you do. Just as you know that Daisy is the only one who can read our customers like a book and have the integrity to sell them something that costs five pounds if that's the right thing to do. We need to diversify and none of us have the ability to lead us through that. None of us apart from Daisy, that is.'

'Oh, this is ridiculous,' cut in Lawrence. 'You can't just go changing the rules of the competition because you've got some sad crush on the poor girl. Daisy was never in the running for this and neither should she be. There is a clear choice, Mother – my design, which fulfils the brief perfectly, or Kit's nonentity.'

Daisy had been staring at the floor again, trying to work out how she felt, but now her head jerked up, anger flaring at Lawrence's words. She was about to say something when Kit laughed.

'You can make fun of me all you want, Lawrence, because I learned a long time ago that what's important to you is just to win, to have, whatever the cost, even if you don't really want something. And just like I worked that out, I also realised that there are some things I care about a very great deal. So where you're concerned, I pick my battles very carefully. So, if you're not prepared to accept that your design is a poor one, let me give you even more proof why Daisy should be at the helm.'

He crossed the room and collected another package from his jacket, handing it to Bea. 'Open it,' he said. 'I think you'll find it very enlightening.'

Daisy felt the colour drain from her face. How on earth had Kit got hold of that? 'I can explain,' she said quietly.

Kit was by her side in an instant, a hesitant hand held out in the space between them. 'No,' he said gently. 'Let me. You have nothing to explain, Daisy, and nothing to hide. Not any more.'

Kit waited until Bea had opened the box and taken out the silver bookmark that Daisy had made and posted days ago. A bookmark on which she had embellished an intricate design of entwined leaves and flowers, leaving a gap at the top where she had cut out the shape of a heart. Suspended within it was the pendant which she had created to nestle against the breast of Nick Carr's girlfriend.

Bea's intake of breath was audible. And then she looked up, straight at Daisy. 'You made this?' she asked, quite rightly deducing its creator.

'Yes, she did,' said Kit firmly. 'She made it for a customer who asked her to make him a present for his girlfriend and, with the aid of only the briefest of descriptions, Daisy made this. She had no idea it was really for me…' He gave her the softest of smiles. 'I even had to go to a friend's house in Chester to pick it up so that she wouldn't guess my identity.'

'I don't know what to say... except that it is utterly beautiful... unique. I'm sure I've never seen anything like it before.' Bea held the bookmark closer, studying the detail, her eyes widening as she spotted the tiny clasp at the top of the heart. 'This looks as if it comes away...?'

Daisy's voice was no more than a whisper. 'It does. The pendant is a separate piece to the bookmark, and I included the chain so that it can be worn. It should be in the box.'

Bea looked again, drawing out the finest of threads. 'Would you?' she asked. 'I'm scared I'll break it.'

Daisy took it from her with trembling hands and slipped the heart onto its chain before laying it across Bea's palm. The pendant was embellished with several tiny flowers – a rosebud curled around the bottom, its stem partially forming the point of the heart, while two daisies nestled between its leaves, every petal picked out in perfect relief.

Bea touched a gentle finger against a detail before looking back at Daisy. 'How long have you been making these?' she asked.

'A few years...'

'But you never told us...'

'No, I...'

Kit's hand slipped into hers. 'Daisy didn't think they were good enough. She thought you would all laugh.'

Sudden tears sprang into Bea's eyes. 'Oh, my darling girl...' Her hug was fierce, pulling her away from Kit, but he let her go, watching her with a gentle expression on his face as he nodded in affirmation of everything that Daisy was. Everything that she had become.

Bertie was next, holding out his hand in wonder, a broad grin on his face. 'I bloody knew it,' he said. 'I knew there was something special about you. That day when you skated on the ice, I saw just a glimpse of it, a lightness of spirit, something set free. That's what this is – imagination set free.'

'So that's it, is it? Just like that.' Lawrence's voice was harsh. 'We're just going to throw everything out the window because Daisy can make a bit of jewellery, are we? It's lovely, but could we possibly get back to the business in hand, and the small matter of who should be running your business, Mother.'

'I rather thought that's exactly what we were doing,' Bea replied, archly.

'Well as far as I'm concerned this doesn't change anything and—'

Bertie cut across him. 'For God's sake, man, can you not see what's in front of you?'

'No, frankly. What I can see, however, is someone who we thought we could trust, but who all along has been waiting to snatch our customers.' He looked directly at Kit. 'And I also see someone else who knew exactly what kind of jewellery Daisy liked. You're nothing but a cheat, Kit. I don't know what's in this for you, but I can guess... In fact they're probably in this together.' He looked Daisy up and down.

'Lawrence! That is quite enough.'

'No, it's okay, Mum. I'm happy to explain.' Kit glared at his brother. 'I think Lawrence has just shown his true colours, so perhaps I should remind you of Daisy's. Right at the beginning of this competition it was actually you who suggested that we each take Daisy out for the day. And may I remind you that it was Daisy who insisted that none of the details of said excursions should be discussed with anyone else. A stipulation that you agreed to. Now, correct me if I'm wrong, but I'd lay money on the fact that you asked Daisy for some insider information on your day out, but she said no...' Lawrence had the grace to look a little sheepish. 'In fact, I bet every one of us tried it on.'

Bertie shrugged. 'He's right, Lawrence. I know I did, and sorry, but after I told them I was pulling out of the competition, I outright asked Daisy to cheat, but she wouldn't. Got pretty angry about it actually.'

Kit continued. 'But the truth is, obviously, I did know about Daisy's jewellery. I found out purely by chance when a friend of mine let slip that Daisy was making a gift for him to give to his partner. He didn't know it was a secret and so the whole thing was just a misunderstanding. And that would have been fine if Daisy hadn't found out that I knew.'

'So, at that point you just cooked this whole thing up between you—'

'No!' Kit gave an exasperated sigh. 'Look Lawrence, will you just let me finish? I entered this competition to win, just as you did, but my intention was always to then pass over the reins to Daisy. All I've done now is simply cut myself out of the equation, because I'm not what's important here. When I found out about Daisy's jewellery-making I knew I had to keep my knowledge a secret so that I didn't compromise the integrity and loyalty she fought so hard to keep. She would have accused me of cheating, and I couldn't run the risk that she would tell Mother and the whole competition would be called off. The other point is that had she realised I knew exactly what her designs were like and how I found out, she would never have made the heart that you're looking at now. And I almost blew it... The other night I let slip I knew and she did just what I knew she would – accused me of trying to wheedle information out of her in order to win the competition and—'

'So you let me think badly of you instead,' said Daisy, her nose beginning to prickle. 'You could have explained how you knew, but you didn't... to protect me...' Her eyes found Kit's. 'You did that for *me?*'

He nodded gently. 'To protect you so that I could bring your jewellery here today, for everyone to see. This is not something that should be hidden away, and neither should you be, Daisy. You have a rare talent and an imagination that deserves to be given wings. It's time for you to shine.'

And he smiled, a smile that went straight to Daisy's heart, that came from somewhere very deep inside of him and met something very deep inside of her. There were tears in her eyes as she saw Bertie nod.

'And Buchanans is the perfect place for you to do it,' he said, coming forward. 'I agree with you, Kit. Daisy is the only one who deserves to run the business.'

He opened his arms to give her a hug and although she could feel the warmth of his embrace, his stubbly chin scratching against her hair, all she could see was the look in Kit's eyes as the enormity of what he had done for her began to sink in. He was watching her now, an expression on his face that she thought she would never tire of seeing.

'So what do you think, Mother? It's time to announce the winner.'

Bea came forward as if taking centre stage and Daisy had a strange feeling that this was what she had planned all along. She daren't look at Lawrence but, as Kit came to stand beside her, his hand slipping back into hers as if it had never been away, she found she no longer cared what Lawrence thought of her. Just as she no longer cared if he did end up running Buchanans. Daisy was already the biggest winner of them all, for Kit had just given her the best present she could ever have wished for. His love.

'Well...' Bea clasped her hands together in delight, her face shining with excitement. 'I had hoped that something like this would happen, but I'll confess this has surpassed all my expectations.'

Daisy stared at her. She'd been right all along – she'd known Bea was up to something.

'Close your mouth, Lawrence, dear, and don't look so surprised. Even you, when you think about it, will begin to understand why I'm doing this.' She took a deep breath. 'As you know, in a little over a week, I will be sixty, and Charles and I will start our new lives together. I've waited a long time for this, but I always knew that the question of what happened to Buchanans would be one that was not so easily resolved. My three darling boys…'

She broke off to look at each of them in turn. 'But how to choose between you? Especially when I knew that the business wasn't right for any of you. You've all served it well over the years, in different ways, but all showing your loyalty, both to me and to your late father's wish that Buchanans should continue long into the future. And perhaps it has simply been that my own change in circumstance has allowed me to see that it was time, not only to set myself free, but to set you all free too.'

She beamed directly at Daisy before continuing. 'I always knew who I wanted to run this place, just as I knew that if I simply announced it, you three would fight me every inch of the way, so I had to show a little cunning… I had to find a way to let you reach that conclusion for yourselves. And by and large that's exactly what has happened…' She changed the direction of her gaze.

'Bertie… I knew that you could never stand to be confined to this place day in day out, your wonderful people skills never quite being given the space they needed to grow. I also knew of course that Luka had asked you to go into business with him, and that all it would take for you to make that decision was a drop of courage and a little bird to point out to you what was important in life.'

Bertie nodded and smiled, shaking his head in amusement.

'And Lawrence… You haven't quite got there yet, but you will, soon. You see, out of you three I always knew that you would fight the hardest, not because you really wanted to run Buchanans, but because you wanted to win, and that is quite a different thing altogether.'

She sighed. 'You've always been that way, and I'm afraid that's my fault, placing so much responsibility onto your shoulders from such an early age, always making you the one in charge... But, now, I hope you will see that your talents too lie elsewhere. You've had some remarkable ideas for Buchanans over the years, but they've never quite hit the spot – but only because you've picked the wrong spot. Go to London, Lawrence. Test out your ideas where there are big budgets and the sky's the limit, that's where you'll find your feet.'

Daisy smiled at him, taking in the stunned expression on his face, but one that showed he was, finally, beginning to understand. He nodded in reply, a small nod, but it was there.

'And finally, Kit... out of you all, the one who knew what he believed in right from an early age and quietly and determinedly set out to live it. You've always known where your strengths lie, and it never has been here... Curious then that you chose to work on the shop floor, day in day out, even when you had other far more pressing things to do. Or rather, not that curious at all, when one of the things you believed in was a young woman. Someone within whom you could see, just as I did, a spark of something very special indeed. It's no wonder you fell in love with her.'

She laughed. 'Of course I knew, Kit, I've known for ages. Trust me, a mother knows these things. What I wasn't quite so sure about was where exactly your feelings were going to take us, but I'm extraordinarily pleased with where they have.'

She paused and looked at them in turn. 'And so, here we are at the end. Or perhaps the beginning... I hope so, because I'm absolutely certain that this is the right thing to do, for all of you. Daisy has more than proved herself the successor of Buchanans. She could have colluded with any of you, at any point, but she didn't. She remained loyal to me and to the spirit of the competition, without even knowing why, and I don't have to tell you how rare it is to find someone with that degree of integrity these days. The fact that she is an extremely talented jeweller has come as the most wonderful surprise and makes what I'm about to do even more special.

'You see, Daisy, I am off to start a new life with everything I could possibly want. But it's also time for us all to take responsibility for our lives, to stand on our own two feet, without Buchanans. And so, I don't just want you to run this place for me…' She looked around her one more time, her hands clasped together. 'I want you to have more than that. I want you to have the very thing that you have never believed you should want but in fact have always needed, and so I'm giving it to you, Daisy. Buchanans is yours…'

Christmas Day

Daisy groaned. 'I have eaten so much,' she said. 'Now I know what all the fuss is about. Even the Brussel sprouts…'

They were snuggled on Kit's sofa, far away from the outside world, warm and cosy inside his log cabin among the trees. She laid her head against his shoulder and stretched out her toes towards the fire.

'I have to confess I wasn't sure if you would eat it,' replied Kit. 'But I could hardly serve you cheese sandwiches and carrot sticks for Christmas dinner, now could I?'

She smiled sleepily, full, contented and happy as he rested his lips against the top of her hair.

'It seems like a lifetime ago that I invited you to spend Christmas Day with me… and yet here you are…'

She twisted slightly so that she could turn and look up at him. 'Yes, here I am. I'm still not sure this isn't all a dream. Or a fairy tale. I feel like a rescued damsel in distress. Actually, that's the second time you've rescued me. I could quite get used to it.'

Kit grinned. 'Well, much as I'd like to continue rescuing you for a very long time to come, I'm afraid that won't be at all necessary. You'd rescued yourself long before I got there.'

'But all I did was start to make some jewellery, Kit, the rest has been down to you. I have a future now I never even dreamed of.' Her eyes sparkled as a huge smile split her face. 'I have a shop! Imagine that...'

'You do. And have you any thoughts yet about what to do with it? You heard what Mum said, no strings attached. You can make it anything you want it to be.'

The time since yesterday afternoon had flown by in a mad whirl and Daisy really hadn't had the chance to take it all in. She did know one thing, however. She pulled a face.

'Not Buchanans... I mean, I might have to keep the name, but not the shop, not like it is now... But I'll sell my jewellery, obviously, and maybe others too, from individual craftspeople like me. I could sell Flora's prints as well... especially now that I can go ahead and make the jewellery to go on them... Oh, and things for The Castle...' She broke off. 'There is so much to think about, so many things I could do.'

'And you can take your time over all of them,' said Kit. 'Work out what it is you really want.'

'I do know one thing,' she replied. 'And that's whatever I do, I will stay true to the things I believe in... the things *we* believe in. And I very much want you to be a part of it all. Will you? Stand by my side?'

'Well, I wouldn't want to be anywhere else. Does that mean you'll be my boss though?' Kit grinned.

'No, it means we'll take it in turns to make the tea.'

'Then you've got yourself a deal, Daisy Buchanan.'

She sat up straight. 'What did you call me?'

He grinned. 'Daisy Buchanan... That is your name, isn't it? Well, it is on Instagram anyway. How else do you think I found your jewellery?'

She rolled her eyes. 'I kept meaning to ask you about that. It was the one thing I couldn't work out.'

'It was pretty easy really. I heard you once talking to a customer about romantic fiction and the subject of *The Great Gatsby* came up... One of your favourite books, you said, a love story, but yet at the same time, not, its beauty corrupted by wealth and power... A book which has at its heart one Daisy Buchanan... So, let me see – your name is Daisy and you work in Buchanans – it really didn't take much to put two and two together and find your account.'

She laughed. 'No, I guess not.' And then she stared at him, a look of dawning realisation crossing her face. 'Oh, I can't believe I didn't spot it – the name you used to order the jewellery – NickCarr1 – Nick Carraway, Gatsby's friend from the book.' She tutted. 'I'm such an idiot!'

Kit gave a slight bow. 'At your service. I couldn't use the full name of course, that would have given the game away far too easily, but Nick Carr...'

Daisy smiled up at him. 'You really did go to extraordinary lengths for me, Kit, and I'm still not sure why.'

'No?' He leaned closer. 'Well, that's really very simple. You see, you make me feel more alive than anyone I've ever known, and in certain lights your skin looks like alabaster. It's so pale that when you arch your neck it makes me want to lay my fingers against your skin to feel your heart beating...'

He gently caught the end of her chin and turned it towards him, his fingers sliding down the curve of her neck to rest lightly on her skin. 'You're the first thing I think about every morning when I wake up, and the last thing at night, and when you smile at me it's like there's no one else in the room.'

'You forgot the bit about not liking frilly stuff except on flowers, and that I'm very tidy and read a lot.'

'Did I…?' His lips just grazed hers as he smiled, his eyes dancing. 'Well, I'm sure there are a million and one things I've yet to find out about you, but I'm certain I'm going to love them all.'

'Are you?' she asked, her mouth millimetres from his.

'Oh yes…' And then he kissed her.

'The perfect present,' she whispered as she drew apart for just a second to catch her breath, her fingers reaching down to feel the silver heart that now nestled just above hers. Kit had placed it there last night as the clock had chimed midnight.

'I wanted to give you something that was truly yours,' he had said. 'Something that would always speak of love. So I gave you my words and you took them into your heart to make something so beautiful it could only ever be yours.'

'That jewellery should speak only words of love,' she whispered.

Kit ran a finger lightly down the end of her nose. 'Daisy Buchanan,' he murmured, leaning in close for another kiss. 'I rather like the sound of that…'

A Letter from Emma

Hello, and thank you so much for choosing to read *The Little Shop on Silver Linings Street*, I do hope you enjoyed reading it as much as I enjoyed writing it – Christmas books are just so lovely, aren't they? I really hope you'd like to stay updated on what's coming next, so please do sign up to my newsletter here and you'll be the first to know!

www.bookouture.com/emma-davies

It's been another hugely busy year, with three more titles published, and among all of that, our eldest daughter has moved into her own home, bought a puppy and I've been criss-crossing the country looking at universities with our youngest. A household of five, which has already shrunk to four, will be reducing to three come September as our son goes off to university, so there have been lots of changes over the last year. I mention this because coming to the end of a series of books is always a time of reflection for me, much like the passing of a year, and a reminder of the journey I've been on – not just in my own reality, but through the worlds I've created in the books I write. And it's always a time of great excitement too, the chance to have a little break, but also to let my imagination have full rein, thinking about ideas for new projects. So I hope you'll be pleased to learn that my head is already percolating with lots of new stories and, by the time you read this, one of those will already be well underway. So, what will it be...? Well, I'm afraid you'll have to wait and see; suffice to say that I'm very, very excited for what the next year will hopefully bring!

I hope to see you again very soon and, in the meantime, if you've enjoyed your visit to *The Little Shop on Silver Linings Street*, I would really appreciate a few minutes of your time to leave a review or post on social media. Every single review makes a massive difference and is very much appreciated!

Until next time,
Love, Emma x

 @EmDaviesAuthor

 emmadaviesauthor

 www.emmadaviesauthor.com

Acknowledgements

'Mum's in the shed' is a fairly constant refrain in our house, the shed being where I write, a six-by-eight space at the bottom of the garden. While that may not sound particularly glamorous, it's really rather lovely, and incredibly toasty in the winter! But of course it's more than just a space, it's a place where I go to be elsewhere, to lose myself in my writing, familiar and comfortable and oh, the places we have been together! So I'm particularly grateful to my family for allowing me the privacy of my shed and for not complaining (well, not often anyway) when I'm there! This is particularly important as I'm afraid I've got lots more ideas for next year... Sorry guys!

I'd also like to thank my other 'family' – Bookouture – who look after me in so many ways and are just a joy to work with, although funnily enough I don't have to ask them to pick their socks up off the floor! They are focused, driven and committed, everything an author could wish for, but also incredibly human too; supportive, encouraging, kind and there through thick and thin. So, thank you, because I'm afraid I've got lots more ideas for next year!

Made in the USA
Coppell, TX
10 December 2022

88591557R00184